Glenn G. Thater's
continues in this tw.... ....,
Kings.

In the *Age of Myth and Legend*, Thetan's Fallen
Arkons raged against their god across the endless
Fimbulwinter, until the Sphere of the Heavens awoke,
ripped open the boundary betwixt Midgaard and the
Nether Realms, and ushered in a new age of horror
where even gods could die.

When Lord Angle Theta and Gallis Korrgonn crossed
swords in Anglotor Tower, good battled evil, villain
fought virtue, man met monster, and only one
survived.

But which one is the hero, and which the devil?

Or are they one and the same?

BOOKS BY GLENN G. THATER

THE HARBINGER OF DOOM SAGA
GATEWAY TO NIFLEHEIM
THE FALLEN ANGLE
KNIGHT ETERNAL
DWELLERS OF THE DEEP
BLOOD, FIRE, AND THORN
GODS OF THE SWORD
THE SHAMBLING DEAD
MASTER OF THE DEAD
SHADOW OF DOOM
WIZARD'S TOLL
DRUMS OF DOOM
BLOOD OF KINGS
VOLUME 13+ (forthcoming)

HARBINGER OF DOOM
(Combines *Gateway to Nifleheim* and *The Fallen Angle* into a single volume)

THE HERO AND THE FIEND
(A novelette set in the Harbinger of Doom universe)

THE GATEWAY
(A novella length version of *Gateway to Nifleheim*)

THE DEMON KING OF BERGHER
(A short story set in the Harbinger of Doom universe)

THE KEBLEAR HORROR
(A short story set in the Harbinger of Doom universe)

GLENN G. THATER

BLOOD OF KINGS

A TALE FROM THE
HARBINGER OF DOOM SAGA

A glorious day for courage,
A better day for the worms.

BLOOD OF KINGS © 2019 by Glenn G. Thater

ISBN-13: 978-1690618690

Visit Glenn G. Thater's website at
http://www.glenngthater.com

September 2019 Print Edition
Published by Lomion Press

The eye of a priest whose word is true,
The blood of a king, eyes of blue,
And the heart of an immortal whose
time comes due,
May awake the Heavenly Sphere, claim
the learned few.

When the Nether Portal tears open,
All Midgaard will cry,
But the Harbinger of Doom will laugh,
While the old gods die.

--Seventh Scroll of Cumbria, verses 66-67.

PROLOGUE

THETAN THE LIGHTBRINGER

The woman's skin was green. Green! Not a sickly shade, but green like springtime, full of life and promise. Thetan had never seen her before, green or not, and she had no business in his tent. And why did he feel groggy, his head pounding? His mind raced. Had he been drugged? Sleeping gas? Sorcery?

His pains and her presence didn't make sense. He went to bed without issue and was the lightest of sleepers — it didn't matter how tired he was or how late the day's toils had kept him. The smallest rodent skulking beyond his tent's wall stirred him. So did a change in the breeze, however mild. There were always two guards he trusted just outside his tent, and the lightest touch upon its flap would spring him fully awake, ready to do battle if need be — a valuable skill for a warrior to possess, but one for which he paid a price, rarely getting the rest he needed, though he needed much less than most men. So you might imagine his surprise when he awoke to a woman's touch upon his cheek.

A green woman. Her hair was green too, much darker than her skin and streaked with yellow. Blooming flowers swayed in her hair, small and delicate, sweet as honey. Her body, slim but

7

shapely. The wisp of a dress she wore, airy and white. Her eyes, blue as the ocean depths. She smelled of the earth, of fresh tilled soil and springtime.

Her face was flawless. Her skin of perfectly even tone; her nose shaped just right; full lips; eyes, large and bright; jawline, strong, cheekbones too. Strange coloring aside, a beauty beyond compare that could move the stoniest heart. Thetan saw and thought all that in but the blink of an eye. Even as he bounded to his feet, the sensation of the woman's touch lingered. She had not the look of an assassin but Thetan would not be fooled by that, for as they say, nothing in Midgaard is as it seems.

Before he challenged her, she waved a hand before his face. That movement and whatever spell it carried with it, pulled down the veil of sorcery that had confounded him. Suddenly, he remembered her. He remembered many things.

Not everything.

Never everything.

But many things.

"We've little time for banter," said Midgaard. "There is somewhere I must take you. Far from here. We must be off at once. Take my hand and so shall we fly."

He thought to question her, or to resist, but what was the point? There was no resisting *her*.

He reached out his hand to hers and she gripped it with surprising strength.

The world went dark. Thetan saw nothing. Air rushed past his face and buffeted his hair. He felt as if he were flying, but not akin to riding a

Targon. He no longer felt the ground beneath him, yet his stomach didn't churn, nor was he tossed from side to side. It was as if he stood still and the world flew by *him*. 'Twas a strange sensation unlike any that he'd felt before, yet somehow it was familiar. Like a forgotten memory. Like so much about the lady called Midgaard -- the mysterious Woman on the Wind.

After a time, when the rush of air subsided, light returned to his eyes. Midgaard stood beside him, their hands still clasped. It was twilight, a strange orange hue to the air.

Before them stood a tree.

The largest tree Thetan had ever seen. Three hundred hand's breaths across was its trunk, limbs equally impressive stretching out to each horizon, though the lowest branches were more than a hundred feet aloft. Its bark, aged and gnarly, but of vibrant color, still vigorous in its health. Powerful and thick green leaves aplenty, but not so many to obscure the sunshine or the tree's lofty branches that carried it upward into the heavens. How high it grew, Thetan could not hope to say. Its heights may well have known the stars.

The tree sat amidst a vast garden. Every manner of fruit-bearing bush, tree, root, and vine imaginable was there aplenty and stretched on and on in all directions for as far as Thetan could see. At the limits of his vision, a thick mist surrounded all.

And all about the garden roamed the beasts of the field in contentment and harmony. Thetan spied deer nibbling at blueberries steps from a brown bear doing the same. A lion lay beside a flock of sheep and a goat who tended her young without a care. Three chattering monkeys rode the back of a striped saber cat, the largest Thetan had known. In the distance he saw horses, camels, olyphants, and more.

The air was thin and the sky was dark blue.

"We're on a mountain," said Thetan. "The summit of a great peak. And that mist be the clouds that hover about its crown. Strange that the air be not chill despite our lofty height."

Midgaard smiled, her teeth white and perfect, her eyes alight. "You never cease to surprise me, my dearest. You are correct. We stand atop the greatest peak in all the world."

"So this is a real place? Not a dream, not a fancy? We are really here? You have not bewitched me?"

"This place is real," she said, nodding, "and we are truly here, in a manner, bewitchings aside. Here for good purpose."

"How did you bring us here? Sorcery? Or some science beyond my ken?"

"Is that not what magic is?" said Midgaard. "I cannot explain to you what you cannot understand, and we have no time for the attempt. The hour is late, and the clock ticks down to your meeting with the false god."

"I hate when you do that," said Thetan. "I can understand many things. I can--"

"I know," said Midgaard. "There isn't time. I've brought you here so you can collect sap from the tree. You need it."

"A most impressive tree it is, but I have no

10

need of sap and nothing to collect it with if I did. I have little patience for these games. Tell me what you are about. Your mystery has lost its shine."

"In the trials to come, my dearest, you will need every advantage, every bit of luck the universe dares gift you. And so I've brought you here, so that by your own hand you may collect a vial of sap from the tree of life itself. Yggdrasil. The first tree. The living heart of this world."

"Do you remember her?" said Midgaard. "Do you remember her garden? You have been here before. Long ago, you knew this place well."

Thetan squinted and looked again about the place. "Familiar it is, I cannot deny, but more like a tale that I once heard than a memory."

Midgaard's face turned sad, but only for a moment. And then in her hand appeared a metal sphere the size of a gauntleted fist -- a container of some sort, with a cap that screwed on. Whence she procured it, Thetan could not hope to say, for her dress left little to modest imagination.

"Take this, and with your knife slice open a small notch in the World Tree's bark, two inches deep, no more, and no wider than an inch across, for I would not have Yggdrasil unnecessarily harmed. Collect the sweet sap that flows with great care, for it be the most precious substance in all creation."

"Why not just bring me a dose and dispense with the drama?"

"I thought it a wonder that you'd want to see with your own eyes and in so seeing, appreciate

11

its value. You might even remember certain things worth remembering."

Thetan shook his head. "A half-truth if I have ever heard one. There be more that you can tell me."

Midgaard raised her chin, turned from Thetan's gaze, and her tone took on a hint of bitterness. "I can interfere in the deeds of man only so much before my ministrations are noticed, even here, in this holy place."

"Noticed by who?"

"By the dark powers that vie against us."

Thetan's voice grew stern. "What dark powers? Name them? Tell me all there is to know."

"I cannot say for the same reasons I could not bring you the sap. Speak of them and they will know. They will hear. And then we would be undone. Your plans and mine, unraveled. I can say no more, and mayhap, I've already said too much."

"And what am I to do with the sap? Spread it upon my bread, drip it into my tea? Don't dare tell me to figure it out myself."

"The sap is the essence of life, my dearest."

"The tree's life?" said Thetan.

"All life of this world," said Midgaard. "One drop by mouth can heal most any wound or cure most any ailment. Diluted in water or wine, its efficacy will hardly decrease. Keep it tightly sealed and add water or spirits to it at your will to keep it full. It will serve you well. One drop only, any more is wasted."

"Any wound?" said Thetan. "Any sickness?"

"It may, or may not, choose to restore a lost limb and certainly won't remedy a severed head, but it can do wonders beyond any healer, poultice, or potion."

"You speak of it as if it's alive, with a will of its own."

"Of course it's alive," said Midgaard. "It's the World Tree. Just don't get too comfortable with it; don't rely upon it. But when you have need of it, it will be there."

"What I need, is a way to get the Sphere of the Heavens to open a portal to Nifleheim when Azathoth is near, for I have no idea how it's to be done, only that it must be done, or else all is lost. Unless, you can tell me some other way that I might overcome him? Know you such a way?"

"I wish I did," said Midgaard. "I wish I could strike him down for you, my love. I've longed to rid this world of him since the moment he arrived. But I know not a way, nor could I even try without breaking rules that must not be broken. Even then, even facing him myself, I don't know whether I could prevail for I know not the depths of his power or the limits of his energies. The Sphere of the Heavens may be your best chance. It may be your only chance. But Worldgates are fickle things with minds of their own. Trust not in them, for they may work against you. That much I know."

"World Trees and now Worldgates?"

"Yggdrasil is the only World Tree on Midgaard, though no doubt other worlds have their own or something else that serves a similar function. As for Worldgates, Midgaard has many. All are ancient and of alien origin. Each can wrench open a portal to this world or that. All the gates are powerful. And all are dangerous. More like living things than inanimate objects, are they. Do not trust them," she said looking around furtively, her voice quieting and quickening, "nor any that advise you of them, except for me, of course."

1

URIEL THE BOLD

Uriel groaned and his face twisted in anguish when his ranal blade sank into Rathgemon's chest. Up until then, Uriel's strikes had been halfhearted – not meant to kill or maim, only to hold Rath off. He didn't want to fight him. He certainly didn't want to kill him, or any of them. He'd hoped that they'd break off their assault, would think better of it. But Rath fought hard from the first. Full of conviction was he. Passion. Battle lust. Just as when he fought the lord's enemies. All the strength and controlled rage that the Arkons unleashed on the heathen hordes that so often opposed the lord, Rath poured down on him.

On him!

As if *he* were the enemy.

As if *he* were evil.

As if *he* had to die.

As if Rath didn't care for him at all or had forgotten they'd been brothers-in-arms for years beyond count. They'd trained together for ages, sparred countless thousands of times; Uriel knew Rath's every maneuver, swing, sidestep, and strike. He knew when he'd take a breath, pause, parry, slash, or thrust. Mind you, Rath

15

was a highly skilled fighter, a sword master by common standards -- all the Arkons were. But Uriel was of a different class.

Rath knew that. Mayhap that explained his aggression -- take the better fighter quickly, throw him off balance from the first. Perhaps he thought that was his only chance. More than likely, it was.

But they didn't need to fight at all. They were brothers, not enemies. Why couldn't Rath see the truth? Why couldn't any of them, Azathoth's loyalists?

The lord had gone mad, or had always been mad. It was *he* that brought it all about — the great rebellion, the civil war. It was *he* that had to be stopped, so clear that was to Uriel. So clear to Thetan, Gabriel, Mithron, and the rest. Why in Helheim couldn't Rath understand it? He was no fool. Why did it have to come to this?

Rath scored a powerful blow, but only because Uriel's heart was not in the fight.

That blow should have ended the duel. But fate spared Uriel that day, for the blade failed to bite through his armor, though its bludgeon numbed his shoulder and sapped the strength from his arm.

That changed everything.

Uriel no longer had a choice. He had to fight to kill. Had to kill his brother. Or else his brother would kill him.

It took but a moment.

Uriel's thrust sheared the chain links at Rath's breastplate's bindings, just below the armpit and sank into his flesh. Rath's eyes bulged; his mouth dropped open. Fear didn't prompt that reaction. Nor did pain. It was shock. Disbelief. Rath knew just as did Uriel -- deep as it was, in that spot -- it was a mortal blow. Rath had walked Midgaard for fourteen thousand years, nearly all of that as an Arkon of the one true god, but now he was done. The people thought of them, the Arkons, more as gods than men – as if a divine spark, some fragment of the lord's essence had attached itself to them, transforming them into something more than mere human beings.

Mayhap it had. Uriel didn't know. He couldn't say. But with that one well-placed blow he had ended it all for Rathgemon.

Rath's sword arm was up for a swing, but it froze, though Uriel kept his eye on it. There was no point in a final strike — Rath had to know that, but then his arm came down hard and fast. One final blow designed to drag Uriel into the afterlife with him.

Uriel blocked it with little effort.

"I'm sorry," Uriel said to the dying man as he swung his sword, hard and fast, and sliced through his brother's neck.

Took his head with that blow. Steaming mist shot from his neck along with the blood as the last air from his lungs escaped into the Fimbulwinter's frigid air.

Uriel didn't have to do that.

He could've let Rath bleed out. Could've permitted him those final moments to make his peace with death, to say his goodbyes to life, to all he ever knew, and ever loved. They could've exchanged final words, be they regrets or curses. Uriel could've begged Rath's forgiveness for killing him. Could've given Rath a final chance to see the error of his ways.

But Uriel didn't have the stomach for that. Didn't have the heart for it. He couldn't bear it. He just couldn't.

If any had asked him why he took Rath's head, he would've said he did it to spare Rathgemon the pain of dying. A mercy it was to end his suffering quickly. To take away his pain. A good thing it was. A kindness.

Who wouldn't have believed that?

That's what Uriel would've said, though no one asked him. And Uriel was not accustomed to lying. Not often. Not for profit. But he would've lied about that killing. For the truth was, he killed Rath quickly, for himself: to spare himself the pain of watching his friend die; of watching him bleed out; of the lingering agony; of seeing the hatred, accusations, and pain in his brother's eyes; the lingering guilt of it all.

He couldn't bear that.

He wouldn't.

So he killed him quickly.

It was better for them both.

Uriel spun about to make certain that no others accosted him.

Not far away, battle still raged. Thetan, Mithron, and Hogar stood back-to-back, a towering circle of steel and muscle that could not be breached. A pile of loyalist corpses heaped about their feet along with the drifting snow. Five more loyalists assaulted them with spear, sword, and axe — the strikes from both factions so swift that even Uriel could barely follow them. Mithron cut one man down; a moment later, he took another.

Uriel's eyes flicked hither and there about the field; all his cohorts still lived, though more than one was battered or wounded. All those they'd fought, dead or dying at their feet; not a one had fled, courageous to the last as was their wont, driven by duty and purpose, corrupt and confused as it was. Zachriel, Zagin, Tahoriel, Maion, Furlac, and Astiro were dead. All of them. Each one, well known to Uriel, some few, friends of long years. They'd fought wars alongside each other, supporting each other, protecting each other's backs, doing the lord's good works. The bond that such conflict formed between men was something hard to explain, a closeness that transcended friendship, and that in some ways, was stronger even than the bonds of blood.

And now they murdered each other.

How had it come to that?

Looking upon the carnage, Uriel's guts felt as if someone was squeezing them, twisting them; the nausea growing in his throat.

Bose wept as he cradled Shariel's limp body in his arms. For a thousand years he'd loved her from afar with all his heart, yet that was the first time he'd ever held her close, for Azathoth's laws permitted no coupling amongst his Arkons, and until of late, Bose had always followed the lord's will, however difficult that duty. But now he'd killed his love. Her blood on his hands, forevermore.

Thetan's sword took Adrapen through the heart. Hogar slammed his blade down on Nacoriel's head; cleaved it in two. Mithron's axe entered Hanoziz's shoulder and came out again at his hip. When his body hit the ground, it joined those of Imriel, Kabriel, Marfiel, Malkuth, Pahta, and some others whose faces Uriel could not see.

The twelve rebels had killed more than twice their number of loyalist Arkons, and at least a dozen footmen of Azathoth's Einheriar Corps. The loyalists had fallen upon them when they'd landed in a glen behind a small hill far from anywhere worth being. How they'd tracked them unseen, Uriel had no idea. The element of surprise did them little good, dead one and all. Thetan had chosen his rebels well; for all their skills, few of the loyalists could long stand against them.

How had it come to this?

2

"**D**id you think that all the Arkons would follow us?" said Mithron, gathered close with his brethren about the campfire as large snowflakes swirled about them and took root on their helmets and cloaks, the frigid wind howling through the wood, the forest's dark looming over them. "That we'd convince them all with a wink and a whispered word and they'd flock to our banners, casting aside everything they hold dear, not to mention -- the lord's grace?"

"I didn't think, and that's the problem," said Raphael, his red cape flowing about him, his long hair and pointy red beard buffeted by the breeze. "And I feel the fool for it. I knew most would oppose us, but I never envisioned fighting them -- at least, not to the death. I still can't believe the anger on their faces. The hatred. Hatred! For us. For me. I thought they'd seek our capture, of course. Drag us before the lord to answer for our crimes. They'd have no choice -- their duty and all. But to kill us on sight, no quarter or parley, no hearing or trial? Never. I'd never have believed it, even if you'd forewarned me. I'd have marked you mad."

"Eager for our deaths, are they," said Dekkar as he stretched to place the cook pot over the fire. No doubt, he'd whipped up a tasty meal out

21

of next to nothing, as was his wont, though you'd never guess it from his look, for not an ounce that didn't belong clung to his lanky frame. "I didn't expect that. My thoughts were fixed on opposing the lord, not our brethren."

"As were mine," said Bose, his eyes downcast, his face sullen. Even his heavy cloak failed to hide his bulk, his weight near to Mithron's though he stood a foot shorter, but still taller than most men. In Mithron's case, it was all muscle, in Bose's, nearly so. "I thought we'd have the chance to convince the others. To build our case. It all happened so fast. Too fast. There was no time."

"There is never enough time," said Thetan, "no matter how long one lives. It's one of the great lessons of life."

"Did you tell her?" said Azrael to Bose. "Did Shariel know about our plot?"

Bose scowled. "I kept the vow I swore on Mount Canterwrought. But I'll regret that for as long as I live."

"Had you told her," said Azrael in a soft voice, "she may well have betrayed us. And if she had, we'd all be dead. You did the right thing."

"Did I?" said Bose, his voice upraised. "I murdered the woman I love. Is that the right thing? Did you know that? That I loved her? All these years?"

"We all knew, brother," said Raphael softly as he placed a hand on Bose's shoulder.

The others nodded.

Bose looked surprised. "I never spoke of it."

"Your eyes gave you away long ago," said

Raphael.

"She gave you no choice," said Azrael.

"I could have let her kill me. Better that, than to raise my sword against her. Better that, than her blood on my hands."

"Had she slain you," said Mithron, "still, she wouldn't have left here alive. You know that. When she and the others attacked us, her fate was sealed."

"And that proves you did the right thing, keeping silent," said Azrael. "If there were a chance that you could've convinced her, if she harbored the same doubts about the lord as we, surely she would've heard us out before attacking to kill. But she didn't, so your words would've been wasted. She would've given us up."

"We'd be dead or in irons," said Dekkar.

"More likely, we'd be under Bhaal's knife," said Mithron. "Penance for our sins."

"You don't know that," said Bose. "Not for certain."

"We know it near enough," said Mithron.

"I agree," said Gabriel Hornblower.

"As do I," said Thetan. "You are not at fault, Bose."

"Would Bhaal do that?" said Hogar, a massive man, as tall as Thetan, but not as tall or broad as Mithron. "To us?"

"He would," said Dekkar. "As would Asmodeus, Iblis, and more than a few others. There have long been many in our ranks that carry out the lord's wrath with enthusiasm."

"With joy," said Tolkiel, the oldest of the

23

group, his beard of white, wrinkled of face but lively of step, and made of stuff as stern as any of the others. "With glee," he said. "It sickens me."

"We all know that Bhaal is a brute," said Raphael. "He is the exception."

"One of many exceptions," said Dekkar. "Exceptions that the lord tolerates."

"More proof of the lord's madness or corruption," said Gabriel.

"Sad it be to say," said Azrael, "but perhaps it was best that it was you who fought her."

"How can you say that?" said Hogar. "The guilt he bears."

"If the deed had fallen to any other, there'd be tension amongst us," said Azrael. "Hard feelings that would linger, that would fester."

"Azrael is right," said Bose. "I wouldn't have forgiven you, any of you, for killing her. I couldn't let that go. How can I forgive myself?"

"Try as best you can," said Azrael. "We will help you if we can."

"You must learn to live with it," said Thetan, "if nothing else. It had to be done, and cannot be undone. Hard this may be to hear, but the sooner that you put her from your mind, the better it will be for you."

"I will not forget her," said Bose. "Not even if I could."

"Remember the good times," said Thetan, "but only in safety, when such distractions won't get you killed."

"Or us," said Raphael.

"Perhaps the fault was in following you in this

mad plan to begin with," said Bose, his eyes fixed on Thetan.

"Perhaps it was," said Thetan. "But that is the path you chose, of your own free will. The path all of you chose. There is no going back, and no time for regrets. Azathoth will slay each of us given the chance. Let's not give him that chance."

"What if we repent?" said Raphael. "I'm not suggesting that we do; I'm merely asking the question. What if we lay down our swords? Beg the lord's forgiveness? Beg his mercy? What will happen?"

"He will slay us all," said Mithron. "I have no doubt of it."

"He's forgiven sinners many times afore," said Raphael. "Vile evildoers who repented their black deeds. Surely, he would--"

"He doesn't forgive anyone who acts directly against him," said Gabriel. "Not ever. Turn away from him — and you can return; stray from his laws, you can be forgiven, but take up a sword against him — there's no coming back from that."

"The die is cast," said Mithron. "We win this or we die. There can be no other outcome."

Raphael nodded. "I agree, and yet I hoped to hear differently."

"How did they find us?" said Hogar.

"Could a traitor lurk amongst the Arkons who follow us?" said Steriel, proud and tall, the only woman amongst the group.

"No doubt, there are many," said Azrael.

"One third of the hosts of Vaeden have rallied

25

to our banners," said Mithron. Many amongst them will be loyalist spies."

"And assassins," said Dekkar.

"They are gathering information," said Azrael, "biding their time, waiting for an opportunity to strike. No amount of caution will safeguard us from those spies, but too much caution will cripple us. Such, no doubt, be their plan."

"This attack was random chance," said Gabriel. "Few knew we'd be about this route this day, we saw to that. If this had been planned, they'd have fallen on us by the hundreds, not a single squadron."

"Have they so many after us?" said Raphael.

"All the lord can muster," said Mithron. "The wind says he's been conscripting folk to his armies from throughout the kingdom and that he's already appointed a thousand new Arkons into training."

"Pressing folk into service?" said Gabriel. "That is new for the lord. A tactic of the barbarians and the heathens."

"Now it seems he's adopted it," said Mithron.

"So he does fear us," said Thetan.

3

JUTENHEIM
ANGLOTOR TOWER
YEAR 1267, 4TH AGE

Uriel the Bold's eyelids fluttered, his mouth dropped open, and he mouthed silent words as the strange relic called the Heartstone pulsed from its chain about Gallis Korrgonn's neck. A meeting of titans it was. One, an Eternal -- an immortal man, ancient and wise as he was deadly -- who had walked Midgaard's ways since *The Age of Myth and Legend*; the other, the son of god himself (or so he claimed) – a mysterious being, enigmatic, charismatic, and yet alien, brimming with powers beyond the ken of mortal man.

The two stood alone in parley on the central spire's top floor within Anglotor Castle, Uriel's redoubt, on the remote Island of Jutenheim. Uriel's apprentice, Kapte, eavesdropped from beyond the chamber's door, fearful for her master. She had never been afraid for him before. Why would she be? He was power incarnate. Strength and skills beyond compare, beyond imagining. No ten men were his match. No twenty. And she felt certain that she had never seen him pushed to his limits, never witnessed the full extent and depth of his powers. But despite all that, she knew -- she knew -- that that day he had met his match.

She prayed that the gods would protect him.

"I am with you, my lord," said Uriel, his voice monotone and weak; in his eyes, a vacant stare, overcome was he by the Heartstone's beguiling magic -- or so it seemed. "Together, we will destroy the Harbinger."

Korrgonn grinned in triumph and gripped the Heartstone all the tighter. "As it is and ever was meant to be," he said. "My father foretold that you'd rejoin us, that Uriel the Bold would retake the righteous path. Glad I am to have you with me in this, for by all accounts, the Harbinger is a terrible foe indeed."

"No one more terrible has ever lived," said Uriel, his voice, stilted and slow. "Of that, you can be certain."

Kapte shrank back from the door in shock. She couldn't believe what she heard, that her master would ally with that invader, that monster. It made no sense. It stunk of sorcery. Even through the door, she felt the waves of magic that spewed from that room -- its nature, alien to her, beyond her knowledge or experience. But she felt it all the same. It passed through her like a cold breeze that chilled her very bones.

But her master was immune to such things.

Above petty magics and even the most powerful sorceries, was he. It made no sense.

It was madness.

She fled down the stairs to warn her sisters, making nary a sound as she went despite her fright.

"Let us descend from the tower as brothers,

just as we discussed," said Korrgonn. "You will pledge your allegiance to me in front of your troops and order them to do the same. We must be swift for the Harbinger is close. I can feel him. I need your forces to hold him back until I open the portal. Nothing must stand in the way of my father's return to this world. Nothing."

4

"They call us, The Fallen," said Bose to his comrades as they sat about their fire, fatigued of mind and body from their recent skirmish. "The Fallen Arkons, thrown down from the heavenly heights of Vaeden for our villainy."

"And they mark us as evil," said Tolkiel. "Not just traitors or rebels, but evil."

"If they win, we'll be called worse than that," said Thetan. "They'll name us demons. Devils. Inhuman monsters, invaders from the *Nether Realms*. Our names will be reviled forevermore, if we're remembered at all."

"I'll accept being marked a traitor," said Hogar, "for that is what I am -- though I feel justified in the act. But evil? A demon? Why lie? Why say such ridiculous things?"

"The truth depends on who writes the histories," said Thetan.

"Alas, that has ever been the way of things," said Azrael.

"The truth is the truth," said Hogar. "It can be nothing else."

"If only that were so, my friend," said Azrael. "What a different world it would be."

"We would not mark *them* as evil," said Steriel. "Why so stain us?"

"Because they believe it," said Gabriel. "They

30

truly believe we are evil. Not all of them, but most."

"How can that be?" said Steriel. "They know us. They know us all, for ages."

"Because now we oppose the lord," said Gabriel. "Because we attacked him. Because we seek to bring down his empire. Didn't we mark for death all those who've done the same over the ages? This is little different."

"They believe they are in the right," said Thetan. "They yet believe that the lord is all good, all love; any that stand opposed must be the opposite. When they attack us, they have no regrets and no reluctance, because destroying evil warrants none. Once you mark someone or something as evil and dangerous, once you are convinced of the truth of that, nothing you do to them is too harsh, too extreme, or ever evil. You can kill evil, true evil, on sight. You can brutalize it. Even torture it. No parley is required. No surrender need be accepted. No mercy granted. You can cut evil down in the public square without shame or consequence. When you destroy evil, no matter your method, you believe you are doing good. You fancy yourself a hero. You expect praise, medals, and accolades. You are proud of the destruction you've wrought; the death; even the torture. This is the folly of mankind — our ability to be brainwashed by others. To believe falsehoods, even those that are patently absurd, that are irrational, or based on the flimsiest evidence. Lies need only be repeated often enough, by enough people, particularly those folk of influence and respect, and we believe. We believe someone is evil or dangerous or stupid or a bigot because others repeatedly tell us so. Others with an agenda, a goal, a plan. Hear it enough, and we believe. We forget to question, to think things through, to make our own determinations. Instead, we take on the positions of others. We filter the "evildoer's" every action through these beliefs, imagining evil intent, foolish decisions, warmongering, or bigotry when it isn't there. We stretch the evidence to conform to the narrative that we've been sold -- that we believe is true because we've been told to believe it. This is how Azathoth ensnared us and kept us in his thrall these many years. For all our skills and knowledge, we are no more immune to such manipulation than anyone else. Even now, he uses the same technique to demonize us. The loyalists believe, and so too will most of the people. That's why they ambushed us. To them, we're monsters. We're monsters because the lord says it is so."

"Then we need only enlighten them," said Raphael. "Make them see the truth. Expose the lies for what they are."

"It's never so simple," said Azrael. "Look at all the years it took us to throw off those shackles. To see the truth. Even when we did, we suppressed it. We toed the line and kept on with our duties. Only when forced to confront the truth and speak openly of it did we accept that we had been duped. If not for Thetan, even now we'd remain the lord's instruments."

"He laughs at us," said Gabriel. "Or rather, he

did. What fools he must think mankind. So gullible. So easily led."

"That's the source of his power," said Thetan.

"And breaking that hold could be the key to our victory," said Azrael.

"Most will never see the light," said Gabriel, "though it shines brightly on their faces."

"How can we clear the fog?" said Azrael. "Is there a way?"

No one offered an answer.

All eyes turned to Thetan.

"It would take years," said Thetan, "perhaps many decades, for the people to see the truth. To accept it. Azathoth will not permit us that time. We must rise to swift victory or else fall to inevitable defeat."

"There will be no swift victory here," said Dekkar, "unless the victory be his. It will take us years to win, if ever we can, and the longer it takes, the less our chances, for his numbers will swell more than ours ever could."

"We know the horrors of war better than any," said Mithron. "Civil war will break the Arkons; our ranks will be decimated, on both sides. There won't be enough of us to patrol the borderlands. We'll lose the provinces. Barbarian hordes and heathen masses will rise up on all sides and, mayhap, even threaten Vaeden. Chaos is what we sow here, even if we win, even if we survive."

"Which seems rather unlikely," said Raphael, "today's skirmish aside."

"That's not why we're doing this," said Azrael. "We're not trying to take over the lord's kingdom. We're trying to remove him from the field."

"If we win," said Thetan, "any chaos that ensues will be but a distant memory a hundred years from now. A small price to free mankind from the yoke we've suffered under for untold ages. Once the false god is gone, Midgaard will be ruled by men, as it was meant to be. At last, we'll be the masters of our fate."

"Or else, the harbingers of our doom," said Raphael.

5

JUTENHEIM
ANGLOTOR TOWER
ENTRY HALL
YEAR 1267, 4TH AGE

URIEL THE BOLD

Uriel's retainers went silent at the sight of their lord leading Korrgonn down the steps to where they gathered at Anglotor Tower's ground level, behind the great doors. Those iron bulwarks were sorely battered, bent about their edges, a hole here and there, the crossbars strained to their limits, but they still held. Not one of the Shadow Leaguers or their minions had breached the ancient tower -- except for Korrgonn who entered via mystical means. No fewer than fifty defenders guarded and bolstered those doors, more than a few battered and bleeding, bandages and splints hastily applied to injuries received earlier in the fray. In the main, they were Jutons, tall and muscular, but there were several each of other races: Dwarves, Gnomes, and Lugron. At least two Elves stood with them, tall and slim; a few Svart, shorter even than the Gnomes, dark gray and spindly; and several Ettin, each nearly ten feet tall, hairy and broader than any man. A Golem of iron stood to either side of the great doors, each nearly as tall as the Ettin and a good deal broader still, but otherwise of manlike form. Each retainer, from Ettin to Svart, wore shirts of dark blue, trimmed in gold, pants to match; Uriel's sigil prominently adorned their chests.

Uriel raised his right hand, palm outward, and called his folk to attention. "My friends, standing with me is Lord Korrgonn. Unlikely as it may seem, he is not a mortal man at all, and not born of Midgaard. He is a godling, the son of almighty Azathoth himself, sent down from the heavens to sunder the veil betwixt Midgaard and storied Nifleheim, to return Azathoth to our realm and restore his kingdom to its rightful place.

"I was there, ages ago, when last such a portal to the *Nether Realms* was opened, and the lord, Azathoth, taken from this world. I witnessed it with my own eyes. Moreover, to my unending shame and guilt, I was one of those who betrayed the lord. Midgaard suffered horrors beyond words for that betrayal, some of which continues even to this day.

"Today, after long and heartfelt debate, to make amends for my olden crimes, I pledged my loyalty to Lord Korrgonn's cause and assured him that each of you would do the same."

"I lied," he said as he spun back toward Korrgonn, a small dagger gripped in his palm, poised to rake Korrgonn's neck.

6

REBEL ENCAMPMENT
FIMBULWINTER - YEAR 1

THETAN THE LIGHTBRINGER

"Lasifer," said Thetan, "I would have words with you."

"Of course you would," said Lasifer. "And long past time. Ply me with a bit of mead, will you, and you'll like my answers better."

Thetan called for a jug of mead and filled two goblets. He wanted information. They settled in their seats in the command tent.

"What is he?" said Thetan. "What is he really?"

"Oh my, now we come to it at last, we do, we do," said Lasifer. "Until now," he said after taking a deep breath and a gulp of mead, "you merely didn't like his methods and questioned his motives, but you now question who or what he is. How far you've come. The big question at last. The important one. It's taken you quite a while to get here, Lightbringer. Stuck in a rut you were for untold ages. But now the floodgates have opened, I see, and you question this, question that, question everything. Oh dear, dear, dear."

"You're stalling, Gnome. Answer my question. I've little patience for your games."

"What do *you* think he is?" said the Gnome. "The *he* being Azathoth, of course."

37

"I don't know. That's why I asked you. You've been around him more than anyone, and you're a master of The Weave; have you no insight into his nature?"

"I have much insight, dear Lightbringer, on this and many topics beyond your ken."

Thetan weathered that, pausing just a moment before he spoke again. "I ask again, what is he?"

"He's a god, just as he claims," said Lasifer, "though, the truth of that depends upon your definition of god."

"How do you define it?" said Thetan.

"A being who wields power so far beyond that of his subjects so as to seem all-powerful or nearly so," said Lasifer. "And that is what he is and does. But being so is less impressive that one might think, if you'll allow me to demonstrate. Let's say that you and I traveled to some backward island where the inhabitants slept in caves, had no use of fire, or the wheel, no farming, and no domesticated animals. We show the primitives your armor, and weapons, the making of such things as fire and whatnot, some sorcery and a bit of sleight-of-hand to go with it. Would we not be gods to them?"

Lasifer continued, "We could dazzle them with wonders on one hand and put the fear in them on the other. And in so doing, could we not easily make them our devoted servants? Even our slaves? Minions that would willingly, gleefully, do our dirty deeds. Would they not believe our words when we told them we created them and that we have a grand plan for their destiny if only they worship us and do our bidding?"

"So, he's played us false?" said Thetan. "He's no god, but rather a charlatan."

"He is exactly what he claims to be," said Lasifer. "A higher power. Or, I suppose you could name him a lower power; it's a matter of...perspective. Of course, one can attain such status through far superior science and technology, or else through trickery, sorcery, or simply deceit."

"So which is he," said Thetan, "a trickster, a scientist, or a sorcerer?"

"Call him what you will," said Lasifer, "it matters not. What matters is, he's played you false. He is not your creator any more than he is your father."

"He's made fools of us," said Thetan. "Of me."

"He laughs at you rock-headed morons for all your gullibility, your need to believe in something greater than yourselves. And so, when he appeared, down from the sky in all his grandness, you believed. He made you his things, his servants, and followers. Minions that lived to do his bidding. Fools."

"But you knew he was a pretender, an impostor, a wannabee deity," said Lasifer, "or you would not have rebelled. You merely needed me to confirm it; to speak the words. The veil is lifted, Lightbringer. See the world as it truly is. Learn how to think critically. To question. The ability — or rather, the potential — to do so is what separates humankind from the monkeys you descended from and from nearly all else in Midgaard."

39

"Why speak you of monkeys?" said Thetan.

"No matter, no matter," said Lasifer. "A bit of nonsense from an old Gnome's maw. You must free yourself from the yoke of ignorance and gullibility. The power to do so is within your mind and your heart. You need not look for wisdom in a book, or knowledge hanging from a tree. Critical thought is your greatest gift, you need merely lift the veil and embrace it. See the world as it truly is. Think for yourself and when you do, if you do, then and only then will you be free. Free as the wind. Free like me."

"You are a strange one, Gnome," said Thetan.

"I take my leave of you now, Lightbringer. I trust that you will not miss me overmuch. When I return we shall have the means to open the portal and rid Midgaard of Azathoth once and for all."

Confusion filled Thetan's expression. "The Sphere can rid us of him, you're certain of it?"

"I am, but only after we learn its secrets. Secrets not easily learned. Despite my best efforts, I expect it will take some time. A good deal of time and with it, an even greater measure of danger. That will be my burden. Yours, to hold out until I return. Remember, until its secrets are ours, the Sphere, well...it be little more than a rock."

URIEL THE BOLD

Uriel the Bold had rarely flown so high riding a Targon, and never for so long, the leather harness digging painfully into his shoulders, waist, and thighs. Hiding amongst the clouds as he traveled wasn't something that Uriel was accustomed to prior to the rebellion, for Azathoth's Arkons hid from no man or beast; they strode boldly forth, doing the lord's bidding and smiting his enemies. These past three years since the rebellion began had changed all that. Many things had changed, not the least of which was the weather. With the rebellion's start came the great Fimbulwinter as it came to be known. Icy temperatures the whole year round, no summer, and scarcely a snap of spring or autumn. The crops didn't grow, the flowers didn't bloom, even the birds, the beasts of the field, and many insects, fled the land, or died in their place, frozen and starving. The old folk whispered that a curse hung heavy over the kingdom, and far afield too, as a consequence of the rebellion. Mayhap they were correct, or perhaps it was nothing but the natural vagaries of the weather.

As in most conflicts, it was the common folk

who suffered the worst – and thus were most likely to cast blame. And cast it they did, squarely atop the heads of the Fallen Arkons, whose names they cursed and reviled. Curiously, few blamed Azathoth for the Fimbulwinter, although many thought he called it down.

Azathoth was not one to let a good crisis go to waste. He had his loyalists distribute food, wine, blankets, and other such supplies to the people, far and wide, and thus purchased their loyalty and thanks. From where he procured the seemingly inexhaustible quantity of supplies, the Fallen Arkons could not fathom.

During the Fimbulwinter, it snowed almost every day. For three years.

Three years!

The wind howled with little respite. Most roads were impassable despite continual vigorous efforts to keep the main routes clear. Many small buildings were lost under the drifts, most others collapsed under the snow's weight during the first year. Entire towns disappeared beneath the white, and small cities were brought to their knees, the populace trapped and starving. The Fimbulwinter claimed fifty lives for each lost to combat during the rebellion. Even the sun feared to show its face, the days short, dark, and of little light; the nights, all the worse.

The higher aloft one went, the colder it got. Why this was so, Uriel never understood, for it seemed that the warmth of the day derived from the sun, so he thought it should grow warmer as one drew closer to it. Why it did not, he could not grasp.

Uriel feared that his Targon would freeze at so great a height, or fail to draw breath enough to remain aloft. He had no interest in plunging three leagues and splattering against the ground if the beast's strength gave out. For all their speed, uncanny strength, and great white feathered wings, Targon were delicate things, thin of limb and narrow of torso, much less robust than a man -- and even Uriel, amongst the most robust of men, struggled with the cold, shivering, his teeth chattered, his skin numb, head achy from the rarefied air. He endured the flight; they both did, though the Targon suffered all the worse for carrying him, five times at least its weight. Uriel and his brethren had little choice but to risk the clouds, for to reach the mustering point at the appointed time they had to traverse great swaths of snow-swamped lands and sky ruled by Azathoth's loyalists. If they were spotted, their best plans might unravel.

Their plan had to work.

All of Midgaard depended upon it.

Or so they told themselves.

8

JUTENHEIM
ANGLOTOR
THE COURTYARD
YEAR 1267, 4TH AGE

Shouts, screams, and crashes filled the courtyard's air. A battle raged within Anglotor Tower.

His eyes wild, Par Keld of Kirth charged Father Ginalli, High Priest of Azathoth and operational leader of The League of Light's expedition. The priest thrust out his arm like a shield to hold the little wizard back. Ginalli didn't bother to make eye contact, instead, he stared overtop Keld's head, at the tower's entry where the red giant, Mort Zag, and the Stone Golem called Mason took turns launching thunderous kicks against the iron doors. Each blow bent and warped them, but they held.

"We've got to get those doors opened, now," said Keld. "Lord Korrgonn needs our help. He can't battle them all alone. It's our duty. There could be hundreds of them in there, the evil bastards. We've got to save him."

"We don't know that it's Lord Korrgonn," said Ginalli, still not looking at Keld.

"Who else could it be?" said Keld. "No others of our men breached the tower, only Korrgonn. You think they've a giant rat problem in there, is that it? They'll kill him, and it'll be your fault, not mine. All the misery we've suffered getting here will be for naught. Don't even think about blaming me."

"Lord Korrgonn entered the tower via mystical means," said Ginalli, "no doubt, he can return the same way, if he so chooses."

"You don't know that," said Keld. "He could be trapped, unable to use his powers. Tortured. Murdered. We've got to get in there."

Now Ginalli's eyes bored into Keld's. "Your babbling won't get the doors opened a moment sooner. Besides, that ruckus is a full company of men battling to the death, not Korrgonn standing on his own. Ezerhauten and his men must've found a back entry; that's what they've been about, why they're not here. Very effective fighters, those Sithians. They'll soon put the last of the tower's defenders to the sword and we'll be on about our business."

"Your mercenary disappeared without leave over an hour ago," said Keld. "He deserted; why can't you see that? He's never been reliable. Never been respectful, especially to me, not that you care. He's running back to Jutenheim Town as fast as his legs can carry him, all that remains of his surly troop with him, derelicting his duty, what we paid him for. Probably took all our provisions too. We'll starve on the way back, mark my words. The man's a coward. I saw it from the first; I warned you, I did. It's not my fault that you were blind to his treachery. You're too trusting. Naive. I did all that could be done. Who could've done more? No one. So you can't blame me. I won't accept it. Look to the Elf for blame if you're set on pointing fingers," said Keld, gesturing toward Stev Keevis; "he's not really one of us. Not a true believer. Can't trust him or his Golem. They're shifty and rotten to the core, the both of them. Anyone can see that. You can't tell me that I'm wrong."

"Have you ever run dry of venom, Keld?" said Ginalli shaking his head. "If you did, you'd probably float away in the breeze, nothing left but an empty husk."

"I didn't do it," shouted Keld. "Don't blame me. I won't have it." He spun on his heels and raced toward the tower's door, squeezing between Mason and Mort Zag. He kicked the doors several times, shouting and grunting with the effort, though the doors didn't notice. Then he scurried away cursing and muttering, pulling at his hair.

A few moments later, the battle sounds within the tower died out. The melee was over. Someone inside worked the doors' crossbars.

Mort Zag looked at Ginalli, uncertainty on his demonic face.

Ginalli shrugged, not a man for tactics, that's what Ezerhauten and his troop were for.

"It's opening," said Mort Zag, his voice a deep baritone. "Get ready."

Ten paces from the great doors the spindly Stowron warriors formed a semicircle several rows deep, staffs and knives at the ready, their faces hidden beneath their deep black cowls. A dozen Lugron, the last of the League's mercenaries aside from Ezerhauten's troop, stood interspersed amongst them. Behind them were all that remained of the League's Archwizards: Ginalli, Par Brackta, Par Rhund, Stev Keevis, and Par Keld. Well to the rear were the prisoners: the one-armed priest, Brother Donnelin, and Sir Jude Eotrus, guarded by Teek Lugron and a few of his ilk.

The tower doors flung open from within. Out plodded an Iron Golem, taller even than Mason. Behind it loomed a second of its kind. Both bore the scars of the recent battle.

Mort Zag, Mason, and the Stowron braced, ready to attack -- a huge axe in the red giant's hand, a great hammer in Mason's. From the tower's shadowy depths, someone stepped into view.

9

URIEL THE BOLD

Victory in such a conflict as they were about to engage in required bold maneuvers. So, Thetan and Mithron, in preparation for the final battle that would decide all their fates, had led them aloft, the entire rebel host of Arkons -- "The Fallen," as they now called themselves. The loyalists coined that term two years prior at the start of the rebellion, and meant it as an insult, but the rebels soon adopted it with pride. "Fallen from Azathoth's grace" or "fallen from goodness" was the loyalists' meaning, but Uriel and his brethren defined it differently. For them, the cloak of lies Azathoth wove so tightly had fallen from their eyes, revealing the truth of his black deeds, of his manipulations and madness, of his corruption.

To Uriel, the whole business felt like a nightmare — something that he'd wake up from, and all would be as it once was, as it should be. Upon waking, he'd bask in the lord's grace and stride through the grand halls of the lord's palace in blessed Vaeden. And the lord...would be the lord. All good. All knowing. All powerful. All wise. The creator. The beginning and the end. The one true god.

But Uriel didn't wake. There was nothing to wake from. The truth was inescapable: he'd broken unbreakable vows and betrayed sacred trusts, turned his back on duty and honor. He'd betrayed the lord, and dared even take up arms against him -- against his god.

For those crimes, Uriel was marked for death by the lord's Arkons, those who had remained true. He had no choice but to fight them — his brothers in arms -- now, his bitter enemies.

How had it come to that?

Had he been fooled? Corrupted by Thetan, he whom the loyalists now named, the Prince of Lies, the Great Deceiver, The Traitor? Had Thetan convinced Uriel by guile or by foul sorcery that the lord's good deeds were evil, that the lord's sage wisdom was madness?

Was that possible?

Uriel pondered that, over and again — the idea never straying far from his mind these past years. But always, he reminded himself that his concerns over the lord's behavior had not been born of Thetan's whispers. They were sown of long years observing the death, destruction, and retribution that the lord wrought and ordered the Arkons carry out in his name. Those deeds happened; there was no denying it.

The killings.

The destruction.

The great deluge, and all the millions that died gasping beneath its unforgiving waves.

The fires. Cities burning, blasted by Azathoth's heavenly fires. Thousands of souls shrieking as their bodies fed unrelenting flames.

Bolts of lightning from the heavens that struck down the heathens, blasted them to blood and bones by the hundreds, by the thousands, with no regard for man, woman, or child.

Uriel had witnessed those wicked deeds, and had brought about much destruction at the lord's command. There was no doubt of that. No denying it. But what were the lord's motivations? Were they justified, part of the grand plan he so often mentioned but refused to explain?

All for the greater good?

Or no?

Could anything justify those murders?

Were the justifications all lies? Were the lord's harsh deeds merely punishment for those who dared defy his will? His domination? Or worse, did the lord do those deeds because he found foul pleasure in them?

How could that possibly be? How could it?

What was the truth? What did truth even mean? Was it a thing, an immutable object that could be known, named, and defined -- like a mathematical formula -- the same for any who studied its secrets? Or was the truth something else? Did it change depending upon who observed it, who defined it, who recorded it for posterity? Was there more than one truth? Or no truth at all? Or did each man have his own truth?

Uriel never thought of those things before, not in all his long years. He'd had no reason to. But now he could think of little else. He didn't even know what was good or evil any longer. It didn't make sense to him anymore. Nothing made sense. He didn't know what side he was on. He didn't know what he stood for anymore. Or what any man stood for. Or what any of it meant.

Was it the lord that had gone mad, or was it he? Was he – Uriel – the insane one, deluded and confused, confounded and conflicted -- he and Thetan, Mithron, Gabriel, Azrael, and all The Fallen? Were they the madmen? The thought of it all made Uriel's head spin.

He decided...to carry on. He had chosen his path, just as Thetan had reminded them. Rightly or wrongly he was on that path, there was no going back or turning about, no chance of forgiveness, no penance enough. He would see it through. And accept whatever fate was in store for him, though he felt increasingly certain that he was destined to come to a bad end.

10

URIEL THE BOLD

"**F**ollow your heart, my darling," Uriel's mother often told him when he was a youth. "Your head may lie to you, your manly parts surely will, but your heart will lead you down the true path. Trust your heart, and follow it, all the days of your life." That's what she told him on the tearful morning she saw him off to Azathoth's service — to enter training to be one of the lord's elite servants, the enforcers of his will, the royal Arkons. A great honor it was; fewer than one in a thousand youths were selected. And a great sacrifice, for forevermore the child was lost to its family — a memory, a story, a point of pride, but little more. Visits were few and far between for most; none at all for many. In all the ages that passed since the day he left home, Uriel had only seen his mother five times -- the last, over a thousand years previous. The long years had taken their toll; he barely remembered her face. He'd forgotten the sound of her voice. Guilt weighed heavily upon him over that. Yet despite the great chasm of time, not having her in his life evoked in him a terrible sense of loss that lingered down through the years. A loss magnified because her love could not be replaced — banned as he was, as all Arkons were, from taking a spouse, having children, or even engaging in intimate relationships be they of no account or great commitment. Such were some few of the weighty burdens of Azathoth's service, for the lord was a jealous god – he'd share his chosen servants' love with no one else.

A terrible thought crossed Uriel's mind. He couldn't fathom why it hadn't occurred to him before.

Had his family been held accountable for his betrayal? Had the lord sent Arkons to seek them out? Throw them into irons? Torture them? Kill them? Was there a record of who his family members were — it had been so long?

The lord would remember. He remembered everything. Time was no barrier to him. Iblis or Makriel may well have led a squad to his mother's home, or to his brother's, or to one of his sisters', or to all of them.

Uriel's heart pounded in his chest as he thought of it. Honors were bestowed on his family for his service. Pride. Respect in the community.

But now what? He'd disgraced them. He'd destroyed his reputation and by association, theirs. They might well be dead for three years already.

And he didn't even know.

When the rebellion began, he dared not visit his family, for fear he'd be seen or be trailed there, and put their lives in jeopardy. He also feared they'd reject him for his rebellion. And why not? Why shouldn't they? To them, the lord was the lord: all good, and so forth. Uriel was the traitor, the villain, the criminal. He couldn't go to them. He couldn't show his face. He dared not. He could not suffer their wrath. And so he stayed away. But it never occurred to him that the lord's wrath might fall on them — or so he told himself.

And now it was too late. Three years had gone by. If the lord had wanted vengeance on them for his deeds, that vengeance was long since taken. What tortures might they have endured because of *his* crimes?

The weight of that guilt hung heavy around Uriel's neck.

When the time came and it was safe to do so, he'd check on them. He needed to know if they were alive or not. He needed to know if they suffered because of him. And he felt a fool, a self-absorbed stupid fool, for not thinking of this three years earlier. But now it was too late to do anything but regret, or mourn, or seek vengeance. It would all play out in time, *if* he survived the coming battle.

11

URIEL THE BOLD

Uriel's heart pounded before he raised his blade against Korrgonn. He didn't know for certain whether he'd fooled the godling. Did Korrgonn believe that his magic had beguiled him, or did he suspect trickery? Was he prepared for Uriel to attack, waiting to launch some devious counterstrike?

And even if he were, did it matter, for they stood at the heart of Uriel's power — in Anglotor Tower with fifty of Uriel's best backing him, including the two nearly indestructible Iron Golems he'd constructed in ages past to safeguard the Olden Dome and do his bidding. The tower doors were barred and wizard warded; Korrgonn's men couldn't get in by muscle or magic, though they'd tried their damnedest.

Korrgonn was on his own.

Uriel had him. He need only make certain to contain him.

Uriel knew he'd at best get one free shot to wound or kill Korrgonn. After that, if Korrgonn

55

was still capable, there'd be a knife fight.

Still, Uriel didn't know who Korrgonn was. He wore Gabriel Hornblower's face – *could he* be Gabriel, gone mad after all these ages? Or did he speak the truth when he claimed to be Azathoth's son, a godling of Nifleheim? And if so, who knows what powers he could possess. Or is he someone else entirely, this all a ruse for reasons yet unknown? The least likely answer, of course, was that Korrgonn was the godling he claimed. But deep down in Uriel's gut, he believed it to be true, the odds be damned. And it seemed fitting that it would come to this. A test or a penance long overdue.

And so, in an odd way, Uriel welcomed the duel, even longed for it. He'd forever lived by the sword, but it had been overlong since he'd faced a worthy opponent. Many of those who invaded Anglotor over the millennia were good fighters, more than a few were great. But great was a long way from challenging an Eternal. Such invaders were dangerous mainly in their numbers.

Might Korrgonn have the skills to challenge Uriel one-on-one?

Uriel was eager to find out. He'd kept up his training down through the long years; hours every day, exercising, sparring, and practicing against Svart, Dwarf, Lugron, Elf, Juton, and Ettin, usually several at a time. Not that this would be a true duel, for Uriel's men would help him and he wouldn't call them off. He welcomed the challenge, but he wanted to survive, and to end the fight as quickly as possible was his best chance at that. Although he lived by a rather strict code of honor, the idea of a "fair" fight meant nothing to Uriel. To fight was to win. To win was to survive. There was nothing else except for tourneys and true duels over honor, women, or other such silliness.

So, Uriel had no doubt he'd defeat Korrgonn, backed as he was and Korrgonn alone, but he didn't delude himself into thinking that it'd be easy. He had to make that first strike count. And he was ready for it, his knife nearly pure ranal, so whether Korrgonn was a charlatan, a mad Arkon, or a true Lord of Nifleheim, that blade could bury him.

Without warning, Uriel raked the ranal blade across Korrgonn's throat. And with that single strike Uriel knew at once that Korrgonn was no charlatan, no wannabe or pretender, and certainly not his old friend Gabriel Hornblower. He was no man at all. He was something else, from somewhere else, whether Nifleheim or beyond, for his flesh was made of much sterner stuff than mortal man's or Eternal's. It was dense and tough. Cutting his exposed throat was more akin to cutting stone than flesh. And so, the ranal blade, even backed by Uriel's prodigious strength, did not sink deep.

Half an inch, mayhap a bit more.

The same cut may well have taken a normal man's head off. But to Korrgonn it was no mortal wound, though a nasty one all the same. Had Uriel's blade been of common steel, however sharp, it would have failed even to draw blood.

Uriel had caught the godling unawares, and

well that he did. Korrgonn lurched back against the stair's wall, a hand reflexively going to his throat, his eyes bulging as white blood oozed from betwixt his fingers, its aspect unnatural.

Uriel's blade never stopped moving despite his surprise at Korrgonn's stony flesh. He aimed his next strike at a gap in Korrgonn's armor, but the godling spun and knocked his hand aside with shocking speed that belied his wound.

Korrgonn flicked his other hand at Uriel and blood spatters doused Uriel's face, his eyes — and burned his skin like acid. As Uriel tried to sidestep, Korrgonn kicked him so hard in the midsection that it lifted him into the air and sent him flying off the stair's side to crash to the entry hall's floor.

A normal man would've suffered multiple broken ribs and been down and out of the fight from that kick, not even counting injuries from the fall. But so too were Uriel's bones made of sterner stuff than mortal man's. Uriel suffered no broken ribs but he'd had the wind knocked out of him and his strength momentarily sapped, such that he couldn't rotate in the air and land on his feet as he otherwise would've done. Instead, he landed hard on his back, but he tucked chin to chest and avoided thumping his skull.

He heard his men shouting.

"Get the intruder."

"Kill him."

Then came an explosion that slammed Uriel's head against the floor. The blast flung the men closest to Korrgonn through the air, knocked

58

everyone else over. Men crashed down all around Uriel. He figured it for sorcery, but how did Korrgonn call it up so quickly?

Uriel made to leap to his feet, but his body was slow to respond; his limbs, rubbery; and he strained to take a breath. He looked up and saw Korrgonn standing on the stair gripping that curious talisman, his other hand clamped to the wound on his neck, trying to keep the blood inside. Uriel wondered if the cut were deeper than he'd first thought, deep enough perhaps to do him in, to bleed him out. Could he be that lucky? Unlikely.

A quick glance told Uriel that at least two or three of his men were dead at the base of the stair. Even the Ettin were down. The Golems, however, were up and plodding toward Korrgonn. They knew an enemy when they saw one. Once they got going and picked up speed, they'd eventually corner him and tear him to pieces.

Korrgonn chanted loudly in some wizarding language that Uriel knew not. In the five seconds it took Uriel to catch his breath and make his feet, Korrgonn completed his spell, and two beams of red light shot from his talisman and struck each of the Golems in the head.

Uriel vaulted for the stair. He didn't know if Korrgonn's magic was strong enough to damage his Golems, but he wasn't going to wait to find out for they were too valuable to lose and too difficult to replace. In a single leap, Uriel's hands caught the stair's edge several steps above Korrgonn. He effortlessly pulled himself up and landed on his feet, pulling out his sword in the process. He swung the blade in a wide arc hoping to catch the godling's neck, but Korrgonn ducked and pulled out his own sword and a wicked-looking curved dagger.

The moment Uriel engaged Korrgonn, he heard shouts of alarm and the sounds of heavy blows being landed below him, at the stair's base.

His men screamed.

12

URIEL THE BOLD

Trailing its innumerable brethren, Uriel's Targon banked hard to the right. The harness dug deeper into his shoulders; after all these hours aloft, he'd be sore and bruised for days.

Uriel knew all too well that any battle might be a warrior's last, so he never let down his guard, never grew careless. It didn't matter how strong you were, how tough, how skilled at arms, or how experienced or confident – a single well-placed sword thrust or arrow, a broken sword, an ill-timed parry, or even a tiny poison dart -- and you were dead. No matter who you were, no matter how well loved by however many, how famous or grand, how important or indispensable, if luck abandoned you, you were dead. Uriel had seen it countless times. He'd witnessed peasants and barbarians of no skill and no consequence bring down great warriors, time and again. Uriel had cheated death a thousand times when others had not. If you asked him how he'd done it, he'd only smile and wink. If pressed, he might boast of his skill at arms or speak of toughness, training, or great gear.

He had those in abundance, there was no

doubt, but those weren't what saved him down through the ages.

It was luck.

Luck.

The most ephemeral of qualities. You can't get better at it. You can't practice with it. You can't hold it in your hand, or buy, borrow, or steal it, but it was responsible for his survival more than anything else.

He knew it.

The same was true of all his brethren. And no one was luckier than Thetan or Mithron; nothing touched them.

Rarely, anything touched Uriel.

Luck.

From where did it spring?

And what kept him cloaked in it? Was it the lord's grace? Was it mere happenstance, pure chance, or something else, something more? Was luck, not Azathoth, the real god of the universe? Mayhap it was luck that man instead should worship. Or maybe luck was nothing more than mere chance, controlled and predestined by nothing and no one. Could that be true? Could a man's destiny, could the fate of the world, rest on nothing more than random chance, improbable happenstance, with no greater purpose, no higher power, no hand of fate? Could that be true? The answers were unknowable and Uriel did not care for that. He liked knowing. Luck was one of the great mysteries he hoped he'd someday solve but couldn't fathom even how to search for the answer. One thing he'd noticed, though -- the people who tried the hardest, who never gave up, often seemed to have the most luck. In everything Uriel did, he tried his best, he strived to win. And he almost always did.

Almost.

In this campaign, best laid plans or not, the odds were against them. Uriel knew it. Some of the others surely knew as well, but none of them admitted it to each other, if even to themselves. Just as he, they were all committed. There was no going back. Only forward toward their fate.

As they swooped lower, angling downward toward their destination, flocks of butterflies danced in Uriel's throat and did flips in his gut, encouraging him to puke, turnabout, and flee. He told the little buggers where they could go, just as he had prior to every bar room brawl, knife fight, skirmish, or all-out war that he saw coming. The pesky things always came back. The only cure for them, battle's first blow. They never survived that. Not once. He need only endure them until then.

13

URIEL THE BOLD

A battle was under way at the stair's base. How could that be? It made no sense, because, save for Korrgonn, no strangers had breached the tower and the doors remained closed — as far as Uriel knew.

Facing most any other opponent, Uriel would've chanced a glance to see what went on, but against Korrgonn, as fast, powerful, and resilient as the godling was, Uriel couldn't risk it. All his focus remained on his duel.

Uriel commanded the high ground and planned to keep it, use it to his advantage. He pulled his dagger and now they both were similarly equipped. Uriel held his sword in his left hand, as did all the Eternals, whereas Korrgonn favored his right.

Then came a furious exchange of blows. Their blades moved faster than the eye could follow and clanged and banged against one another like thunderclaps. Normal blades, even of the finest steel, would've shattered under those impacts, but Uriel's ranal weapons could withstand most anything and maintain their edge. What Korrgonn's weapons were made of, Uriel could not guess. They both parried, ducked, or dodged most every blow. Korrgonn countered even the boldest and most obscure techniques, and Uriel tried one after another, but scored only a few minor hits.

Uriel attempted to force Korrgonn down the steps, into his men's clutches. There was no chance Korrgonn could fend off him and them simultaneously; only a matter of time before they took him down.

But no men rushed to Uriel's aid.

And the roaring, bellows, and battle cries below grew the louder.

Those cries soon told Uriel what was happening: the Golems had set upon the Anglotorians! They'd turned against them, but whether in wild madness or in purposeful attack, Uriel knew not. Regardless, they were killing his men.

His soldiers, for all their skills and courage, had not the tools or training to destroy a single Golem, little less two acting in concert. Now, instead of Korrgonn's defeat being inevitable, Uriel wondered if *his* was.

Uriel knew of no means by which a wizard could wrest control over another sorcerer's Golem; their mystical ties to their master could not be severed while the master yet lived, and Uriel was still quite alive, or so he figured.

How had Korrgonn turned them?

For every second that ticked by Uriel and Korrgonn exchanged two or three blows. Both opponents had been sliced and pricked, but they'd landed no heavy blows.

In that exchange, Uriel learned four important things.

Wounding Korrgonn was next to useless. Cuts and stab wounds didn't slow or stop him. He didn't cry out and he didn't tire. Uriel figured, he either possessed extraordinary healing powers or was immune to pain, or both.

Korrgonn was faster than him; not by much, but by enough.

Korrgonn was the stronger by a goodly ways.

Fourth, although Korrgonn was one of the greatest fighters he'd ever fought, Uriel was the better. He nicked him, pricked him, sliced him, and jabbed him. Unfortunately, it was all to no end for Korrgonn came on relentlessly, never slowing, crying out, or tiring.

Korrgonn repeatedly tried to move up to the same step as he, but Uriel refused to give up that small advantage and beat the godling back over and again. When Korrgonn moved back a step to catch his balance, Uriel retreated a step, took a moment to catch his breath, and chanced a glance below. At least a score of his men were down. Broken. Probably dead. All the rest were on the Golems, attacking them like mad, working together: sword, axe, and hammer. The Ettins mercilessly bashed the Golems with clubs.

The Golems were slashed and battered but nothing could stop them.

"Golems, stand down," shouted Uriel. He didn't think that would work, but he had time for nothing more.

Even that took too long.

In those moments, Korrgonn touched his talisman and a beam of yellow fire shot from it and struck Uriel in the chest. The blast knocked him back against the stairs, though it failed to burn him; no doubt, his Ankh safeguarded him, reliable as always. Suddenly, Korrgonn's magic pulled him into the air and suspended him above the stair. How it lifted him, he knew not; he felt nothing grab him.

The sorcery suddenly slammed him into the nearest wall, a terrific impact. His dagger dropped from his grasp and his head spun, dizzy. "Coward," he shouted as he squirmed to get free, but there was nothing to get free from, nothing to push away or hit. "Fight me, you bastard."

Korrgonn made no response.

Uriel was helpless as the unseen wizardry turned him on his side and sent him flying into another wall.

He threw his sword at Korrgonn, but the godling dodged.

Then the magic slammed Uriel into another wall. His vision clouded and his limbs refused to respond. He tried to reach for his Ankh, but before he grasped it, the magic flung him again, headlong into another wall.

And another.

And another, until Uriel saw no more.

14

URIEL THE BOLD

Uriel had been up higher than the others, flying alone deep amidst the clouds since they'd set out that morning from the depths of Taramor Forest. Other squadrons joined the main flight along the way, but he'd paid them no heed, leaving troop coordination to others. Happily without duties until the battle began, he remained lost in his thoughts amidst the rarefied atmosphere, nothing but the rushing air about him, while he tried to make sense of it all.

When he finally dipped below the lowest clouds, he enjoyed a commanding view of The Fallen's aerial host. He'd rarely seen so many in flight at one time. Thousands, in all their majesty and plumage, ornate armor of every color, reflecting dawn's light to the heavens and blotting it out for any below.

Seeing all those Targon, Uriel recalled the looks of shock on novice Arkons' faces when they first saw one up close.

Shock, followed by disappointment. Every time.

Not until the solemn ceremony of "the wings", did novices learn that the wings they'd receive were not theirs at all, but those of a flying beast,

68

their Targon, who would join them in their service to the lord, much as a knight's horse or war hound. Before that, novices assumed that the lord would wave his hand, speak a blessing, and great wings would sprout from their backs, ready to carry them aloft on their holy duties and allow them to frolic at will amongst the clouds. The truth was kept close by the Arkons by long tradition.

At first, novices hung by the harness like baggage, their limbs and stomachs flopping, carried about by the noble beasts. But an expert rider could coax a Targon into wondrous acts of agility, speed, and daring maneuvers unmatched by any other mount on land or air. Masters fought while flying -- jousting with lances, long and deadly.

From above, Uriel could see the Targon that carried each man, though their bodies were thin and translucent, save for their feathered wings. A beautiful sight it was. From below, the Targon's bodies, save their wings, were entirely hidden, making it appear as if the Arkons themselves had wings. It added to the Arkons' illusion of being heavenly beings, set apart from man, — that of course being the source of the novices' preconceptions.

From Uriel's vantage, most of The Fallen were dim specks in the distance, a horde of mosquitoes dive bombing the idyllic snow-covered land far below. He saw frozen lakes and rivers, hills and forests, valleys, crags, and far-off peaks. They'd flown high, their strategy to remain unseen by the loyalists and the lord until they reached Vigrid Valley, deep in the heart of the lord's territory. Vigrid was the anticipated scene of the great battle.

Thetan had marched his ground troops to muster at the eastern edge of the Plain of Vigrid. They'd gathered in secret, troop by troop, company by company, corps by corps, these past weeks, trudging through the snow, the aerial corps to join them at the appointed hour.

At last, the valley came into view. Approaching Vaeden from the east, one *had* to pass through it. A great road kept passable by the lord's minions stretched down the center, the terrain flat and inviting, no natural dangers of distress. The valley was surrounded by picturesque hills and small peaks. Nothing grand, merely a pleasant valley nearby Azathoth's storied capital.

But no longer. From that day forward it would be infamous. A place of blood and death and wasted lives, and if The Fallen won, the site of Azathoth's twilight. But if they lost, no doubt, the battle would be forgotten, and all their names struck from the rolls, never to be spoken again.

Uriel had rarely seen such a gathering of military might. The great campaign against the northern barbarians two hundred years prior had put great numbers in the field, so had the easterly expeditions of fifty years back, and the push to expand the lord's kingdom to the southern sea and the islands beyond, five hundred years prior. There were not yet so many on the Plain of Vigrid, but before they were done, there would be more. More than ever before. The battle to end all battles. Uriel wondered how many of his brothers would survive it. How many would fall?

What if Thetan fell?

Or Mithron?

Both?

Would one of the others take up their mantle? Could they?

Or would the rebellion fall to chaos? Uriel didn't relish command, not of a vast group under dire circumstances.

Was Azrael up to the task?

Dekkar? Yes, Dekkar could do it. He'd step up if the need arose.

Hogar had not the words or Raphael the depth of resolve. Bose had not the temperament. Tolkiel could carry the mantle, though he wouldn't want to.

The world's fate hung on so flimsy a thing -- a well-placed sword thrust, an arrow, a catapult blast, or a single throw of javelin or dagger.

Uriel would take command if he had to.

If it came to it.

But he prayed that it wouldn't.

The trouble was, he didn't know who to pray to. It was one thing to cast off Azathoth's yoke, but another entirely to take up with some pagan deity and begin worshipping trees or water, the sun, the moon, or the stars. He was above the foolishness of deities birthed by superstition. Azathoth was different. He was tangible. You could see him, hear him, follow him. And that's what Uriel had done, for Uriel was never a man of faith. He didn't trust in some invisible and mysterious guiding hand greater than man.

Azathoth *was* something greater, and he had been right there before his eyes, and so, Uriel believed. How could he not? But what did he believe now? Who did he believe in now?

Thetan?

His brethren?

Himself?

Or nothing at all?

All those thoughts and more spun through his head, but he cast them aside as they reached their destination. He'd keep them at bay until the troubles were done, for the moment his Targon set foot on the Valley of Vigrid, his thoughts would focus on nothing but battle and victory. Such was his training, such was his mind, for in so doing he maximized his chance of victory, and of survival, and of his precious luck holding out.

Thetan, Mithron, Tolkiel, and Dekkar had planned it all so well. They assembled their host for one great push to end a war that had gone on too long. A day of infamy and of greatness. And if all went well, they'd throw down the gates of Vaeden and march inside in triumph, many folk cheering their banners, knowing that their arrival meant freedom from the yoke long hung around their necks.

The Fallen had made certain that Azathoth and his minions heard tell of their plans and were ready for them.

The Fallen knew what Bhaal and Asmodeus would do. They'd set a trap. They'd come at them with all their strength from the West, from Vaeden, and from the South, up through the forest of Bissel. Mammon would come in on Targon, perhaps from the North, mayhap from the West, and they'd converge on The Fallen from at least two sides, mayhap three, in a vise grip that could not be sundered. They'd come in with all their worth: Mikel, Iblis, Makriel, Hecate, all leading their legions. They'd destroy The Fallen in one fell swoop. Such would be their plan. It had to be. They could not afford to draw out the war any longer, for fear the people might turn on them. They needed to bring it to an end, to save face for the old god.

The Fallen counted on one thing, their plan depended upon it -- that Azathoth would take to the field himself. And when he did, Thetan would deploy the Sphere of the Heavens to open a portal to the *Nether Realms.* And once that portal lay open, they need only find a way to throw Azathoth through it.

They would find a way.

Uriel would find a way, or die in the trying.

15

JUTENHEIM
ANGLOTOR
THE COURTYARD
YEAR 1267, 4TH AGE

Korrgonn was battered and bloody; dripped with sweat; haggard and unkempt; his clothes, ripped; his armor, dented and gouged; bloodstained, hair to boot. His right hand held his sword, and his left dragged a limp man by the collar -- Uriel the Bold: broken, bloodied, unconscious, or dead.

"Master, master," shouted Par Keld as he pushed through the ranks and threw himself at Korrgonn's feet. "Praise almighty Azathoth that you are well. I never doubted your victory; I only wish I could've gained entry to help you, try as I might, my knuckles bloody, the doors would not yield."

Korrgonn ignored him and sought Ginalli's eyes. "The keep is ours," he said, his voice like a growl. "We must find the inner sanctum at once. Bring forth the Orb, for time grows short."

Ginalli rushed up to Korrgonn, the other Leaguers a step or two behind.

"My lord, you are injured," said Ginalli. "We must treat your wounds, give you time to rest, and take sustenance. You must have your full strength for the conjuring that is to come."

Korrgonn waved him off. "The Harbinger of Doom approaches. I can feel him. His power. His malevolence. Close on our heels is he, closer than ever before. He may be here within minutes, hours at most."

"But my lord," said Ginalli, "Master Thorn sent six hundred Stowron to intercept him. Surely, the Harbinger hasn't enough men to get past such a force? If they don't slay him outright, he'll have to go to ground or retreat, giving us all the time we need."

"Thorn's Stowron are already dead," said Korrgonn. "You still don't understand the Harbinger's power, the evil that he embodies and represents. All the Stowron in Midgaard could not hope to stop him, little less slay him. He is evil incarnate. His power, beyond mortal understanding."

Ginalli's face went pale; he was at a loss for words.

"We must be swift," said Korrgonn. "Bring the prisoners."

"Who is that?" said Ginalli when he finally found his voice, a finger pointed at Uriel as the others began to march into the tower.

"A devil from the ancient past," said Korrgonn as he shook Uriel by the neck, though the man hung limp and lifeless. "Once beloved of my father, he betrayed the lord and all the good people of Midgaard. He has hidden here in this far-off isle for untold ages, festering in his own evil, wallowing in his deceit, corrupting the local populace, and desecrating the very land itself. Look upon him with trepidation, for his is the

75

face of true evil. There is no end to his depravities, his wicked and foul deeds, or his malevolent desires. A key henchmen of the Harbinger is he. Without this demon, the Harbinger is weakened, and that is good."

"Such a foul creature," said Ginalli as he looked at Uriel. "Praise Azathoth that you bested him."

"There could be no other outcome," said Korrgonn.

16

EAST OF VIGRID VALLEY
FIMBULWINTER - YEAR 3
THE AGE OF MYTH AND LEGEND

THETAN THE LIGHTBRINGER

Thetan sat on a rocky snow-covered ledge that overlooked the thick forest east of Vigrid Valley. His brethren sat stoically to either side and behind. The forest was alive with movement, filled as it was with myriad troops -- all those who came when The Fallen called their banners. Tens of thousands of them. An exact count, even Thetan did not yet possess.

No one atop the overlook spoke.

This was their stundar-mal, the quiet time before a battle -- the time to clear one's thoughts of all else but the upcoming conflict, or, for some, the time to remember, reflect, or to say their goodbyes. So too, it was a time to breathe the clear crisp air, to appreciate life and all creation, to remind oneself of the many things worth living for.

The Arkons ordered that the troops and militias that rallied to their banners respect the stundar-mal, but many amongst them lacked the discipline. Men's nerves rattled before battle, energy aplenty. Nervous men made noise -- shuffling, talking, even laughter here and there. They made much less noise than most armies, but too much for The Fallen's ears. It put them on edge, some more than others.

Thetan heard footsteps approach from behind. He didn't turn until Gabriel, who sat at his right hand, gripped his shoulder.

"Markon," said Thetan. The Fallen's chief scout had returned.

Markon was of slim build for an Arkon, lanky, rugged, and weathered. One of Thetan's oldest friends amongst the Arkon corps; they'd both served Azathoth from the beginning.

"Lord Thetan," said Markon standing at attention, his eyes fixed on his leader. "The Northmen are in position along Percipion Ridge as agreed, late though they be. They will march at dawn to support us."

"How many have come?" said Mithron, who loomed like a great bear at Thetan's left.

"All of them, it seems," said Markon. "they swarm the forest's northern reaches like ants. Even Wotan's chieftains did not know their number, but they claim no fewer than sixty major clans have come, though they can't or won't say how many men per clan despite my pressing. I'd place their number at more than fifty thousand, but understand, that is little more than a guess."

"Could there be only twenty thousand?" said Thetan.

"That is possible," said Markon, "but unlikely."

"Could there be as many as one hundred thousand?" said Thetan."

"I cannot say," said Markon shaking his head, "but that too is possible."

"So we have no idea how many there are," said Mithron, "other than *many*."

"Fifty thousand, or thereabouts," said Markon, his voice louder, eyes now on Mithron. "I spied the edges of their encampment; their density; heard their noise, smelled their stink. It's guesswork, as I've said, but not based on nothing."

"No disrespect, brother," said Mithron, "but we can't rely on a guess. Too much is at stake. If there are only twenty thousand, it changes our plans."

"Wotan was there?" said Thetan. "And Donar?"

"I saw them both," said Markon, "though both were too important to speak with me, despite the weighty messages passed to and fro. These barbarians think themselves quite grand. Two of their chieftains took my measure: one, as big as Hogar, name of Heimdall -- he asked after you, Thetan; the other, called Loki, scoffed at your name. That Loki had a queer look about him -- the scion of a strange bloodline that I cannot place, save to say he is no common Northman. The eyes of a fox, he has; the tongue of a serpent. Not a man to be trusted. He shadowed my every move. I thought it best not to linger lest a dagger find my back."

"Well that you did not," said Thetan. "We've held here longer than planned already. Wotan is three days late. What delayed him?"

"Weather and unfamiliar terrain, they claim."

"Not loyalists?" said Gabriel.

Markon shook his head. "They believe they've

gone unnoticed, though they spied several airborne scouts. I would not count on their stealth. My former brethren are...skilled."

Thetan nodded.

"But if true," said Gabriel, "no better news could you bring. If the Northmen enter this campaign in surprise, the loyalists will rout or else be overrun, just as we planned. Could we be so lucky?"

"A man makes his own luck," said Uriel, "by smart planning and sound judgment."

"Or by bold action," said Mithron.

"I'll give you that," said Uriel.

"Another scout," said Gabriel, pointing to where another slim man had landed his Targon nearby.

"It's Cephalon," said Uriel.

The scout hurried confidently toward the officers.

Thetan nodded, granting him leave to make his report. "My lords, the Northmen are on Percipion Ridge as planned, though I trust you already know that, since brother Markon is amongst you. I saw him depart their camp just as I arrived. I lingered to get the best count I could of their numbers, hard as it was to make them out through the trees. Judging by the span of the camp and the thickness of their groupings, no fewer than sixty thousand warriors, I'd warrant -- half again as many in their train. But there could easily be eighty or ninety thousand of them packed into those woods. A barbarian horde the like of which has not been seen in an age."

"That settles it then," said Mithron, nodding to both scouts in turn. "Wotan has delivered as he promised with more than we could've hoped for. We may prevail in this mad adventure after all."

"I've said this before," said Dekkar, "and I'll say it now once more. We cannot rely on the Northmen to support us *after* we are fully engaged. If they delay, or turn tail or coat, our forces may well be slaughtered. Better that we give up the element of surprise and have the Northmen attack from the northern flank simultaneously with us."

"We've been through this a dozen times," said Mithron. "We know your reasoning and it's not unsound, but we have voted, and the majority agrees that a surprise charge by the Northmen is our best chance to break loyalist lines and pull Azathoth into the fray. It's in that confusion that we might strike him down. We must not forget that our goal is not to vanquish his armies – for goodness' sake, they are our brethren. Our goal is to bring Azathoth to the field, where he's vulnerable; to pull him out of his palace where he's strongest.

"And I say," responded Dekkar, "we can break his lines with a simultaneous assault, and he'll still venture to the field just as quickly. That will be our chance, and at much less risk. Why can't you see that?"

"There is not a right or wrong in this," said Azrael. "There is merely a judgment to be made, sound reasoning on both sides. We've all considered the arguments and cast our votes as best we could. The matter is settled; let it not distract us henceforth. There is much work to be done."

"Aye, aye," went the Arkons.

17

JUTENHEIM
ANGLOTOR TOWER
YEAR 1267, 4TH AGE

JUDE EOTRUS

Sir Jude Eotrus's stomach churned as Teek Lugron led him by the arm to the doors of Anglotor Tower's entry hall. The bulk of the Shadow League's expedition massed just past the doors while their scouts spread out in all directions to scour the tower's interior. The torn dead lay heaped about the hall, broken, slashed, and crushed – their ruined bodies a mockery of their living selves. The floor drowned in blood, awash in dismembered limbs, decapitated heads, and shredded torsos of dozens of soldiers: Jutons, Gnomes, Dwarves, and Ettin, all in common livery -- the defenders of the tower, not a single Leaguer corpse amongst them.

Up in front, Par Keld shouted and cursed, but at whom, Jude couldn't tell. The little wizard began to cough and retch from the stench of death that hung over that place until he leaned forward and launched a plume of vomit into several Stowrons' faces, spattering many others. The Leaguers backed up, cursing. Even the normally silent Stowron grumbled, their weird voices, alien and haunting.

"They haven't respect enough to move the bodies," said Brother Donnelin. "Trampling them. Standing atop them as if they're garbage, and they expect us to do the same. Deserve some common decency. What a disgrace."

Jude wanted to agree. He wanted to shout in protest over the whole thing: the slaughter. But he believed if he dared open his mouth, his stomach's contents would follow even more forcefully than had Par Keld's. Best keep it in, tired and weak enough, he figured.

What had those men done to the League?

Nothing.

And yet the League laid siege to the place and put the inhabitants to the sword, no quarter or mercy. Not even for the women. Thank the gods he'd seen no children about. He prayed someone had spirited them to safety. He'd not stand by and watch children slaughtered. He'd sooner die than see that.

"Steady there, Judy Boy," said Teek. "You've gone white as a bonnie lord's new bedsheets. Puke on me, and I'll pummel you cold, so keep your stuffing on the inside where it belongs," he said in his comradely banter.

"Some of these boys," said Teek pointing to the corpses, "got sent up Valhalla way by a great big bladed weapon: slashed, stabbed, and whatnot – Korrgonn's doing, the big boss man, the high-and-mighty. How you figure he done all that killing on his lonesome, Judy Boy? He be a swordmaster, can't argue, but there ain't no man alive what can chop down thirty, forty trained-up

84

men all coming at him at once from every which way. But he did. That make you a believer, convinced of his godliness?"

Jude shook his head. Couldn't chance answering aloud even though his stomach was settling.

"He had help," said Brother Donnelin. "Many of the bodies are crushed. Heads and chests staved in. The Golems' handiwork."

Teek nodded his agreement. "Curious thing, them ironsides turning Leaguer, following what the big boss man tells them, like pet puppies, don't you think? Took them over he did. Enslaved them to his will. How you figure he did that, Judy Boy?"

Jude shook his head and shuffled his feet, the congealing blood sticky beneath his boots.

"All your fancy schooling ain't got you no answers, do it, lordling?" said Teek. His voice was a whisper when he spoke again. "I ain't so fancy, and I ain't got no schooling to speak of, but I see things clear enough. I've heard tell, Golems only do the bidding of he who made them. Magicked up by wizards they are, one and all. Since they're doing the boss man's bidding nowabouts, it follows he's got more magic than the boss of this place did, the poor bastard. That makes our boss man a high wizard or a sorcerer or some such, but not no godling."

"My brother saw him come through a magical doorway from Nifleheim," whispered Jude. "So did others."

"Aye, laddie, maybe so," said Teek, "but traveling from the *Nether Realms* to Midgaard is more wizard's work -- black sorcery, I'd mark it. Chaos magic some would call it. Working *The Weave* don't make him a godling, but it does make him dangerous."

"He's not human," whispered Donnelin. "That much I can tell. I can feel it."

"Can you now?" said Teek. "Carve him up in his sleep, did you? Augur his innards whilst chawing on fresh-boiled newt's eye? Then I bet you sewed him up all right and proper, him never knowing nothing nohow? Or did ya get your feeling from tossing the bones a time or two when no one was none the wiser? I know you've got a set of old grays, seen you fidgeting with them." Teek shook his head. "You don't know dung, priest, nor do your bones. That old boy's a humbug with spells. Delusions of grandeur is what he's got. And Ginalli and his bunch are just the kind of nutters to believe him. He can't fool me, not old Teek, I've been around, farther afield even than hereabouts. You fancy boys are weak-minded and provincial. That comes from soft living in your fancy castles and frilly clothes, you know. Not getting out enough, not seeing all the wonders and all the dung what Midgaard has to offer -- a lot of both, I'll tell you. Things you wouldn't believe, not even after this adventure. Open your eyes and see things the way they are; you'll be the better for it."

18

AZATHOTH'S PALACE IN VAEDEN
FIMBULWINTER - YEAR 3
THE AGE OF MYTH AND LEGEND

Tall, lean, thin faced, and heavy jawed, Mammon approached the broad table where his fellows sat eating and took his place. "Our spies report, the traitors gather in the eastern woods."

The others paused their meal and gave him their attention. "How many gather?" said Iblis, a lanky hawk-faced man with spiky flaxen hair.

"The whole lot," said Mammon. "Tens of thousands strong. This is it. The deciding confrontation. Our chance to finally put an end to this madness."

"Even after all this time," continued Mammon, "I didn't think they'd take it this far. To question, to defy the lord, is one thing -- a grave sin in and of itself -- but one I could comprehend, though not condone. But what they did in the throne room, and all these attacks, months -- years -- of terrorism and strife, there's no making sense of it. And now they march an army against us. A horde! Against the lord. What madness has taken Thetan?"

"Do not speak the traitor's name," said Bhaal, a giant of a man, taller and bulkier even than Mithron, his cheekbones high, features chiseled as from stone. "Not in my presence. Not ever again."

Mammon rolled his eyes. "I will speak as I choose, unless the lord orders otherwise."

Bhaal's breathing was like a wolf's warning growl. He did not look at Mammon when he spoke, his eyes to his meal. "Be careful, brother. Be very careful."

"The Lightbringer truly believes he's in the right," said Arioch, until lately one of Thetan's inner circle. It was he who exposed Thetan's plot to the lord, betraying the betrayer. "They all do."

"So they're not traitors?" said Mikel, a barrel-chested man of rippling muscles.

"They raised their hands against the lord, you fool," said Bhaal. "They're traitors, no doubt of it. No coming back from that. No forgiveness, not even from the lord. I'll kill the traitor and the other Fallen on sight, you mark my words."

"Not if I get to them first," said Iblis as he twisted his knife, menacingly. "I would know the truth. I would know their minds. If it were only the Lightbringer, and mayhap a few followers, then madness I could call it. But since there are so many of them, there has to be more to it than that. This is a plot long in the making, but to what end I cannot grasp."

"I would know that truth before I see any of more of our former brothers dead," said Mikel.

"I will pluck the truth from their tongues," said Iblis, "even if I must take their tongues with it. Their crimes cannot stand."

"The lord could've killed them all in the throne room," said Belfaneor, a gaunt man with a pointed black beard. "You all know that, don't

88

you? He could've stopped the plot the moment it was birthed. Could've smote them from on-high at any time since this rebellion began. He has chosen to let them live. I struggle with that."

"He loves them," said Mikel. "The Lightbringer, Mithron, and the Hornblower have always been amongst his favored sons, just as we here have that honor. He wants them to return to the fold."

"Their crimes are unforgivable," said Iblis. "They deserve –"

"The lord will decide what they deserve," said Mikel. "You and Bhaal overstep your places. Mayhap the lord will forgive them if they repent, prostrate themselves before him, and beg mercy. He loves them well."

"They went too far," said Bhaal through gritted teeth. "No forgiveness this time, not for those crimes. Pay and pay dearly, they will. I will see this done."

"Only if the lord so orders it," said Mammon. "If you go rogue, you'll be as guilty as they."

"Sometimes, the lord's heart is too soft," said Bhaal. "I will not stand by and let him be betrayed again. I'll not take the chance that some magic those maggots uncover might harm him."

"None of us want that, brother," said Mikel. "But in this, as in all things, we must follow the lord's lead."

Bhaal hung his head low, his jaw clenched. He did not respond.

"The Lightbringer was ever the most beloved of us, but the least worthy," said Asmodeus. "His mind is and has always been troubled. He knows not the difference between good and evil, between loyalty and deceit. He is the Prince of Lies, and the Lord of Fools. He was given everything by the lord, yet appreciates nothing."

"Hear, hear," said Bhaal.

"Mithron is no malcontent," said Mammon. "He's respected by all. He sat this table countless times, broke bread with us, exchanged good cheer and counsel, as one of us. He did not set himself apart like Thetan."

Bhaal's fist slammed into the tabletop. "Don't...speak...his name."

"Brother, you've had enough wine for the evening, I think," said Mammon. "And I've had enough of your threats."

"Enough squabbling," said Asmodeus. "We can't afford more dissent in our ranks."

"Mithron never earned his place," said Bhaal. "The lord handed him his position, and I say that he was never worthy of it. The others...are nothing."

"The Lightbringer does evil and calls it good," said Asmodeus. "The lord does good and the Lightbringer calls it evil. He's a madman, Iblis. Root around in his brain or his guts all you like and you'll find no more than that. He walks through life in a fog, seeing things upside down and backwards. The best we can do for him and for all Midgaard is to put an end to him. It would be a mercy."

"The lord will not allow that," said Mikel.

"Then mayhap we should decide for him," said Bhaal. "In the heat of battle, men die. The traitor should die. He *must* die for what he's done. Imagine if he repented and the lord forgave him. Imagine having to suffer his presence at this table, at our council."

"If the lord allowed him to keep his position," said Iblis, "we may well be under his thumb again. I'll not have that. I suffered that for all too long. The most unworthy amongst us as a leader? Never again."

"I agree with that," said Mammon.

"The Lightbringer has holes in his mind," said Arioch. "Great swaths of time and events he fails to remember. Hit in the head too many times, in too many battles, if you ask me. The lord tried to heal him, but he's so far gone that even the lord has had only limited success."

"That's not it at all," said Asmodeus. "It was the lord who created the gaps in his memory."

Every man at the table perked up at that.

"Says who?" said Arioch.

"Says I," said Asmodeus. "I've served the lord near since the beginning, soon after he revealed himself to us. The Lightbringer has ever been a murderous rogue, out only for himself. The lord took him on as a project, a challenge, and tried to redeem him. He wiped from Thetan's memory some of his greatest crimes, and in so doing, tried to change his character. Tried to meld it into something better. And that sadly failed."

"Of what crimes do you speak?" said Mikel.

"Wanton murders," said Asmodeus. "Unnatural lusts, abuse of the weak, the elderly, women, even children. In times long past, all these things he did. The lord sought to save him, heal him, redeem him. And he's proven unredeemable. He was the worst of us. The most evil being in all creation. The lord kept all this secret, even from Thetan himself."

"How do you know this?" said Arioch. "I know Thetan better than any of you and I know nothing of this."

"I know it," said Asmodeus. "The lord believed that if he redeemed Thetan, if he brought him out of the darkness and into the light, then he could do the same for anyone. For a great length of time, it worked. Thetan served him well, though he always was of little faith, often defiant, a troublemaker."

"I know nothing of any of this, said KithKarmon, a muscled man of dark complexion. "Though I know Thetan as well as I know any of you. When it comes to it, he will not murder his fellow Arkons -- he will not murder *us*. I don't believe that could ever come to pass."

"Brother," said Asmodeus, "your faith in that foul traitor is woefully misplaced. His rebels have killed many of our brothers these past three years. Given the chance, he would kill you dead and shed no tears about it."

"Kith," said Iblis, "do you think the gathering horde is dropping by for tea? Do you think they'll assault us only with words and threats? Don't be a fool. They're here to kill us. They plan to pull the lord from his rightful throne and throw him down to the dirt. The lord! My brothers, this will be a battle, a battle unlike any other. Brother against brother, sword master against sword master. No more skirmishes and backstabbings in the night. No more hit-and-run tactics. This will be a stand-up fight, the battle to end all battles. Their madness is proven by marching upon us. They're outnumbered five, maybe ten, to one. And we have our fortifications. Our siege weapons. And the Brigandir."

"Hornblower has a mind of his own," said Mammon. "So does Mithron. Dekkar is a master strategist. Raphael, Azrael, Tolkiel, they all have brains upon their shoulders. I don't understand why they follow him, but our understanding is not needed. All we need do is end this thing, and safeguard the lord's kingdom."

Asmodeus nodded. "Yes, that is our duty. And we will do it even if some of us do not survive the day. Even if all *of them* do not survive the day."

"Such is our duty," said Mammon. "The right and proper thing to do."

19

JUTENHEIM
ANGLOTOR TOWER
YEAR 1267, 4TH AGE

JUDE EOTRUS

When the Shadow League's expedition entered Anglotor Tower, the going was slow, several starts and stops. The place was slick as ice with blood, the footing treacherous. Worse, every breath gifted them the nauseating, pungent stink of a battlefield – that distinct and unforgettable combination of blood, sweat, and men's innards. There was no way to avoid stepping on the bodies, or in the pools of blood.

Across the entry hall lurked an old stone stair, narrow, dark, and steep, that wound down into the bowels of the tower. A good many of the Leaguers headed down, caution and torches aplenty. The bulk of the Stowron stayed behind to guard the tower's entry hall.

Donnelin stepped closer to Jude and Teek and spoke quietly so no one else could hear. "You know where that leads, don't you?" he said gesturing toward the stair. "Down to whatever unholy altar pollutes this place. To the spot where they'll cut Jude open and drain him dry to bring back their foul lord. That's what they're about, what they've planned from the first. Is that what you signed up for, Lugron?"

"It ain't, holy man," said Teek. "I don't follow their religion, but I'm a mercenary, bought and paid. I got me orders, and if I don't heed them, these blokes will kill me dead and gift someone else the duty. Someone else less friendly. You're best off with me, I figure."

Jude swallowed hard, found his voice. "Teek, I played you square from the first, fair to say you've done the same with me and I thank you for it, but you've got to get us out of here. This is our last chance."

"Aye, I expect it is," said Teek. "But if a real chance comes, help you I will. You've got me word on that. I'm not your enemy and I'll do you no harm, League orders or not. But your best chance is if that witch woman of yours steps up and takes your side. If she don't, I don't think there's any getting out of here for either of you, my help or not. If it comes to it, I'll see they kill you quick. You're a good lad, Judy Boy. Damn good one. I'm proud to have fought at your side against those fish folk and them Black Elves. Even old one-arm here ain't so bad, for a Volsung anyways, and I never liked priests."

"I suppose I've known worse Lugron," said Donnelin.

Jude's eyes searched for Par Brackta. He'd lost track of her amongst the throng. Behind, stalked a half-dozen Lugron and a squadron of Stowron. Somewhere way back was Par Rhund -- a true believer in the Leaguer cause as best Jude could tell. There was no getting by that crowd. Not even if Jude had his sword, Donnelin his staff, and Teek threw in with them. Jude resolved to not go quietly to Valhalla or wherever else men went when they got murdered.

He'd fight them at the end. He'd go down as a warrior, not trussed up like a pig or a side of beef. He'd give them what for, tooth and nail, and die on his feet like a man, and not as a victim, cut up on a table, or as a sacrifice to some ancient god or demon or whatever that Azathoth was. He'd make his father proud.

20

AZATHOTH'S PALACE
FIMBULWINTER - YEAR 3
THE AGE OF MYTH AND LEGEND

"The lord lashed out in the throne room," said Mammon, "his wrath on full display. He hit Thetan and the others with blasts of power that should've turned them to ash. And yet still they stood, unharmed and defiant, the bastards. How? What could possibly shield them from the righteous wrath of the one true god? I want that answer, I need it, and though it has troubled me greatly since that day, I dare not ask the lord."

"I have your answer," said Arioch.

Mammon and the others turned to him in surprise. "They carry the Shards of Shadow," he said.

"What say you?" said Iblis.

"The Shards are strange tokens that the traitors wear about their necks," said Arioch. "The lord told me of their nature. Before man walked Midgaard, mayhap before there was a Midgaard, at the very dawn of creation, there was another great power in existence to rival our lord. But where our lord is good and just and loving, this other power was evil and treacherous, without mercy. Everything the lord created, the evil one sought to destroy. The lord could not coexist with that creature. The universe, for all its vastness, could not contain them both. And so came to pass a battle beyond our understanding, and witnessed not by any man, but remembered well by the lord, of course. He told me not the details of that conflict, save to say it cost him dearly. In the end, he utterly destroyed his foe. Nothing was left of the evil one but sorry fragments resembling black stone or charred wood or metal, and even those bits were scattered to the stars. Every once in a long while, such fragments fall to Midgaard as shooting stars. The Shards of Shadow, the lord calls them.

"Those fallen shards hold a measure of the dark lord's sorcery, and far worse, they are tiny fragments of his corrupt soul. He who possesses such a relic, if he has the talent and the training, may well tap into that dark magic, though he is doomed to be corrupted by it. The Shards' lingering sorcery is what saved Thetan and his fellows in the throne room that day, and may well explain their fall from grace. The influence of the Shards may be what drove them to this."

"You wore a Shard about your neck," said Iblis to Arioch. "I remember seeing it -- a strange thing like a twisted rune made of stone or wood -- which, I couldn't tell."

Arioch nodded. "Thetan calls them Ankhs after the heathen symbol that they resemble. He knows not their true nature, so far as I know. I resisted the Shard's effects, and turned it over to the lord."

"So, can they be saved?" said Mikel, his face brightening. "Brought back to the light? If we wrench the Shards from their grasps, will that free them of the evil influence, return them to their senses?"

"Mayhap they're not responsible for all they've done," said KithKarmon.

"Such is the lord's hope," said Arioch. "I believe that's why he hasn't smote them. As we've said, he loves them so; if there's any way to return them to the fold, he'll do so, if even at great cost. The depth of his love for them would make me jealous, save that I know he'd do the same for each of us. He risks himself, the lord does. He risks his kingdom and mayhap all creation to spare those few Arkons, to give them a chance to overcome the evil that possesses them and return to his bosom."

"How were you not corrupted by the Shard?" said Iblis with narrowed eyes.

"I feared the Ankhs at first glance," said Arioch, "appearing as they did, my memory clouded as to the events of their arrival. I smelled dark sorcery at work. The others did too, but they lusted for the Ankhs' power whereas I did not. I feared it. And so, only once did I place the Ankh around my neck, the first day we returned with them from the mountains. That's when you must have seen it. At all other times, I kept it in a pocket, wrapped in layers of cloth, never touching my skin. And well that I did, for if I'd worn it against my bare chest as did the others, it surely would've corrupted my mind and heart the same as it did to them. I turned it over to the lord. Once he discerned its nature, he blasted it with fire and lightning, but to no effect. He threw it in Vaeden's largest furnace, but it would neither melt nor burn. All else exhausted, the lord ordered me to weight it down with stones and drop it into the depths of the eastern sea, never to be seen or held again by the hand of man. I did as he commanded, and the Shard is forever lost, and good riddance to it."

21

JUTENHEIM
ANGLOTOR TOWER
YEAR 1267, 4TH AGE

JUDE EOTRUS

Jude's heart beat ever faster as they trudged down the worn stone stairs. With each step, his chance of escape grew more remote and he grew more anxious. The narrow stair was dark despite the Leaguers' torches and the sconces they lit at each landing. The air grew colder as down they went, damper too, harder to breathe, though why that was, Jude couldn't fathom. At least the narrow confines left little chance of a fall, stout walls on both sides. After they descended several flights, the men grumbled and looked from one to another, for the stair seemed endless.

It nearly was.

It took the better part of an hour before they reached the bottom, which opened into a large round chamber -- dim, dark, and dreary as the stair itself. The place was empty – nothing but bare, cold stone, echoey and lifeless. How many hundreds of feet below ground they were, Jude couldn't hope to guess, but surely at least as deep as the Black Elf tunnels.

Three stone passages led off in different

directions. Owing to the darkness and their pace, Jude couldn't discern whether they were natural tunnels or carved by the hand of man or some forgotten race of old. The Leaguers headed down one tunnel with little pause or study -- why that one, Jude had no idea, for to his eyes it appeared as featureless and uninviting as the others. They left Stev Keevis behind to guard the tunnel's entry. Just as Jude ducked entering the tunnel's mouth, Keevis called out to Par Rhund to stay behind as well, Korrgonn's orders.

Jude didn't have much hope left. If he made a run for it, how could he get past Keevis *and* Rhund, Archwizards both? And if he did, he'd face a wild run up that endless stair, the Leaguers hot on his heels. If he outpaced them, what strength would he have by the top, squadrons of Stowron awaiting him, that is, if they didn't hear the commotion and charge down to intercept him. Oh, and the guards up top had two Iron Golems...

There was no way to escape whence they'd come. He had to put all thoughts of that aside, or they'd become dangerous distractions.

He could only go forward. If the luck of the Vanyar were with him, maybe there'd be another way out.

There had to be!

That's what he'd keep a sharp eye out for. It was his only hope -- and he had to cling to it, or else fall to despair, which would ensure his demise.

The tunnel's ceiling was little more than six feet high, its rocky surface uneven. Jude ducked over and again, yet repeatedly bumped his head on the unforgiving stone. He missed his sturdy helm, long now lost.

The stone tunnel was as endless as the stair. From the torchlight ahead, Jude discerned that it didn't lead in a straight line, but neither did it turn sharply or curve about itself. And it led steadily downward -- as if they weren't deep enough.

They marched for a long time before halting. Jude figured Ginalli had finally called for a break; they'd had only a few mouthfuls of water as they went, canteens and water skins passed about sparingly. But no such luck. They'd reached their destination. The end of the line, for Jude.

Another chamber.

The chamber.

The inner sanctum as Jude heard them call it. The room in which they'd open the dread gateway to Nifleheim. The room in which he'd die.

22

EAST OF VIGRID VALLEY
FIMBULWINTER - YEAR 3
THE AGE OF MYTH AND LEGEND

THETAN THE LIGHTBRINGER

The rebel leaders gathered under the eastern forest's thick canopy. The officer in charge of every regiment was there, every battalion commander, every local chieftain. The twelve original Fallen Arkons were at their head, with them, a hundred more of what were once Azathoth's finest lieutenants.

Thetan stood atop a boulder so that all could see him.

"The day we have long worked toward is here," he boomed. "The world's enslavement is at an end. All good people, born and unborn, rely on us this day to remove the yoke that has shackled them in servitude to a false god. Everything hinges on what we do today. On your bravery, on the strength of your arms, and that of your resolve. But we must steel ourselves, for this will be a red day unlike any other. Brother will kill brother, sister will kill sister; Old Death will envelop us as never before. Not one of us, least of all me, wanted it to come to this. But know well my brothers and sisters, this must be done. This...*must*...be done. Rally your troops. Bring forth all your strength and hold nothing back in the conflict to come, for our enemy will surely do the same. Most of all, remember well, that no matter the events of this day, there can be no retreat and no surrender. We fight on until victory or Old Death takes us. And it *will* be victory."

"Victory," boomed Mithron.

"Victory," shouted Gabriel.

"Victory," shouted the troops.

23

JUTENHEIM
ANGLOTOR'S GATEHOUSE
YEAR 1267, 4TH AGE

Theta knelt low over a spindly cloaked figure that lay bleeding beside Anglotor's sundered outer gates. Theta gripped him by the throat, arms pinned, sword bloody. Several similar figures, dead nearby. A smoky haze hung about from the remnants of fires that engulfed several of the keep's buildings.

The bulk of the Eotrus Expedition jogged down the road to Theta's location, sweating and winded.

"He squeal?" said Ob the Gnome. "There are more of them buggers, you know, creeping on the walls, like roaches. Same scum as what jumped us out yonder. They might've swarmed you, Mister Fancy Pants, had we not come along all timely."

"Calls himself a Stowron," said Theta. "Says the League are in the tower's underhalls."

"How many they got?" said Ob.

"It doesn't matter," said Theta as he twisted his arm and the Stowron's neck snapped. Theta stood up and faced the expedition. "We head for the underhalls."

"Where did that bugger from up the wall get to?" said Ob as the expedition crept cautiously past the gates. Scores of bodies littered the courtyard. "Disappeared like a rat."

"The central tower," said Dolan Silk, Theta's manservant. "Lookouts from the east and west walls scurried that way too; they've ceded the place to us."

"No stomach for a standup fight, these Stowron," said Ob as he examined one of the bodies. "Can't blame them after this bloodbath. A couple hundred dead, I figure. Nasty battle, only hours old."

"But who won?" said Dolan.

"The League," said Claradon Eotrus, the expedition's young commander.

"We don't know that for certain, my boy," said Ob. "The Stowron didn't come in on *The White Rose*, so they must be locals. If this be their keep, they wouldn't have sallied forth to take us on unless they wiped out the League and they thought we were with them. But like I always say, we won't know nothing about nothing until we get our butts in there," he said, pointing to the tower.

"I sense great power emanating from that building," said Par Tanch as he pointed toward the stone gatehouse.

"And I sense horse poop spewing from your mouth," said Ob. "Speak plainly, Magic Boy, or not at all."

Tanch ignored the Gnome's barbs. "Either the most powerful wizard this side of Grand Master Pipkorn is holed up in there, or else several archmages are, or an entire company of common wizards, not that any of my ilk are common," he said adjusting his tunic. "I think it's

107

in there that we'll find the leaders of the League of Shadows and hopefully, Master Jude."

"Then that's where we're going," said Ob.

Theta, with a hand on his Ankh, said, "The temple of power lies deep beneath the central tower. That's where I must go and with no time to lose."

"We can't afford to split our force, laddie," said Ob. "We're tired and beat and there's not enough of us left. If we get hit hard again, with a split force, we'll be in the deep stuff. Best we stick together. Take things slow and smart."

"The enemy split their force," said Theta. "Some to the tower, some to the gatehouse. We must do the same. I want no archwizards on my back while I'm rooting through that tower, and we can't afford the time to clean out the gatehouse first. Claradon, you and the Eotrus flush out whatever's in that building while the rest of us head to the underhalls." Without pausing for debate, Theta turned and marched toward the tower. The Eotrus men looked to Claradon while the balance of the expedition followed Theta.

"High and mighty, Mister Know-it-All, stinking foreign fancy-pants bastard," mumbled Ob. "Always spouting orders, making proclamations, acting like he's in charge."

"No offense to Claradon," said Sergeant Artol, "but Theta *is* in charge."

"Grak you, Mister Too Tall," said Ob. "If I want your stinking opinion, I'll pull it out your behind, otherwise, keep your trap shut."

Artol rolled his eyes.

"Claradon will be deciding what we're to do," said Ob, "not that no-good foreigner, nor anybody else. And Claradon has decided that we're heading into the gatehouse to see what's what, am I right?"

"We need to find Jude," said Claradon.

"That we do, laddie," said Ob, "but he may well be in the gatehouse with whatever big baddie is making Magic Boy pee his pants. If he's not, we'll wring the big bad's neck, quick as a cat, and be on after Theta."

"Sounds like a plan," said Claradon.

24

EAST OF VIGRID VALLEY
FIMBULWINTER - YEAR 3
THE AGE OF MYTH AND LEGEND

THETAN THE LIGHTBRINGER

Thetan's first challenge: force the lord to appear on the field. Next, pass the Brigandir who'd surround the lord during any battlefield trek. The Brigandir were his royal bodyguards, brutes raised by Azathoth's priests in Vaeden's grand palace of Himil. They held no love for the Arkons, Fallen or otherwise, and knew nothing save for service to the lord, and the only service they provided was security. Not that the lord needed it, for the Arkons never allowed anyone of ill intent near him. So, the Brigandir guarded, trained, and occasionally ventured to the field with Arkons on holy missions -- real world training being necessary to hone one's skills. The Brigandir were fearsome foes. Thetan had seen them fight. Their style was unconventional, though they all used the same techniques, battling as a unit, whereas the Arkons were more adaptable – fighting in precise and coordinated battle lines whenever needed, but as individuals when circumstances warranted. Who taught the Brigandir their martial skills, even Thetan did not know, for their barracks and practice grounds were closed to him, and the lord dodged such questions when asked. Mayhap the lord himself trained them. Or another Arkon, whose combat style Thetan did not recognize. A mystery. One of many.

Thetan never liked or trusted the Brigandir. He sensed their jealousy whenever Azathoth called him to council: their eyes bore into him with hatred, envy, contempt. From where such feelings sprang, Thetan never understood, but something or someone stoked them. Thetan gave them wide berth and rarely ran afoul of them.

The palace had long whispered that the Brigandir were as well-schooled with magic as they were with the sword. Raphael swore that he once saw, through a momentarily open door, a Brigandir turn invisible during a sparring match. Raph oft indulged in too much Vaeden Red or Cherubin Brandy, so Thetan had always been skeptical of that tale. But if it were true, the upcoming battle may well be unwinnable. Thetan had no interest in facing invisible foes — he'd fought one three years prior — the guardian of the Sphere of the Heavens. One of the toughest fights he'd endured, though in the end, he'd killed the otherworldly creature.

Thetan long suspected that Lasifer's true purpose in Azathoth's court was to train the Brigandir in the mysteries of the Grand Weave. The old Gnome never admitted it, and instead, passed himself off as "a special adviser" to the lord, though he'd hinted at the truth after he'd joined the rebellion. Perhaps the Gnome had taught them invisibility. Of course, that meant the Gnome had that power too, which may well explain his abrupt comings and goings.

For all their worth, Thetan didn't consider the Brigandir the lord's greatest shield — the Loyalist leaders were: Bhaal, Iblis, Asmodeus, Mammon, Hecate, Stromriel, KithKarmon, Fathromfar, and Arioch -- that foul traitor. They were Arkons of the highest order, the best of the best fighters, heroes even amongst their kind.

Thetan needed *his* best men to deal with that wrecking crew, while he concentrated on Azathoth. Even the greatest among the Fallen followed Thetan's lead, though many believed he led them to certain doom. More than likely, they were correct. But that didn't change his plan. He was doing what needed to be done, though he, his friends, and much of the world might die in the doing.

Though Thetan believed Azathoth a false god, he yet had no hope to bring him down by force of arms. His powers, too great, beyond even Thetan's understanding. The Sphere of the Heavens was his only chance. Yet, he did not trust in that alien artifact, a thing of which he knew nothing until old Lasifer spoke of its potential use. The Gnome had withheld the details of the Sphere's activation, claiming esoteric magics were involved that only he could employ, all his energies focused these last three years on procuring the needed charms from parts foreign and frightful.

The Sphere's function however was quite clear. It could wrench open a portal betwixt Midgaard and the *Nether Realms* -- or so claimed

Lasifer. It was a door to another world; a place of hellish nightmare. All knew of the Nine Worlds of creation, but Thetan never thought any but Midgaard were real places, the rest, fireside tales and fancy, no different from the myths of the heathens. Mayhap myth it was, and the "doorway" a mystical portal that would drop Azathoth somewhere on the other side of the planet. In the end, would that do any good?

Thetan knew the lord had the power to appear at will where he was not moments before. He also had the power to levitate and to fly, appearing in far flung places swifter than any Targon could carry him, though not instantly, not nearly — there were limits to his powers. But if Lasifer were correct, and a door to another world could be opened, then open it he must. Push Azathoth through by hook or by crook, and their long servitude would be over. Assuming, of course, travel betwixt the worlds was beyond Azathoth's powers. If not, mayhap he could instantly come back, or travel back over time. Who knows? There was great risk and great uncertainty in this endeavor. But Thetan had hope that it would work. A man had to have hope, useless a thing though it be.

If all else failed, he'd find a way to rip Azathoth's head from his shoulders. That would end him.

He hoped.

And then the world would be free.

25

JUTENHEIM
ANGLOTOR TOWER
COURTYARD & ENTRY HALL
YEAR 1267, 4TH AGE

"**W**e should check the outbuildings," said Blain Alder as Theta and the Eotrus Expedition advanced across the bloody courtyard toward Anglotor's central tower. Theta's group included Harringgolds, Malvegils, Alders, Kalathen Knights, and crewmen off *The Black Falcon* led by Captain Dylan Slaayde and his chief bullyboy, Little Tug. "We'll be in a fix if we barrel in and another force skulks up behind us. This place is large enough to house hundreds."

"There is no time," said Theta.

Blain turned to Milton DeBoors, the famed Duelist of Dyvers, until lately in his employ.

DeBoors shrugged. "The man says there's no time."

"Their lookouts marked us when we cleared the tree line," said Dolan. "I figure, if they had much left, they'd have stepped out to greet us, arrows and iron. They haven't, so that big troop we killed out yonder must've been the last of their best."

"Agreed," said Theta. "Let's get the doors open." He spoke louder, so that all the men heard. "Form a skirmish line and be ready. We

114

don't know who, what, or how many will be come calling when those doors open. I want half our archers covering our backs. Give a yell at any sign of movement. Any sign."

While the men formed up as directed, Dolan examined the battered tower doors, then scrambled back to Theta. "Barred up nice and tight, Lord Angle. Heavy gauge steel, the frames too. Designed to keep out an army. And it's wizarded up."

"How do you know?" said Theta.

"My ears went all tingly," said Dolan as he tugged on one of his pointy ears.

Sir Seran Harringgold turned towards his squad. "Find something we can use as a ram."

"Somebody already did that," said Dolan pointing to the mangled doors, "and they couldn't get through. They're still solid despite the dents."

"We'll take it down," said Seran.

"There's no time," said Theta. He pulled his hammer, stared at the runes inscribed on its head and handle, drew it close and whispered to it. No one heard his words. The runes flashed bright white for an instant — anyone not looking directly at them wouldn't have noticed or known. Theta marched up to the tower, lifted the hammer high and slammed it against the doors with all the power of his mighty thews. The hammer struck the joint where the two doors met. And when it hit, there was a sound like a thunderclap, the courtyard shook, and the doors crashed inward with a skirling rending of metal.

Strange voices from within cried out in an

alien language, and a dark shadow appeared near the threshold, a lumbering bulk far larger than a man. Theta backpedaled. Out into the courtyard stepped a ten foot tall construct of iron.

"Oh shit," said Dolan.

Theta slammed his hammer into the thing's knee. There came a loud clang as if he'd struck an anvil.

The Iron Golem dropped to one knee, but its massive hand shot out, grabbed Theta about the chest and neck, and effortlessly lifted him into the air.

And then Little Tug was there. Even he was small beside the Golem. He swung his massive maul, Old Fogey, with both hands, his back and hips pivoting to maximize the blow's power. He caught the Golem amidst its back, a strike strong enough to fell a fifty-year oak.

Old Fogey rebounded. The Golem wasn't knocked forward as it should have been. It didn't even notice the blow. Tug staggered backward several steps and fell on his rump, his arms shaking, legs rubbery. Old Fogey fell from his grasp.

The Malvegils let fly their arrows, useless against iron. Harringgolds rushed in with spears, equally fruitless. DeBoors tried to call them off as dozens of Stowron scurried from the tower.

The two groups went to war.

Behind the Stowron lumbered a second Golem. It stopped at the doorway; its purpose clear — bar any entry into the tower.

Theta struggled to free himself, still held aloft

by the Golem's massive arm. As the Golem pivoted to swing its other hand in a deadly punch directed at Theta, DeBoors grabbed its arm and halted the blow.

Theta kicked and punched the thing over and again, each blow of gauntleted fist and metal-shod boot sounded like a hammer striking a dwarven forge, but the Golem did not stop, did not loose its grip. When the Golem tried to grab Theta with its other hand, it dragged along DeBoors who still clung to its arm like a tick.

And then Little Tug was there again. He wrapped his massive bulk around the Golem's forearm and tried to hold it back. It was clear to anyone that one punch from that thing would crush a man to pulp.

Theta touched his Ankh to the Golem's hand. Instantly, the Golem went still as stone, all energy and life fled from it. Theta twisted and dropped from the creature's grasp. And when he did, the Ankh dropped with him, no longer touching the Golem. That freed the creature from its spell. But now, it was disoriented, as if it didn't know where it was.

DeBoors' Kalathen Knights, the Malvegils, Harringgolds, and the rest were locked in a deadly battle with the last of the Stowron army conjured up by Master Glus Thorn. The battle was bitter, the Lomerians and the Stowron well-matched in their skills and determination. But the Kalathens were in a different league. Their swords worked up and down, and side to side, like scythes. They cut through Stowron staffs, turned aside their blades, and chopped down one spindly man after another.

Dylan Slaayde wielded his saber like a madman, his eyes afire, his white hair flapping side to side. He growled like a wolf as he stabbed, cut, and chopped. The Stowron recoiled from his fury.

"How do we take it down?" shouted DeBoors to Theta.

"Drop it into a pit," said Theta as he slammed his hammer into the thing's chest, producing a visible dent. "Pin it down, wall it in, or beat on it until it stops moving."

"We've no pit handy," said Tug, "but we could use ropes, like we did with them things in the Dark Elf tunnels."

"We'd need steel chain for this bruiser," said Theta, "and the other wouldn't sit still while we truss up this one."

"There may be more of them in there," said Tug as he slammed his maul against the back of the Golem's ankle. The blow pushed its leg to the side, the Golem overbalanced, and tipped. The men scrambled out of the way as it fell. When it hit, the courtyard shook. But any thought of trussing it up, or pinning it down was immediately abandoned, for the thing rolled over in a flash, made its knees a few seconds later, and then its feet quick enough, ignoring further hammer blows along the way.

"We can do it," said DeBoors. "We've several ropes, we'll find chains, we have to. We'll put this thing down and the other after it."

"There is no time," said Theta. "I need to get in there and stop that ritual before they open the gateway, or all is lost. Send a runner for Par Tanch. He has a ring of power. Mayhap he can use it to wrest control of these Golems from their master."

"I'm going in," said Theta. "Follow me if you can, but if you can't, keep these things occupied and off me."

"Even *you* can't go in there alone," said DeBoors. "Not against the Nifleheimer. And what of the servants he commands, Archwizards all?"

"I will do what needs be done," said Theta.

Theta marched to the tower's entryway, slipping through the wild melee that went on all around. When he drew close to the door Golem, it reached down and swung its massive arm. Theta dodged the blow, spun, and slammed his hammer with all his strength to the side of the Golem's foot. It overbalanced the same as had the other, and toppled to the ground with a huge crash. Theta stepped up and over it, Dolan following in his footsteps.

26

EAST OF VIGRID VALLEY
FIMBULWINTER - YEAR 3
THE AGE OF MYTH AND LEGEND

THETAN THE LIGHTBRINGER

Thetan gazed one last time upon the gathered troops. He kept a confident look on his face and in his bearing, though he felt a lump in his throat, and his stomach churned, for he knew that many of them -- mayhap all – would soon be dead. Some, he didn't know; others, only in face, name, or reputation; others, he called friend, and some few were as brothers to him. That would make no difference, of course, in the dying. That made it all the harder. His order to charge would be the start of it. The day of reckoning. The red day beyond all red days. He'd brought the world to the brink of destruction.

The world.

He was responsible for all of it. All those troops followed him. Believed him. Trusted him. It was all on him.

And he knew well, that even if victory was theirs that day, even if they brought down the mad god, uncountable thousands would die in the doing. All thanks to him. His rebellion. His betrayal. His treachery. And for that, his heart hung heavy and his spirit was low.

But he took pride in the sea of shining helmets

arrayed behind him in precise rows, many men deep. A thousand professional soldiers stood in Thetan's formation -- the best of the best, heroes amongst heroes. Half were Arkons, most of the highest orders, fallen with him from Azathoth's grace, adorned in polished armor of varying hues, and carrying rune-inscribed weapons of rare metals, of a craft and worth beyond those of the greatest of common kings. Some of the Arkons were lanky, others, tall and bulky, some few were slender and small, but all were strong and stern, battle-hardened, and combat trained to a skill level beyond common understanding. Each one, a hero, a titan among men, worth a hundred common soldiers. The balance of the troop were rugged warriors of weathered visage and worn weapons, muscles and courage aplenty -- each, a named man or woman, of fierce and worthy reputation; their faces, hard; their eyes, cold. Most had served with Thetan for many a year, on campaigns across Midgaard, doing the lord's bidding, as was ever their wont and duty.

To either side of his gallant regiment, for as far as Thetan could see, the rebel units gathered, nearly one hundred thousand strong, braving the biting wind and swirling snow of the Fimbulwinter. They were assembled into battalions, regiments, and companies. Most of the units were gifted with but a single Fallen Arkon in command, larger contingents had two, three, or half a dozen. Only the most important units boasted a squadron or more.

The majority of the soldiers were footmen:

some, well trained and equipped Einheriar, professional soldiers defected from Azathoth's legions, but the bulk of the troops were common folk from all corners of the realm who for one reason or another, no longer, if ever, loved Azathoth -- and felt so strongly about it that they were willing to risk their lives in a mad endeavor to unseat him.

A portion of the common soldiery were local militiamen with second-rate equipment, limited training, and no combat experience. A quarter or more of the host, however, were little more than untrained rabble, not conscripts, mind you, for the Fallen pressed no one into service -- that was against all they stood for. These were peasants accoutered with scraps of homespun armor and farmers' weapons: wooden staffs, iron daggers, firewood axes, or common pitchforks. They were simple folk who took to the field of free will, fighting for their freedom, freedom to do and say what they will, to be the masters of their destinies – but most of all, to escape the suffocating laws of Azathoth's kingdom. Boys of twelve to old men marched amongst that throng. There were women fighters too. Some young, strong, and brave as any man, others were wives and mothers, strong of spirit, ready to fight and die to protect their broods and their freedoms.

Thetan's heart was heavy allowing such folk to join his ranks, for what chance did they have against the loyalist Arkons and their Einheriar? Little more than fodder to the slaughter were they. *But a man has a right to fight for what he believes*, argued Gabriel. The Fallen did their best to distribute the common folk amongst the militias, so that they stood beside others with some semblance of training and discipline. Many folk would hear nothing of it. They gathered in groups of their cronies: fathers, sons, brothers, sisters, cousins, and neighbors, banding together to fight and die side by side. The thing was, they didn't think they were going to die; these folk knew nothing of war -- its horrors and pain. The Arkons had been fighting on their behalf for so long, and so effectively, that the common folk had grown weak and soft compared to the peoples of less civilized lands.

The forest road could not contain that host. The Fallen Arkons spread their forces along the whole of the Valley's width, drifting snow be damned. Well-trained and equipped units anchored the host's flanks, the best units marched in the center, the militias and rabble in between and behind. Troops of horsemen patrolled either flank, outriders beyond them.

Although nearly all the Arkons were equipped with Targon, a dedicated aerial force of one thousand were ready to take flight at a moment's notice, many scouts already aloft.

Thetan chose to keep his closest brethren at his sides where another general might have dispersed them, gifting them each a battalion to command as was their wont and due, owing to their unparalleled skills and vast experience. Yet close he kept them, so that by his side they'd be when he faced the lord in the final confrontation that would decide the world's fate -- assuming, of course, the lord deigned to take the field, which was not at all certain. If he didn't, there could be no victory for The Fallen. A wise leader might well stay away for that reason alone, but Azathoth did not think himself vulnerable. He had no personal fear of The Fallen, or, at least, never showed it. He feared only what havoc they could wreck upon his kingdom, and havoc they had wrecked those last years. But the Ankhs no doubt gave him pause. Those otherworldly artifacts cloaked Thetan and his cabal from the lord's magic, protected them when otherwise they'd have been burned to ash by the lord's vengeance.

Thetan didn't know what the Ankhs were, nor why or how they'd come to him and his. He only knew that they fell from the sky that cold dark night when he and his brethren conspired atop Mount Canterwrought and hatched their rebellion. No coincidence was that. But what force or being sent them those odd boons, he'd no idea, though, strangely, he felt he should know, did know, but had somehow forgotten. He'd forgotten many things from long ago, important things. He knew that, and it greatly troubled him, but to have forgotten something important *and* so recent was truly disturbing. Sorcery was at work, it had to be. The only question was, did it come from without – some person or entity attempting to manipulate him – or did it spring from within, from a troubled mind, his brain eroded over the long years by the insidious perils of sorcery? He was no master of those esoteric arts, far from it. But he had an inexplicable aptitude for its mysteries. And he had dabbled in the magic, sometimes, more than dabbled. It dwelled within him, that power did. Simmering. Lurking. Waiting for its rare chance to be unleashed, and pushing for that to be more often. But he had a sense of sorcery's perils. It burned his skin when he threw it; his hands felt afire, his head throbbed. Scattered his thoughts, it did. Eroded his judgment. He feared if he used it regularly, he would lose himself; he would go mad. So he rarely used it these last many years. Had the damage been done even with only occasional use? Could that account for his memory loss? Was it getting worse? He had to put those thoughts aside. So long as they didn't affect the imminent battle, he'd file them away to ponder later, if later ever came.

Regardless of why he didn't recall the Ankhs' origins, he believed he was being manipulated by some being of great power. He didn't care for that, not one bit. After all, that was at the core of his reasons for rebellion. He'd no interest in doffing the yoke of one master only to don that of another.

He'd have cast his Ankh away, and bid the others do the same, save he chose to think of them as gifts.

Gifts given with good intent should be valued and honored. And so he kept his Ankh close. After it had saved him from Azathoth's wrath, he decided not only to keep it, but never to take it off. Never be apart from it.

His brethren did the same. Each of the dozen Ankhs were different from the others, yet much the same, similar to the Arkons themselves. Thetan believed that his Ankh had other powers that had yet to reveal themselves, but he'd had too little time to experiment with it. What few experiments he'd tried were fruitless; the thing lay there like a rock or a slab of metal and reacted not at all to anything he did or said, the same as any other inanimate object. But Thetan felt its power, sensed it with every fiber of his being. It carried within it a magic of great potency and of a nature quite alien to him. In time, he was certain that he'd unlock its secrets and bend it to his will. But he was determined to be cautious, for magical things oft carried a will of their own -- and were notorious for their mischief. Not that Thetan knew much of such things. No one did in Midgaard in those days, save mayhap Azathoth or the Gnomish wizard, Lasifer. Magic was not common in the world. In fact, it was quite rare. WFrom whence it sprang, Thetan knew not, but Lasifer spoke of The Grand Weave of Magic, which as best as Thetan could discern was a wellspring of power that existed in some other place -- beyond Midgaard, beyond the Nine Worlds themselves, though he could not say where exactly that was or what it all meant. Thetan suspected that Azathoth knew a means to tap into that power, and manipulating it was the source of his wonders, much the same as it was Lasifer's. Mayhap the only difference betwixt the two was Azathoth's far greater mastery of The Weave, and mayhap his lust for power and profound need to be worshipped. Lasifer had neither failing so far as Thetan knew.

27

JUTENHEIM
ANGLOTOR'S GATEHOUSE
YEAR 1267, 4TH AGE

"**S**top eying me," said Par Tanch. "If you think that I'm going in first just because there's a wizard in there, then you'll be sorely disappointed. Scouting and skulking are not my specialties, no Sir, not at all. I'm a scholar, not a warrior. And my back's been killing me; I can hardly walk. You people may be used to this life but I'm not. This is Helheim for me, and I've saved you all, more than once, at great pains to myself, I might add, and if you think..."

"Pipe down, Magic Boy," said Ob, "and try not to shit your pants this time. All I need to know is, is that stinking wizard you sensed anywhere near this door or not?"

"It doesn't work that way," said Tanch. "I've no idea–"

Sergeant Artol's boot crashed into the gatehouse's door just beside the handle. The wooden frame splintered and gave way, and the door crashed open. The Eotrus dodged aside to avoid any missiles that might fly from within.

A dark hallway is all that greeted them.

"Did you even check if it was locked?" said Ob.

Artol shrugged.

Ob shook his head. "Might as well strike up a merry tune, boys, because we've announced

127

we're coming, yet again. Dumbasses, one and all."

The men kept a wary eye on that hallway, but no one moved toward it. None of them wanted to go in first. Not that they were afraid. Most of those men weren't afraid of much; some of them, weren't afraid of anything. But an archwizard, lurking in the dark, waiting for them — well, that was a frightening thing for anyone, no matter your courage, your resolve, skills, or strength. They'd all seen what Par Tanch could do, and as impressive as that was, his reputation was by no means "great". There were wizards whose powers purportedly far exceeded his. Nobody wanted to be fried to dust or turned into a toad or something even worse.

"Hold for a moment," said Claradon. "Glimador, prepare your shield spell – the one you used to block the Brigandir in *The Falcon's* hallway. Set it up to block *this* hallway, but to move forward in front of us as we go in. Put all the power you can into it. I'll back you up and lay a mantle of protection over us. Tanch, you stand ready with a bolt of fire should our shield come down. Waste no time in letting it fly if our magic drops." To the others he said, "If the shield falls and you see a wizard or someone that looks like a wizard, or maybe possibly could be a wizard — other than Tanch — I want you to rush him. Jump on him. Knock him over. Throw stuff at him, whatever it takes. That'll disrupt whatever magic he's doing. Then it will be knife work. You with me, everyone?"

"Aye, aye," said the men. Kayla smiled and

128

nodded her approval. Ob smirked with pride.

Glimador Malvegil and Claradon spoke their mystical words from the *Militus Mysterious* and drew down their magics from *The Grand Weave.*

Glimador's shield wall was visible only in the light of the doorway. It was like glass, translucent and tinted blue. You could see through it as clear as day, but nothing physical could pass it; it was solid as a wall of stone, yet Glimador could push it forward by will alone.

Glimador stepped forward with both palms outward but not touching the wall. Claradon kept a hand on his shoulder, his sword in the other. The hallway was narrow but two could go side-by-side if pressed, but not with comfort. Tanch walked close behind. The hall had a strange design, some twenty feet long, no doors on either side, and ended in a tee. Ob trailed closely behind Tanch, Artol behind him. Then came Sir Kelbor, Ganton the Bull, Sir Trelman, Sergeant Lant, and four Eotrus troopers. Sergeant Vid remained outside to guard the rear with Kayla and two more troopers.

The men lit a torch and passed it to Claradon. When they reached the hall's end, they saw doors just around the corner to the left and the right. Both were closed, no sign or sound of any movement.

"If we turn either way," said Glimador, "we expose our backs to the opposite door. I can't extend my shield down both ways; it's one or the other."

"Do we gamble or try to draw them out?" whispered Claradon to Ob.

"They know we're here," said the Gnome. "Better for us to draw them out. Let's make some noise and see what happens."

And so they did. They shouted and threatened. They banged on the walls and stamped on the floor. They pushed forward just enough to throw rocks and a javelin at each door. All to no avail. No response of any kind.

"They're laying low on us," said Ob. "Either afraid or they've got a trap well set."

"We hit one door at a time?" said Claradon.

"If I was holed up in there, as soon as you went through one door, I'd hit you from the other, catch you with your pants down, maybe put you in a vice, if I had men behind both. That's what I'd do, so I assume they'll be just as smart. So we've got to hit both doors hard, at the same time."

"Glimador and I will go left," said Claradon. "Ganton, Kelbor, Lant, and two troopers are with me. Ob, you break to the right with Tanch, Artol, and the rest."

Glimador was able to rotate his mystical shield so that Claradon could reach past and grab the left door's handle. It was unlocked. The door on the right was locked tight. Artol's boot was at the ready, his hammer was backup.

They went through both doors at the same moment.

For a split second Claradon saw a tall, pale, white-haired man on the far side of the room. The man's arm was outstretched and pointed toward him. Then something unseen slammed into Glimador's shield, struck it like a charging

130

Olyphant.

And then the world turned upside down.

Claradon felt himself flying through the air.

28

VIGRID VALLEY
FIMBULWINTER - YEAR 3
THE AGE OF MYTH AND LEGEND

THETAN THE LIGHTBRINGER

Some two miles across the valley from the rebel Arkons' position, the loyalists massed.

"For every Arkon we have," said Mithron, "stand two opposed. For every soldier that stands with us, stand five against. Where most of theirs are Einheriar, all too many of ours are ill-trained rabble."

"He's gathered all his strength from across the kingdom," said Gabriel, "from the Eastern Plains to the Western Marches, from the Northern Steppes to the Southern Sea and beyond, from Trafilgden to Tanis Myreem, and all the lands between. How could he have done it so quickly?"

"The lord has his ways," said Uriel, "always has. We've seen him do the impossible more than--"

"Gabriel," said Thetan, "make ready to sound the charge."

Mithron leaned to Thetan's ear. "We cannot win this, brother," he whispered such that only Thetan could hear. "Not even with the Northmen. There are too many loyalists, far more than we dreamed he could muster this quickly. We are undone."

"Henceforth, our power only wanes," said Thetan. "Time is on his side. We'll get no better chance than this, so we must take it, even if this proves to be our last day."

Mithron's jaw stiffened and he took a deep breath. "Aye," he said. "It must be done now if ever it will."

Gabriel Hornblower unclipped the brass horn from his belt and pressed it to his lips.

"Now," shouted Thetan.

But before Gabriel blew the signal, a different horn sounded from across the field. Not from the loyalist camp, but from another rebel unit. A moment later, yet another horn sounded from elsewhere amongst the rebel lines, and then another, and a dozen more. Four short pips, then one long one. Thetan didn't know what it meant. It was not one of their signals. Something was amiss.

Owing to some preternatural sense unique to Thetan and his ilk, he spun around with every ounce of speed he could muster while simultaneously drawing his falchion and dropping into a defensive crouch.

Not a moment too soon.

A sword slammed into his blade with such force it drove his arm back against his breastplate and pushed him back. So powerful was that thrust, if his sword had not caught it, his breastplate may well have been skewered.

Markon's sword had done it. Markon! His friend. A man who was like his brother. As close to him as Uriel or Hogar or Azrael.

Markon's face was filled with equal mixtures

of shock and anger. He hesitated only a moment before he maneuvered to attack again.

In that half a heartbeat of hesitation Thetan would normally kill his opponent, but not that time, for Thetan hesitated too. He couldn't believe what he was seeing. He expected traitors in the ranks. There had to be. Spies for Azathoth. Assassins. But not one of his closest friends. Not Markon.

Thetan didn't want to kill him. There had to be another way.

"Stop," Thetan boomed. "Brother, stop!"

"Traitor," shouted Markon.

Though he dared not look about, Thetan heard the sounds of battle erupt from all around -- howls, yells of anguish and alarm, and war cries, wild and deadly...from all across the rebel lines.

Azathoth's assassins had planned their attack well.

Thetan had to end it quickly. His sword sliced by at incredible speed. Markon dodged, moving faster than any but the greatest of Arkons could move, and sent in his own strike.

Thetan's dagger was in his opposite hand, no time to draw his scimitar, no hope for his shield; Markon was too fast and would give no ground for that. Markon gripped a main gauche in his offhand and on he came, blades whirling faster than a common man could see -- but Thetan was no common man. His blades lashed out just as fast and with even more power.

Despite his uncanny focus on the duel, Thetan realized that Markon would've stabbed him through the back. Tried to. Would've killed him dead without the courtesy or honor to look him in the eye and let him know what fate had befallen him.

The thought of such disrespect, such betrayal, such dishonor, unleashed the anger from Thetan's core, from the deep dark that welled inside him. Thetan's blows came all the faster, all the stronger, for neither quarter nor mercy would they pause.

A clash of steel.

A symphony of death. Around they danced, two gods of the sword, but the battle did not last overlong, though ten heartbeats was an eternity for such a contest.

Blood spouted from Markon's neck.

His hesitation had been slight, no one but a sword master would've even noticed it, but it was enough for Thetan's dagger to slip under his and sink two inches deep before Thetan pulled it back. Then a sweep of his falchion battered Markon's sword aside and a thrust skewered the man's breastplate -- the sword sinking deep into his rib cage.

He might have survived it, those wounds. And in another time or another place, Thetan may well have spared him. Not that day. Not after what Markon had just done.

To his credit, Markon never yielded, his strength never gave out. He fought until the last, but Thetan took his head *and* both his forearms with a single swing as Markon tried to protect his neck.

All around Thetan was chaos.

Thetan spoke the proper command and his Targon unfolded its wings, immediately took to the air, and hovered above the din. The entire battalion was engaged, brother against brother, a wild melee, no way to tell who was who. From the east side of the field to the west, nearly every company, troop, battalion, and regiment were much the same. Thetan didn't know what to do, who to attack, who to defend.

Gabriel fought Cephalon; Mithron battled Tastagor while Fromen and Firestall lay dead at his feet; Uriel dueled Delanor; Raphael rolled on the ground, hands locked around Hariel's neck.

And then the world shook. Thetan turned, and saw Azathoth's armies charging toward him at breakneck speed: foot, horse, and Targon. Seven minutes and their horse would be upon him, a third of that for the Targon -- if they came straight on. Before then, he had to reform the battle lines and brace to meet the loyalists' charge, or they'd be overrun and their forces scattered.

By the time he was able to swoop down to aid Gabriel, Cephalon was on his knees and out of the fight, bleeding from neck and chest. Thetan shifted to his left and sank his falchion six inches into Hariel's back, grabbed him by the collar, and flung him off Raphael. Then Uriel was at Thetan's side. Azrael too. Thetan found himself offering each a sidelong glance, wondering if they were on *his* side or the other. Azathoth had him doubting even his closest friends, an ingenious plot to foster chaos and dissent.

In but a few more moments it was over. More

than one hundred dead in Thetan's battalion alone. Hundreds more, mayhap thousands in total, throughout his host. It appeared that his unit had been hit the hardest, which made sense, for Azathoth would want to concentrate his assassins near the core of the rebels' leadership to maximize the damage that they might do.

"Reform the line," shouted Dekkar. "Get back into position, now!"

"This is madness," hissed Gabriel. "Our own brothers. How could they do it? Foul traitors."

"Backstabbers," said Hogar.

"No doubt, they thought the same of us," said Azrael.

"Hornblower," said Thetan.

Gabriel scrambled for his horn, fallen to the snow. He picked it up and blew it. The same call echoed from every unit within the Fallen host. As one, they charged headlong across the valley of death to meet their fate.

29

JUTENHEIM
ANGLOTOR'S GATEHOUSE
YEAR 1267, 4TH AGE

CLARADON

Claradon figured that he had blacked out for a few seconds. Before he got his bearings he felt and heard men running past him. He didn't know if they were going towards that room or away, or even whether they were his men or the enemy's. It was dark, his head was spinning, everything hurt, and he couldn't take a breath, as if a great rock lay upon his chest. His arms and legs weren't responding. For a moment he feared he had broken his neck or back and was paralyzed. But after but a second or two, he was able to inhale, though everything hurt all the worse for it. He tried unsuccessfully to pull himself up. He heard men shouting.

"Laddie," said Ob as the Gnome appeared at his side and helped him to a sitting position. "Get in there, you sniveling coward," shouted Ob to someone, probably Tanch. "The wizard is tearing them apart. Get in there. Laddie, laddie, are you with me, boy? Dammit, your head's bleeding but good."

The world came back into focus. Claradon's mind cleared. It felt as if he'd had an hour or two's rest, though it had been but moments. A strange sensation and no accounting for it. "Get me up." By the time Claradon made his feet, Artol appeared in the doorway looking battered and in pain, shaking his head.

30

VIGRID VALLEY
FIMBULWINTER - YEAR 3
FIVE HOURS AFTER THE INITIAL CHARGE
THE AGE OF MYTH AND LEGEND

THETAN THE LIGHTBRINGER

Death. That's what that day was.

Arm weary, Thetan swung his sword and sliced into KithKarmon's chest, tearing through his breastplate, the metal screaming where the man did not. As KithKarmon staggered backward, shock filling his face, a javelin pierced his neck, another his leg, the Fallen close about Thetan, protective of their leader, though in all history there was no man more capable of defending himself. *Another dead friend*, thought Thetan, this one, amongst the loyalists' best.

That blow left Thetan's sword badly notched and broke inches off its tip. "I need another blade," he shouted in the loudest voice he could muster, mist rising with his breath. Even still, only those closest heard him through the din, his voice, crackling and dry from hours of shouting orders.

Bodies piled high on all sides of the rebel formation. Thetan stood at the van, blinking blood from his eyes as he'd done a hundred times that day, and inched his unit forward against terrible resistance. His arms felt like tree trunks. His shield, the sixth he'd picked up, was a broken mess. He tried to control his breathing but he sucked air faster than was his wont. He'd numbed to the battlefield stench as much as he could. The blood scent was nothing, it was the nauseating miasma that men's innards released that sickened all within its sphere.

"A shield," he shouted before he spied one before him standing on edge in the snow. It was Gravfilgar's, he knew his sigil well; a loyalist, but an old friend even still. He chanced a glance about but didn't see his body. He wouldn't have abandoned that shield. Somewhere he lay dead and trampled. A good man. One of countless that fell that day.

Because of him.

Hogar handed him a sword -- an Arkon's blade, long and bloodied, ranal born, with a thick ornamental haft. He didn't recognize the sigil or the flourishes, and he was glad for it, the guilt already unbearable.

31

JUTENHEIM
ANGLOTOR'S GATEHOUSE
YEAR 1267, 4TH AGE

MASTER GLUS THORN

Thorn dreamed of somewhere pleasant, but he couldn't say where. Most anywhere was better than Jutenheim – that godforsaken backward continent that slumbered far from civilization's edge and boasted myriad ways to kill even the most powerful and pious of men. How long he'd been asleep, he had no idea, other than it felt not long enough. He needed more rest to restore his energies, and most importantly, to stave off the Wizard's Toll. He'd never come so close to succumbing to it: his body still felt afire, arms shaking, hands blistering, perspiration drenching him, muscles twitching, head to toe, head pounding, and ears buzzing. He hadn't felt worse in years. Of course, he'd never conjured six hundred and fifty Stowron from halfway across Midgaard before. That took a feat of strength that fewer than a handful of wizards in all Midgaard could accomplish – or so Thorn told himself. And that, only shortly after fighting off an army of Giants, Lugron, and their minions and beasts. But for his efforts in that battle, the expedition would've collapsed. Even Lord Korrgonn may not have escaped.

So Thorn was quite annoyed when someone tried to shake him awake. A tentative tap on the shoulder is all it was, but more than enough to disrupt his dream and pull him back into unwanted reality. He wasn't ready for that yet. Not in the mood or in any shape to help the League's slackers out of any more trouble. He'd helped enough. Six hundred and fifty Stowron! They could hold off the very hordes of Helheim for a few hours at least. He should be able to sleep, for god's sake. They should have some respect. Some deference. And a healthy dose of fear.

He'd ignore them. They'd go away eventually. Probably just Ginalli wanting confirmation he could take a shit, or Keld wanting to rub his feet or kiss his behind.

But he kept his ears pricked in case Korrgonn's name was mentioned. If the lord's son wanted him, he'd bounce up and do whatever needed to be done, such was his devotion to their quest, and to the lord, of course.

But short of that, well, the rest of them could go straight to Helheim. That sniveling worm, Ginalli -- high priest, indeed — he could throw a spell or two, there was no doubt, but he was a snake-oil salesman if Thorn had ever met one. Let him handle things on his own for once. *He* was supposed to lead the expedition. Thorn wasn't even meant to be there. He joined of his own accord after the Eotrus began their pursuit.

He had to make certain that Lord Korrgonn was properly protected and that the mission was successfully accomplished. Bringing the lord back to Midgaard was the most important thing in all the world. And until the lord arrived, Korrgonn was the most important person. And so, Thorn trudged through endless muck and monsters those last months, albeit intermittently, since he routinely traveled back to Black Rock Tower via his mystical coach, the *galdr vagn*. But the coach was safely stowed on *The White Rose*, there being no way to pull it through the tunnels of Svartleheim or the damnable jungles beyond.

Thorn was quite done with monsters, mayhem, and endless trekking. He wanted to get back to Black Rock, to his experiments, and to the solitude that he so valued. He had plans that needed to be worked on. Deep, deep plans.

But they wouldn't stop shaking him, the slackers. He ignored them until the shaking became violent and he heard a voice call his name. It was Nord. He knew better, the Stowron did. It must be important, he wouldn't dare otherwise.

Thorn opened his eyes. He sat straight up, stiffly. Nord was at his side. He didn't recognize the room, but it had to be somewhere in Anglotor. He didn't remember how he got there. He'd passed out. That meant the Toll had nearly taken him.

"Violation here," said Thorn.

"The devil comes," said Nord in his grating accent, so strange were the Stowron voices.

144

"They're at our door; it will not hold."

Thorn looked around, just the two of them in the room. Three doors, two were closets. No windows. Nothing for a barricade. No way out but the main door. "Where is everyone?"

"The temple they went," said Nord. "Way down low, in the heart of the mountain."

"We're alone here?" said Thorn. "I was left unconscious and unprotected?"

"In this building, yes. My brothers guard the tower's ground floor. And the Golems serve."

Thorn looked around again searching for something, anything that would be of use. "What good does that do us?" he said. "That stinking traitor, Ginalli. I'll put him right on the floor."

"There is no way out but the way they come in," said Nord. "And nowhere much to hide."

"I do not hide," said Thorn as he turned and put his feet to the floor, his boots still on. He tried to stand but grew dizzy and dropped back on the cot. "Dammit all. I finally get to face the Harbinger, but I'm at my worst, my weakest."

Nord cocked his head as if listening. "They come."

Thorn's eyes narrowed and he went silent and still, and reached out with his art. "They have sorcerers amongst them, men of some power, though nothing of concern to me – but in the state I'm in...dammit all. Let them come. Let them come."

Soon they heard a racket. Taunts and curses. Banging on the walls, pounding of many feet.

"Cowardly barbarian scum," said Thorn. "Afraid to come straight at me, they are. Trying to work up their courage, rile themselves into a frenzy. Ha, even the Harbinger's greatest minions are afraid of *me*. As well they should be. Must sense my power, know that I'm here, just as I know of them. But the Harbinger isn't amongst the group that entered here. There's nothing like his power out there, just common men of uncommon skill. That won't be enough, not nearly. Let them lurk until they find their courage. And when they do, they'll pay. They'll pay for disrespecting our lord and for all the vile deeds they've done in the Harbinger's name."

Thorn got to his feet with Nord's help. He prepared his sorceries. Most wizards, even archwizards, needed time for such preparations. Often, considerable time, and all sorts of talismans, accouterments, and spell components, to ready their magics. Thorn needed none of that bunk. He thought the right words of the *Magus Mysterious,* supplemented on occasion with a gesture or two, and he'd create wonders, or throw death in all directions, whichever he fancied.

The door burst in...

VIGRID VALLEY
FIMBULWINTER - YEAR 3
THE AGE OF MYTH AND LEGEND

THETAN THE LIGHTBRINGER

It was all coming apart, Thetan's great plan, his historic rebellion, his glorious chance to free the world.

And to atone for his sins.

To a certain extent this was to be expected, for in battle, the one thing that you can count on is that it won't go as planned.

Ever.

No matter how carefully you plan. No matter how many contingencies you have.

That said, those who plan best, gain an advantage over their opponents. An advantage that can sometimes counterbalance other deficits. But to win, the main parts of your plan have to work out. If not, you're doomed, or at best adrift amongst the winds of fate.

Thetan's battle plan counted on two things. That the Northmen would join the rebels on the field in timely fashion, and that one way or another, he'd draw Azathoth to the field, get the Gateway opened, and push Azathoth through it.

The problem was, the battle was nearly over, and none of those critical events had happened.

At first, things had gone much as Thetan had

planned. Despite the sneak attack of the loyalist's fifth column, the rebels broke the lord's initial charge and left a regiment of Einheriar loyalists dead on the field. That sent the lord's advance guard scurrying back to their main force, broken and bloodied.

With little respite, Azathoth sent in his strike force: a full corps of Vaeden footmen — elite Einheriar -- who advanced from the west, and two full corps of footmen from the south, the latter up from Trindinland and Mercum. The southerners were spearmen clad in bronze armor, well trained and battle hardened, but their equipment was no match for an Arkon's or even a Vaeden Einheriar's. They were fodder sent to probe the rebels' resolve and siphon their strength.

Simultaneously, the lord sent a dozen flights of Targon swooping down from the north, dropping javelins by the hundred, while several other flights soared in from the east, from behind the rebels – though that was no surprise to Thetan, he'd prepared for it. He'd left half his aerial force in the rear waiting for that maneuver, counting on it, in fact, for it was an opportunity to cripple Azathoth's fliers in secret. The rebels soared to the attack, surrounded the loyalist Arkons who came in from the east, and in less than five minutes, not a single loyalist remained in the air. The bodies of hundreds of white-winged warriors crashed into the snowy ground, broken and torn, and turned the white drifts red. That engagement took place well away from the main, and concealed by the

148

Fimbulwinter's bluster it no doubt took some time for the lord to learn of their defeat. That too was part of Thetan's plan.

As soon as Azathoth's strike force engaged the rebels, he sent forth from Vaeden the core of his strength, his armies moving east, northeast, and southeast simultaneously, attempting to envelop the rebels while they were distracted and pinned down.

Exactly as Thetan anticipated he would do.

Thetan sprang his trap. His heavy cavalry thundered from the northern woods and the southeastern marches. Half his Targon sprang up from the woodland and engaged Azathoth's aerial force head on. The rest of his fliers, fresh from their victory in the east, dropped from the clouds and attacked Azathoth's Targon from the rear.

The loyalists were unprepared for such a fearsome, coordinated, and multi-pronged assault from the much smaller force. They fell by the thousands for it. By the tens of thousands. But it wasn't enough, not nearly, for the Fallen and their allies were far too few.

33

JUTENHEIM
ANGLOTOR'S GATEHOUSE
YEAR 1267, 4TH AGE

MASTER GLUS THORN

Thorn was not at all surprised when the door burst open. The first man through was a Church Knight called Glimador Malvegil, a cousin to the Eotrus, and first son and heir to his storied House. Thorn knew him at once; he had a talent for names. A gift he was born with. He had a way of reaching into a man's mind and plucking out bits of information. Not much, mind you. He couldn't read a man's thoughts, not without casting complex sorceries. But innately, he could read one's emotions, even those concealed, and he could extract a man's name from his mind or mayhap the ether, he never knew which. And occasionally, he plucked other useful tidbits.

He noted at once that Glimador had thrown up a formidable shield spell. 'Twas a physical incantation of impressive power that most archwizards could not match. The thing about Church Knights is, they are one-trick ponies. They can throw a spell or two, sometimes three or four, sometimes to great effect, but that's it. They had no magical repertoire to speak of, no style or system, no depth of understanding of the arcane. But what they could do, they did competently, and sometimes quite well indeed, considering.

And Glimador could throw a darned powerful shield spell. It had a fatal flaw though, as most spells of amateurs do — it wasn't anchored down. Push on it hard enough from the other side, if you could withstand whatever shock it gifted you, and you could move it. Thorn ascertained all of that in about one heartbeat.

How could he do that?

He was a wizard, that's how. And not just a common one. He was a sorcerer supreme.

Behind Glimador came another Church Knight. This one, protected by other magics common to his ilk. Thorn figured they'd charge forward and try to pull him down. He'd not give them the chance. He immediately extended his arm, index finger pointed, and spoke a single word from an old dialect, a precursor really, to what modern practitioners called the *Magus Mysterious.* An invisible bolt of force rocketed from his hand, called down instantly through the ether from the Grand Weave of Magic, and crashed into young Glimador's shield wall.

The two sorceries were not evenly matched, of course. Glimador and his Church Knight friend, one Claradon Eotrus, went flying backward whence they came, and crashed into and through their fellows, who fell like dominoes. Thorn had put them all on the floor. That made him smile out of the corner of his mouth, a look that most men would call a sneer.

Claradon Eotrus? How interesting, thought

Thorn. Come all this way to find his long-lost brother? Oh, how interesting. How loyal. Thorn admired that. And quite convenient too, for it now meant they had a backup for the blood of kings if good Sir Jude proved insufficient or if he somehow slipped their grasp.

Thorn wanted to shout some appropriate taunt, but the breath caught in his throat. Everything tightened up. Smoke wafted from his fingers; the backs of his hands and his forearms felt afire, blisters forming. His ears tingled, as did his toes.

Nord stood beside him at the ready. The Stowron was so scared Thorn wondered how he kept from peeing himself. But the old boy stood his ground, made no show of cowardice. Quite reliable that Nord, which is why he'd kept him around these many years. It was no vice to be afraid as long as you did your duty, as long as you stood up for what you valued. The vice was in turning tail on what was important to save yourself. Nord showed no sign of that. Never had. And Thorn would be surprised if he ever did.

Next came Sergeant Lant. A veteran bruiser of House Eotrus, Troopers Manley and Voss at his heels, a handsome duo, tall and muscled. That Lant was a confident one. Frightened but confident. Thorn knew at once he had to put him down quickly; not tangle toe to toe, not backed as he was by capable men. No doubt, Nord could take him on, but then Thorn would face the troopers alone. On a good day, that wouldn't bother him, save for the indignity of battling commoners, but that day he wasn't in any shape to go hand-to-hand with anybody.

And so, Thorn extended his hand again as Lant charged forward. He pointed his index and middle fingers at the soldier and then gestured toward the ceiling, a favorite maneuver – quick, deadly, and intimidating.

Lant was halfway across the room already; the man wasted no time.

But then the magic took Lant from his feet, his momentum redirected. He shot straight up, head first, into the room's stone ceiling. Didn't even have time to bring his hands up to protect himself. He slammed into the stone with an ugly thud. He had a helmet on, but Thorn didn't think it did him much good. Thorn twisted his arm and Lant flipped over and shot headfirst into the floor with speed. Admirably, the man tried to put his arms out to protect himself this time, but they were as effective as wet noodles in arresting his fall.

Thorn sensed a nobility about that soldier. He wasn't some crazed zealot or vile barbarian heathen. A noble savage if you will. On a better day, Thorn would've twisted his wrist and his sorcery would've snapped the man's neck, to put him out of his misery. But he couldn't afford to expend that energy, not with the Wizard's Toll hounding him. Lant would have to twitch on the floor until his heart gave out. There was nothing else for it. A shame.

Nord intercepted the Eotrus troopers. His staff caught Manley in the head. The man tried to parry but was too slow, pathetic actually. That was to be expected for Nord was a Stowron staff

153

master, one of the best of his ilk. Nord swept out Voss's legs. Dropped him heavily on his back and then thrust the staff into his neck, crushing his windpipe. The trooper never had a chance. Quite efficient was Nord when need be. Quite reliable.

Trooper Manley was up right quick, no doubt his head pounding and foggy. Scrappy that one. Made a couple of swipes with his sword -- of course, neither hit Nord, while Nord hit him about ten times to the head, chest, and privates. Manley made the mistake of falling to his knees, which gave Nord a convenient target. He bashed his staff quite forcefully to the back of Manley's neck. And that was the end of him.

34

THE AGE OF MYTH AND LEGEND
VIGRID VALLEY
FIMBULWINTER - YEAR 3
EIGHT HOURS AFTER THE INITIAL CHARGE

The falcon's eyes were shiny silver -- a match to its feathers, talons, and beak -- and took in all the bleak terrors below as it soared over the battlefield, banking, twisting, and dodging to avoid the occasional arrows that sought to send it spiraling to its doom. Though it held the face and form of a great falcon of the northern mountains, it was not a bird, not a living creature at all, but a product of metal and man's boundless ingenuity. Born and guided by the fallen Arkon Blazren's hand, it soared and spied at his bidding alone. None but he could mark it a construct of science or sorcery, for Blazren had long labored at both in private laboratories far removed from the prying eyes of Arkon and Azathoth alike.

"Get your metal bird aloft," Thetan had ordered during a brief respite between the onrushing waves of loyalists that pounded their lines. "I must know how our forces fare and can spare no more Targon for the duty, for our former brothers pluck them from the skies with abandon."

"Our forces are decimated," said Raphael, his face dirty and bloodstained, his locks and shirtsleeves uncharacteristically disheveled. "You need no tinker's bird to tell you so; plain as day. We walk a field of death."

"The field is vast," said Thetan, his eyes affixed on Blazren. "The battle may go better elsewhere. Get it aloft."

"I care not to lose Silver to a lucky archer this day," said Blazren. "Best wait until dusk or later when *his* eyes grow sharper and the archers' dimmer."

"We'll be dead by dusk, like as not," said Bose, looking tired and sweaty but none the worse for wear.

"Stow that talk," said Tolkiel sharply, his arm bound in bandages, dripping red in two places. "Don't let the men hear such words," he said, his voice quiet such that only the closest could hear.

"She took me years to make," said Blazren.

"I'll not ask again," said Thetan sharper than was his wont. "I'll not lose any more of our scouts while that toy remains unused."

Without a word or perceptible gesture, the metal falcon leapt from Blazren's shoulder and took flight with no more effort than a living bird of its type. Blazren pulled strange spectacles, another of his inventions, from a pocket with practiced ease and put them on as Silver sped toward the heavens with speed astounding even for a true falcon, the swiftest of birds. Blazren's spectacles featured a clear glass lens over his left eye, opaque over the right. Thick lenses stood vertically to either side, another overtop. It had straps that fastened around his ears and the back of his head, securing them in place even during combat or vigorous activity. How the contraption worked, no one but Blazren knew, but it allowed him to see through Silver's eyes. He'd witnessed many a grim and gruesome sight through those spectacles in the years since the bird's creation. Azathoth had oft had Silver scout and spy for him in times and places when Targon scouts were impractical or indiscreet -- against the heathen hordes, of course, but perhaps surprisingly, more often against the faithful, watching for willful transgressions, vile blasphemies, fomenting of revolt, or worst -- the rise of pagan idols in any of their many forms. Azathoth would not suffer graven images, not for a moment.

Many a time, Silver had overflown a battlefield at Blazren's behest, but invariably the field was strewn with dead from the opposing side. Truth be told, the Arkons did not win every skirmish or small engagement. They occasionally were overwhelmed by force of numbers or sometimes stepped into a trap smartly sprung -- but the big battles, the ones that mattered, Azathoth's Arkons always won. That day was no different...save that this time, Blazren fought on the opposing side. The losing side.

Blazren called out all that he saw through Silver's eyes, but no louder than needed for his closest comrades to hear. Thetan knelt beside him. So too did Gabriel, Azrael, Uriel, Tolkiel, Dekkar, Bose, and Mithron, all huddled about, thick as thieves.

What was left of Thetan's troop numbered no more than five hundred and were surrounded by ten times that number of loyalists, but beyond that cordon of steel, lay nothing but the torn dead for a quarter mile around. A man couldn't take a single step within that killing field without treading on a dead or twitching body or sinking his boot into a shallow pool of congealing blood.

Blazren spoke of a sea of shattered helmets not far from their position: red, blue, green on gold. Armor to match. Limbs broken, bloodied, strewn in hopeless search for their ravaged bodies. Elements of the Fourth and Fifth Einheriar Corps were they -- Azathoth's regulars, the pride of his holy army -- felled by the swords of the rebel's 53rd Regiment and the berserkers of Bargos Tel, bannermen of The Fallen — dead in the hundreds by their sides.

Myriad shafts and spears stuck up at every angle all across the field. Here and there they propped a lifeless body in a macabre scene of undeath. Burnt and shredded banners and pennons flapped in the breeze to a chorus of disembodied moans that droned continually from all directions. So too came shrieks from those who until lately believed themselves invincible. Pleadings for water or wine or the lord's forgiveness -- the usual battlefield dirge the rebels knew too well, but this time sung by beloved brothers on both sides. Men that should not have died that day or for countless years to come. The devastation was beyond belief, its scope unimaginable. The dead, uncountable. From on high, the entire field had a red and white cast from the snow and the glistening blood betwixt the bodies and staining the armor and shields of the fallen.

Blazren recited the names of regiment after regiment, battalion after battalion, belonging to both sides, but now killed to a man, or nearly so. The list went on far longer than any of them wanted to hear, but they kept listening, dreading the mention of some unit to whom a dearest friend was assigned. They kept listening in the same way folk passing a crashed cart on the road stop and stare and cannot turn away until they've seen whatever there is to see, however sad or gruesome. This time, there was no end to the dead.

As Silver flew higher, other skirmishes came into view. In desperate attempt to avoid being overwhelmed, the rebel Arkons grouped in turtle formations -- a circle of soldiers fighting back to back, sword, spear, and javelin, shield wall all around and on high, cramped together in an unbreakable line of muscle, grit, and steel. The Arkons employed that maneuver only in the most dire circumstances, when all was lost, the only hope, to hold until reinforcements arrived or providence interceded.

Those desperate formations were all they had left, save for what few Targon fliers remained amongst them. All the flashy and deadly war weapons, engines, and tactics were exhausted early in the battle. Batteries of catapults, scorpions, and ballistae, that launched flaming or explosive projectiles, all now overrun, abandoned, or destroyed. Hidden pits, acid bombs, flaming oil, trips and traps of myriad types had taken countless victims, many more on the loyalist side than not. Now it was down to muscle, sweat, and steel. The outcome determined by numbers, skills, courage, and of course, luck.

Two turtles battled battalions of loyalists not far from each other, but miles north of Thetan's men, both formations much larger than his, but sorely beset. Ten more turtles fought to the east, a half dozen to the south, all of varying sizes and compositions. Silver spied not a one to the west. Thetan's men had made it farthest west of all, closest to Vaeden, capitol of the realm.

Most of the surviving rebel units had a squadron of The Fallen at their core, which is likely why they yet fought on, where the bulk of the rebel army's units had been wiped out or dispersed. Some of the peasant units broke and ran as soon as the dying started. They hadn't expected it, the death. To them, war was a foreign concept, no more dangerous than a tavern brawl. When they saw the blood, the guts, the horror, and heard the screams, their courage faltered and they fled. Whole families fled. Entire companies. Others stood their ground and were slaughtered together for the loyalists gave them no quarter, showed them no mercy. Thetan and his brethren expected that, and it pained them more than they could say, but they needed the numbers, needed every man that they could get if they had any hope of fighting through to the lord himself and using the Sphere of the Heavens.

Thetan's brigade had lost about two-thirds of their original compliment, though they'd augmented their numbers with survivors from several other units. Of Thetan's five hundred troops, about two thirds were Arkons and most of those were amongst the best of their ilk. They were Thetan's spearhead, with which he'd hoped to crash through the gates of the holy city of Vaeden, perhaps even into the palace itself.

Any hope of that was over.

If Wotan did not arrive within the hour, capture would be Thetan's best chance to survive the day. And capture was something he would never endure. He knew the tortures that Iblis would gleefully inflict; better to face the void than that. He had brought his men to ruin. They'd followed him to their deaths. His comrades were correct when they named him the Harbinger of Doom.

JUTENHEIM
ANGLOTOR'S GATEHOUSE
YEAR 1267, 4TH AGE
MASTER GLUS THORN

More men moved in the corridor, grunting and cursing the way barbarians do. They'd been battered when the Church Knights crashed into them, or else more would've attacked already. Thorn could kill one more with his sorcery, mayhap two, three, or even four, if he were lucky, but somewhere along the line, the Toll would take him, and the Eotrus would win, Nord's help notwithstanding.

Thorn was not about to let that happen. He figured his best chance was to use what energies he had left to make his escape. He could cast a variation of his Stowron summoning spell to send himself and Nord elsewhere. He should've thought of that the moment that Nord warned him of the infiltration. But he hadn't. His mind had been clouded and sluggish.

It still was.

His best bet was to transport himself into the tower and rejoin Lord Korrgonn. And he tried to do just that for a full five heartbeats before he realized it was impossible. There was something about the tower, something in the stone. It prevented his magics from penetrating. He couldn't transport himself there, not even if he were at full strength, and he was far from that.

Alternately, he could drop himself outside the building, outside the tower, somewhere on Anglotor's grounds, or in the woods beyond, but what good would that do? He'd be alone and unprotected and unable to use any further magic for a goodly while. He needed more rest than Anglotor would afford him. With the Eotrus running around, he'd be as good as dead. Might be better to save the energy from that spell, and make his last stand in that room, he and Nord, fighting to the end for the lord. Martyrs to the holy mission.

He also couldn't chance a portal back to Black Rock Tower — for that would require far more energy than he could safely spare. The spell may well fail due to his sorry state, or more likely result in his death along the way from the Wizard's Toll.

The only other option was to transport himself back to his *galdr vagn*. There he'd be safe, and could recuperate as needed, and travel wherever wished, including home. The problem was, that would take him out of the fight. He wouldn't be there for the lord's arrival. He wouldn't be able to make certain that the portal was opened properly.

So he was left with two choices: either abandon the holy quest and save himself, or die there in that pathetic little room by the blades of his enemies or by the Wizard's Toll, whichever took him first.

If the Harbinger had been there, he would

have stayed. He would have gone down fighting that bastard. But he wasn't there.

Better to live to fight evil another day.

Just as he began the invocation to send him to the *galdr vagn*, more Eotrus stormed in. There wasn't time to complete the spell, not even if Nord interposed himself, which he surely would. Several big men stormed in. One was a giant. Artol the destroyer they called him. Thorn knew of that man's reputation. A wild sell sword -- a drunkard and womanizer, he'd heard — that had long served with Gabriel Garn, the man whose body served as a vessel for Lord Korrgonn. At another time it might be quite entertaining to see that man tangle with Nord. Who might come out on top, Thorn wasn't certain. But Artol was backed by numbers while he and Nord were on their own.

Thorn spoke two quick sounds and simultaneously punched with both fists. Twelve feet away, Artol and The Bull were each hit by an unseen force of titanic might. A force that flung them through the air to the far wall. The third man, one Sir Kelbor, came on unaffected. But good old Nord was there to stop him. Then came quite an exchange of blows, sword and shield against a staff master's might. Thorn didn't see much of the duel, the summoning spell requiring the bulk of his concentration, but he caught glimpses enough. That Eotrus knight was one well-trained barbarian bastard. He gave Nord a run for his money, he did. Of course, by the time the spell was ready, Nord had dropped the knight and vaulted back toward Thorn at his behest.

Thorn merely rolled off the side of the cot into the black shimmering portal that he created on the floor, and disappeared, Nord following him through. Two heartbeats later, no trace of that mystical portal remained.

36

THE AGE OF MYTH AND LEGEND
VIGRID VALLEY
FIMBULWINTER - YEAR 3
EIGHT HOURS AFTER THE INITIAL CHARGE

THETAN THE LIGHTBRINGER

"**C**an we regroup?" said Gabriel. "Are any of our units close enough?"

"Stragglers here and there," said Blazren, "most of them dead on their feet or hiding in trees. We might be able to pick up a hundred men, though it will likely cost us just as many to get to those. The closest formations are to our east, about a half mile through the trees and they're getting pounded, worse off than us. A tough slog if we head back that way."

"Can we make it to them?" said Gabriel.

"I think so," said Blazren, "but it will cost us dearly, and we'll yet be miles away from escaping this valley."

"This position is untenable," said Mithron as he wiped the blood and gore from his sword with a stray scrap of cloth. "We must take to the air before they bring in more fire bombers. Why they haven't doused us already, I cannot fathom."

"They may have none left after the trouncing we gave them at the first," said Raphael.

"They want us alive," said Dekkar.

"The air is our only way out," said Gabriel.

"Nearly half our number have no Targon," said Raphael, "and we cannot carry them in these conditions. They'll be slaughtered if we leave them behind." Raphael leaned against the large chest that contained The Sphere of the Heavens. Neither he nor Bose moved more than a step from it during the battle.

"And we will be slaughtered if we stay," said Uriel.

"They knew the risks when they signed on," said Dekkar.

"No easy choice," said Azrael. "Hold here, and the Northmen are our only chance -- *if* they're on their way, which I now strongly doubt. Take to the air and we abandon our comrades to certain death, but we live a while longer, mayhap to fight another day."

"The moment we take to the air," said Thetan, "loyalists will do the same. We'll be attacked from all sides, no shield wall to safeguard us. Safer to hold this formation unless and until we decide to abandon the field."

"If all that yet remain of our forces abandon the field," said Azrael, "even then, there won't be enough of us left to carry on this campaign. The rebellion is finished."

"Better that we were dead than that," said Bose.

"They'll track us down, no matter where we go," said Uriel. "There will be nowhere to hide. I'll not squirm under Iblis's knife. Better to die here, a warrior's death, clean and honorable — if honorable we yet deserve."

"It will not come to that," said Thetan.

"It's already come to that for most of our men," said Uriel.

"Where are your barbarians?" said Mithron to Thetan. "We'd not have launched this offensive today but for their promised support."

"The Northmen are not *mine*," said Thetan sharply. "And Wotan is a man of his word."

"So you have said," said Mithron, "but relying on them has brought this ruin upon us. We should have followed Dekkar's counsel and waited until the Northmen were in position to strike simultaneously with us."

"There's no sense in rehashing that now," said Dekkar, "but perhaps in the future, you geniuses will pay a bit more attention to my advice on tactics."

"What future?" spat Raphael.

"We know that some of our scouts were traitors — Markon, Cephalon, and mayhap others," said Thetan. "They likely passed Wotan false information that caused his delay or withdrawal. Or, he may have been waylaid by a large loyalist force."

"Who'd have thought Markon would've turned on us?" said Uriel. "He was one of the first to rally to our cause. A beloved friend of long years. I trusted him. He would've been with us that night on Mount Canterwrought but for other duties that kept him away."

"And who'd have thought we'd take up swords against the lord?" said Tolkiel. "Or that Arioch would turncoat on us? No man can be trusted, no matter how loved, that is what this venture has taught me."

"Such thinking will tear us apart," said Azrael. "We twelve must trust one another come what may, or all will surely be lost."

"Aye," said Mithron, his voice calming. "A hard day, brother," he said to Thetan. "Worse than we feared."

"It's not over yet," said Thetan. "Neither the day nor the cause. Blazren, look to the north; find those Northmen."

Gabriel put his hand on Thetan's shoulder. "The war is lost, my friend. Even if Wotan appears now, our armies are broken--"

"Not broken," said Raphael. "Dead. There is no recovering from dead. We walked into it here, never should have come straight on."

"Even if Wotan has a hundred thousand screaming barbarians with him — and they show up right now," said Uriel, "we still can't win this. The lord has more warriors even than that, fresh and ready, that haven't even entered the fray yet. The best we could hope for is to merge with Wotan's forces and make a run for it, to the Northern Mountains. Live to fight another day."

"I yet see nothing over the northern woods," said Blazren, "not for miles out, a day's trek at least. If they're still coming, this battle will long be over before they arrive."

"Mayhap they never left Percipion Ridge," said Uriel.

"Mayhap they never even arrived there," said Azrael. "We had them there only by Markon's and Cephalon's accounts."

"That confirms it; we're on our own," said

Steriel. "Let's take to the air and get gone from here while we yet can."

"Send your bird in low, amongst the trees," said Thetan. "The Northmen are stealthy, even in their numbers. They may be closer than you imagine."

"We must fly before the lord tightens his noose," said Mithron.

"The day is lost," said Gabriel, his voice quiet, calm.

"There's only dying left to do," said Dekkar.

"It be not lost," boomed Thetan as he rose up to his full height. "It be not lost! I cannot...I *will not* be defeated."

"There is only one thing for it, my brothers," said Dekkar. "A decapitation strike. We go aloft. Have the bird find Azathoth and descend on him with all we have. He hasn't shown himself, so we go looking."

"And then, we use the Sphere if we can--" said Gabriel.

"Or swords if we must," said Steriel."

"A blaze of glory," said Uriel. "If I'm to die this day, that's how I'd prefer to go."

"And I," said Tolkiel.

"Aye," said Mithron. "Other than retreat, it be the only option left to us. What say you, brother?"

"Let's not be hasty," said Azrael. "All Midgaard depends upon this mad venture. If we end here today, Azathoth remains in power, forevermore. We cannot defeat the loyalists, the Brigandir, and the lord too, with so few, no matter our resolve. We don't even know how to activate the Sphere and the Gnome is as absent as the Northmen. We must flee north and regroup and try again another day. It's our best chance to win, to defeat him. That's the purpose of all this, don't forget. It's not to die in battle, it's to banish the lord. We must survive this. You must survive this, Thetan."

Thetan paused for some time considering those words before he spoke again. "Recall your bird," he said to Blazren. "We rely on the original plan to use the Sphere, or die today in the trying. It was always to come to that in the end. The false god will not be far. Blazren, you'll likely find him perched atop some hill within sight of this field, gloating over his victory. Find him for us so we can have done of this. Today, we slay a god."

Raphael shook his head. "God help us," he said.

37

JUTENHEIM
ANGLOTOR TOWER
THE TEMPLE OF POWER
YEAR 1267, 4TH AGE

JUDE EOTRUS

The sanctum had a stone door, once polished, now marred with spidery cracks and inlaid with odd geometric patterns that were hard to look upon. The Stowron turned their heads from them.

Donnelin leaned toward Jude and whispered in his ear. "The doors be relics of the *Nether Realms*, brought over by fools like Ginalli and his people. Stone they may look like, but they're made of stranger stuff not meant for Midgaard. Not meant for the eyes of man. Let your gaze not linger upon them or risk madness, you will."

The hairs on Jude's nape stood when he heard Donnelin's words, but his curiosity and thirst for knowledge compelled him to look. The shapes he saw were foreign to him. He couldn't name them. The angles were too sharp, but yet curved in a way that made no sense. Looking at those alien patterns for but a few moments made him grow dizzy and his stomach churned. How the mere sight of them caused that, Jude didn't understand.

The sanctum appeared deserted. As Jude stepped across its threshold, his stomach churned again, all the worse. He noticed the others had a similar reaction, the Stowron no exception.

The chamber was sixty feet square. Doors at each of the four corners, located at the points. How they closed and fit at those angles was hard to say. Each door boasted the same unnatural look, but Jude pulled his eyes away lest he puke. Still, he felt unsteady, stomach flopping. He did his best to act natural; had no interest in showing weakness, not to anybody, not even Donnelin. He was Aradon Eotrus's son. He'd make no fool of himself, and no one would make sport of him, not even there at the end.

Especially not at the end.

Jude knew that unless some miracle happened, he'd soon be dead, bled dry by maniacs in a stinking dungeon on the backside of the world.

How had it come to that?

He was a warrior, a nobleman, a Northman. This was not the way for him to die. Murdered there, would he be granted entry to Valhalla or be forever barred from Odin's halls? Would the Valkyries find him in those tunnels, in that far-off land, or would his spirit be cursed to haunt his rotting corpse, forevermore? To watch helpless as the maggots devoured his flesh and the rats gnawed his lonely bones. No Northman deserved such a fate.

Teek put a firm hand on Jude's shoulder. "Steady there, laddie," he whispered. "Make no false move, for there's no good end to it here. Bide your time. Deliverance may yet come."

Korrgonn sent Stowron through each door with orders to root out any of the tower's defenders hiding thereabouts.

The Leaguers lit wall sconces, dozens of them, brightening the sanctum, though that did little to reduce the unnatural chill that abided there and strangely failed to banish the black shadows that lurked about the room's edges and its heights.

The floor was of carved stone -- great blocks laid in a geometric pattern, expertly cut, one against the other, no mortar to be found. The stones were of varied shades of black and gray, brown and red, arrayed in a swirling, mesmerizing pattern as hard to look upon as that of the doors. The dark gray walls were rough, and adorned with glyphs and runes of similar esoteric pattern as the doors and floor. Above them, an odd domed stone ceiling loomed high in the blackness. It came together at wild angles and misshapen curves, a dizzying chaotic effect that caused Jude to stumble and turn away. He wished they hadn't lit so many sconces; the light made it all the harder to bear the unnatural sights of that bizarre non-Euclidean geometry.

Jude's breath hung steaming before him, though the air felt mountaintop thin, hard to catch one's breath. Sound was strangely amplified in the forlorn space: echoing and reverberating in ways grating to the ear, confounding to the mind. The chamber was empty save for a stone altar: ponderous, wide, and imposing, which resided at the room's center. A great black basalt slab it was, rough but shiny, supported by two stout plinths of similar stone -- stone born of a different place and a different time than that of the chamber.

Save for the expedition, the sanctum was devoid of life. Not a cobweb or creepy crawly hid in any corner; no rat or bat dared brave the place. No evidence of occupancy or passage, recent or distant, marred the loneliness of that peculiar place. It was as if no man had ever ventured within, but Jude doubted that were true. He imagined that the place had seen no end of horrors in its day -- gruesome sacrifices upon that unholy altar; innocent lives offered up to foul demons, monstrous fiends, forgotten gods, or bizarre alien creatures. And perhaps, more recent horrors took place there, carried out by the master of the tower and his sorry dependents.

At Ginalli's command, Teek and the Lugron ushered Jude and Donnelin toward one wall, guarding them closely. Par Brackta moved near to them, her eyes sad, or so Jude imagined.

Mort Zag tossed Uriel's limp form against another wall. The Stowron had carried two wooden beams into that place, and at Korrgonn's direction, they lashed them together into the shape of a cross. They laid Uriel's unconscious form upon the cross and tied him to it: ankles, wrists, and neck. Their tasks done, Korrgonn banished the last of the Stowron from the room. Apparently, they weren't worthy to welcome Azathoth home.

"Prepare the ritual," said Korrgonn to Ginalli. "Waste no time about it, but make no missteps. Mort Zag, return to the surface and lead the defense against the Harbinger. Be on guard, for he will be here at any moment, if even he has not arrived already. You must hold him at bay until we get the portal opened."

"How will we know when you've succeeded?" said Mort Zag.

Korrgonn smiled. "When you hear the world sigh in relief, you will know. You'll feel it in your heart, in your very bones. No one will need tell you. Afterwards, we'll rejoice together and bask in the lord's glory, forevermore. But that will only come to pass if the ritual goes uninterrupted. You must not fail me."

"I will not, oh great Lord of Light," said Mort Zag.

"Even if it means your death?" said Korrgonn.

"Even so," said Mort Zag as he departed.

Par Keld placed a large leather bag atop the altar, opened it, and rummaged about. He removed several strange tokens and assorted wizardly paraphernalia. Ginalli hovered over him, and in hushed but sharp tones, questioned and criticized his every move.

Korrgonn turned toward Jude, made eye contact with him and Donnelin. Then he closed his eyes, held his hands out before him at waist height, palms down, deep in concentration.

Before Jude's eyes, Korrgonn transformed.

38

THE AGE OF MYTH AND LEGEND
VIGRID VALLEY
FIMBULWINTER - YEAR 3
ELEVEN HOURS AFTER THE INITIAL CHARGE

THETAN THE LIGHTBRINGER

"**I** found the lord," said Blazren. "Four miles northwest, atop that large hill at the forest's edge, the one with the little waterfall on the southern side. I don't think he saw Silver, not with all the crows."

"How many does he have?" said Mithron.

"The bulk of the Brigandir and two or three score Arkons. A few hundred Einheriar on the slopes."

"A steep hill, if I remember," said Gabriel. "We'll need to fly in all the way or else get bogged down."

"Their bowmen will cut us up," said Bose. "I'd rather slog through them on foot, even with them on the high ground."

"If we come at them quick," said Steriel, "we can push through."

"If we don't engage Azathoth straightaway," said Thetan, "he'll flee, fly, or rain down death on us from above. We've got to contain him. Flying in fast is the only way."

"Dekkar, what do you think?" said Raphael.

"As the Lightbringer says, it's the only way,"

said Dekkar.

"Agreed," said Mithron.

"Bhaal is with him," said Blazren. "Iblis too."

"Wonderful," said Raphael.

"Enough talk," said Uriel. "Let's do this."

"Make ready," said Dekkar.

Thetan's heart was heavy as he and his Arkons prepared to take to the air and abandon their brigade. His footmen, for all their skills and bravery, would be quickly overwhelmed by the surrounding loyalist forces. His men would never surrender. They'd be killed to the last.

Yet he must abandon them. It was his only remaining chance to stop Azathoth.

But that didn't lessen his guilt.

He looked at his soldiers, his expression grim.

"Go," said a white-haired trooper that had fought at his side for the last hour. The man had read his face, his mood. Thetan didn't know his name. Didn't even know his face prior to the battle. He must've come over with a remnant of another troop. The man was like iron and fought without fear as they battled the loyalists side by side; skills to match the best Arkons. And now he'd leave him to his death.

"Go," said another man. Then another. Then began a chant repeated by all the soldiers, "go". That must have confused the loyalists.

Thetan nodded respectfully to his men. Those brave veterans knew they'd be slaughtered to a man after the Arkons took flight.

And yet they urged them to go.

It made Thetan proud, and sad, and guilty, all at once.

"You will be remembered," was all he could say. He wanted to say more, they deserved to hear more, but he couldn't find the words and dare not spare more time in the searching.

In the crowded turtle formation, pressed on all sides by loyalist forces, Thetan and his men had no room to maneuver, or for their Targon to outstretch their wings, run forward, and launch into the air as was their wont. If they launched from a standing position, they'd rise too slowly - - easy targets for several seconds for archers and javelins; many had already fallen that way. But they'd trained for this; they knew what to do. They cleared what space they could at the formation's center and three large and sturdy men went to hands and knees, one behind the next separated by a goodly stride. A fourth man knelt on one knee, his back upright, beyond the other three.

Uriel stepped quickly up on the back of the first man and strode forward picking up speed as he stepped on the backs of the second and third men in turn. When he reached the last man he stepped up onto his shoulder and leaped into the air, his Targon's wings unfurling in an instant. Those wings flapped majestically and fought against gravity for but a moment before Uriel shot forward faster than the swiftest eagle. Arrows flew late, javelins slow, and Uriel the Bold made good his escape.

Two steps behind Uriel went Gabriel, then Steriel, Hogar, Dekkar, and the rest. The formation's size shrunk as more and more Arkons launched themselves into the air. Most

179

sped clear but javelins and arrows aplenty tore through majestic wings and some few pierced armor and flesh. Several Arkons plummeted and crashed amidst the throng of enemies only to be torn to pieces. As the rebel ranks thinned, the loyalists pressed their attack; the last score of rebel Arkons had no time or opportunity to take flight and were left behind.

Thetan's Targon rose eagerly into the air, joyful to be aloft and free from the claustrophobic battle formation and the sickening stench that hung over it. Thetan felt much the same. He held a lance at the ready, certain he'd need it, the loyalists' Targon closing in on them. Hogar flew beside him, as did Dekkar, Raphael, Uriel, Gabriel, Tolkiel, Bose, and Steriel. He'd lost sight of the others amidst the throng.

"Lances ready," shouted Dekkar. "Here they come."

Thetan lowered his lance and held it steady against the buffeting wind as he sped headlong at the nearest loyalist that blocked their path. Marthiel was her name, a long-time acquaintance of Thetan's. Had Azathoth's restrictions been not in place, she was a woman Thetan would have wanted to know better, having long admired her strength and beauty from afar. He sensed that she too thought fondly of him, but he was never certain of it; no such words were exchanged, for even that would have raised Azathoth's ire and broken his laws. The lord's jealousy ran deep.

Thetan would have chosen another opponent,

most *any* other opponent, if he'd had the chance, but his comrades flew close about him; to turn aside would have disrupted their formation and endangered them all. He grit his teeth and flew on.

Thetan and Marthiel's eyes met for a split second as their lance points passed.

Thetan put his lance through the center of Marthiel's chest; an instant kill.

Simultaneously, Marthiel's lance veered wide, *too wide*, and missed Thetan entirely.

She'd missed on purpose; there could be no other explanation for she was far too skilled for so clumsy a run.

He'd always wanted to know how she felt about him, but now the knowing hurt a thousandfold more than not. The broken haft of his lance fell away and his stomach churned, a groan of anguish that no one heard escaped his lips. He watched for a moment, only a moment, as Marthiel spiraled down, his fractured lance protruding from her chest, to crash upon the snowy ground far below.

Did she expect that gruesome end, that betrayal of all that they wanted but never had? Or did she think or hope that Thetan would spare her, his feelings the same? Or did it all happen too fast; too fast to think at all?

He'd never know. Again, he'd have to live with not knowing. Another horror to push from his head until the day's deed was done. Another weight to carry on his conscience, forevermore.

A glance to either side and back confirmed his cadre was still with him, and the Sphere still intact. The loyalists had crumbled under the rebels' lances, dropping from the sky like falling stars.

Normally, Thetan would have swung about and attacked again, finishing off any enemies that might still pose a threat, but he couldn't do it. He just couldn't.

"Look there," shouted Uriel, his arm pointing to the northeast, toward the forest. "The Northmen!"

At first, Thetan saw nothing but the swirling snow and swaying trees, but when he looked longer, he spied a tide of white moving amidst the forest floor. The Northmen were cloaked in white furs that made them almost invisible amidst the fallen and whirling snows.

"That's no scouting party or advance guard," said Gabriel. "The entire forest is alive; it's the core of their strength. Wotan has joined the fray."

"We're not done yet," boomed Bose.

"The Northmen are with us," shouted Steriel, and a cheer went up amongst the rebel ranks.

"Mithron," shouted Thetan, "fend off the incoming with Third Flight. First and Second Flights, turnabout, and follow me. Back to our brigade," he shouted as he pulled another lance from its sheath.

"To the brigade, you bastards," shouted Dekkar.

Though but few minutes had passed since their departure, the remnants of Thetan's brigade had been decimated. Fewer than fifty rebels stood in a wavering turtle formation as the loyalists swarmed them on all sides, the dead of both factions piled high.

Thetan swooped down and his lance crashed into one loyalist's head, then a second, third, and a fourth as he sailed across their lines, killing each man with that single blow. Beside him, Dekkar, Hogar, and Uriel did much the same.

When his lance snapped, Thetan retracted his wings and plunged into the loyalists' midst, sword and shield working. The other rebels followed his lead. The surprise and fervor of their assault panicked the loyalists. They had no idea how many rebels attacked, only that they did so without fear, as if they had the numbers on their side. Almost immediately, most of the loyalist units broke and fled. Those who remained fought tooth and nail against Thetan and his men. Talmikron of Tavers Bay, a royal Arkon of the first order, commanded the main loyalist unit. He gave no ground and refused to yield. Dekkar cut off his head.

When the skirmish was over, no more than a score of Thetan's footmen still lived and he'd lost near a fifth of First and Second Flights.

"Why did you come back, my lord?" said the white-haired soldier to Thetan. He bled from a shallow gash, hairline to chin. "The mission."

"The Northmen will be here within the hour," said Thetan. "If only we had spotted them sooner."

"The fog of war, lord, is a fickle thing," said the man.

"I would know your name, warrior," said Thetan. "I should know it already, methinks."

"I am called Partell," said the man. "A marcher lord from distant Trenton Heights, out east over the Asher Range. We rallied to your banners last winter only lately hearing of your rebellion."

"I know your land, Lord Partell," said Thetan, "and your reputation. You and your sons have held the eastern borderlands against the wild for many a year."

"No longer, I fear," said Partell, "for all my sons fell over yonder with the rest of my regiment, all the strength of The Heights. I am the last of my House. The last of my name."

"I have no words," said Thetan.

"You need none," said Partell. "Your cause is just and your actions speak for themselves. Continue to lead us by example as you have done; that is all I or anyone can ask. Freedom is worth any price, even death."

39

JUTENHEIM
ANGLOTOR TOWER
THE GREAT STAIR
YEAR 1267, 4TH AGE

THETA

It took a moment for Theta's eyes to adjust to the relative darkness of the entry hall. In those seconds, he and Dolan were vulnerable, but the chamber proved empty, save for the torn dead. Dozens of them and only recently fallen. At a glance, Theta discerned they were of diverse types: Jutons, Elves, Svart, Ettin, perhaps others, but all wore common livery. These were the defenders of the keep. The Stowron, were the invaders — no doubt, agents of the Shadow League.

"Which way, Lord Angle?" said Dolan as he glanced warily at the entry Golem, even now rising to its feet.

Theta paused a moment longer, tightly gripping his Ankh, and then made directly for the downward stair. Just as they reached the stair, the entry Golem was up and had spotted them. It lumbered toward them and squashed the dead to pulp beneath its feet.

Theta thrust open the stair's door into that even darker space and headed down, his falchion held before him. Dolan slammed the door behind them and wedged a spike into the frame.

"It will only hold a moment, but it doesn't matter," said Dolan as he glanced about the stair, "for I think its too big to fit through, and the stair's too narrow. We may be clear. How far does this go down, can you tell?"

"A long way," said Theta, still gripping the Ankh. "The temple of power still feels far off. The rock dampens the signal. It must be deep below us."

Dolan looked over the side of the stair and he could see that it wound down and down and down as far as even his sharp eyes could see. "Several hundred feet at the least."

"Someone's coming up," said Dolan after they'd gone down a few dozen steps. "A big man in a shaggy red coat. Never seen red fur like that. He's bigger than Tug."

Theta turned to Dolan, a quizzical expression on his face. "Red fur, you say?" He gripped the Ankh once more, and spoke words into its ear. "Oh, shit," he said after a moment.

"What's happened?" said Dolan. "What now?"

"It's a Red Demon of Fozramgar," said Theta.

"A red demon of what?" said Dolan. "Why should we happen upon a demon? Can't we just stumble across some bats? Or a large rat or two? Why does it have to be a demon?"

"You sound like the Gnome," said Theta.

"Do I need to be worried?" said Dolan.

"Yes," said Theta.

40

VIGRID VALLEY
FIMBULWINTER - YEAR 3
LAST DAY OF THE AGE OF MYTH AND LEGEND

"**I'**m quite disappointed," said Lasifer.

Thetan, his lieutenants, and the leaders of the Northmen spun around, surprised. Wary though they were, they hadn't heard the old Gnome approach, and no one had leave to disturb them, save to warn of imminent attack.

"I thought your forces would fare better against those of the false god," said Lasifer. "I fear I've thrown in with the losing side. That won't do it all; no it won't."

The northern lords Donar and Heimdall pulled their weapons and took a step toward the Gnome, a stranger to them.

Thetan motioned to halt. "Stay your hands; he's one of ours."

Lasifer shook his head, a disapproving look on his face. "Swords first, questions later, always the same with you brutes," he said.

"The old bone thrower you spoke of?" said Wotan, king of the Northmen and father to Donar.

"Aye," said Thetan, "such as he is."

Lasifer raised an eyebrow. "How else would I be?" he said. He looked more wrinkled than usual, though that seemed quite impossible. He wore his pointy blue hat, white tassels fluttering in the breeze, his flowing robes of black and yellow rumpled as usual but not the least bit soiled from the day's events. His appearance, quite the spectacle despite his diminutive height.

"A hard day for brutes," said the Gnome, "and not over yet, not nearly. Before the sun sleeps, we'll see your true mettle, we will, what you're all made of, one way or the other."

"From where did you spring, Gnome?" said Thetan.

"Have I been missed?" he said as a mischievous smile formed, birthing even more wrinkles.

Thetan held his gaze until the old Gnome spoke again, the wizard's voice a bit sterner.

"I've been here, and there, and everywhere, observing this debacle. I decided I'd best offer a bit of advice before you all end up in the afterlife sooner than expected. It won't do to show up early for that party; there's more fun to be had first."

"We've no time and I have no patience for jesters or fools," said Wotan. "You value this one's counsel, Lord Thetan?"

"He has his uses," said Thetan. "Tell us now the secret of the Sphere," he said to the Gnome. "How do we use it? You've held too much back."

The Gnome appeared surprised by the questions.

"What?" blurted Mithron. "Are you saying, you don't know how to work it?"

"The Gnome knows," said Thetan. "Or he'd better."

"Of course I know," said Lasifer. "You'd all be

doomed if I didn't. Well...doomed sooner."

"Are you mad?" said Mithron to Thetan. "We launched this attack without the means of finishing it? What if the Gnome hadn't showed up? What if he'd been killed? What if Azathoth had taken to the field already? How would we finish it?"

Thetan looked confused.

"Thetan would find a way, of course," said the Gnome. "He always does. Quite resourceful."

"Why didn't we wait?" said Gabriel. "I thought you knew how to use it. This was reckless."

"Insane is what it is," said Bose. "Why have we been lugging this thing around if you didn't know how to make it work?"

"We're getting far off track," said Lasifer. "We should—"

"Perhaps a better question," said Azrael, "is why didn't any of us think to ask about its use. How could that be? We prepared every element of this plan, debated it at length. I fear that--"

"You didn't ask because you trusted Thetan, of course," said Lasifer loudly, his fingers fluttering the way a wizard's sometimes do. "As well you should, and he trusted me, as well he should, to uncover the Sphere's secrets in good time, which I lately have, and informed him of my success well before your attack began. Your plans haven't been delayed even a moment, so the matter is quite settled and we're moving on."

"Not that you care," continued the Gnome before anyone could speak, "but it wasn't easy learning the Sphere's secrets. Perhaps you thought I had an old tome moldering on my

189

bookshelves these last millennia that describes precisely how to open magical gateways and banish false gods, all instructions clear and simple, illustrations aplenty, in color no less, plain as day even for such dullards as you? You think that's what I've got up my sleeve?" he said, holding up his hands, showing he concealed nothing. Before he lowered his arms, an assortment of playing cards fluttered from his sleeves. As he tried to catch them, out fell a pair of Spottle dice and a small frog. "Pay no attention to those," he spat. "Tools of the trade, nothing more."

"Now," said Lasifer as he tried repeatedly and unsuccessfully to stomp on the wayward frog, "the knowing of such things as heavenly spheres demands lengthy and perilous delvings in the mysterious corners of Midgaard; forbidden places that would make your skin crawl and your hair stand on end -- if you were lucky. If not, it'd go all white or fall out entirely. I have only now returned from such places, where I went on my lonesome I might add. There, I consulted with...things, creatures worse in their way than Azathoth, though less bold in their plans, all to acquire the answers that you seek. I've not held those answers back, not for a single day, since as I said, I've only lately returned, having risked my life, and my very soul, if you can believe it, serving our common cause, playing the part that only I can play, that not one of you could hope to fulfill."

"I've learned the truth and it has cost me dearly, though I admit, you might not tell it from my pretty face and well-coiffed look. I've suffered as much in this endeavor as any of you and my ordeals have lasted for longer than just this single bloody day. I've been out there for three years obtaining this information. Three years!"

"What have you discovered?" said Thetan.

"Oh, no need to thank me for my arduous efforts," said Lasifer. "Let's put *all* pleasantries aside and get down to business and—"

"You've rambled overlong," said Thetan. "Tell us what you've found."

"Lightbringer, some days you're mildly entertaining, but today, you're no fun at all."

"Will our plan work?" said Gabriel. "Is there a way?"

"The eye of a priest," he said sharply, looking about to each of the gathered men, "and the blood of a king," he boomed. "That's what the Weave of Magic demands in recompense for opening a portal to the *Nether Realms.*"

41

JUTENHEIM
ANGLOTOR TOWER
THE GREAT STAIR
YEAR 1267, 4TH AGE

MORT ZAG

Before Mort Zag saw it, even before he caught its putrid stench, he knew it was there, on the stair above him.

That vile murderer.

That incarnation of evil.

The *thing* that had ruined his life.

The so-called Harbinger of Doom.

He could feel it, but he didn't know how. Mayhap he somehow sensed the creature's unholy power, or else, perhaps he detected the foul malignancy that consumed the Harbinger's soul and radiated out, corrupting all within its sphere.

But Mort Zag preferred thinking the forewarning a boon from the Lord, granted him for years of loyal service, the better to exact righteous vengeance long overdue.

Until he spied it creeping down the stairs, trailed by its pointy-eared familiar, Mort Zag wasn't certain that the feeling was real, that he wasn't imagining things. But when he caught sight of it, he knew and he remembered: the fabled armor, so bright and beautiful, the mirror opposite of its owner's black heart; and the infamous weapons of countless atrocities. Those cursed slayers born of Helheim: the hammer that only the soulless could lift; the curved sword coated with insidious poison, indiscriminate and cruel. But where was the soul-eating spear — lost to the long years or gifted to one of its vile minions?

Mort Zag tracked the Harbinger and his brethren for years before becoming a disciple of the one true god and joining the League of Light. But no matter how hard he tried, no matter how fast he traveled, the Harbinger always eluded him, ever moving, restless in his wanton ways, his plots and schemes, hunting down hapless victims, extinguishing innocent lives, wiping out whole tribes, entire races, genocide.

Sometimes, Mort Zag fell a month behind, the trail cold save for the decaying corpses it left behind, often in neat rows, heads on pikes to terrorize him, to create fear and hesitation, anything that would give *it* an advantage however small when we finally meet. Those atrocities disgusted Mort Zag and rather than deter him they emboldened him to quicken his pace.

The dead always pointed the way. He need merely follow their spoor.

Often, he drew within a week or two of the Harbinger's heels, and sometimes he closed the distance to only a few days. More than once he'd come upon the Harbinger's campfire, still warm or smoking, coals aglow, though why a Lord of Helheim yearned warmth, Mort Zag couldn't fathom.

Close as he came to his quarry, he'd always been late. It was a game, of course. The Harbinger knew he was following, and toyed with him, no — tortured is a better word for it. Denying Mort Zag even a chance at vengeance, at justice, was the worst thing the Harbinger could do to him, so that's what he did. Over and again, for years. What malice. What evil. Its depths, limitless.

Mort Zag had only laid eyes on the Harbinger once — on the day of death, that's what he named it -- though the Harbinger's evil visage was forever burned into his mind's eye. Ever since that red day, time and again he wondered if the Harbinger were only a myth his mind had conjured in its grief, a mere will-o-the-wisp as insubstantial as the morning mist.

But in his heart, Mort Zag knew the Harbinger was no hobgoblin, for he witnessed it in action. While he watched, helpless, the Harbinger and its minions sacked his home and murdered his people. His family. All that he ever loved.

The Harbinger slaughtered the Fozramgar, all their strength, skill, and bravery, to no avail against the fiend and its hounds. The Harbinger called no parley, granted no mercy. It charged in and killed: males, females, children, elders, all. No quarter, no prisoners, no decency. Only death did he sow.

The Harbinger's minions were well trained and equipped and they caught Mort Zag's tribe by surprise. Would've been different had it been a standup fight, not that his folk engaged in such battles with the spawn of Midgaard. They kept to themselves, hidden away in the high mountains, venturing from their hideaways only to forage or hunt. But the Harbinger would not leave them in peace. It stalked them at every turn, killed them on sight. And now, it found their village. It was determined to kill them all.

Mort Zag was but a wee youth then, four feet tall, barely into his fur, and untrained as yet in the ways of war, unprepared to deal with the evils of the Volsungs and their allies. From a hidey hole his mother had dropped him in, he watched his father duel the dark blue knight that his people called the Harbinger of Death. His father was Dharma Gog, the chieftain and greatest warrior of the Fozramgar.

Dharma Gog fought with the golden staff of power, a product of Abaddon's forges, sharpened on both ends, blades beyond the skill of mortal men. One blow from that sacred weapon could take down a tree. He watched the duel as it raged on and on, thunderous blow crashing against thunderous blow, until at last the Harbinger plunged his evil blade into his father's chest where it stuck fast.

Dharma Gog, who had never before been defeated, dropped to his knees, blood gushing from the fatal wound, his heart, skewered. But the Harbinger wasn't done yet. He pulled out his cursed hammer and brandished it, laughing, as Dharma Gog knelt there, bleeding, helpless, dying.

And then the Harbinger smashed that hammer into the side of his father's head. The horrible sound that it made haunted Mort Zag's nightmares, forevermore. And the look on the Harbinger's face: the maniacal eyes, and the mocking laugh that went on and on. It was more than Mort Zag could bear.

But that was long ago. Mort Zag was now as tall and strong as his father had been, and he'd battle trained every day of his long life, schooled by those few survivors of the slaughter, and by others of skill he paid for with mountain gold. A thousand battles he'd fought down through the years, and he'd not suffered a single defeat, discounting of course the recent debacle with Dagon of the Deep.

In battle, Mort Zag was fearless and peerless. But when he saw the Harbinger loping down that stair, his heart fluttered, his breathing quickened, and sweat dripped from his pores. He wanted to turn and run screaming down the stair into the dark. He almost did. But there was no point. He knew the Harbinger would find him.

Only one of them would leave that place alive.

Rotten luck that they met on the stair. It was so narrow, Mort Zag had to turn his torso at an angle to climb the steps, no way to maneuver, and the Harbinger had the higher ground. He thought of withdrawing and facing the fiend at the stair's base, but quickly realized the Harbinger would prove faster of foot than he. If he fled, the beast would backstab him. He couldn't risk that. He must face the Harbinger head on and make him pay. He owed his father that, owed all the Fozramgar.

And so, Mort Zag boldly charged up the stair

to meet his fate, knowing in his heart of hearts that he was last scion of the Fozramgar — a proud and noble race of warriors born — once of fabled Abaddon, long now trapped on this puny world of vicious hairless apes.

42

VIGRID VALLEY
FIMBULWINTER - YEAR 3
LAST DAY OF THE AGE OF MYTH AND LEGEND

"**A** jester, he marks himself," said Donar. "Eyes and blood? Throw the fool out, and let's finish our plans."

"No jest, Northman," said Lasifer. "I've deciphered every ancient tome and crumbling scroll from Vaeden to Valadon to Myhrr. I've consulted the eldest and the wisest and the shades of what once were, and all who knew have advised the same. The eye of a priest whose heart is true and the blood of a king whose eyes are blue."

"That's quite particular," said Gabriel.

Lasifer's head rocked from side to side. "I added the bit about the blue eyes -- it rhymes quite nicely, wouldn't you say? The rest is true -- the eye and the blood, without those, you can beseech the Sphere for forever and a day or smash it to bits if you like, but no mystical portal will ever open. You'll have naught but a broken Sphere, perhaps a bit of an explosion, perhaps more than a bit, but Azathoth will not be killed by it, nor banished, and you'll be no better off than you are now. Worse, in fact, considering he'll no doubt kill you dead."

"And if we had such an eye and such blood," said Azrael the Wise, "what would we do with them?"

"And there's the rub, of course," said Lasifer. "Magic is a wanton thing, not to be trusted or relied upon. It has its ways, its goals; some say, its own sense of humor. Others call it madness, but no matter -- for sorcery sets the terms, we must comply, or it does not do the deeds. One might say that it is we who serve it rather than it that serves us. To open the portal, we must pluck out the eye of the priest and place it on the Sphere as a sacrifice. We--"

"A sacrifice to whom or what?" said Azrael.

"Disappointed again," said Lasifer shaking his head. "Of all, I thought *you* would pay attention. To the Weave, of course. What else?"

"After which, we drain the blood from the king and let it drip upon the Sphere until its thirst is quenched. And when it's had its fill, the Worldgate will open."

"How much blood is needed? " said Wotan.

"Doubtless, more than a noble northern king can spare, I fear," said Lasifer, "however broad his shoulders or surly his disposition. There's always a chance, of course, that if the man be made of stern enough stuff, he might survive it. Not much chance, mind you, but some, a trifling."

"How will we know when it's had enough blood?" said Gabriel.

"Have you been asleep this whole time, Hornblower?" said Lasifer. "You're being quite dense today. Quite dense. When the portal *opens*, of course."

"How does it know to open a door to the

Nether Realms after it gets the eye and the blood," said Hogar, "instead of doing something else, like making a chicken appear out of the air, or some nonsense like that?"

"I certainly hope that you're an especially skilled fighter, dear Hogar," said Lasifer. "Elsewise, I truly can't imagine why the Lightbringer lets you hang about."

"I'll hear your answer," said Dekkar, his voice stern.

"Obviously, Mr. Happy Face, because the doing of other things requires *other* rituals, other sacrifices. Not that the Sphere can do anything that you can dream up. It's not a ring of wishes out of some old fable, you know. Hmm. Does anyone have one of those, by the way?"

Some of the men shook their heads; most just stared at the Gnome.

"Pity," said Lasifer as he scribbled something on his sleeve with a quill that appeared from nowhere. "The Sphere has its purpose and its limitations. One of its purposes, mayhap its primary purpose, is to open portals to other worlds. That's what it does. World Gates are what they're called. And when it opens one, whoever and whatever is nearby gets sucked through by a great wind or some such. My sources are quite vague on the details, but clear enough that if you're close by, within a dozen yards, let's say, you'll get sucked through that yawning portal and gifted a one-way ticket to the *Nether Realms*. Nifleheim, Helheim, Abaddon, or elsewhere -- not quite clear on that, but does it matter?"

"I'd try to catch Azathoth unawares if I were you. I've a feeling if he anticipates what's coming, no wind, however strong, will push him an inch, little less through the portal. Now, not all the Spheres create a vortex, some open quite gently, relatively speaking, but our Sphere is a wild and willful one."

"There's more of them?" said Hogar.

"I see you've woken up," said Lasifer. "How delightful. No doubt, you'll want your eggs and bacon."

"The more I listen to this," said Thetan, "the more it sounds like nonsense. You best not have played us false, Gnome. I warn you, if you have—"

"This is madness and foolishness," said Gabriel. "Pluck out a man's eye? Bleed a king? Ridiculous. Why not bleed his bloody frog or speak a riddle to make the crops grow? Nonsense, all of it."

"Not nonsense," said Lasifer. "It's madness, just as the Lightbringer said. Magic is madness. Or rather, better to call it chaos. If you don't believe me, go ahead and try to coax the Sphere to open the Worldgate now. Beg it, bribe it, threaten it, or smash it to bits, if you will, and see what happens. Problem is, you've only got the one Sphere, and thus, if you damage it before meeting its terms, well, it's all for naught, now isn't it? Unless you locate another Sphere, and you've no time for that. So, you have to find the priest and the blood, and do as I've spoken, or all is lost, madness or no. Take it or leave it, there simply is no other choice."

"What other counsel do you offer?" said Thetan. "What other details, wisdom, or mad ravings can you gift us this day?"

"Are you done with me, already?" said Lasifer. "Heard what you needed, and now you usher me away like the misbehaving whelps. Is that all old Lasifer is worth to you, Lightbringer? Surely, I'm valued a bit more than that, methinks. But don't bother yourselves about me. Oh, no, don't bother. I'll stand in the corner, quiet as a mouse. You'll not even know I'm here. But if something happens that might warrant my feeble insight, I may dare to speak up, albeit meekly, so as not to disturb your greatness and grandeur."

"Do we believe this?" said Gabriel.

"Can we afford not to?" said Mithron.

"He's always been flighty and arrogant," said Raphael, "but I've never known him to be a liar nor truly mad."

"The bone throwers of our people speak of such rituals," said Donar. "Not the same as which he spoke here but of things similar."

"Mystical nonsense," said Dekkar.

"Is there truth to it or only tapestry?" said Gabriel.

"The bone throwers have often spoken true," said Wotan. "They proclaim things they could not know, but that yet came to pass. This Gnome of yours, if his power be true, may speak the truth. Is his power real, or is he but a humbug?"

"His power is real," said Thetan, "but his words may yet be false, but why, I cannot say. Azrael, what think you of this? You've dabbled in magic."

202

"Truth be told," said Azrael, "I've more than dabbled. Far more. Mayhap more than anyone save for Lasifer. Sorcery defies logic and reason, defies science and nature. It is a thing of itself. It makes its own rules, has its own structure, though much of it is beyond our understanding, mayhap beyond our ability *to* understand. So I say to you, it doesn't matter if the method of which Lasifer speaks makes any sense. It's either true or it's not. It'll either work or it won't. But as he said, we only get one chance. And so, we have little choice. We must find us a willing priest and a king with blood to spare," he said glancing at Wotan, "or more than likely, all our plans are undone."

"I have done many things under Azathoth's banner of which I am ashamed," said Thetan. "Things that I would never have done of my own accord. This rebellion is about ending that, establishing free will for all people, being beholden to our consciences and values, and never again bending to a tyrant's will. I am not going to pluck out a man's eye to satisfy a mad Gnome and whatever shades he squeaks to in the dark."

"It must be done," said Mithron, "unsavory as it is, for as Lasifer said, we only have the one chance. We cannot defeat Azathoth; we knew that going into this. We knew that with certainty, all the more so now after the losses we've suffered. As mad and as unlikely as it sounds, this plan is our only chance. Our only hope."

"God help us," said Raphael.

43

JUTENHEIM
ANGLOTOR TOWER
THE TEMPLE OF POWER
YEAR 1267, 4TH AGE

JUDE EOTRUS

As Jude watched, Korrgonn grew taller by several inches, his shoulders widened, limbs thickened -- until his bulk was twice that of Sir Gabriel's and of nearly solid muscle; his skin, of golden tone. His armor transformed to bright, bold, golden plate, stylish and thick, all sharp angles and polish. His sword grew longer, thicker, its sides inlaid with strange runes of black and crimson. And his eyes! Dead gods, his eyes -- they became golden, bright and shining. A golden crown-like helm appeared atop his head. And from his back sprang great wings of golden feathers that stretched out first above his shoulders and then to the sides, out and out, farther still, until they reached a span of twenty feet. Regal and beautiful was he, shining and bright as the noonday sun. Chiseled from stone were his features, angelic, godlike. A scion of the gods themselves.

Everyone stared, mouths agape. Ginalli and Keld stopped their work, awestruck.

Korrgonn stepped towards Jude, golden eyes

locked on the young knight. "My true form, revealed," he said gesturing at himself. "The form I carried hereto now was but a mask to ease my passage through the realms of man. Such subterfuge is no longer needed."

"An illusion?" said Donnelin.

Korrgonn nodded. "Necessary to avoid unwanted attention."

"So what of Sir Gabriel?" said Jude. "What became of him? Does he yet live or no?"

Korrgonn's expression softened as he looked to each prisoner in turn. "You deserve the truth, and to know your part in it, at long last. So tell you, I will, though our time is short and there is much to tell. Nearby your home, as you well know, Thorn and Ginalli wrenched open a mystical portal -- a Worldgate -- much as we will do here today, for the sole purpose of returning my father to his rightful place in Midgaard. In our exile in Nifleheim, we'd awaited that opportunity for ages: for the stars to align, for the signs and portents to be just so, and for someone of Midgaard to have the knowledge and strength to act. What a joyous day it was when we felt the Worldgate stir. When we knew our deliverance had come. We sprang at once to our designated places, long planned, long practiced. I was at the vanguard, alongside our bannermen, when the Harbinger and his minions attacked. Your soldiers were duped. They thought they were stemming an invasion, protecting their lands.

"They were fed an evil lie.

"The Harbinger used dark sorcery to confound

your men -- to make me and mine and even the holy temple itself look like things out of hellish nightmare, though to us, we looked our normal selves and were oblivious of the foul magics that enshrouded us. We marched through the Worldgate expecting to be greeted with love and adoration by my father's faithful, but instead, were assaulted with deadly force, no quarter or parley offered by the Harbinger and his minions, Gabriel -- chief amongst them.

"Gabriel was not the simple soldier that you knew. He was more -- much more. He betrayed my father long ago, when the Harbinger and his followers were cast out of the holy realm of Vaeden for their crimes, their unspeakable blasphemies, their acts of wanton depravity.

"That night in the Vermion Forest, despite my divine powers, I barely escaped, the Harbinger's trap so shrewdly set. But escape I did, and I killed the traitor Gabriel and cast his corrupt soul down to Helheim. A fitting end for the ancient fiend.

"You didn't know his true nature. You thought him a good man. And once, long ago, a good man he was, or so my father believes. But he was corrupted by the Harbinger, just as are all who linger within his sphere.

"Gabriel squandered his long years, lurking about your keep, insinuating himself into your House so that if ever acolytes of my father came to open the portal, he'd be there to stop them. He waited forever for that chance; he hated our lord that much.

"Jealousy. That's what it stems from.

"The root of evil.

"When I escaped from the temple that night, I knew that I could not walk about Midgaard in my true form. The Harbinger's minions would be at me at every turn. I had to hide amongst you, and I chose the form of Gabriel...I'm not certain why. Looking back, perhaps it was a foolish decision, his form so well known, but yet it commanded respect in voice and bearing, and I judged that would serve me well. And it worked. We made it here, to this far-off isle, to this place of power where we can complete the task we began in the Vermion.

"Do you understand now?"

"I understand your words," said Jude, his voice strong, unafraid, "but that doesn't mean I believe them. I've seen and heard tell of far fouler deeds committed by you and yours on this quest, not the least of which was kidnapping me and putting all my men to the sword, murdering them, my friends, my father."

"Much of what you believe," said Korrgonn, "has not happened the way you think. The Harbinger counts many tricksters amongst his minions: wizards, warlocks, witches, Gnomes, and Svart. The hallmark of their magic, their mastery of deceit and illusion. Spun a thick web of it about you, they have, though you can see it not."

Korrgonn leaned in closer. "The Harbinger is the Prince of Lies.

"He is evil incarnate. The lord of chaos.

"It was not my men that attacked you on the North Road. It was the Harbinger's minions. His illusionists hid in the wood, beguiled you with sorcery. Tricked you into believing The League attacked you.

"We saved you. Mort Zag pulled you from their clutches. Had we arrived but a few minutes earlier, we would've saved your whole troop. That tardiness I will long regret."

"You've kept us prisoners for months."

"To my shame, that I have, though I believe you have been treated well," said Korrgonn. "Do you know why you are here? Why the Harbinger wants you dead?"

"You need my blood for your vile ritual," said Jude.

"Not my ritual," said Korrgonn sharply. "It's the Harbinger's ritual. He created it. He locked the Worldgates. The sinister sorceries that he spun about them, sealed them forever, even to the lord -- such is Harbinger's power. The Worldgates can be reopened only when blood is spilled."

"But why my blood?" said Jude.

"The ritual requires the blood of kings, and that is what flows through your veins. That is why the Harbinger wants you dead. You are descended in direct line from Odin, just as your family legend tells. In olden days, Odin was called Wotan the Great. Wotan the Destroyer. Wotan of the Northmen, and a hundred other names. He was no god then, and he is no god now, despite misguided beliefs. He was merely a great king of men, but not great in his goodness but rather in his strength, and the measure of his armies, and the might of his sword. But alas, he was also an enemy of the lord. It was Wotan's blood that tore open the great veil betwixt the worlds once before, long ago, and it must be his blood this time again. But he is naught but dust and memory, living on only in song and story -- and in you, his descendant. That is why you are here. That is why we must take your blood. It is all for the greater good. For the glory of god. But it was not us who set these conditions. It was the Harbinger. He's behind it all."

44

VIGRID VALLEY
FIMBULWINTER - YEAR 3
LAST DAY OF THE AGE OF MYTH AND LEGEND

THETAN THE LIGHTBRINGER

"**I** am both chieftain and high priest of the Aesir," said Wotan. "I'm no holy man but I preside over religious rituals of importance, always have."

Donar said, "Father, do not--"

"There is no other priest here, my son. And no other king. Is there? Willing or not, is there another? Anyone at all?"

"Every priest of Azathoth has sided with him," said Azrael. "Not one has joined our cause. We have no other priests. And we have no king."

"Then we'll capture one of his priests," said Donar. "And pluck a king from some heathen realm. We'll capture a dozen if need be. I'll drag them back here myself."

"We've no time to search for foreign kings," said Azrael, "and all the local priests are with Azathoth, gathered close about him, or hold up in Vaeden, beyond our reach. We cannot hope to snare one unless and until we mount a final assault on his position or the city itself."

"So be it," said Donar. "When we attack, I will grab one, rip his head from his shoulders, and pluck out his eye with my own fingers. I would

210

do that to every one of them a thousand times over before allowing my father to be so defiled. I will not abide that. Never."

"That yet leaves us short one king," said Azrael.

"I'm an old man," said Wotan, "well past my time. I--"

"You are eternal," said Donar. "You have ruled for an age and can yet rule forevermore. That is your destiny. Age will not stop that and if ever it did, I would take up your mantle."

"As you will do now, my son."

"I will not," said Donar.

"I will," said Loki. "If Donar dares defy you, All-Father, I will not. I support you in this, though my heart be heavy. I will take up your mantle if my good brother lacks the courage or resolve."

"You sniveling bastard," said Donar. "Were we not in the midst of a battle, I would thrash you from here to Norguardt."

"You think too highly of yourself, brother," said Loki. "You always have and always will. You're an impetuous, brash lout who fails to see wisdom when it stands before him. Listen to our father, you hot-headed fool, for this must be done. If you don't have the courage to see it through, then get you from our ranks, slink back to Asgard, and hide behind your mother's frock and tresses."

Donar balled his fists and stepped toward Loki, murder in his eyes.

Wotan held out his hands to restrain them both. "I will not have this, not now of all times. You must stand together. You must learn to work together, for if this ends as it now appears it will, you will soon be without me. There must be no hot blood between you. Do you understand me? No treachery and deceit," he said looking towards Loki, "and no pointless anger or foolish bravado," he said looking toward Donar. "You must be the men I have taught you to be, the leaders I have taught you to be."

"To lead is a terrible burden and sometimes one must sacrifice much for the good of their people, for the greater good of all. I do not look forward to this...sacrifice, but do it, I will.

"I hope that such sacrifices are never demanded of either of you, but that if they are someday, you will do what's right. And so too I hope that you are loved enough by those you love that in that sacrifice their hearts would hang heavy and mayhap in private even shed a tear for you as you may well do for me when the time comes. We've no more time to squabble over this. We must draw closer and be ready. I will give one eye and as much my blood as need be for this deed that we do. Thetan, it falls to you to ensure Azathoth is cast through the gateway when it opens -- even if you must pass through with him. Just as I, you must do what needs be done."

"I can do no less," said Thetan.

Blazren burst into the gathering. "He's taken to the field. The lord. He's here!"

45

JUTENHEIM
ANGLOTOR TOWER
THE TEMPLE OF POWER
YEAR 1267, 4TH AGE

JUDE EOTRUS

"**S**o to bring my father home to Midgaard," said Korrgonn to Jude, "I must become what I have fought against my entire life. I have to do evil. That was the Harbinger's design. His method to prevent any true Azathothian from bringing my father back, because no true follower of his would do the evil that must be done to open the Worldgate. And so the Worldgates have remained locked. That has ever been the Harbinger's plan. And it worked for millennia. Until at last, the League of Light rose to power -- Glus Thorn and Father Ginalli in command. Only they had the strength and courage to open the gateway despite the terrible price that it cost: your father's blood; your father's life. His sacrifice enabled my passage to this world. But you believe that the League ambushed and murdered your father. They did not."

"Then what happened to him?" said Jude glancing sidelong at Donnelin.

"I was there," said Donnelin. "I witnessed the

attack -- the creatures. You're the trickster. You're spinning a web of lies. We will not be fooled by your golden tongue."

"Your memories of that night," said Korrgonn, "are the lies. The Harbinger's minions bewitched you, confounded your mind with false memories of monsters that exist only in fable."

Korrgonn turned back toward Jude. "Aradon Eotrus was a noble man. Master Thorn met with him in the wood. And not by chance. A secret meeting but long planned. Thorn revealed the truth about the Worldgates and the blood of kings. He convinced Eotrus that the only way to bring back the lord was through the sacrifice of his blood. Your father was wise. He knew the value of the lord's return. He marked well the evil that has overrun Midgaard these last years. He knew these troubled times must end. That man must once again look to the divine for guidance, and love. That people must acknowledge and honor that which is greater than themselves. That we must move back toward the true faith of old, and away from false religions. And so, your father agreed to the bleeding, willingly. He wasn't tied down to an unholy altar. He wasn't murdered. He and Thorn acted in good faith and clasped hands in friendship.

"The hope was that your father would survive it, the bleeding. That the ritual would not require enough blood to kill him or do him grievous harm. He was a strong man -- with a constitution far beyond his peers. If any could survive it, it would be he.

214

"But alas, the Harbinger had cast his curse all too well, ensuring that any descendant of Odin would die from the bloodletting however strong he might be. Your father sacrificed himself for the lord. For Midgaard. For all mankind. What a horror that such had to be done. That such a man -- a hero -- had to die. But it was the Harbinger that brought that all about. He is your enemy as much as he is ours. You want revenge, young Eotrus? Then look to the Harbinger."

"My father followed Odin," said Jude. "Not your demon lord of ancient days. I do not believe this. I will not."

"Though he never revealed it to you, your father was schooled in the old ways. *All* the nobles of the old northern Houses are."

"This isn't true," said Jude. "I've never heard of such a thing."

"You have an older brother," said Korrgonn. "The lord of the House and his heir are so schooled. That is longstanding tradition even though you know it not. On the face of things, the Eotrus worshipped Odin and his pantheon of barbarians – just as all Northmen appear to do. The truth is somewhat different."

"Don't listen to this trickster, Jude," said Donnelin. "His tongue is golden but his heart is black as pitch. Our patrol was attacked by a horde of creatures. They came –"

"No," said Korrgonn. "After the ritual, the Harbinger's minions, Gabriel at their van, attacked your patrol just as they later attacked Jude's. Killed them to a man -- except for you.

"Do you think your skills saved you?

215

"Or luck?

"It was neither. They wanted you alive so that they could fill your head with false memories, and thus create a web of lies -- a fiction -- to throw you and yours off from the truth. You and the Eotrus would be out chasing monsters while the true villains -- Theta and Gabriel -- remained in your midst."

"Gabriel was off hunting when my patrol was attacked," said Donnelin.

"Part of the fiction, was that," said Korrgonn.

"Gabriel was with you. He led you into a trap and slew your men. Thorn's men found you, but not in time, the damage to your mind, already done. Thorn had no magic on hand to counter it, but he could not have you return to the Dor telling that false tale, and so you were taken captive. It had to be that way. You thought the Leaguers were your enemies, so they had to tie you up and treat you as a prisoner to keep you from running away, and for their own safety. No doubt, you'd have killed to escape. Thorn and Ginalli tried for days to clear your mind, to lift that foul sorcery from it, as did I, but all to no avail for the Harbinger's sorceries run deep and are of a nature that I cannot grasp. Gentlemen," he said, looking to Jude and Donnelin, "I am here to tear down the veil of lies that has hung heavy over all Midgaard for untold ages. To bring back truth, justice, fair play. Yes, the blood ritual is a vile thing. We will not repeat the tragedy that was your father's death. That's why we've bled you over and again these last weeks, collecting the blood so that we have a large store

216

of it, magics to preserve it," he said pointing toward Keld who held up a large stoppered flask of blood, another atop the altar beside him. "The hope is that we won't need to cut you during the ritual, that there is enough stored blood to break through the barrier. No one here wants to harm you, young Eotrus."

Jude's mouth hung slack and his head shook. Donnelin was wide-eyed, a confused expression on his face.

"Everything I have told you here tonight is the truth as best I know it," said Korrgonn, "believe me or not, but this is the way of things. My father must be brought home. The madness that has overtaken the world must end."

"I've seen things along this trip," said Jude. "Evil acts. Things that no goodly man would do, but were done by you and your men."

"Deceit and illusion is what you saw," said Korrgonn. "One amongst our expedition is a minion of the Harbinger. A dark sorcerer of the first order."

Ginalli and Keld both grunted in surprise.

"Who?" said Jude.

46

VIGRID VALLEY
FIMBULWINTER - YEAR 3
LAST DAY OF THE AGE OF MYTH AND LEGEND

THETAN THE LIGHTBRINGER

When the fourth bolt of crackling lightning exploded upon the battlefield, it seemed to Thetan that the entire valley shook. Men were thrown from their feet hundreds of yards from the impact site, and far away as he was, flying near as high as the lowest clouds, still he was violently buffeted by the shock wave. Death is what it wrought.

Just as with the first three blasts, the latest left a crater a dozen yards in diameter and some ten feet deep. Natural lightning didn't cause such destruction, but Azathoth's fiery bolts invariably did. The earth within the crater: molten, bubbling, fires licking up all around. Men ten yards from the crater's edge spasmed in agony, their bodies afire, burning from the inside out, no hope save for a speedy death. Those closer were instantly killed, and that was a mercy. The ones closest to the rim had all their bodily fluids consumed in a fraction of a second, leaving behind little more than desiccated husks. Those within the crater's boundaries were incinerated to dust; no trace lingered to mark their passing.

Thetan had seen such death before, more

218

times than he cared to remember. Azathoth's wrath it was. The lord had many ways to kill, though bolts of lightning were amongst his favorite for they were flashy, showy, intimidating, and quite effective.

On those occasions when a barbarian horde or foreign army defied him beyond his tolerance, Azathoth took to the field and displayed his power. He'd stand on high ground for all to see, shout words or threats if his mood so moved him, and point to the sky, to the heavens. Thetan always felt it coming: something in the air smelled different; a static charge appeared on his clothing, and the hairs stood on his neck and arms. And then the lord would point his right index finger at whomever he decided to smite. With that, a bolt of lightning, as if spawned from the greatest storm, would plummet to the earth from on-high and explode, slaying anyone near. Azathoth's aim was unerring. No one escaped his wrath; it was hardly worth trying. Rarely did Azathoth call down more than one bolt in a single engagement; one being more than sufficient to rout the common rabble, or the wild men of the world who were too foolish to grasp the futility of defying him. Sometimes, a professional army would require a bit more convincing. They'd grow suspicious and wonder, however powerful, mayhap that single blast was all that Azathoth could throw. And so, they'd keep up their assault. On such occasions, the lord would grow angry and gift them a second bolt. That would do it. Every time. They'd turn tail, call for terms, white flags and whatnot. The war, swiftly over;

they'd cede territory, cough up their riches until it hurt, provide any and all labor the lord required, and contribute their finest to his legions.

As effective as was the lightning attack, Azathoth rarely employed it. Though he chose not to share his mind on the matter with Thetan, mayhap, on common occasion, he simply preferred not to get his hands dirty. Better that the Arkons did the dirty work for him, though in the end, that caused a far greater death toll. Thetan wondered many times of late, if that's what the lord wanted. The death. The mayhem. The chaos. The suffering. What kind of person was Azathoth to lust for such things? Pondering that, gave strength to Thetan's purpose.

Over all the years, Thetan had never seen the lord's powers employed against his own forces. He never had reason to. There had never been a rebellion before, and barely any hint of dissent. What little there was, Azathoth...smoothed over. There was no doubt he had a way with words. No one was more persuasive, or more charismatic than he. He could defuse most any situation, no use of force, or even implied threat required. He had "smoothed over" Thetan's concerns many times over the long years.

With hindsight, Thetan wondered why the lord had had such patience with him. Why not just strike him down and raise up a more agreeable servant, one who had fewer questions and more faith? Did the lord indeed think fondly of him? Or was he a valued tool, worth a bit of trouble now and then to keep in working order? Maybe a bit of both. Mayhap he was just a favored pet.

"Four bolts," said Bose. "Never seen that before. He's out for blood. They'll break in a moment."

"Shock and awe," said Dekkar. "Stun the troops. Kill some leaders. Demoralize the rest. Break our spirits; make us pay. The usual tactics."

"They're not breaking," said Azrael. "Death raining down all around them and they're not breaking. Even the Northmen, they're holding fast or charging on."

"Of course they're not breaking," said Dekkar. "Our men are the best there is."

"They've proved their mettle," said Bose. "I'd not have believed it. You were right about this last push," he said to Thetan, "all our strength focused and unleashed."

"The outcome is all that matters," said Thetan. "Courage and honor, for all their worth, won't be remembered if the other side wins."

"We don't have the numbers," said Mithron.

"Don't need them," said Dekkar. "Just need to tire him, rough him up a bit. Then we drop in with the Sphere and Thetan and the Gnome work their magic."

"Look beneath Azathoth's shadow," said Bose, pointing. "Mammon's brigade; Asmodeus's too, fresh and ready. Our boys won't get past them. It's on us."

"As we expected," said Azrael.

"Our van has broken through," shouted Dekkar. "They're on Mammon!"

"Now?" said Bose.

"Not yet," said Thetan.

"Our men are dying," said Azrael.

"We hold until my command," said Thetan.

"They're fighting to the death," said Bose. "Every one of them."

"A glorious day for courage," said Mithron.

"A better day for the worms," said Dekkar.

47

JUTENHEIM
ANGLOTOR TOWER
THE TEMPLE OF POWER
YEAR 1267, 4TH AGE

"**I**'ve tried to unmask the spy," said Korrgonn to Jude. "I've cast my suspicion across our wizards and mercenaries alike, but dark magics cloak the spy and hold me at bay. Throughout our journey, the spy has cast a veil of lies before your eyes, to make us appear as villains, hoping against hope that somehow you might escape, or that you might kill me or Thorn or Ginalli, or that you might destroy the Orb, or else do something, anything, to disrupt the ritual, where he apparently cannot. Such are the Harbinger's methods. He yearns for a world enslaved by his illusions and deceit."

"I would've explained everything to you, but for weeks after my arrival, my mind was troubled: my thoughts, clouded; my judgment, impaired -- the price of passage through the Worldgate, it seems.

"That is past now, my mind, clear.

"But also, I didn't think that you'd believe me. I thought you'd flee us or fight us or who knows what. Easier to keep you captive, drag you along. This quest is too important. And so I made myself and my father's followers, kidnappers -- a crime for which I must confess to my lord, and beg forgiveness.

"I will receive it, I am certain, but there will be a price to pay. A weighty penance for my ill deeds, however noble their purpose. I will pay that penance, whatever it is."

"And why am I here?" said Brother Donnelin. "Need a wee bit of priestly blood too, do you?"

Korrgonn's jaw stiffened. He didn't want to answer. "Some say, in addition to the blood of kings, to open a Worldgate, one also needs...the eye of a holy man.

Donnelin's voice went cold and sharp; his face paled. "Sick, demented barbarians."

"Not my doing," said Korrgonn quickly, "the Harbinger's ritual, as I've explained. But if the stories prove true, then take your eye, I will. A terrible thing, but you will not die from it."

"Who gave their eye in the Vermion?" said Donnelin.

"An ancient priest of my father's, lately one of Ginalli's faithful," said Korrgonn. "I'm not convinced that taking his eye was necessary, but with you here, we are prepared, if it is. If there proves no need for such sacrifice, you will remain unharmed, I promise you. Either way, should one or both of you live through it, you'll be afforded the opportunity to bend the knee before the lord and pledge your loyalty. With the lord's grace and blessing, you'll take your places amongst his chosen people, and be afforded positions of great honor and standing, as is only fitting, owing to the trials you've faced."

"If we refuse?" said Jude.

"Then you'll go free, free to return home. The lord compels no one to his service."

"I do not do these deeds lightly," said Korrgonn. "My conscience weighs heavily upon me and has from the moment the fog lifted from my eyes. I hope that someday you'll find it in your hearts to forgive me for what I've done, no matter how things turn out here today. But I'll understand if you cannot. You've been through an ordeal no man should suffer. I promise you that the lord will make this right. He'll reward you beyond your dreams for your sacrifice and the hardships you've endured - I know he will.

"Ginalli is almost done with the preparations. I will soon place you upon the altar. I cannot remove your bindings for I will not take the chance of the ritual going awry. But I beg you to gift your blood willingly *if* our reserve proves insufficient. Please, sacrifice that bit of your lifeblood for the lord your god. You will be rewarded both in this life and the next."

"But if I don't give it willingly, you'll take it anyway, won't you?" said Jude.

"I beg you," said Korrgonn, "do not let it come to that. Do not curse me with that choice for it cannot be a choice. I must bring back the lord to Midgaard. Even if so doing destroys me. Even if it destroys you. Bringing him back is the right thing to do for the world. For the world! It must be done. The world has gone astray -- endless wars and strife, famine and plague, butchery and villainy, illusions and lies. The lord can put an end to that. He can usher in a golden age of peace and harmony the like of which Midgaard has not seen in recorded history. You hold that possibility in your hands.

"Be a hero.

"Risk yourself for the lord.

"I beg you. I beg you!"

48

VIGRID VALLEY
FIMBULWINTER - YEAR 3
LAST DAY OF THE AGE OF MYTH AND LEGEND

THETAN THE LIGHTBRINGER

This time, unlike all the others that Thetan had witnessed, Azathoth called down his bolts while hovering in the air. He rode no Targon, sat no flying carpet, nor winged horse. He simply floated in the air upright moving about at speed by means unseen and undeterminable. What strange method of locomotion he employed, no man could say. Few had ever seen Azathoth in such a pose; Thetan had seen it a few times, but it was no less impressive. And when he called down the magic -- or whatever it was from wherever it came -- it did not push him back or buffet him about, or affect him in any way. He was in complete command of his location, his movement, his momentum. The Arkons could mimic that behavior to far lesser extent, but it was the beating of their Targons' great wings that held *them* aloft.

More than a few Fallen Arkons made a run on Azathoth, trying to push through Mammon's brigade. Brave, brave warriors were they. Although the lord's attention was focused on his magical blasts, he was in killing mode. Thetan knew that a frontal assault meant almost certain death.

Trontiel, one of the Arkons' finest lancers, dived toward the lord at incredible speed, his lance lowered, four other Fallen Arkons on his heels. Azathoth saw them coming, of course. He extended his right hand, palm forward. Red and yellow fire, as deadly as that of the greatest fire drake of legend, blasted from his hand and engulfed everything within a hundred yards of his position, including Trontiel and his men.

Moments later, when the flames cleared, Thetan fancied he saw ash drift down and disperse in the breeze. Nothing else fell. No bodies. No Targon, not a feather. No fragments of armor, molten metal, or flaming bits of anything. In truth, Thetan wasn't certain he'd even seen the ash. Mayhap, there was nothing left of them at all. That made Thetan's blood run cold.

But a moment later, Azathoth swooped down to the field at eagle speed, his bodyguards following on his heels. Azathoth landed amidst the rebels and had at them with his wooden staff, whirling about, clubbing any within his range. The rebels swarmed him with lance, sword, axe, hammer, and dirk.

And died for it by the dozens.

Thetan saw the opportunity. The lord was distracted and fully engaged. *Now* was the time for a frontal assault; he'd be able to get close. This might be the chance they'd been waiting for. He turned toward his men who soared behind him. "Charge!" he roared. He urged on his Targon and sped towards the fray. His comrades followed, the Sphere of the Heavens with them.

Thetan had flown but a hundred yards when Azathoth extended both hands, palms outward. From them spouted cones of fire every bit as large and deadly as what had lately laid low Trontiel's cadre. Hundreds of men, rebel and loyalist both, disappeared within the flames.

When the fire died, the loyalists remained untouched, albeit shocked and disoriented. The rebels they'd been fighting were gone. Incinerated. Even the worms were deprived.

A great ballista bolt crashed into the center of Azathoth's chest. He staggered backward, wide-eyed. The impossible had happened — Azathoth had been caught unawares. He hadn't seen the bolt coming, few did, fired as it was from close range by men that fortune had sheltered in a narrow wedge betwixt the two recent cones of fiery death. Mind you, Azathoth wore no armor, no mail, merely his customary robes of white. He was not accoutered for war, never was. No helmet did he wear. No shield or sword did he carry, only his long staff. He needed nothing else, if even that.

The bolt that struck him was of no common variety. Its tip was made of ranal, sharpened and polished, as deadly an edge as existed in the world. At that range, it should have gone clear through Azathoth, leaving him impaled if not run through entirely, the bolt exiting his back. That's what it would've done to any man. Even the heaviest armor would likely have failed.

But in this case...it merely bounced off his breast. The great shaft dropped useless at the lord's feet, its tip shattered. Shattered! And the bolt's wooden shaft with it, broken lengthwise through its core, cracked and pitted, shriveled and desiccated. That made little sense. Ranal could be bent if it hit something hard — a wall of stone, a door of metal. But nothing could shatter it. And what could do that to wood?

Nothing natural.

But what of the unnatural?

The icy cold of Nifleheim — the frozen wasteland of the *Nether Realms* — could do it, Thetan figured. But Azathoth was not of Nifleheim. Or was he? He had not done a thing to the bolt. Didn't even see it coming. He was merely struck by it, a victim of it, yet woe was its fate. How could Thetan face such a foe, a foe that could destroy without even a thought? Azathoth took to the air again, rising far out of reach of the rebels. Thetan and his squadron halted their advance. Removed from the wild melee, Azathoth would see them coming and gift them a fiery death. Thetan would have to bide his time a bit longer.

Above even the din of battle, Thetan soon heard a strange droning. He looked about to locate its source. That's when he saw it. An amorphous black cloud just above the treetops. It was moving toward the battle.

"More lightning?" said Hogar.

"Those are no storm clouds," said Uriel. "They are locusts. Millions of them. Billions."

"By all that's holy," spat Dekkar.

"Gabriel, have the reserves advance into the fray," said Thetan. "All of them, and quickly."

230

"It's too soon," said Hogar. "There's no break in our line, though the lord has weakened our center. We may need the reserves elsewhere."

"Thetan wants our men mixed in with the loyalists," said Dekkar. "The insects won't know one from another, so our men should be safe from them. If they remain where they are, they'll get swarmed, scattered, or chewed to pieces."

"A smart play," said Uriel.

"The only one that makes sense," said Dekkar.

49

JUTENHEIM
ANGLOTOR TOWER
THE TEMPLE OF POWER
YEAR 1267, 4TH AGE

JUDE EOTRUS

Jude's mouth hung open, his eyes wide, his heart pounding in his chest. He didn't know what to believe. If Korrgonn's words were true, who was the spy, the illusionist, who had meddled with his mind?

"Can what he says be true?" Jude whispered to Donnelin.

The priest looked as confused as Jude felt.

Donnelin shook his head. "I don't know what's real anymore," he whispered. "I know what I remember. But that entire night in the Vermion was and is a fog. Everything felt strange, surreal. More like a dream than reality. Perhaps it was an illusion implanted in my mind. I don't know. By Odin, I just don't know anymore. My head spins."

"Don't believe the Korrgonn, laddie," whispered Teek. "Spins a pretty tale, he does, but he's a false prophet. I don't believe him for a second."

As Teek spoke those words from just behind Jude, the hairs on Jude's neck stood up and he shivered. At that moment, he wondered whether it had been Teek all along. The Lugron dullard, no dullard at all. A wizard. An illusionist. A minion of the Harbinger, he had to be -- he was the only one close enough to Jude throughout the voyage to have done it.

No.

He wasn't.

Jude's eyes flicked to Brackta. No one had been closer to him than her.

Why was that? Why was she so...eager?

Was he so pretty that a League Archwizard would risk her station, her very life, for a love affair that could have no happy end?

Or was it but an act to get close to him, so she could better weave her spells about him?

Dead gods, who could he trust?

Not her, not with those doubts in his mind.

Not Teek.

Donnelin?

How could he even trust the priest, when he couldn't trust his own mind, his own memories?

Dead gods, what madness.

Jude now understood why the Harbinger was so reviled, so universally hated down through the ages. What greater crime than to invade one's mind, manipulate memories, defile the spirit, make one doubt and mistrust all those around them?

If Korrgonn's assertions were true, there was only one thing Jude could do.

Aid him.

Give up his blood, even if it meant his life, to bring the old god back to Midgaard so that he could put down the Harbinger and free the world

233

of his evil.

But what if Korrgonn was the liar, the trickster?

Why would he be? For what purpose? He was already a prisoner. No chance of escape. Korrgonn needn't convince him of anything. All he need do is tie him to the altar and cut him. No agreement from Jude was necessary. None at all.

So why bother?

Why create such a ruse, such an elaborate story? What was the use of it? It made no sense.

So it had to be true.

It had to be!

Dead gods!

Everything that Jude believed had been a lie.

His father was *not* murdered.

And it was the Harbinger that had killed the Eotrus men.

Dead gods...

50

VIGRID VALLEY
FIMBULWINTER - YEAR 3
LAST DAY OF THE AGE OF MYTH AND LEGEND

After the ballista bolt struck the lord and he withdrew from the field, Thetan and his fellows pursued him from on high to his command post on a rocky hill at the valley's edge — a hill that swarmed with the lord's elite troops. Thetan could wait no longer. He took the time only to call for reinforcements to converge on the hill before he launched his attack.

The hail of missiles was fierce and furious and caught all too many of Thetan's fellows as they dived towards the lord's position at best speed, wings tucked tight against their sides. Arkons' armor was quite immune to common arrows, but not invulnerable to the cold-forged steel-tipped shafts launched by the thousand Einheriar who guarded the slopes below the lord's position. Far more fearsome though, were the great ballista bolts -- seven feet of fire-hardened oak, two inches thick, steel tipped and sharpened to a razor's edge, much the same as the bolt that had lately struck the lord.

The missiles came in waves, their crews precise in aim and timing -- trained by KithKarmon and Bose in better days. Even at goodly range the bolts had the penetrating power to cut through the stoutest steel, sometimes even the ranal plate favored by many an Arkon.

Thetan shifted his head to avoid an arrow intent on his eye; its tip shrieked as it grazed his helm. He chanced a glance to one side, then the other, and an arrow pinged off his shield, another off his leg armor. He'd seen them coming, but they didn't concern him. Everything moved in slow motion, or seemed to, as often it did for him in battle, and that of course gave him a singular advantage for he could more easily spot attacks coming and react to them far quicker than others. So quick in fact that he seemed superhuman, even godlike in his prowess. Thetan knew some few of the Arkons possessed a similar ability, which no doubt gave rise in part to the common claim that Arkons possessed a divine spark or heavenly heritage. Thetan called it "battle sight" -- as good a name as any, he figured -- though it worked whenever he needed it, battle or no. He didn't know whether it was a natural skill he and the others shared, or some product of untold years of martial training, or a gift from Azathoth, but he felt he should know -- in fact, that he had known, but had forgotten for reasons he could not explain.

Arrows pinged off armor all around like summer hail on the metal roofs of the palace's minarets. Stakatiel took an arrow to the neck and careened into another flier. A ballista bolt hit Pluriel in the gut and exploded out her back, sent her spinning head over heels before plummeting from sight. Many others were hit less severely

236

and soldiered on, but more than a few fell from the skies. Intent on his mad purpose, Thetan had no time to give thought to them. Not until the battle was over, assuming he survived it. Then there'd be time for grieving, regret, and guilt.

Mammon must have withdrew from the main battle for he stood now beside the lord with a troop of Brigandir, his shining orange and black armor proclaiming his presence to all within a mile. Curious that they thought the false god needed such protections, immune as he was to any weapon, magic, deed, or craft of man.

Iblis met The Fallen in the air, a hundred handpicked Arkons on his flanks, lances poised, jaws set, and eyes hardened. They gazed on the Fallen with the same confident, righteous expressions that they gifted the heathen hordes when they swooped down and smote them on the lord's behalf. Now they considered Thetan and his men no better than foreign barbarians who bowed before pagan idols and practiced blood sacrifices and other unspeakable blasphemies. That hurt and angered Thetan more than any weapon that had struck him that day.

Thetan lowered his lance before they made contact with Iblis's squadrons. Most Arkons, however skilled, aimed their lances at the center mass -- the chest or belly -- so as not to miss. Thetan aimed for the neck — a much more elusive target, but which, except for the most glancing of blows, yielded an instant kill. That time was no different. He caught his opponent in

237

the throat; his lance snapped, so strong was the impact, and Thetan barreled past, deflecting the other's lance with his shield. But a moment later, his muscles still atremble, he pulled another lance from its sheath, even as he deflected a loyalist's lance with his shield.

His second lance broke against a shield but sent the man tumbling away, his Targon's wing broken with Thetan's passing. As Thetan reached for his last lance, he caught a glancing blow to the shoulder, barely saw it coming, while simultaneously, another lance broke against his shield. His weapon caught a Loyalist in the neck, and he blasted past him, blood spurting his tabard. Even with his battle sight, flying at that speed, helmets on and visors down, he couldn't name his opponents. He didn't know whether he'd just killed friends or strangers. Breathing heavily, his muscles aquiver, he banked down, moving inexorably toward the lord's position. He hoped one of his men had taken out Iblis – that bastard deserved to die for many foul deeds over the ages. Thetan's peripheral vision told him the core of his strength was still with him; they'd broken through the loyalist charge, unsurprising since they far outnumbered Iblis's troop. Now came the hard part. The Brigandir and the most elite of the loyalist Arkons. It would be knife work, long and bloody. And if they made it through, Azathoth would be waiting.

51

JUTENHEIM
ANGLOTOR TOWER
THE TEMPLE OF POWER
YEAR 1267, 4TH AGE

JUDE EOTRUS

Jude pointed to where Uriel lay bound. "And what of him?" he said loudly.

Korrgonn turned his attention from the altar. "The last component of the Worldgate's binding," he said. "Another hurdle set down by the Harbinger eons ago. The blood of kings, the eye of a holy man, and the heart of an immortal. What a diabolical mind to craft such a binding. Cruel, evil, perhaps insane. Legend says, without all three, the Worldgate can never be opened, but as I said, I am skeptical about the eye."

"An immortal?" said Jude. "You mark this man a god?"

"Some few Midgaard folk age slowly enough," said Korrgonn, "as to be fairly called immortal, by human standards, though they are but men -- possessing no special powers or wisdom, no divine grace or lineage. Such folk have always existed; far fewer now than in olden times. They call themselves, Eternals. Hoarders of wealth and power are they. Most fancy themselves grand -- more gods than men. And they encourage that thinking in others. A corrupt lot in the main, selfish, ruthless, egomaniacal; pagans, nearly all. The priest I mentioned was one of them. The best of them. An outlier. He spurned their cabal, devoted himself to the lord. Willingly gave his eye and his heart for the lord. Long will he be remembered."

"And he," said Donnelin, gesturing toward Uriel, "is one of these Eternals of which you speak?"

"Uriel the Bold is his name," said Korrgonn. "One of the original thirteen Arkons that betrayed the lord during *The Age of Myth and Legend*. One of the chief minions of the Harbinger is he. He's lurked here, these many years, guarding this Worldgate, just as Gabriel guarded the other, so deeply does his hatred run."

"You're going to cut out his heart?" said Jude. "Is that what your god would have you do?"

"He is your god as much as mine," said Korrgonn, "no matter your denials or ignorance of it. The lord would never ask such a thing of me, of anyone. And he'd never condone it. It's my choice. My sin. Once I do it, I know not if the stain upon my soul can ever be cleansed. Can such an evil act be forgiven, no matter the import of its ends? I don't know for certain.

"None of you will aid me in this. The sin, mine alone. After the lord arrives, I'll beg his forgiveness for this terrible deed. And his forgiveness I may yet garner for Uriel is a black traitor, rotten, evil to the core, nearly as bad as the Harbinger himself. No doubt, the lord would smite Uriel for his transgressions, so in killing him, I may yet be forgiven.

"I hope.

"I pray. But if not, I shall weather any penance the lord inflicts upon me. We are too close. His return is too important. This must be done, whatever the cost."

"Sell your snake oil, demon," said Uriel, his voice weak. "The only buyers are fools. You are a joke."

"There are no falsehoods in my heart or my words," said Korrgonn, "though yours are filled with nothing but. I hope, for the sake of your soul, that the evil within you was birthed of the Harbinger's trickery, as it was in so many others. If so, you may yet find the path to salvation, if not in this life, then in the next."

Uriel laughed. "You people never give up. Why not just speak the truth? Convince others to follow your cause by the weight of your arguments, not by the sleight of your tongue."

"It's because your arguments have no merit, of course," continued Uriel. "Evil means and selfish ends is all that you're about. Normal folk won't abide that, so you lie. If you had any honor, you'd let me die as a warrior, sword in my hand."

"You're no warrior," said Korrgonn, "you're a butcher. A vile murderer, slayer of children, women, old folk."

"Yes," continued Korrgonn, "I know of all your black deeds. Your unspeakable abuses of women and of children. And an assassin you are, a minion of evil. Uriel the Bold – even your name is a lie -- you only strike from the shadows, spring from the gutter, and weave your evil threads in secret. You disgust me so, my guilt wanes to naught."

"I was there when Azathoth was banished from this world," said Uriel. "I saw the gateway open, what came through, what it means, where it leads, the plague it unleashed. Don't believe him, boy," Uriel said shouting at Jude. "A monster in a man's suit, he be. His purpose is to destroy us all."

Korrgonn stepped close to Uriel. "I will not let you do this," said Korrgonn. "Those men have been through enough," he said gesturing toward Jude and Donnelin. "I'll not have their minds muddled by your poison. All--"

"Don't believe him," shouted Uriel, "or all will be lost."

Korrgonn bent over and with little effort lifted the cross upon which Uriel lay. He stepped to the nearest wall and leaned the cross against it.

Uriel groaned and cried out in pain as he hung from his bindings. "You see what he does?" said Uriel. "A monster, he is. A demon of accursed Nifleheim."

"Stop with your lies," said Korrgonn. "You're finished. It's over. Good has finally prevailed. The lord will soon return. Renounce your sins and perhaps your soul can yet be saved."

"I will never give in to you and your kind," said Uriel. "I will fight--"

Korrgonn punched him in the abdomen, once and then again, silencing him.

"You men," said Korrgonn to the Lugron that

242

stood nearby Jude. "Gag him. I'll hear no more of his poison. Bind him tightly and spare our ears."

"No matter," said Uriel coughing, "I've no more strength to bandy words with you, demon. Thetan will stop you; he will cut off your head and mount it on a pike for all to see and the crows to feast on."

"We shall see," said Korrgonn.

"If the Harbinger is the monster that you claim," said Jude, "how is it that he once followed Azathoth? How was the great god deceived and betrayed by such a creature?"

"Betrayed he was," said Korrgonn, "but deceived, never. My father knew what the Harbinger was. He knew his black heart, his evil bent. But in my father's goodness and mercy, he believed he could change him, redeem him, for some good abides in all men, no matter their faults.

"But my father was wrong.

"Some evils run too deep.

"Even the one true god can be wrong on occasion. And he's paid a terrible price for that error. All Midgaard has."

VIGRID VALLEY
FIMBULWINTER - YEAR 3
LAST DAY OF THE AGE OF MYTH AND LEGEND

Thetan groaned in anguish when his falchion sheared Belipheron's sword in two.

So went his helmet.

And his head.

In the moment before his body dropped lifeless and Thetan wrenched his blade free, their eyes met. Shock is what Thetan saw there. The shock of betrayal, and of course, that of Belipheron's newfound mortality. Thetan stepped over his dead friend even as he bashed his shield into Feliel's face. She shot backward two yards, feet off the ground, before she crashed to the snow, unmoving, her helmet staved in, blood spouting.

Thetan's men formed a tight wedge protecting The Sphere of the Heavens. Gabriel was close on Thetan's right, working sword and shield, Mithron on his left, doing the same. Tolkiel and Uriel were directly behind, guarding Raphael and Bose who hefted the Sphere's case between them. Hogar and Dekkar defended their flanks. Azrael, Blazren and Steriel protected their backs. The rest of Thetan's troop fought all around, their larger wedge formation only partly intact, such was the fury of the loyalist's attacks. Hundreds of Brigandir swarmed them supported by dozens of Azathoth's best Arkons.

Thromriel and Boriel rushed at Thetan; others came at his comrades, two or three to one. Thetan parried a strike with his sword, took another on his shield, then another, and another. Punched with the shield and heard a sword shatter against it, though he didn't know whose. A blade slammed into his side, squealed as it raked his armor. He had enough time to parry it, but let it pass to focus on Thromriel's more deadly overhand chop. The slight twist of Thetan's torso was enough to insure the side strike failed to penetrate. He stabbed with the falchion's point and caught Thromriel in the face, the blade sinking deep. He pulled it free, spun about, and sliced Milaliel's throat with the sharpened edge of his shield even as Dekkar ran him through from the back.

Mithron cut down Boriel, and Frantiel, Bockereel, and Sminteliel. Gabriel did similar damage to the loyalist ranks. Thetan and his men were killing everyone they'd known, everyone they'd served with over the long years.

Too many close to Thetan filled the ranks of that loyalist troop. That was no happenstance. They'd been pulled from multiple units posted near and far. Azathoth's design, it was, of that, Thetan had no doubt. Mayhap the lord thought fighting so many friends might give Thetan pause, might make him decide to surrender rather than kill those beloved of him. Or perhaps, the lord hoped he'd simply hesitate -- for hesitation in battle was a soldier's undoing. It oft got one killed.

No matter, the strategy would not work. Thetan remained focused, intent on his quarry. Any who blocked his way, whether former friend, foe, or stranger, fell bloodied before him never to rise again.

'Twas a terrible battle even for men who had fought countless battles before. Thetan was accustomed to cutting through heathen hordes with little effort, even when far outnumbered. Unskilled warriors against ones such as he and his, were of no consequence and would barely hinder their advance. But Thetan was also accustomed to epic duels with Midgaard's greatest warriors. But even in such contests of champions, he typically only fought one great warrior at a time. Occasionally, he'd encounter two or three or four of skill in some battle or skirmish. On rare occasion, he was even pressed and battered. But this time, this battle, was unlike any other. Every opponent was a weapons master. Each ranged from highly skilled to world-class combat expert. Not skilled only in sparring or tourney games, mind you, but in killing. Thetan wasn't accustomed to that sort of a fight. In truth, no man was. There had never been a battle quite like this before. Thetan's spirits were buoyed by the skill of his brothers in arms. Those closest to him – the conspirators from Mount Cantorwrought, twelve strong, not counting the traitor, Arioch -- were amongst the best of the best, the elite of the elite, champions of champions. Had such warriors not been at his side that day, how much tougher it would have been. The Brigandir may well have overwhelmed him and pulled him down by force of numbers. He who could not be defeated may well have tasted defeat. Even so, the battle was a close thing, and far from over.

53

JUTENHEIM
ANGLOTOR TOWER
THE TEMPLE OF POWER
YEAR 1267, 4TH AGE

"**M**y lord," said Ginalli, "We're ready for the Orb."

Korrgonn walked to where Mason stood. Still as a statue was that man of stone. In his hands, the wood and iron-bound box that cradled the fabled Orb of Wisdom, that arcane relic without which the gateway could never be opened -- blood, eyes, or immortal hearts notwithstanding.

Korrgonn placed the box atop the altar, close to one end, unlatched several catches, and carefully lifted its lid. The box's sides dropped, revealing the Orb in all its glory: a sphere of utter blackness that emitted a persistent, humming and vibration and maintained a grayish, aural glow hovering close about it. Waves of cold poured from the Orb despite the sanctum's still air.

Ginalli and Keld fled from it, backpedaling to the wall -- fear and surprise on their faces, shivering from the unnatural chill. Keld retched, doubled over, and puked against the wall. Korrgonn seemed oblivious.

The preternatural cold devoured the room's heat, ravenous in its hunger, and chilled Jude to the bone; how, he couldn't fathom.

Korrgonn turned toward Jude once more. "You've heard the truth from my lips, best as I can tell it. Sometimes, in life, truth lies in perception more than reality. Only you can decide what you believe, what cause you'll fight or die for. I know my path, what I must do, but you have yet to choose. The hour grows late."

"No matter my choice," said Jude, "you'll tie me to that altar, cut me wide, and drain my blood. What difference does it make what I say? What I think?"

"It makes a great deal of difference to me," said Korrgonn, "and to the lord. "If you say "no", if you disbelieve, if you have no faith, and our blood reserve fails us, then you'll be a victim, and I'll be a murderer. But if you open your heart to the lord -- and have faith, stand true to what's right and noble, then, if the worst happens, you'll depart this life as a hero, doing the lord's work for the good of us all. And selfishly, I say, you'll save me from becoming a murderer. I beg you, spare me from that fate. I cannot bear the thought of it."

"And yet you'll cut out that man's heart?" said Donnelin.

Korrgonn looked stricken and took a deep breath before responding. "A different thing to put down an immortal demon than to take the life of a young man with all the world to live for."

"There's no need for a charade here," said Jude to Donnelin. "If his words were false, he'd slit my throat and be done with it. Why create drama, put on an act, especially when so pressed for time? His words must be true, don't you think?"

Donnelin shook his head and shrugged, as confused as Jude.

Korrgonn started, turned about abruptly, his eyes wide.

"What is it, my lord?" said Ginalli through chattering teeth.

"He's here," said Korrgonn. "The Harbinger of Doom is here."

Par Keld, still coughing and spitting, sucked in a deep breath, and ground his back against the wall as if to push through it and find some hidey hole to escape into. His face, pale; terror in his eyes, his mouth opening and closing, but only muted grunts and squeals escaped.

"Mason," said Ginalli, "off with you now to Stev Keevis and Par Rhund. Hold the stair's base with them even unto death. Let nothing and no one pass. The lord is counting on you. We all are."

"Do my duty, I will," said Mason in his deep halting voice, "as the Keeper taught me. As long as a spark of life remains in me, no evil will reach this chamber." And with that, Mason was through the door, bounding down the passage with speed astounding for one of his bulk. Keld rushed to the door, slammed it closed, tried to lock it but found no lock.

"We've got to barricade it, and wizard-it closed," he shouted. "It's our only chance. There must be a spell, an incantation to do it, some stinking cantrip or charm. Something. I can't think. We've got to block it. The Harbinger! Dead gods, the devil himself, coming for our souls. For my soul! I don't deserve this. I'm innocent. I did nothing. Nothing!"

And then the entire chamber shook.

Everyone looked about fearfully.

"Dead gods," shouted Keld. "He's bringing the mountain down upon us. Take cover!" The little wizard dived to the floor and rolled into a fetal position, hands covering his head. The Lugron warriors dropped, some to a knee, others prostrate, fear and confusion on their faces.

"There's no more time," said Korrgonn to Jude. "Let your heart guide you, but make your choice, now."

"Do what you have to do," said Jude, "but try not to bleed me to death."

"Yes, yes," said Korrgonn, a smile fast to his face. "First, the blood reserve, and then, only if needed, a cut to one wrist. I'll take not a drop more than I must, believe me. Come forward now, the both of you."

"Put these in your mouth," said Brackta as she held out a handful of blueish-green leaves, "and chew on them."

"Why?" said Jude as he stepped toward the altar. His stomach churned as he neared the Orb; he felt the bile rise in his throat and his head went foggy. Donnelin groaned beside him; Teek, the same.

"The leaves will help with the nausea; take them quickly," said Brackta as she handed a few leaves to each of them. "Swallow the juices, but not the leaves -- keep them against your cheek."

Jude didn't know whether to trust those herbs

251

or not, but the nausea and dizziness was overwhelming. Donnelin popped the leaves into his mouth and began to chew; Teek did the same. Jude wondered if it were poison; would Brackta do that to him? Or else, something to put him to sleep? He had to chance it. He couldn't function. He was sweating profusely, the chamber's plunging temperatures notwithstanding.

Then came a great blast in the distance – an explosion that rattled the room; dust fell from the ceiling, stone shards followed, and the sounds of cracking stone came from everywhere.

"Hurry," hissed Brackta.

"And you, priest?" said Korrgonn as he traced runes in the air above the altar, preparing the way for the ritual.

Donnelin looked uncertain. "Try your ritual with only the blood," said Donnelin, "and see how things go. I've grown quite attached to both eyes these many years."

Korrgonn nodded. "The ritual's details are foggy -- what's actually required, what's truly in the binding, not fully known. Perhaps you can be spared. We shall try. Ginalli, begin the incantation, quickly now, we've lingered overlong."

Ginalli stepped to the opposite side of the altar, his jaw clenched; face, pale and drawn, lips stained blue -- Jude figured from more of the medicinal leaves. He chewed the ones Brackta gifted him - a sickly sweet taste they had, tinged with bitterness. His stomach settled; the dizziness and weakness waned. Ginalli raised his hands above the Orb and chanted in a wizarding language unfamiliar to Jude, his words, short, sharp, and harsh. The priest's eyes were closed; he droned on and on, ignoring all else.

Par Keld frantically cast spells at the chamber's door, cursing and complaining with each throw, two Lugron supporting him, though they could do him no good, save as objects of his ire.

Korrgonn uncorked the glass bottle that held the bulk of the blood reserve. He too began to chant in an unknown language, but one altogether different from Ginalli's mystical tongue. Korrgonn's words were strangely melodic, soothing to the ears, beautiful and uplifting, a song of the heavens.

Jude's heart beat ever faster. He didn't know whether to hope for failure or pray for success. Success would usher forth Azathoth, for good or ill, and failure would have him bled and mayhap dead, and still, Azathoth might appear. His thoughts spun chaotic, his breathing labored, mouth dry as dirt despite the leaves. He didn't know what was right. What was real. But he knew he wanted to live.

Had he made the right choice? Or were there only wrong choices?

Korrgonn passed his hands over the blood-filled bottle – a blessing of some sort -- and then tilted it overtop the Orb until the reddish-brown liquid began to flow. Jude's eyes were glued to it. Korrgonn jerked his hand up when crackling frost appeared on the flask's bottom and spread up its sides, the Orb's chill threatening to freeze the flask and its precious contents, which were already dry and congealed. Holding it as high above the Orb as he could reach staved off the ice, but the blood fell unnaturally slowly, more than could be attributed to the cold. 'Twas as if time or gravity fought against that flow – nature itself impeding it.

Korrgonn's voice grew louder, his tone commanding, and then, as if in response, the blood flowed more freely -- a continuous stream doused the relic without sound or splash. The Orb absorbed it. Devoured it.

Every drop.

54

VIGRID VALLEY
FIMBULWINTER - YEAR 3
LAST DAY OF THE AGE OF MYTH AND LEGEND

THETAN THE LIGHTBRINGER

His falchion notched and bloodied, his shield battered and gouged, armor crusted of gore and dented helm to boot, Thetan stalked toward the lord, who stood stoic on the rise. All about, battle raged, brother slaying brother, death on a scale the world had rarely seen. But curiously, between Thetan and the lord, there was no one, dead or alive.

Their eyes met and Thetan advanced. When he drew within ten yards, the lord's right hand gestured. A humming arose from everywhere and yet from nowhere. And suddenly appeared a dome-shaped barrier of translucent energy centered on the lord. Its peak stood high overhead; its base extended to the ground and enclosed several thousand square feet. One could see through it, but little sound penetrated. No one stood within the dome's extents save Azathoth...and Thetan. The Fallen Arkon deduced at once that it was meant either to keep all others out, or him in. A troubling development, but he trusted to his fellows to breach it, for they must, to bring into play The Sphere of the Heavens and let loose their mad plan. It now fell

255

to Thetan to buy them time, however much needed, even if he purchased it with his very life. He had not expected to face the lord alone, and had taken pains to avoid it — the risk of failure too great. But perhaps it was fitting for it to end this way. Fitting for them both.

"Beloved Thetan," said Azathoth, his voice soothing and calm yet earnest, "stand down and hear me."

Thetan paused in mid stride, though it was not his nature to hesitate in such circumstance. He cared not for banter and not often for parlay. It was his wont to approach those who needed killing and do the deed, quick and direct, which was what he planned for Azathoth, however mad the notion and unlikely the outcome. He had no interest in engaging the lord in debate, his silver tongue unbeatable. But Thetan need only delay; keep the lord talking until his men tore through the shimmering wall, or until he crept close enough and wounded the lord, causing the wall to drop - he hoped. Either *had* to happen, if not, The Sphere would remain too distant to serve its function — dooming his rebellion to inevitable defeat and he and his fellows to certain death.

"Your mind is troubled," said Azathoth. "Your conscience weighs heavy. Strange forces tug on your will, influence your actions, stoke your anger, and vie for dominance over you. I know that you sense it. You must accept that it comes not from within you, but from without."

"My mind is my own," said Thetan. "My actions, my own, for the first time in long years."

Azathoth shook his head. His eyes, sad,

glistening, on the verge of tears. "You know not what you do or of what you speak," he said. "You must hear me now if you have ever heard me. You are under the influence of dark powers. Around your neck hangs a strang e talisman that you think serves *your* purposes and provides you protection, though you understand not its nature nor its origins — and that alone should give you pause."

"I tell you," continued Azathoth, "the thing is false. It is not a tool that serves *you* – *you* are an unknowing puppet that serves *it*. It is no mere magical bauble. It be a Shard of Shadow — a mystical thing of evil beyond your comprehension. It has existed since the very dawn of creation, drifting betwixt the stars, seeking somewhere where it might work its evil. It corrupts all that venture within its sphere. And now, my beloved, it is your master. It poisons your mind and enslaves your spirit though you know it not. My heart breaks at the very thought of it. And my anger swells. You, and my greatest followers, ripped from my bosom and twisted to serve the darkness, the evil, the chaos — all that I have fought against from time immemorial, all that I have taught *you* to fight against. And now you serve it. You serve the darkness!"

Azathoth's face grew deep red and he shook all over. "If I did not know for certain that it had beguiled you, I would smite you where you stand — turn you to dust for such treachery."

"But I know you better even than you know yourself," said Azathoth. "You'd never do what you've done of your own accord. You'd never turn from the light, from goodness, from *me*. Never. It *has* beguiled you; you're under its thrall. That's why I've allowed this rebellion to persist. I could have put it down at any moment. I've let this play out, hoping to find a way to save you from the Shard and bring you back into the fold. I've sacrificed much to provide you that chance. Only I can save you, if you cannot save yourself. You must see the light and the truth and separate them from the darkness. Listen to your heart, it will not deceive you and will ever remain true to your nature. Examine your feelings. Delve deep into your memories. You are not evil, Thetan. At your heart, you are good. You serve the light, not the darkness. Order not chaos. You are strong. You can yet overcome the Shard's influence. Come back to me. Please, beloved, come back to me, and stand proudly at my side once more. Cast the Shard from your person. Throw it down and forsake it, for now and forever. And then fall into my loving embrace," he said, his arms outstretched. "I offer you forgiveness, reconciliation. All can be as it once was. You need only cast the evil aside and all will be forgiven."

Thetan's mouth opened as if to speak, but no words came out. His mind raced. Confusion took hold for a moment. And then, Thetan's jaw stiffened, his eyes narrowed, and his sword grip grew all the tighter.

"My heart is broken," said Azathoth, not missing those tells. "My kingdom crumbles. Do not make me strike you down. I have sacrificed so much to stave that off since this foolish conflict began. Please Thetan, first of my Arkons, you who I love best, gather all your strength, all your free will, and fight the alien influence that plagues you. Be the man that I taught you to be. The good in your heart can yet overcome the evil that assails it. Cast it out, Thetan. Cast it out. Let me help you. Let me destroy the Shard, as I destroyed the thing that it once was."

Thetan paused, confused. He knew the Ankh held a mystical power beyond his understanding. He knew a cloud over his mind concealed its origins, prevented his recall of how it had come to him. But he felt it must be his; that it belonged with him. That it was, in some inexplicable way, a part of him. And, perhaps most importantly, that it was the only thing that had thus far saved him from Azathoth's wrath. What he didn't understand was whether the Ankh was his protector or his curse. Did Azathoth make his claims to save him or to trick him into casting it aside, thereby making him vulnerable to his magics. He knew not what to do. He expected not such confusion. His mind raced. His head swam. All his will was bent on stopping the mad god, but who was it that was mad? And why was there a hole in his memory?

He didn't know. His anger welled. He wanted to put all thoughts aside and fight, just fight.

"Let not that rage devour you," said Azathoth. "The strength to overcome the darkness abides within you. I can see it. I can feel it. I always have."

Sweat drenched Thetan, and his breathing was heavy; both arms shook. He knew in his

259

heart, the Ankh belonged about his neck. But the lord's words bore into him and confused him.

"You have asked me many times to fill the hole in your mind and memory, Lightbringer. I promised you that I would, and yet I have delayed. I have failed you, and for that I deserve your ire. To my shame I have not told you everything, though I had good reason for it. All to protect you, to help you, out of my love for you."

"You know what took my memories?" said Thetan, surprise on his face. "From where I sprang, my ancient history?"

Anger grew within Thetan's chest, within his heart, and mind. "Darn it all," said Thetan. "You've always known." He barely held back from rushing Azathoth and tearing him to pieces.

"Lightbringer, some truths are best left forgotten. But you leave me little choice."

Within that force dome, beyond the hearing of any other, Azathoth told Thetan the story of the Lord of Shadows -- he who was Azathoth's counterpart, his nemesis, his opposite. And when he was done, he said, "You wear a piece of the Lord of Shadow's heart around your neck. Nothing less could have staved off my magic that day in the throne room. A magic I never would've used had I recognized the Shard for what it was. Only after I studied its twin that Arioch turned over to me, did I discern its nature. Before that, I thought you had betrayed me of your own will, that you had become corrupted; that there was no hope for you. I'd rather see you dead than live on as a thing of evil. And so, I tried to destroy you.

"To free yourself of its evil influence, you must first accept that the seeds of the rebellion sprang not from you, but from the Shard. It has brought this misery upon us. Yet, I sense that you feel a kinship to it. But you don't know why. I will tell you – though I wish that it had not come to this."

"When I destroyed the Lord of Shadows, I destroyed everything he had built. His evil empire crumbled beneath my righteous wrath. Every evil servant, dead."

"Except for one."

The breath stuck in Thetan's throat. He could only stare at the lord and await his next words while his heart raced.

"You are the Prince of Shadows, Thetan. You are the son of the dark lord himself. A spawn of evil."

Thetan shook his head; his face, drawn; his jaw, slack.

"Once, long ago, your name was not Thetan — the name I gave you. Your birth name was gifted you by the Shadow Lord. And that name was Sa-tan — a name that defined evil but thankfully, is long now forgotten. I sought to save you from your birthright, from your evil nature. I sought to nurture you to goodness. So I took from you those memories of your father, of all his foul deeds.

"And of yours.

"I was determined to save you from yourself. To make you into the man that you could be, if properly guided and trained. A leader. A man to be admired.

261

"A hero.

"And I did. It worked all these long years. You've served me well. You've served the people and Midgaard well. You have been a hero, Thetan. You have made me proud. But when you defied me, rebelled, and sought to take my life, I thought your old nature had reasserted itself. That some spark of the evil that was once in you had reignited. I knew that after all these eons, if you had turned back to the darkness, I could not redeem you. Not again.

"And so I tried to slay you where you stood.

"I was wrong.

"And I am sorry, my beloved. It was not you. Not you. So long as you carry the Shard, you cannot tell right from wrong, good from evil. So, I beg you once more, cast it off. I will help you if I can, but it must be your choice. Trust in me. Have faith in me one last time."

55

JUTENHEIM
ANGLOTOR TOWER
THE TEMPLE OF POWER
YEAR 1267, 4TH AGE

JUDE EOTRUS

How long it took the blood flask to empty, whether half a minute or half an hour, Jude couldn't guess. Was it the eerie atmosphere of that alien chamber, and the magics old and new that swirled about it, that distorted his sense of time, or was his mind simply muddled from stress and fatigue?

Regardless, after all that blood, something should've happened: some strange vibration; electricity in the air; a tingling of the flesh or a curling of the hair. Something. Anything. But there was no hint that the mystical portal was stirring, that the long lost god was awakening. And with that realization, Jude knew despair, for that first flask held half again as much blood as did the second.

The reserve wasn't going to be enough.

Not nearly.

Korrgonn shook his head, as dissatisfied with the lack of progress as was Jude. The chamber rattled again, another blast, well off in the distance, perhaps on the keep's grounds or mayhap within Anglotor Tower's walls.

"It may take some minutes, my lord," said Brackta. "The magic works in its own time. Master Thorn said--"

"We don't have minutes," said Korrgonn sharply. "The Harbinger pounds at our door. Our sentinels cannot stop him. Even now, they pay for these moments with their lives."

Korrgonn uncorked the second flask of blood – the last of the reserve – and poured it over the Orb even as the room violently shook from yet another explosion, this one, nearer than the last.

"It's not working," screeched Par Keld, but whether he spoke of the ritual or his attempts to magically seal the room's door, Jude didn't know. "Stand the door with me," Keld shouted, "all of you; we have to hold them back. They'll kill us all, send our souls to Helheim -- to eternal torment. Do you want that? We've got to brace the door, for Azathoth's sake! I'm trying to save you, you fools! Why won't anyone listen to me?"

"Bleed him, my lord," said Ginalli, momentarily halting his chanting, although Korrgonn was still pouring the second flask, holding it steady to ensure every drop landed atop the Orb. "That congealed blood is useless," said Ginalli. "I warned Thorn of that. Fresh blood is what the binding demands. You must bleed him. Quickly."

The second flask, now empty; Korrgonn tossed it aside, studied the Orb, his golden eyes locked on it.

"There's no more time, my lord," said Ginalli. "Let not your compassion bring us to ruin. Do what you know must be done. Quickly now, I beseech you. 'Tis a small price to pay for the lord's return."

"So say you," mumbled Donnelin.

"Lay your forearm on the altar," said Korrgonn to Jude, urgency in his voice, his jaw clenched. Teek had a hand on Jude's shoulder and stood close enough that Jude felt the Lugron's breath upon his nape.

"Hold it steady as you can," said Korrgonn. "Lugron -- help him. I'll make a precise cut, no deeper than need be. Have faith in me, but there will be much blood. There needs to be. I'm sorry."

Jude felt Teek fidgeting behind him, one cold, clammy hand gripping the back of his neck, the other, holding down his hand.

"Do what you have to do, just don't cut my darned hand off," said Jude, his entire body atingle, so close was he to the godling. He felt Korrgonn's power; it poured off him much the same as the cold poured from the Orb. Jude clenched his jaw, braced himself for the knife.

Korrgonn's cut was as promised.

The blade was sharp, a deep but clean cut. Jude's blood hurried out, but aside from its warmth on his wrist, it took some seconds for Jude to feel anything.

Then it hurt like hell.

Brackta had slipped a wooden bowl beneath his wrist to catch the flow. She didn't look at him when she did it. Guilt? Or didn't she care about him at all? Or mayhap, she was still worried about her standing in the group — about giving away that there was something between them.

The bowl filled far faster than Jude would've liked but slower than perhaps need be. The blood reserve had indeed proved useless for the portal still hadn't stirred. He'd suffered through all those bleedings for nothing. Worse, if only fresh blood worked, then they'd have to bleed him dry.

Just as they'd done to his father.

Was Aradon looking down on him even now from Valhalla? Was he proud of his son for making the same sacrifice he made? Or did he mark him a fool for throwing away his life? Jude had felt his father's presence whenever he thought about him, whenever he pictured his face. It was as if he were always there, invisible, watching over him, guiding and protecting, judging him. He was always there. But now, when he needed him most, he couldn't feel him at all, couldn't sense him in the least. In that chamber, he was cut off, somehow. Isolated from his ancestors. And that made it all the harder.

Jude glanced around the chamber, best as he could with those gathered close around him and a dusty haze in the air. He wanted to see whatever there was to see, hear whatever there was to hear, because those may well be his final moments. He had to face that. He was out of time, at the end of his road. And that wasn't fair. He hadn't had his chance at life: happiness, a wife and children of his own. Robbed of it all, and for what? Dying for nothing? The ritual wasn't even working. Was he doing the right thing? Did it even matter?

If only his father were alive and with him. He'd know what to do. So would Sir Gabriel and Master Ob. But he was on his own. Even surrounded by the Leaguers, he'd die alone. No one back home would ever know what had become of him and Donnelin. No legacy, and no brave tale to be told. He'd soon be forgotten, mayhap even by his brothers.

56

VIGRID VALLEY
FIMBULWINTER - YEAR 3
LAST DAY OF THE AGE OF MYTH AND LEGEND

THETAN THE LIGHTBRINGER

Azathoth's words echoed in Thetan's head, over and again. "*You are the Prince of Shadows. The spawn of evil.*" He felt numb, barely conscious. His mind raced through a desolate foggy expanse.

Could it all be true? It seemed impossible, yet so many disparate pieces of Azathoth's claim fit snugly together.

Or was it all a trick? An epic web of lies to lower his guard?

But Azathoth spoke true when he said that Thetan felt a kinship with the Ankh. He did. It was as if it were a part of him. Was the rest equally true? *Was* he the son of the Shadow Lord? And if he were, then he wasn't a man at all.

"What am I?" he said, though his words were a mumbled whisper. His arms shook. He barely kept hold of his sword. His shield hung limp.

Azathoth wore a gentle smile of love and benevolence. His arms outstretched, palms forward, a look of peace and caring on his face.

Or so it seemed.

"That's it, my beloved. Come forward into my

embrace with open heart and empty hands, and retake your place of honor in my kingdom, as was always meant to be. Throw down the Shard and all is forgiven. We will dine tonight together in Vaeden's great hall and mourn those we've lost."

Thetan took a step toward Azathoth, unsteady though he was. A second step, now quicker.

And then a disembodied voice whispered in his ear, and with it came a scent of springtime: a flowery breeze and fresh tilled soil. A woman's voice it was, soft and melodic, but with an urgency to it. "Touch the Ankh, my love," she said. "It will yet save you. You've only a moment; do not hesitate."

He knew that voice, but he could not name it. He trusted it, and in some way he could not explain, he loved it. He pulled on the cord that held the Ankh, and lifted it from beneath his breastplate.

"Yes, that's it," said Azathoth. "Tear the cord, throw down that blasphemous thing at once, and resume your rightful place at my side."

Thetan wrapped his hand around the Ankh, and the moment he did, his mind cleared.

Or so he thought.

He knew at once who he was, where he was, and what was his purpose. In the blink of an eye he'd covered the thirty feet between him and Azathoth, sword and shield on the attack.

The lord's eyes went wide in shock and horror.

57

JUTENHEIM
ANGLOTOR TOWER
THE TEMPLE OF POWER
YEAR 1267, 4TH AGE

The inner sanctum shook again. Stones fell from the ceiling. Dust choked the air.

"I hear him coming," shouted Keld, his ear close to the chamber's door. "Come and listen," he said, waving the others forward, though no one complied.

The sounds of battle reached Jude's ears.

A clash of arms.

An exchange of spells.

"They're at the stair's base," shouted Brackta, "maybe closer."

"The Harbinger," wailed Keld as he fled from the door and staggered franticly about the room, pulling out clumps of his hair; his eyes, surrendered to madness. The Lugron guards cowered at the room's far side, all pretense of bolstering the door cast aside.

When the bowl was filled of Jude's blood, Brackta exchanged it for an empty one and handed the full bowl to Ginalli who opened his eyes and halted his chanting.

"By this sacrifice of the blood of kings," chanted Ginalli in a voice now loud enough for all to hear, "may the veil betwixt the worlds be sundered; may the curse be lifted, and the joyous path to heavenly Nifleheim at last be opened again."

The priest poured the blood onto the Orb. It didn't splatter or splash. Instead, the Orb's surface absorbed it, every drop, and turned a deep red. When the bowl was empty, the room shook again.

Par Keld continued his antics, screaming, "the Harbinger, the Harbinger," as he tore at his hair. "The devil is coming, the devil. I don't deserve to die. I haven't done anything. Anything! I'm not a villain! I'm not! You're all against me! Why?"

"It's not enough," said Korrgonn. "I'm sorry, boy, but we'll need another cut. There's no time to waste, the Harbinger is upon us. Hold out your other hand."

Tears welled in Jude's eyes; he didn't know why. He started to feel dizzy. But he was committed. It had to be done. He knew now where he stood. He'd been deceived all along, fighting for the wrong side, angry with the wrong people. At least he'd die a hero.

He put out his right hand.

And Korrgonn slit his wrist.

This time, the cut was deeper than before; the blood flowed all the faster.

"I'll try to do this without you," said Korrgonn to Donnelin. Then he stepped over to Uriel who hung upon the cross, pale and weak, though somehow his gag had fallen away. Uriel struggled against his bonds, but so tightly was he pinned with thick ropes at neck, waist, legs,

271

and arms, he could not even shift his weight. He had no chance to escape, but the ropes, as thick as they were, groaned as he pressed all his strength against them. Korrgonn drew a dagger from his belt, held it up before Uriel. "Father," said Korrgonn, "forgive me now for what I must do."

"Curse you back to Helheim," said Uriel as he struggled to catch enough breath to speak. "You lying, no good, inhuman scum. Cut me down, give me a sword, and let me die fighting. If you had any courage...not like this, dammit all. Not like this!"

Korrgonn raised the dagger.

"Wait," shouted Uriel. "I have—"

Korrgonn plunged the dagger into Uriel's chest.

Uriel stiffened and his eyes went wide but he continued to struggle, and he spit in Korrgonn's face.

Korrgonn plunged his dagger in again. He sliced the blade across Uriel's sternum, down, around, and back again, cutting and sawing and breaking bone. The terrible sounds of those cuts haunted all who heard them.

Uriel's face contorted in agony, and his eyes rolled back in his head, but he did not scream.

And then, via some feat of strength or force of will beyond the ken of mortal man, Uriel the Bold's left hand snapped the rope that restrained it.

His fingers found Korrgonn's neck.

And squeezed.

That grip should have been feeble. What

strength could Uriel have left, injured as he was, bleeding out, hanging from a piece of wood, no leverage, and only one arm brought to bear? And yet, Korrgonn, for all his inhuman strength, struggled against that grasp, such was its power -- the power of an Eternal, a man who had been old even during the far-off *Age of Myth and Legend*.

Korrgonn tried to wrench himself free, first with one hand, but then with two, the dagger dropping to the floor. As the titans struggled, blood poured from Uriel's chest, his face pale and sallow, but his eyes fixed on Korrgonn – hatred burning in them, his will indomitable.

"My lord," called out Ginalli, shock in his voice as he turned and moved to help his master.

"Now's your chance, Judy Boy," whispered Teek in Jude's ear as he wrapped a cloth about one wrist to staunch the blood flow. "Get you gone by the back door while they be distracted."

Jude looked over his shoulder at Teek and shook his head. "This is where I need to be. The Harbinger is the enemy, not the League."

Teek's jaw dropped and his face scrunched up in puzzlement.

"Jude," said Donnelin, "We've got to go, the chance we've been waiting for."

"Get your head on straight, Judy Boy," whispered Teek. "These black hats are about to kill you dead, you darned fool. Skedaddle, whilst you can. I'll cover you. You've only a moment, now move!"

"My head's on straighter than it's been in a long time," said Jude as he looked to Teek and

273

Donnelin in turn, though he had to brace himself against the altar, the dizziness worsening.

"I'll drag your butt out of here," said Donnelin.

"Don't try it," said Jude.

Teek shook his head. "If the fool won't go, we can't make him. We'll move too slow carrying him and they'll be on us in a flash."

Korrgonn wrenched Uriel's hand free and Ginalli helped him to pin it against the wall. And then, without a moment's hesitation, Korrgonn plunged his other hand into the gaping wound at Uriel's chest.

This time, Uriel screamed.

Korrgonn rammed his fingers deep into the wound, farther and farther, bone breaking, blood spurting over all three men. Uriel howled, thrust his neck forward and tried to bite Korrgonn, his jaws snapping. But he fell short.

He had no weapons left.

Korrgonn's hand plunged wrist deep into Uriel's chest, pulled and twisted, as Uriel screamed. Then came a terrible sucking sound when the Nifleheim lord withdrew his hand and pulled out the still beating heart from Uriel's chest.

VIGRID VALLEY
FIMBULWINTER - YEAR 3
LAST DAY OF THE AGE OF MYTH AND LEGEND

THETAN THE LIGHTBRINGER

Thetan's bound was so swift, so sudden, and so unexpected that Azathoth had no time to react. Thetan's falchion came down with blinding speed, all his strength behind it.

And struck Azathoth, face and chest!

Had he been a mortal man or any creature of nature, that blow would've cleaved him in two.

But Azathoth was neither. He was something else. His eyes morphed to red in a flash; the look of love fled even faster.

The falchion sank but a fraction of an inch into his flesh, and stuck there as if embedded in stone. The assault pushed Azathoth back: one small step and then another. Before the lord raised his hands in defense, Thetan pivoted and raked his shield's sharpened edge across his neck. That should have opened his jugular and been the end of him.

Instead, it barely broke the skin. Black blood, not red, dribbled from that wound; the same from his cheek and chest.

Azathoth's hand flicked out and Thetan felt himself flying through the air at great speed. He could not say whether Azathoth had struck him or whether he was flung via sorcery, but flung he was. He crashed hard against the force dome's wall, but had time to tuck chin to chest, and thus avoided a cracked skull. He fell to his rump, back against the dome, the breath knocked out of him.

Thirty feet away stood Azathoth, no anger on his face. He looked sad, defeated. Azathoth's right hand reached down and took hold of the falchion's hilt, the blade still embedded in his chest, and pulled the sword free without even a wince. More black blood oozed from the wound but he paid it no heed. He held the sword on display before him, making certain he had Thetan's attention. Beginning at its tip and running down its blade, the falchion disintegrated to ash.

Thetan scrambled to his feet and charged again. Halfway there, Azathoth's arm arced in his direction and an unseen force caught Thetan by the throat. It lifted him into the air and his feet dangled well above the ground. Thetan tried to shield bash whatever it was that held him, but his shield met no resistance. With his left hand he tried to pry off whatever held him, but found nothing to pry. But something was there, squeezing the life from him, holding him aloft. The pain was terrible; all his weight suspended from his neck. He couldn't take a breath. Not a single breath. He'd black out in moments. He remembered the Ankh that dangled from its cord. He grabbed it even as his vision grew dim.

And then he was falling.

Fifteen feet to the ground. He landed on his

feet, and with nary a moment's respite, he leapt again, and reached Azathoth in a single bound. The resulting impact was like nothing Thetan had experienced. It was more akin to running into a great oak than a man — such was the lord's inertia. Nonetheless, over fell the lord, Thetan atop him. Azathoth crashed to the ground and sank some three inches into the hardened soil. To do that, his weight must have been tenfold that of a common man.

Thetan's hands found the lord's throat. He squeezed with all his might; a grip that could crush a bear's neck. Azathoth's flaming red eyes bored into him but Thetan stared back, defiant, unafraid. From the corner of Azathoth's eye dripped a tear, black as tar.

For all Thetan's titanic strength, he could not compress Azathoth's throat in the slightest. His attack, useless. Azathoth grabbed him about the breastplate, lifted him up and off, and rose to his feet, holding Thetan aloft with one arm as if he were a small child. At that, Thetan knew that a fly had more chance to defeat a dragon than he had to defeat Azathoth. A man, no matter his attributes or resolve, cannot battle a god and hope to win.

As Thetan dangled, Azathoth spoke and softened his grip. "Alas, there is no hope for you, you who I loved best of all. Destroy you now I must, all of you, and in my shame, I will begin anew, and make those in my image all the better the next time."

"What can bleed, can die," snarled Thetan. He kicked Azathoth in the face with all his strength,

277

but it did the lord no harm. What it did do, was distract him for a moment. Time enough for Thetan to press the Ankh tightly against the lord's arm.

Azathoth screamed.

59

JUTENHEIM
ANGLOTOR TOWER
THE TEMPLE OF POWER
YEAR 1267, 4TH AGE

JUDE EOTRUS

"**D**ead gods," whispered Teek when Korrgonn ripped out Uriel's heart. "Should've got gone while you had the chance, Judy Boy, darned fool you are. Now we're done for, the three of us. It's all gone to shit."

The room violently shook, the battle now raged just beyond the sanctum's door. Jude heard shouting in the tunnels from more than one direction: not just from the main door, but also from the others. That didn't make sense. He couldn't trust his ears any longer, weakness from blood loss overtaking him.

Blood-spattered, Korrgonn lurched back to the altar, bloody heart in hand. He placed the heart atop the Orb. No frost accosted it, for even the Orb's otherworldly magic dared not mar the Eternal's heart. Strangely, the heart did not balance where he placed it, nor did it slide off.

It sank.

Sank into the Orb as if the sphere's surface were not solid, yet, the surface did not deform; it remained spherical even as the heart sank through it, defying all logic and sanity.

After the heart dropped from sight, the Orb pulsed with an eerie light and its humming grew all the louder. The pulsing came faster; the light, brighter, then darker, then brighter again, over and over. The lights scrambled Jude's mind, his head swam, and a terrible nausea washed over him, his stomach churning. The room shook so violently, Jude barely kept his feet.

Par Keld screamed.

Jude's eyes fluttered, his knees buckled. Teek held him up. Brackta switched out the basin, now full again. Full of his blood.

Did he have any left?

Korrgonn snatched the basin from her and held it up.

"Father, please let this be enough," Korrgonn said as he poured the second bowl of fresh blood overtop the Orb. Again, it absorbed every drop, pulsing red, lights flashing, the room spinning. Jude went numb all over, a ringing in his ears, fatigue dulling his mind, weakening his limbs; he was cold, freezing, shivering. He could only stare straight ahead - at the Orb - at the pulsing lights. His will, sapped. The world closed in on him, his hearing dimmed.

And then, the image of a great black and yellow eye appeared on the Orb's top surface.

Korrgonn gasped and his eyes flicked to Donnelin. "I'm sorry, priest," he said. "The legends hold true. The ritual requires an eye. The eye of a holy man."

Donnelin shook his head in disbelief, his eyes wide, his breathing, quick. "Pluck out your own, son of Azathoth. Or take his," he said motioning toward Ginalli. "I'm not very holy, all things considered, especially compared with you lot. And I'm a heathen by your accounting. He's the true believer," he said indicating Ginalli.

A great roaring filled the room. What it was, where it came from, Jude couldn't fathom; the lights wouldn't stop flickering, he wasn't certain where he was any longer. A moment later, a deafening popping sound assaulted his ears as Stev Keevis and Par Rhund materialized just inside the door and collapsed to the floor, a bluish glow surrounding them. Magics they wielded passed them through the closed door, Keld's wards notwithstanding. Both men were battered and bruised, clothes torn, hair eschew, their hats gone, packs too. Rhund was bloody down his right side, shoulder to boot, though Keevis seemed intact. They scrambled from the door on their rumps as best they could, refusing to give it their backs for even a moment, their hands outstretched before them, luminous magics crackling betwixt their fingers.

A thunderous impact struck the door. Dust and stone shards flew in all directions.

"It's him," shouted Keevis. "The Harbinger!"

"My bindings!" screeched Keld.

And then the heavy stone door exploded -- exploded because Mason was thrown against and through it with incredible force. The door disintegrated, shards flying into the sanctum, and Mason crashed to the floor -- directly atop Par Rhund. Rhund tried to save himself, his hands aglow, crackling with some reflexive magic, but whatever the incantation, he failed to launch it quickly enough; it never left his fingers. Jude imagined he heard a nauseating squishing sound as Mason's bulk crushed the wizard to pulp, but with all the noise, and his head foggy, he couldn't be certain of anything.

Korrgonn's hand rose and he mouthed strange, painful words of mystical power, but to what effect, Jude knew not.

What remained of Jude's blood froze in his veins when from the passage's gloom, strode the devil himself: Thetan, the Harbinger of Doom.

VIGRID VALLEY
FIMBULWINTER - YEAR 3
LAST DAY OF THE AGE OF MYTH AND LEGEND

THETAN THE LIGHTBRINGER

The lord screamed in agony.

Screamed.

A sound too horrible to hear, too wrong to be real.

An impossible, horrific sound that could not be Thetan's doing.

But it was.

It was all his doing.

His sin.

A betrayal beyond imagining or forgiveness. An atrocity. An evil.

As the lord screamed, Thetan screamed too, and fell free from the lord's grasp, but held tightly to the Ankh -- that curious *thing* that had proved effective against the lord where all else had failed. Why that was, he could not say. Perhaps, it truly was a Shard of Shadow and the antithesis of Azathoth, or mayhap it was a shard of light and Azathoth spoke in the opposite. Or maybe, it was something else entirely, merely a random substance that was poison to him. Thetan knew not the truth that day; he could not cut through the web of lies that spun around him. But he knew well that if he won the day, he'd be named the godslayer, proving himself a worthy heir to the Shadow Lord, his name reviled by much of Midgaard forevermore no matter what goodly future deeds he might do. And if he lost, he could expect naught but eternal torment writhing in the hellfires of Abaddon, or else, if the lord proved merciful, he'd be cast adrift in the endless nothingness of the void, spinning aimlessly, alone, for all eternity, until madness broke his mind and shattered his spirit.

He could yet have turned from that dark path. He could've repented, bowed down, begged forgiveness, pleaded for mercy.

But he did not.

Instead, he pushed his conscience aside, all his doubts along with it, and resolved to battle the lord to the death.

The lord staggered back, obviously in great pain. His arm smoked; the flesh burnt, melted, where the Ankh had touched it.

Azathoth slapped the wound as if to douse flames that Thetan could not see, though mayhap they existed in some ethereal realm beyond his sight.

Thetan heard a great crackling behind him. He turned and saw Gabriel pass through the dome's wall whilst carrying Wotan upon his back -- an almost comical sight, for despite Gabriel's large frame, the Northman was thicker and near half again his weight. The hole they'd made immediately sprang closed behind them, sparking and booming. Gabriel dropped the Northman, who landed on his feet, clearly unharmed. Thetan deduced Gabriel's Ankh had somehow passed them through the dome's magic. Perhaps Azathoth's injury had weakened not only him, but the dome as well.

A moment later, Raphael and Bose pushed through the force wall, the same as Gabriel, the ornate box that held The Sphere of the Heavens gripped between them, and old Lasifer crouched atop it, cackling, his hair and beard wild, eyes wilder. Other men pounded on the dome's wall, trying to breach it, to no avail. An Ankh in hand was the price of entry.

"The eye and the blood?" said Thetan.

"I will be ready," grumbled Wotan. "Give me a moment, for all that's holy."

"Gabriel," said Thetan, "stay with Wotan and see that it's done. You others are with me." Thetan extended his Targon's wings and leapt forward with all speed. He crashed again into Azathoth who still staggered and howled in pain. The lord went down hard on his back again and sank into the hardened clay. Thetan's fists pounded the lord's face without mercy or quarter. Thetan threw those punches. He felt the impact and yet, he didn't. It was as if someone else controlled his body and he was trapped inside, helpless witness to the impossible horror. But he refused to fool himself. He knew no one controlled him. He was responsible. No other. Still, it was surreal.

"Lord forgive me," said Bose as he slammed his axe into Azathoth's leg.

Thetan's first instinct was to strike Bose, but he stayed his hand when he remembered that they were in it together, Bose carrying out *his* orders.

"For freedom," shouted Raphael as tears streamed down his face and he repeatedly stabbed Azathoth's abdomen with his dagger. Thetan couldn't look at that. But he kept punching. He couldn't stop. He dare not. Tears dripped down his cheeks. Or, was it merely sweat? Or blood? Did it matter? The world had gone mad. Everything was upside down. He was lost. Lost. Better that Bose put that axe through his head, Raphael's dagger across his neck. At least then the nightmare would be over.

61

JUTENHEIM
ANGLOTOR TOWER
THE TEMPLE OF POWER
YEAR 1267, 4TH AGE

When the Harbinger stepped into the sanctum, Jude saw him for what he truly was, his natural form at last revealed, his illusions either dispelled by that holy place or dropped by his choice, having served their purpose. A great hammer he gripped in his left hand -- mystical runes aplenty, dark magics cascading up and down its unholy haft. Seven feet tall was the demon, features hewn of stone: a long, sharp nose, high cheekbones, square jaw, and heavy brow. A great horn amid his forehead, two more rose from the sides of his head, spiraled upward like a ram's. Two dagger-like tusks protruded from his mouth; his feet, cloven hooves beneath shaggy legs, armor-clad; his skin, corpse gray; eyes, black as pitch. A spiked tail dragged behind him. Broader than the door were his shoulders, nothing but muscle and rage. A monster out of darkest nightmare. Evil incarnate. The doom of us all.

Jude couldn't believe it. Everything the Leaguers had told him was true. This Harbinger of Doom -- Thetan, as they called him -- was the devil himself. A creature so evil, so malevolent, that merely to look upon him, stained one's soul. How had he been such a fool to think the Leaguers his enemies? How had he not seen the truth? What a blind fool he was.

"Slay the beast," shouted Ginalli to his faithful, what few remained. "Send him back to Helheim."

Brackta's eyes met Jude's for but a moment before she turned to her duty, fear and determination competing for her features. And in that moment, Jude's heart ached for he knew that neither of them would survive the day.

"Priest," shouted Korrgonn, "your time has come."

Donnelin nodded, his face a mask of fear, barely able to turn away from the monstrosity at the door. Same as Jude, he could no longer deny the Harbinger's evil. They'd been on the wrong side all along. Ginalli gripped Donnelin's shoulder, held him fast, his jaw set, his face grim. No hint of compassion softened the high priest's eyes.

"Dead gods, save me," said Donnelin. "Do it, do it now. Do it."

"Stop," boomed the Harbinger in an inhuman voice that rattled Jude's ears. Its eyes bored into Korrgonn, even as blasts of fiery plasma, one after another, a veritable swarm, launched from Par Brackta's hand and crashed unerringly into him, exploding on impact, shock waves taking everyone nearby from their feet.

Even positioned well behind Brackta, the blast rocked Korrgonn, but the moment he steadied himself, he plunged his dagger into Donnelin's

288

eye. Jude knew that blow was coming, but was shocked all the same at its sight, the breath catching in his throat. Korrgonn withdrew the dagger at a steep angle, Donnelin's eye coming with it.

Donnelin howled and dropped to the ground, clutching his face as blood poured from the socket. Jude tried to help him, but Teek held him fast, his wrist still dripping blood into another bowl. All he could do was put his other hand on Donnelin's shoulder; meager comfort.

Korrgonn placed the eye atop the Orb but didn't wait to see what happened. "Complete the ritual; let nothing stop you," he shouted to Ginalli as he moved around the altar, wiping the blood from his hands, and drew his battle blade.

As Ginalli chanted, Jude watched the eye sink through the Orb's surface just as had Uriel's heart. He had to watch -- his fate, and that of all Midgaard, may well depend upon it, or so he told himself. Or mayhap, he lacked the courage to gaze again upon the devil's face, though that did him little good, for the Harbinger's evil visage was forever inscribed upon his mind's eye.

Through the dusty haze that now hung heavy in the chamber, a preternatural light appeared -- a fiery, pulsing luminescence born of the misshapen Ankh that hung about the Harbinger's neck. What that accursed thing was, Jude dared not contemplate.

Brackta's magic had stopped the devil in its tracks for a few moments but did it no lasting harm. The Harbinger roared and made to charge when brave Stev Keevis hit him with a titanic blast of yellow fire that leapt from his fingertips. The sorcery crashed into the Harbinger's chest and exploded with eldritch might, engulfing the beast, horn to hoof. The vast power that the Elven Archmage plucked from the Grand Weave of Magic pushed the beast back, first one step, and then another, as it howled with rage.

Before the beast steadied itself, Par Brackta's voice rose up and drowned out all else. She chanted cruel words in the *Magus Mysterious*, her face flushed from the magics she'd lately thrown, her shaking hands upraised before her, her body floated upright, toes kissing the ground, her eyes rolled back in her head -- only the whites on display. And then flew her most deadly magic, a stream of numinous energy the like of which she'd never cast before, far more powerful even than what she'd thrown against the leviathan of Dagon's Isle. Her sorcery rocketed at the Harbinger, in whose hand appeared a great battle shield -- blacker than black, seen more by its absence of color than by its shape. The magic exploded against the shield -- a persistent blast that lingered, siphoning endless energy from the Grand Weave -- and pummeled the shield with a force that would've brought down and pulverized the most stalwart castle's walls. Flaming tendrils of mystical energy rebounded off the shield and cascaded in all directions, setting ablaze all it touched, hither and there. The deadly magic pushed the demon back, and back again.

But it did not fall.

It did not flee.

It did not cry out or beg for mercy.

And when at last the spell's energies were expended, the Harbinger still stood. He lowered his shield and cast an evil smile of yellow teeth and mocking eyes. Par Brackta staggered back and fell on her rump. She convulsed and twitched as smoke rose from her exposed flesh, red and blistering, stealing her beauty and devouring her life force. Her arms shook uncontrollably. Her legs too.

Stev Keevis heroically stepped before her, his eyes defiant, his jaw set, and blocked the Harbinger's path. His arms inscribed a circular pattern in the air, and a field of bluish-green energy projected from him, rectangular in shape, vertically oriented, crackling and sparking at its edges. It stretched to the ceiling and to the chamber's walls -- a magical barrier, translucent but unyielding.

The Harbinger's hammer crashed against it, the blow so swift few marked its coming. When it struck, a cracking sound filled the room, like glass shattering. For all the hammer's preternatural power, the barrier stopped the blow, but it collapsed and dissipated. Keevis's jaw hung slack and he stepped back but one step before another blow from the Harbinger struck him across the chest and sent him flying. The Elf crashed against the chamber's far wall, slumped down, broken and unmoving.

Now only Korrgonn stood between the Harbinger and the holy altar where Jude bled and Ginalli frantically chanted his ritual. The portal betwixt the worlds stubbornly remained closed. Fitting it was, Jude figured, that the world's fate depended upon the lord's son. No doubt, that's why the lord had sent him on ahead, to do the deed that only he could do: to bar the devil's path, even if it meant his own life. But could even the son of god put down that monster that bristled with evil powers unknown, that destroyed Golems and Archwizards with a single blow?

Before those titans converged, the doors on the room's far side burst open. In streamed the League's mercenaries to join the fray, Lord Ezerhauten at the van. Behind him, the best of his knights -- hardened veterans all, their weapons blood-soaked, sweat dripping from their brows. And from the main door, behind the Harbinger, streamed more Sithians, bloodied and battered, no doubt from putting down the Harbinger's evil minions.

The Sithians rushed into the room, dozens of them -- weapons at the ready, all eyes on the great beast that menaced the chamber.

Jude was weak, dizzy, his back against the altar, Donnelin beside him, moaning, overcome with pain, but Jude's heart leapt at the sight of the stalwart mercenaries. He saw the broad smile form on Ginalli's face and heard both Teek and Keld shout, "Yes!"

Now they had a chance, for Odin's sake. Even if they couldn't destroy the Harbinger, mayhap they could pin him down by force of numbers, or at the least, delay him until Ginalli completed the ritual, and the gateway to Nifleheim lay wide and yawning, ready to usher through the long lost god and his heavenly host.

Ginalli raised his voice so that all could hear. "Lay down your arms and beg mercy, Harbinger, and the Lord may grant you a swift death," he said, a broad smile on his face. "You are sorely outnumbered, you alone against the lord's son, me and my wizards, and scores of my best men."

The hairs stood up on Jude's neck as a gravelly voice from over Ginalli's shoulder boomed, "Count again."

VIGRID VALLEY
FIMBULWINTER - YEAR 3
LAST DAY OF THE AGE OF MYTH AND LEGEND

THETAN THE LIGHTBRINGER

Gabriel removed the top of the ornate container that held The Sphere of the Heavens and placed the open box in front of Wotan. Wotan stared down at it but made no move.

"There is no time," said Gabriel as he glanced over at the nearby melee. "You must do it now or I will do it for you," he said, his right hand now gripping his dagger's hilt. "Make your choice."

"Stay your hand," said Wotan in a fearsome voice as he brushed Gabriel's hand away, "and speak no threats against me, Arkon, or it will be *your* eyes that are cut out. I will suffer nothing today. I am chieftain of all the Aesir, and the lord of shining Asgard, may she gleam forever. I will do what must be done. I need no promptings from you or anyone." Wotan pulled a bejeweled dagger from its sheath, a blade that in later days would be known as *Wotan Dal.*

"Destiny is all," he said, and with barely a moment's hesitation, plunged the dagger into his own left eye. He groaned, grit his teeth, and bit his tongue until blood spurted from his mouth. He turned and twisted the blade and roared as he did so. He kept that up until his eye popped free of its socket, which mercifully took but a few long seconds. Wotan's remaining eye was clouded of tears and blood. "Guide my hand," he growled. With Gabriel's aid he positioned the eye directly over the Sphere.

"That's close enough," said Gabriel. "You must not touch the Sphere. Open your hand and let it fall."

Wotan did. The eye's fall, which should have taken no time at all, took many seconds, defying all natural laws, it fell in slow motion. When it hit the Sphere's glassy surface, it clanged like a great hammer striking an anvil. And then it sank into the glass as if its surface was liquid. Then it was gone. The eye of Wotan was gone.

Wotan winced, held his hand over his empty socket. "Guide me closer," he said to Gabriel through gritted teeth.

"What I do now, I do not only for all *my* people, but for all mankind."

"Your name will be remembered," said Gabriel. "We will see to that. Ten thousand years from now, they will know you still, Wotan of the Northmen. Make haste and fare thee well."

Wotan sliced deep into his wrist and red blood spurted.

"Put your hand over the Sphere," shouted Lasifer. "Quickly now, don't waste a precious drop."

Wotan dropped to one knee and held his wrist overtop the Sphere, careful not to touch it with his bare flesh. The stream of blood struck the Sphere with an overloud plop, much the same as his eye had done. The blood did not sink as had

295

the eye; it spread across the Sphere's surface as if some alien will required it to cover every square inch. More and more blood streamed down, but not a drop dripped off or pooled about the Sphere's base.

"How will we know when it's had enough?" said Gabriel to Lasifer.

"We'll know, I'm sure of it," said Lasifer. "Patience, now. Patience. All is as planned."

Nearby, Azathoth kicked Bose and launched him twenty feet through the air. Then the lord flicked his hand, and an unseen force slammed into Raphael and sent him tumbling as if run over by a galloping horse.

With his Ankh gripped in his fist, Thetan continued to pummel Azathoth's face. Each time the Ankh's edge touched the lord's flesh, it sizzled and smoked, and the lord roared in anger and agony. The touch of that alien thing sapped Azathoth's strength; he could not summon enough to throw Thetan off or stave off his fists.

Thetan knew that it was only the Ankh that preserved his life. Without it, the lord would've long since turned him to dust. Thetan shifted his grip and pressed the Ankh to Azathoth's forehead, wincing as he did so. The lord let loose an inhuman wail the likes of which Thetan had never heard before or since. 'Twas a sound that could not come from the throat of any man or any *thing* remotely close to a man.

Azathoth shook and quivered in a seizure. His forehead's flesh melted away, face twisted in agony; his eyes glowed red with pain and hatred.

296

Hatred is all that Thetan now saw in those eyes. He steeled himself and pressed the Ankh down all the harder. Footsteps approached from behind. Friend or foe, he didn't know. He didn't care. He wouldn't let up; didn't turn to find out.

It was Gabriel. He carried the Sphere, still within its box, though it had grown in size and burst the box's seams. It pulsed with a bright red light and hummed as if it were alive.

"The eye?" said Thetan.

"It is done," said Gabriel. "It's ready."

Holding the Ankh pressed tight to Azathoth's forehead, Thetan reached out and grasped the Sphere with his other hand.

63

JUTENHEIM
ANGLOTOR TOWER
THE TEMPLE OF POWER
YEAR 1267, 4TH AGE

Three things happened at once.

Ginalli's eyes widened in panic, his mouth dropped open, and he turned his head toward the menacing voice behind him.

Thetan bellowed, "Those aren't *your* best men, they're mine!"

Ezerhauten's sword burst through Ginalli's chest.

And chaos ruled the room.

The Harbinger of Doom bounded across the chamber, bat-like wings fluttering, mammoth hammer swinging with inhuman power and blazing speed. Korrgonn, the son of Azathoth, charged, his otherworldly sword slicing the air, howling as it went, angelic in his bearing, the heavens smiling full upon him, the lord's grace bolstering his every action.

Their weapons crashed together with lightning sparks and deafening thunder from which sprang a concussive blast that took all present from their feet, and sent both titans careening back.

Korrgonn's sword was blasted to bits, its preternatural forging to no avail.

VIGRID VALLEY

FIMBULWINTER - YEAR 3
LAST DAY OF THE AGE OF MYTH AND LEGEND

THETAN THE LIGHTBRINGER

The moment Thetan's fingers touched The Sphere of the Heavens, he heard an odd voice in his head. It sounded like his own, but it spoke words that were not his.

The voice demanded attention.

He believed that it sprang from elsewhere of its own accord, or mayhap, at the behest of the Sphere itself. Could that be? Could that strange relic have a mind and purpose of its own? Were its esoteric energies sentient? Or was it a channel to something else, a conduit to somewhere else, something communicating with him from afar? From another world? From the Heavens? the *Nether Realms*? Or elsewhere in the Nine Worlds? Could that be?

Or had he finally gone mad?

He wanted to drown out its words, ignore them, but they refused to relent.

Place your other hand on the Sphere, said the voice several times, though he resisted.

Use me, went the voice, but he ignored it.

Then the voice changed. Where it had mimicked Thetan's voice, now it sounded old. Alien. It crackled and warbled. Its pitch changed: high and then low, and back again. One voice, yet many, overlapping and competing to be heard: a high-pitched skirling voice; a deep gravelly one; the wild cackling of a crone; and myriad more, each distinct and bizarre -- a legion of creatures, a raucous cacophony of otherworldly voices -- a demonic chorus that crawled from the depths of hell.

Place us near the Old One, said one voice. *Near Azathoth.*

Close as can be, said another.

Do it swift, said yet another, then came more. The hair on Thetan's nape rose and a chill sliced through him as the eerie voices haunted him. His heart fluttered, breathing quickened.

Quickly now.

Closer now. We must be closer to it.

Place it atop us or us atop it.

Let us touch it.

We must touch it.

Consume it.

We are hungry.

Devour its energy.

We thirst.

Drink its power.

Revel in it.

Every instinct warned Thetan to smash the infernal Sphere to a thousand bits and flee howling while his soul still remained intact. And then he wondered, was it all a ruse? More of Azathoth's trickery? Was it actually the lord who spoke to him, masquerading as the Sphere, making him believe it was alive and evil? So convinced, Thetan would throw down the Sphere and abandon his plan. Wasn't that exactly what the lord wanted?

Thetan was so far beyond his ken he knew not what to do or what to believe.

Let the Old One touch us and we will rid you of it, said one of the Sphere's voices. Then more spoke in turn.

It will be with us.

With us!

Where it belongs.

Home.

Again.

With us.

We want it. We need it.

Hungry.

And then, *who will be king, Thetan?*

Who will be king?

You, Thetan? Are you not worthy?

Who else but you? No other. No other.

No other, it repeated, each time in a voice of different pitch, a cackling crone, a whining child, a pitiful wretch.

And Thetan knew they spoke the truth, about that at least. There would a void to fill after the lord was overthrown. Thetan was the leader of the rebels, for good or for ill. Who better than he to continue to lead?

Who better? said the Sphere in a low gravelly voice.

Who better? said the crone, high-pitched and crackling.

But not king, no, no, no. Such a puny title for a titan. No, not worthy, not worthy at all.

You will be god. God. God. God, each time, a

different voice.

No other.

No other.

Thetan will be god.

Yes, yes, thought Thetan. Midgaard must have a leader. A shepherd to watch over it. And who better than me?

No one, said the Sphere.

Power we will grant you.

Power we will gift you.

Limitless.

Power over all things.

Even over life and death.

"Yes," said Thetan. "Yes!"

VIGRID VALLEY

FIMBULWINTER - YEAR 3
LAST DAY OF THE AGE OF MYTH AND LEGEND

"**Y**es, now I will be god," boomed Thetan, and all Midgaard shuddered.

Yes, said the Sphere. *Give yourself over to us.*
Body and soul.
Blood and bones.
Life and limb.
Sanity and sin.

Gabriel's eyes widened, not understanding Thetan's words because all that had transpired between Thetan and the Sphere had happened within the blink of an eye, unheard except within Thetan's mind.

But Gabriel was wise. His thoughts raced and he put the pieces together. He slunk away from Thetan, one step and then another, shock and fear washing over him. "What have we done?" he muttered in horror, his eyes wide.

As Thetan gazed down upon The Sphere of the Heavens and contemplated godhood, he had a vision. A glorious vision. He stood atop a mountain plateau clothed in flowing robes of purest white, standing twice his natural height. The Sphere was now a glowing jewel -- a diamond of mammoth size -- and affixed to a crown set atop his noble brow. From that jewel his power flowed -- a conduit it was, to the limitless energies of the multiverse, a chorus of heavenly voices to advise him on every decision, their infinite wisdom imparted to him alone. A grand palace of which Vaeden's brightest halls were but a dim shadow stood behind him, ornate chambers gilt of gold, treasure vaults of fire drakes' envy, majestic minarets of wizardly wonder, slender towers that reached for the heavens and beyond, and stone walls to withstand every onslaught of man or nature. An army of titans attended him and proclaimed his glory, conquering all in his name, crushing the lowly heathens underfoot and assimilating them into the fold. A thousand wives begged for his embrace, and battled over it, living only to serve his every desire. A hundred slaves on hand at every moment to do his bidding, his every want and whim attended to. And all the people of the world to worship him. To exalt him. All glory to his name. The god of peace they named him. The lord of light and love they called him. Choirs sang joyous songs at the mere mention of his name. Kings prostrated before him. More loved was he than Azathoth ever was or could ever be. The king of kings they marked him. All bowed down before him, willingly, happily, with joy. No one dared defy or deny him. He loomed over them, the little people of the world, the common rabble, and he knew, beyond all knowing, that this was the way things were meant to be. His destiny. The world's destiny. The inevitable outcome of Thetan's grand plan, that which his puny cohorts could never comprehend.

He need only embrace the Sphere.

Join with it.

Become one with it, and the vision would be a vision no longer. It would come to pass as surely as the sun would rise the next morn.

And Azathoth, the false god, would be swept aside, a feeble memory, soon forgotten. After all, Azathoth was little more than an unworthy charlatan, a wannabee god of infinite failings and boundless avarice. He -- Thetan, was the true god.

The one true god.

66

JUTENHEIM
ANGLOTOR TOWER
THE TEMPLE OF POWER
YEAR 1267, 4TH AGE

JUDE EOTRUS

Jude's eyelids fluttered, his vision, cloudy. He'd fallen unconscious, for how long, he knew not. He hurt all over. He tried to catch his breath and get his bearings, but the room was filled with the clangor of battle and a dusty haze that impeded his sight and clogged his throat. Men were shouting, movement all around, hard for him to see.

And then he witnessed the towering knight, Frem Sorlons, step through the murk and pluck Ginalli from the floor by the throat, the priest bleeding profusely from back and chest where Ezerhauten had skewered him for reasons yet unknown. Had the Harbinger's dark sorceries turned Ezerhauten, or had he purchased the mercenary's loyalty with ill-gotten gold?

And where had Frem come from? Jude had long thought the big knight dead, cut down in the accursed tunnels of Svartleheim with so many other brave souls. How had he survived that place and reappeared at that crucial moment?

Haze or no, the power of Frem's grip was plain to see as he bore down and squeezed Ginalli's throat. But the priest had fight left in him; he was not ready to yield, though his wounds were surely mortal. Jude had thought Ginalli a weak man who wore a façade of bluster and bravado overtop charlatan's robes; little more than a trickster, a purveyor of snake oil and secrets. In the end, it seemed, he was a bit more than that. His feet dangling in the air, Ginalli placed the palms of his hands against Sorlon's chest and unleashed a burst of magic from his fingertips. Numerous bolts of red fire slammed into Frem's sternum, a lightning storm of deadly magics, crackling and blazing, a barrage to bury a squad of heavy horse or troop of stalwart, fearless footmen.

On Frem, it had no effect.

None at all. How that could be, Jude had no idea.

Frem grabbed the priest's ankle and flipped him over; held him upside down as if he weighed no more than a small child, Ginalli cursing all the while. And then, with shocking speed and deadly power, Frem swung Ginalli headfirst into the wall. As Jude looked on in horror, the priest's head burst like a melon. As quick as that, the League of Shadow's great leader was dead, murdered by a mercenary sworn to do his bidding. It all made no sense. It felt surreal.

From nearby, Jude heard Stev Keevis scream. He turned and saw Par Keld drive a dagger down through Keevis's neck into his spine. Jude knew that Keld hated Keevis, but he never expected he'd murder the Elf -- at least not during battle with the Harbinger when they needed all the power they could muster. The Elven Archmage never had a chance, for he still lay slumped against the wall, broken and bloodied, as the Harbinger had left him. With his one arm that still worked, Keevis tried to staunch the geyser of blood that shot from his neck, an artery severed, to no avail. After but a few moments, he lay still, his eyes open but sightless. Jude wondered for a moment whether in death the Elf would see his old mentor, the Keeper of Tragoss Mor.

Somehow, through the battle's din, Jude heard Brackta's brave voice rise up above all else, her mystic words brimming with power and determination, all her energies focused into one last volley of arcane power the likes of which she had never before mastered. She directed her eldritch energy at the Harbinger, a sustained attack that pelted him over and again with voluminous missiles of deadly might, some erupting from her fingertips, others, speeding down from on-high, the Weave bending to her power, submissive to her will -- if only for that fleeting moment. All to no avail, for the Harbinger withstood it all.

Brackta's skin turned a fiery red, blisters erupting all over -- her beauty marred, perhaps forevermore, the magics she wielded, too much for the human form to contain, no matter her sorcerous skills or wizardly will. She shook uncontrollably, the last of her magics spent, she stumbled and fell to her rump, smoke rising from her exposed flesh.

Jude disbelieved. It couldn't be real. Couldn't be happening.

Brackta turned toward him, her eyes seeking his; her face, filled of anguish. Her skin turned dark red, almost to black. Smoke rose thick about her. Her blisters flaked off, crumbling and dessicated; her body shuddered. Her eyes, wide and sad, locked on Jude, filled with what could have been, but was never meant to be. As the smoke rose thicker, her skin wrinkled, flaked, peeled, and fluttered away. Her flesh turned to ash, disappearing before Jude's eyes.

He wanted to run to her. Comfort her. Save her. But he was too weak to move. Too weak to stand. It couldn't be happening, he thought. A fevered dream is what it had to be. He was unconscious, dying from blood loss, imagining it all -- he had to be.

And then, what remained of Par Brackta...blew away.

Disappeared to nothing but ash.

The Wizards Toll...it took her. Jude's face, the last that she saw.

And in the horror of that moment, Jude understood all that had happened. It was all the Harbinger's doing, the chaos that he wrought, the insidious evil out of Helheim. That's what he was...chaos incarnate.

Evil.

The lord of it.

That's what he did. He turned friend against friend, brother against brother. His mere presence, a poison. All within his sight moved to violence, to madness.

Jude finally understood. The evil.

The evil.

Mercifully, he blacked out again.

VIGRID VALLEY
FIMBULWINTER - YEAR 3
LAST DAY OF THE AGE OF MYTH AND LEGEND

THETAN THE LIGHTBRINGER

Thetan kept the thought that he was, is, and ever would be the one true god foremost in his mind's eye, concentrating all his will on it to the exclusion of all else...until he uttered the forbidden words of magic that Lasifer had taught him; the words of mystical power that wrenched open the portal betwixt the worlds and denied the demonic voices the godly meal they had longed for and the new alliance they proffered.

Thetan would not be god.

Nor a dictator.

And certainly, he'd never allow himself, or the world, to be enslaved by an alien relic and whatever unholy *things* that whispered their lies through it.

Thetan would not be corrupted.

He *could* not be corrupted.

Not for all of everything.

He had brought the world to ruin to save it. For freedom's sake. Not to replace one despot with another. He'd fooled the Sphere. And it was easy enough to do so, for such things never dream a man could be beyond corruption. So few are or ever have been. Such is their nature, the way of things. But Thetan was different. Always was and always would be -- come what may.

JUTENHEIM
ANGLOTOR TOWER
THE TEMPLE OF POWER
YEAR 1267, 4TH AGE

FREM SORLONS

Frem's heart raced as he slammed Father Ginalli's head against the stone wall. Horrible thing to do. He didn't want to do it, but he had to kill the priest quickly. The man was too dangerous -- a sorcerer of terrible power, resourceful and crafty. His ilk could oft turn blades with their tricks, and Frem had no time or stomach to choke him out. On impulse, he did what he did, and figured it had to be done. In battle, you had to do whatever it took to survive.

He dropped Ginalli's corpse and immediately turned his eyes away. The Pointmen and the other Sithians had taken out the last of the Lugron guards: killed a few what put up a fight, captured the rest. Frem couldn't believe Ginalli was dead. Couldn't believe that he'd done it, though, in truth, Ezerhauten deserved the credit, for erelong, the priest would've bled out from the wound Ezer had gifted him. Frem didn't think any more on it; couldn't afford to let it distract him, not in battle.

He saw Theta shrug off a terrible barrage of

battle magic -- the kind that could take out a whole troop. It barely slowed him.

"Let this be our final battle," boomed Theta as he squared off against Korrgonn. The great knight's appearance looked normal to Frem -- no horns, wings, tail, or demonic accouterments to be seen. Only shining armor, blue and polished, cape of midnight blue, chiseled features, muscles bulging, stature imposing to behold by any standard. But a man he was, not a monster.

"Victory will not be yours, Harbinger," shouted Korrgonn as he drew two curved daggers from his belt. "I possess all the knowledge of Nifleheim *and* that of Gabriel Hornblower. I know your strengths and weaknesses better than you know them yourself. I've honed my martial skills these many thousands of years preparing for this day, for this very moment. You cannot defeat me, nor can the combined might of all your petty mortal minions."

"Gabriel Hornblower was born on the slopes of Mount Canterwrought a thousand centuries ago," said Thetan. "Before that mountain sprang from Midgaard's loins, on that very spot lay a plain of endless grass, before that, a deep blue sea, and before that sea was born, in the time before time began, I was already old beyond words or imagining. At long last, today, you meet your doom."

Theta swung his hammer but Korrgonn ducked, his speed incredible -- so fast, Frem barely saw him move. Frem wondered if he should help, join in the fight. But he knew that Theta wouldn't want that. It was his battle to

314

win, or lose, such as the Norns decree. Not that Frem believed in them, or in anything, save himself, and his brethren. He knew that deities and demigods came and went as civilizations sprang up, grew old, and died, their mythologies with them. It was only he and his brethren that endured down through all the ages of the world. It was only they that were eternal.

Theta, Frem knew, had a destiny born of his ancient actions -- an inevitable confluence of events as unavoidable as the turning of the heavenly spheres. He'd want to destroy Korrgonn himself, and bask in whatever fleeting solace that victory afforded him. So Frem stood down. Ezerhauten wisely did the same.

Distracted by the titans, Frem didn't notice the air above the altar begin to stir and shimmer. The temperature plunged. A ring of blackness formed and hung in the air above the Orb. Without warning, a gale burst forth from above the altar, where the air had been stagnant only a moment before. The impossible wind hit Frem like a galloping horse, flung him through the air and slammed him into the chamber's wall, the breath knocked out of him.

Disoriented, Frem gulped the air and smelled a foul pervasive scent -- sulfuric, alien, bestial. Frem didn't know what had happened; wasn't certain what had hit him; blinked and looked around in attempt to get his bearings. Men were strewn about the chamber, groaning, bleeding, some few were still as stone, lifeless; the blast, whatever it was, had struck them all. Even Theta and Korrgonn were not immune. They'd been knocked against the far wall, weapons gone, hands locked about each other's throats in death grips.

Frem snatched up his sword, which thankfully was at arm's reach, and scrambled to his feet as he searched for the source of the bestial smell.

That's when he first heard them: screeching, howling, barking, and gibbering, monstrous baying and roaring -- the wild cacophony of Helheim.

Frem shuddered and his blood ran cold for he'd heard those sounds once before, long ago, and hoped never to hear them again. And then, he spied the breach: a great black hole centered above the altar from which no light entered or escaped. Ginalli had done it again, the mad bastard. He'd ripped open another gateway to the *Nether Realms* -- one that if not promptly closed would herald the end of human life on Midgaard.

Jude Eotrus lay unmoving on the floor beside the altar, Teek laying protectively over him, the Eotrus priest beside them. The foul smell spewed from the breach, a strong wind blowing it, though nothing compared with its initial blast.

From the breach sprang a creature of darkness. A demon of the *Nether Realms*. A multi-legged fiend, all claws and fangs, three eyes across its broad forehead, a dozen legs, black and shaggy -- its aspect far more akin to a spider than a man. It leapt with speed astounding, and pounced on one of the Sithians, caught him unawares, his eyes transfixed on the dueling titans. It crushed him to the ground and battered him, its fangs puncturing the back of his neck. And in that moment, fleeting though it be, Frem froze. How unlike him that was, battle-hardened veteran, fearless in all things, yet in that moment, a terror unlike any that he'd felt in an age gripped his heart and rooted his feet as if he were entombed in a block of ice.

And then, from the gateway leapt another creature, this one wholly different from the first. Another monstrosity, an outré being from beyond the pale.

And then another appeared, different still from the first two.

The breach then spewed a fourth.

A fifth.

More, and more still.

No end to them.

An endless horde of otherworldly death.

Frem shrugged aside the paralysis that held him, raised his sword, and charged howling into the fray.

VIGRID VALLEY
FIMBULWINTER - YEAR 3
LAST DAY OF THE AGE OF MYTH AND LEGEND

THETAN THE LIGHTBRINGER

As the portal to the *Nether Realms* began to open, Azathoth's force dome dropped, and all the Sphere's voices screamed in unison so loudly that Thetan thought his head might burst.

No!

Not our will, shouted one voice after the others died down.

Not our desire, said another. Myriad others spoke up in turn.

How know you those words?

Secret words.

Forbidden.

Only for us.

Now you're doomed.

Doomed.

Betrayed us, you have.

Traitor!

You've betrayed yourself.

All mankind.

Traitor!

Prince of Lies.

Harbinger of doom!

Curse you.

Curse your name, forevermore.

Your line is ended.

Torment.

Forever.

Now we won't just take him, we'll take it all.

All that, Thetan heard in but a fleeting moment.

The Sphere pulsed and a great wind sprang from nowhere and yet from everywhere at once. The gale blew toward the Sphere. Thetan turned his gaze upon Gabriel and spoke but a single word.

"Run."

And Gabriel did. Thetan too, though his Targon was unresponsive, mayhap injured or dead. Raphael extended his wings and fled, battered and bleeding though he was. Gabriel scooped up Bose under one arm as he took flight.

In moments, the wind grew so strong that it threatened to drag Thetan back toward the Sphere. Without his Targon he was too slow to escape its pull. He scrambled behind a granite boulder, the only refuge in sight, meager though it was. He peered past its edge and gazed upon the lord's struggles against the torrent. Azathoth had made his feet and stood mere inches from a circular portal as black as death that hung suspended in the air nearby the Sphere. No light passed through it. No light survived it. It consumed the wind and all else within its grasp. Hungry for all and everything.

What lurked beyond that bleak veil, no man could say, but Thetan knew it was from somewhere within its Stygian depths that the

Sphere's voices sprang. A hell that no man was meant to travel to or even contemplate lest he lose his sanity and his immortal soul.

Thetan hunkered down and still gripped the Ankh within his hand. When he repositioned it, to stow it for safekeeping, to his surprise it burnt his fingers. The pain was sharp and intense, but he did not drop the relic. He would not. Perhaps, he could not. He soon realized the burning arose not from the Ankh itself, but from seared bits of Azathoth's flesh that clung to it. He wiped them off against the ground, gripped the Ankh all the tighter, and looked again at the lord. He wanted one last look. He wanted to see him pulled through. He needed to know for certain that he was gone. If he didn't see for himself, there'd always be some lingering doubt hanging over him. That would haunt him for all his days. He couldn't have that. He needed to see him go. He needed to be done with him once and for all.

And when he looked, the Ankh's powers revealed more to him than he'd seen before — more than human eyes were meant to see. Tendrils of spectral energy reached out from the void. They were no random sparks or tongues of flame, they were appendages — pseudopods, if you will — akin to those of a giant squid or octopus, but each one different from the next, varying in shape, size, and feature, as if belonging to myriad creatures, but all a ghostly gray and strangely transparent. What relationship those tendrils had to the voices he lately heard, he knew not. Were the creatures one and the same, or altogether different, rivals or allies or whatnot? Thetan did not know. He hoped he'd never know.

The tendrils sought to grasp whatever life they could. They hungered for it -- ravenous and wild.

And Azathoth was their prey.

They wrapped around him: foot, leg, waist, arm, neck, and head. They squeezed and tugged with strength that no man could resist, no flesh could withstand. But Azathoth was a god, or so he claimed. He fought back with supernatural strength beyond imagining.

And while he did, from all sides — on foot and wing — swooped the loyalist Arkons to his rescue. They'd broken off their assault with the Fallen and swarmed toward the gateway the moment they'd realized their lord was hard pressed.

Unfortunately for them, the gateway's hunger knew no bounds.

The preternatural gale funneled the loyalists towards the gateway, while dozens more ethereal tendrils, invisible to the loyalists' eyes, lashed out and scooped them up at lightning speed. Powerful as they were, the loyalists had no defense against those otherworldly attacks and could offer no resistance of note. The tendrils retracted the moment they'd snared their prey, and pulled them to the brink. When they reached the portal's surface, their plunge paused for a moment before they were pulled through, sinking as if through a liquid's surface, plopping sound and all. A dozen were lost every moment.

Thetan saw Arioch pulled in. Mobius and Mammon too. Asmodeus, Hecate, Mikel, and a hundred more, too quick to count, too fast to mark all their faces and their names. As the moments ticked by, hundreds more were ensnared, Azathoth's best Arkons, his Brigandir, his priests, and Einheriar aplenty.

Several loyalists inadvertently slammed into Azathoth, buffeting him about and nearly taking him from his feet, making his attempts to save himself all the harder. And then Bhaal charged forward roaring and cursing the wind. Iblis flew just behind him. Bhaal slid to a halt and braced himself against the wind, no doubt realizing it was unsafe to advance any farther. But Iblis was unable to stop in time and slammed into him. Together, they rocketed forward on the wind and crashed into Azathoth. Their momentum was so great, the lord tumbled backward and Bhaal and Iblis careened into the portal and plunged through. Whatever godly strength had anchored Azathoth thus far, failed him. The tendrils whipped him back against the portal. He hung there, feet dangling, his arm outstretched, reaching for Thetan who was hopelessly beyond reach. His eyes were locked on the Lightbringer. And in that gaze Thetan saw anguish. Disbelief. And fear.

A thunderclap shook the world and Azathoth shrieked as the tendrils pulled him through that infernal portal to the *Nether Realms*, or whatever hell to which it truly led.

VIGRID VALLEY
FIMBULWINTER - YEAR 3
LAST DAY OF THE AGE OF MYTH AND LEGEND

THETAN THE LIGHTBRINGER

The impossible had come to pass. Azathoth was gone.

Thetan had won.

But danger remained. A danger so vast, so alien, it threatened to swallow the world. The howling wind thundered toward and through the gateway from all directions. It grew stronger by the moment. Thetan crouched behind a nearby boulder and gripped it with every ounce of his strength. He barely held on, feet planted but slipping, knuckles white. He strained to breathe, struggled to see as the air rushed past and threatened to lift him aloft and suck him into the breach. The roaring in his ears drowned out the world.

The unholy portal that loomed before him, that fell gateway to the dread realm of Nifleheim, demanded he yield to its embrace; its call, nigh irresistible.

It wanted him.

It hungered for him, just as it had hungered for Azathoth. It was a yearning that he could sense: a tugging at the edge of his consciousness that became a whispering not in his ears, but in his mind.

The voices returned.

Let go, said one voice.

Do not fear, just let go, said another.

Come to us, it said, pitch changing, growing higher and higher, ever more shrill.

It's not too late. Come to us.

We need you.

Faster and faster came the words of the demonic chorus.

Let go! You belong with us. You are one of us.

You can still...be...god.

God!

Come home to your kingdom!

What have I done? thought Thetan. That portal be an alien thing of ancient evil with motives dark and foul. What terror have I unleashed upon the world?

An evil far worse than Azathoth

It had to be thus. Or else, he was truly mad. Mad beyond all redemption or recovery.

A dread hung over him, helm to boot. The hairs stood on his arms and nape. And he felt fear. Not the butterflies that plagued him before a battle, but true fear. The kind that common men so often felt, danger looming. The feeling, wholly alien to him. Whence it sprang, he knew not, save to say, its origin was not within him. 'Twas an unnatural fear. Palpable -- it seeped in, polluted, corrupted. Foul sorcery it was, and of a nature beyond his ken. He pushed it from his thoughts, forced it back with indomitable will. When the portal first opened, that had been easy to do despite all its temptations, its promises of glory and grandeur -- what with Azathoth railing before him and death beckoning on all sides. No sorcery, however foul, could garner more than his slightest notice. But now, on the brink of falling into the gateway itself, the fear overtook him. The demonic voices grew in power and influence by the moment. They sought to distract and overwhelm. To paralyze. To make him their *thing*. Their slave. He'd never allow that. Not Thetan. Never. The notion of it was absurd, yet his instincts warned him that those mumblings were underpinned with dark sorcery of frightful power. Power that might well be his match.

The roaring torrent flung everything nearby at the gateway's maw whose surface was darker than dark, blacker than pitch; a dozen feet in diameter, its lower arc cut off by the ground. A fallen shield hurtled toward it, but just as had every object before it, it inexplicably slowed and crashed to a halt against its surface. When the shield slowed, the portal's surface reached for it of its own accord, fingering outward, gray, wriggling, amorphous tendrils of living liquid or energy, dense but yielding, covetous and malevolent -- the embodiment of the voices of the damned. Thetan knew now that the voices and the tendrils were one and the same. They enveloped the shield and sucked it through the veil betwixt the worlds into whatever uncharted madness lay beyond.

Uncharacteristically, Thetan hadn't thought through what would happen after he banished Azathoth. All his energy had been focused on putting the Sphere in the right position, getting Azathoth close enough, getting the portal opened, and somehow pushing the lord through. That was the end of the plan. An impossible plan. But against all odds, it succeeded. Azathoth was gone. Banished from Midgaard, hopefully forevermore.

But the yawning portal to the *Nether Realms* lay wide.

And hungry.

How to close it?

Thetan knew not.

And even if he knew a way, he could take no action, lest he lose his grip and hurtle into the abyss in Azathoth's wake. Perhaps that was a fitting fate, an appropriate end to his story, the skein of his life already overlong.

71

JUTENHEIM
ANGLOTOR TOWER
THE TEMPLE OF POWER
YEAR 1267, 4TH AGE

FREM SORLONS

Frem charged the Nifleheim beasts, courage bolstered by the ranal blade he wielded, lately gifted him by Ezerhauten, his own weapons of long years forever lost in the deeps of Svartleheim. All the Sithians carried at least one ranal blade, rarities in the modern world, their ancient purpose and forging long forgotten, even disbelieved, by all but the learned few.

But the Sithians -- Theta's men -- hadn't forgotten ranal's singular purpose: to smite inhuman invaders from the *Nether Realms*. Where honest steel and common iron faltered and turned aside, no matter the power behind the blow, ranal bit deep. Why that was, was hard to say for they were half the weight of common steel and no sharper, though they held their edge thrice and more as long. Some said ranal's special efficacy derived from the extraterrestrial origins of its key component -- that strange metallic obsidian, an esoteric substance found only at the site of fallen stars, never once recovered in a natural vein, not even from the deepest mines or tunnels. A substance of the Outer Spheres was it – what better to put down beasts of similar otherworldly origin. Frem rarely pondered such things overlong. For him, it was enough to know, ranal worked.

A monster out of darkest nightmare was the arachnidian fiend that fronted Frem, fire and bloodlust in its inhuman eyes, no spark of mercy or love in its stony heart. Frem had never seen its like; not that its aspect was any worse than many others he'd fought, just...different. Until lately, he'd forgotten he'd faced such beasts before, his memories suppressed by sorcery, and later restored after he escaped the Svart tunnels, though ironically, he couldn't recall how.

The Nether creature lunged with shocking speed, its forelegs swiping, claws dripping putrid ooze, deadly poison promised by its fangs. Frem's kick was faster. Slammed his boot to its chest as it reared up; stopped it in its tracks. He slammed the sword's pommel just above its central eye -- a crushing blow that shattered bone.

The creature staggered, legs rubbery. Frem stepped forward and plunged his blade through its back. It squealed and quivered, legs skittering, black blood dousing the floor.

Another fiend came on, the first's death throes incomplete. This one, a monster, taller and broader than Frem, shaped like a man, but with four arms and skin of shiny black pitch, hairless, muscles bulging, great horns sprouting from head and shoulders -- a devil of the Stygian depths. Frem slashed its chest twice, making deft use of his sword's range -- the first blow deflected, the other opened a deep gash, though strangely, Frem saw no blood flow.

The horned creature roared, a mouthful of gleaming fangs. It lunged inside Frem's reach and its claws raked his borrowed armor, ripped away steel plates and knocked the ranal blade from his grasp with a strength far beyond mortal man, resilience to match.

Undeterred, Frem kicked, punched, pummeled, spun, and kicked again. His uppercut caught the fiend's jaw -- a blow that would've snapped any man's neck. The creature staggered back. In a flash, Frem scooped up his sword, and thrust; took the beast through the abdomen. He yanked the blade out, spun, and swung for its neck. The creature raised a bony arm. The ranal's cut severed the limb, stunning the creature, but failed to strike its head. Frem chopped twice, and two more demonic arms polluted the floor -- a yellowish goo that was its blood, oozed from its deepest wounds.

Frem's next blow split its head in two.

As he watched it drop, Frem felt alive again, the battle lust taking hold, the adrenaline rushing through his veins. His heart pounded, lungs strained. He knew who he was again. What he was fighting for. What he fought against.

He fought monsters again in defense of Midgaard -- just as he was meant to do, just as he had always done at Theta's side...at Thetan's side. He was not merely Sir Frem Sorlons any longer -- as he had been those last three score years. He was more than that again -- at last, himself again. He remembered his name of old, the moniker he'd carried for ages beyond count.

He was Hogar the Invincible, the Eternal who stood at Thetan's side from the beginning -- one of the original thirteen rebels, one of The Fallen. And he was with his comrades as he was always meant to be. Ezerhauten was there, once called Dekkar so long ago, another of The Fallen. And Putnam was there, fighting tooth and nail. So was Royce and Carol, Lex and Ward, Bradik and Grainer, Torak and Wikkle, Borrel, Stanik, and good old Moag Lugron. Even Ma-Grak Stowron still fought at their side, all but he trained by Frem, and Ezerhauten, and Thetan himself. They, and two score more Sithian knights battled like berserkers against the monsters from the void, the creatures from the pit.

The Arkons' training had elevated the Sithians' skills far beyond that of other mortal men. It was only that training that had seen them through the darks of Svartleheim, the horrors of the Isle of Dagon, the subterranean vaults beneath Tragoss Mor, and all the other horrors they'd weathered on that fateful mission. And unlike the Eotrus who fought the Nifleheimers months before in the Temple of Guymaog, every Sithian held ranal blades, and with them, could injure the Nifleheimers as if they were ordinary creatures. And that, of course, changed everything.

VIGRID VALLEY
FIMBULWINTER - YEAR 3
LAST DAY OF THE AGE OF MYTH AND LEGEND

THETAN THE LIGHTBRINGER

Only because he'd been farther from the gateway than Azathoth, and not been taken unawares by its opening, had Thetan so far staved off the lord's fate, for the gateway's unnatural pull reduced with distance for reasons he could not fathom. Still, but for a random boulder's presence, Thetan would not have stayed his slide; he'd have followed Azathoth and his henchmen into the void. He felt the fool for not preparing better. He was always ready for anything. Five steps ahead of any opponent, every contingency marked and ready.

But he'd never betrayed *god* before. That made things more...complicated.

More bits of armor and weapons flew past Thetan and plunged into the gateway. So too did the bodies of the nearby dead, those lately fallen in the great battle between Azathoth's forces and Thetan's rebels. More than a few living men flew by him too, screaming and cursing, begging and howling, praying for help or deliverance.

But Azathoth was gone.

What god remained to hear their prayers?

In the chaos, Thetan could not tell who they

were: loyalist, rebel, or Northman.

His only hopes were that the gateway might close of its own accord, or that Lasifer might launch some sorcery that would bring it crashing to a close. But if swallowing a god was not enough to sate the thing, then what would be? Devouring the world itself? More? The moons? The stars of the heavens? The whole of the firmament? How deep was its hunger? How far might its power stretch?

Thetan tried to think amid the maelstrom. What could he do to close the portal? What could he do to save himself? What help could he hold out for? He arched his neck and narrowed his eyes against the wind to look back toward his men, though he saw little through the gale and cloud of snow flurries it arose. He hoped for an outstretched hand. A dangling rope. Anything to grab onto, to anchor himself. To crouch behind something larger than his boulder. Anything. But what few men he saw were in the same straights as he, even a dozen yards farther afield, holding on to whatever they could for dear life.

Thetan's endurance was rarely tested, but was not without its limits. Erelong, his grip would falter. His bag of tricks held no escape that he could conjure...save for perhaps the Ankh. He resolved to hold it outstretched before him if he fell. If luck was with him, perhaps the infernal portal would reject that artifact and bar it and him at its entry. A foolish hope perhaps, based on nothing but conjecture, but it was all he had, unless Lasifer appeared and offered deliverance. But the old serpent was nowhere to be found, and in truth, could never be found, except when he wanted it. The king of elusive lurkers was the old Gnome wizard. He could hide forever in a man's own shadow.

And then, as if his mind had conjured him up, Lasifer appeared by his side and struggled too against the gale, sliding forward despite his best efforts. Thetan reached out, grabbed his hand, and pulled him close behind the boulder.

"You know what to do?" shouted Lasifer, his voice quavering as he struggled to be heard over the wind.

"How in Helheim would I know what to do?" said Thetan. "We talked only of opening this thing, not closing it. I thought it would close of its own accord when he fell through."

"A foolish shortsighted notion," said Lasifer. "Why would you think that?"

"How can we close it?" said Thetan. "Will its power wane over time or not?"

"You must destroy the Sphere, of course," said Lasifer. "Smash it to a thousand bits. It can't work after that, now can it?"

"I can't get to it," said Thetan.

"Of course you can...if you have the courage. I'd use your hammer if I were you."

That was enough for Thetan to deduce the rest. He must let go of the boulder. Let the wind take him. And as he flew toward the portal, he must smash the Sphere to bits and hope that the gateway collapsed before it pulled him through or sliced him in two as it closed.

"Ha, ha," cackled Lasifer. "Have you the courage to do what must be done, Lightbringer?

Have you the courage?"

The Sphere hovered several feet above the ground beside the gateway, unaffected by the wind or any of the many things that had crashed into it on their way to the portal. It hung there, immobile, immovable, eternal. And it had to be destroyed.

Thetan tied the Ankh to his right hand with a thick cord. He pulled out his battle hammer, held it in his left hand. He looked at Lasifer, he didn't know why. Mayhap, for some word of encouragement, or to give the old fiend the opportunity to wish him luck.

Lasifer leered at him and said, "This is your chance, *son of man*, to show us your mettle, prove yourself worthy."

Thetan cared not for the Gnome's words and less for his tone, and didn't respond. He had proved himself a thousand times over, or so he believed, and had no desire or need to impress the wizard or anyone else. Just as he always did, he would do what needed to be done.

Thetan stood, leaned forward into the wind, and let it take him. Arms outstretched before him, he flew headfirst, no way to stop, no way to steer, no control. Somehow, he had to maintain his angle or all would be lost. He felt the acceleration as he drew closer to the portal. Overcoming the wind, he pulled back his hand and swung the hammer with devastating power. A skilled warrior could've swung that weapon a thousand times in similar circumstance and never hit the Sphere, such was the madness of that situation: the breakneck speed, the pain, the disorienting cacophony. But Thetan was no normal man, no normal Arkon, no common hero. He was something different. Something special. And when his hammer came down, it struck the Sphere. Not straight on, mind you, a glancing blow but one from a Titan such as he was powerful indeed.

The Sphere shattered!

Black shards of crystal flew in all directions, the Sphere's blood red tinge now gone.

With the Ankh held before him, Thetan slammed into the portal.

The gateway did not yield.

The abyss that it was half a moment before was now solid and impassable, but whether the instantaneous change was due to the Sphere's destruction or the mere presence of the Ankh against its surface, who could say? All that mattered was that the portal did not swallow Thetan.

A few moments later the wind dissipated. The gateway was closed.

JUTENHEIM
ANGLOTOR TOWER
THE TEMPLE OF POWER
YEAR 1267, 4TH AGE

"**D**estroy the Orb, now," shouted Theta to his men as he battled Korrgonn, "or Midgaard is doomed!"

Theta's hammer had fallen away, no time to draw a sword in that close combat, but he managed a dagger: Wotan Dal -- Odin's blade -- a fitting weapon for the contest.

Korrgonn attacked Theta with the Nifleheim dagger that cut the heart from Uriel the Bold and slit the throats of a hundred innocents in a Tragoss Morian temple, or so claimed Ob and Tanch.

The titans slashed and stabbed with their short blades, punched and kicked, their movements a blur. Thrust and parry, dodge, block, spin, sidestep, and stab — they wove a dance of death the like of which the world had rarely seen. Unlike in fiction and fairy tale, such battles rarely lasted overlong. Most duels, even amongst well-matched masters, lasted but a handful or two of heartbeats before a decisive blow was struck. But Theta and Korrgonn's contest raged on and on, each blow parried or dodged despite its speed or power. Blood droplets showered the floor, but whose, no witness could say. Neither combatant slowed, faltered, or paid heed to any injury, grevious or small; their energies, boundless.

As they battled, the foot soldiers of dread Nifleheim vaulted through the yawning portal promising naught but horror and death to all they encountered. With them came a nauseating bestial and brimstone stench so foul it was a weapon in itself. Those disparate creatures of nightmare, one more horrible than the next, came on as if they'd been lined up, crowded together, waiting for their chance to invade the world of man and savoring the opportunity to sate their hunger for blood and souls. They soon outnumbered the humans, two, three, and four to one, no end to them.

His attention fixed on Korrgonn, a six legged Nifleheimer crashed into Theta's leg even as a massive tusked and snouted creature, more swine than man, leapt at his head, its agility belying its bulk. The six leg's bone-snapping pincers and claws clacked like mad as they assaulted Theta's armor, denting and rending where even Dyvers steel would've faltered. Ignoring the six leg's attacks, Theta caught the swine midair, spun, and flung it at Korrgonn. The terrific impact staggered the godling and sent him reeling backward several steps.

Wotan Dal slammed through the skull of the six-leg, instantly killing it, but three of its fellows took its place, one much larger than the rest. As they pressed Theta toward the wall, he worked his blade up and down, crushed their defenses,

337

and sliced through one skull, then another. The last creature shrieked in agony as its powerful jaws bit through Theta's leg armor, which was an alloy of iron, carbon, and ranal — the last, a poison to the Nifleheimer and all its ilk.

Poison or no, another moment and the Nifleheimer's teeth would tear away flesh and sever arteries. Before Theta could smite the creature, Korrgonn flew at him like a missile, his Nifleheim blade extended before him; its unholy runes — the foul script of the *Nether Realms* — glowed red as death along the midnight blade. The Nether Script's geometric patterns were comprised of shapes and angles that confounded the mind and scrambled the senses, painful to behold, anathema to mortal man. Peer too closely for too long and insanity would take hold, its grip relentless.

Korrgonn crashed into Theta with a squealing rending of metal, and drove him so hard against the wall that the rock crushed and crumbled under the impact, stone dust and shards flying. A common man's sternum and ribs would've snapped under that assault, but Theta merely groaned, his breath lost, and his eyes wide.

Theta found the strength to slam Wotan Dal through the last six leg's eye, which killed it, but stuck fast his blade. Theta abandoned it and a split second later, punched Korrgonn with such power that the godling flew backward several feet and crashed to the floor.

But the damage had been done.

Having rent a hole through his fabled armor, Korrgonn's Nifleheim blade was stuck to the hilt through Theta's abdomen, red blood pouring forth, the blade hissing and sizzling where it touched his flesh.

VIGRID VALLEY
FIMBULWINTER - YEAR 3
LAST DAY OF THE AGE OF MYTH AND LEGEND

Thetan felt as if he were floating on his back, pulled by a river's current, white water roaring and splashing. He wanted to open his eyes, swim for the shore however far it was, the frigid water be damned. The shore was far away, tired as he was, mayhap farther than he could reach. But he couldn't even try. His eyes wouldn't open, arms wouldn't work. He was lucky he wasn't drowning.

Water rushed around him, the current picking up.

Or was it wind?

Indistinct, growing louder. It was wind. Then a firm hand gripped his shoulder, spoke his name.

It was one of his brothers, he knew the voice, but he could not name him or recall his face.

His brother called his name again and shook him harder. For a long time, Thetan struggled to open his eyes. And when he finally did...he was back in the world. He sucked in a deep breath and felt the pain of being alive, of all the wounds he'd suffered that day: body, mind, and spirit.

He lay on his back — on firm ground. He must have lost consciousness when he crashed against the gateway. Gabriel knelt by his side, it was *his* voice he'd heard. Lasifer was with him, a grin on his wrinkled face.

"Are you badly hurt?" said Gabriel.

"Did it work or did I dream it?" said Thetan as he tested his limbs. Everything hurt but still functioned.

"It worked," said Gabriel. "I saw him fall through and all his cronies with him: Bhaal, Iblis, Arioch, the lot of them. And you broke the Sphere. How you scored that strike in that maelstrom, I cannot fathom. Luck shined on you this day. On us all."

"Not with the dead," said Lasifer, "and there's far more of them about than not."

"Courage begets luck," said Thetan.

"Only when it doesn't get you killed," said Lasifer as he looked around. "I wonder if they'll get up. The Sphere is capable of stranger things, you know."

"Who will get up?" said Gabriel.

"The dead," said Lasifer. "Pay attention. And I didn't say they will, only that they might."

"Have you gone mad, Gnome?" said Gabriel. "Dead is dead."

"Until it's not," said Lasifer. "Given all the sorcery adrift in the ether hereabouts this day, if they're hungry enough, they may well get up," he said as he looked around again, concern on his face. "That could get quite messy. Quite messy, indeed. Best we get gone from here while the getting is good."

"I don't fear the dead," said Thetan.

"You should," said Lasifer. "When they are hungry, they are relentless."

341

Thetan struggled to a sitting position and looked to the portal. Still there, black as pitch. Closed. Solid. No opening to be found. "Help me up," he said.

Gabriel offered him a hand, hoisted him up. A bit unsteady, Thetan stepped to the side of the gateway...and it disappeared. The gateway had no thickness, and from the rear it was not there at all. One could see it from the one direction only. From all other directions, the space it occupied appeared empty. "A strange thing this is," said Thetan as he studied the portal. "What of Wotan?"

"No tougher man has ever lived," said Gabriel. "He survived the bleeding, last I saw him. Headed back to his troops under his own power."

"What he did took courage few could muster," said Thetan. "I don't even want to think about being in his position."

"Most would say the same about what you did, brother," said Gabriel. "You stood alone against the lord himself. And won."

"I did what needed doing, the same as always. The same as you did, and Wotan, and the others. At long last, we're free to make our own choices. Or we will be once this battle is over. It yet rages in the distance, I see."

"The field is vast," said Gabriel. "No doubt, most do not yet know that the lord is gone, his lieutenants lost. Once reliable word reaches them, the loyalists will lay down their arms and disperse. Leaderless, they'll have little choice. Many will flock to our banners. We've won. It's over, or near enough."

"Ha, ha, ha, ha," cackled Lasifer. "You fools. It's not over. Not by a long shot. The fun has barely begun."

Thetan and Gabriel both looked to the Gnome quizzically.

"What are you babbling about now?" said Gabriel.

"Take a look," said Lasifer, pointing at the closed portal.

"It remains closed," said Gabriel. "We shut it down. The thing is dead."

"Aargh, you're blind and deaf, the both of you," said Lasifer. "I told you, dead isn't always dead. That gateway is hungry and it's not through with you yet, my boys, oh no, not yet."

And then Thetan heard a muffled rumbling akin to a far away avalanche: stones rolling over stones down a distant hillside. A bulge appeared in the portal's center, as if the darkness were reaching out, pushing through, trying to re-enter Midgaard.

"Will it open again?" said Gabriel, panic in his voice. "Lasifer, what do you know of this? Speak plainly now."

"Spare us any riddles," said Thetan.

Lasifer shook his head in frustration. "Worldgates are fickle things," he said. "Who knows what excitement it has in store for us before it's done for the day."

"How do we shut it down?" said Thetan, "permanently, this time. Tell me quick and true, Gnome."

"I'm certain that you'll find a way," said Lasifer coldly. "There's always a way. That's how the multiverse works. Best to remember that. Though finding the way may not be as easy as you would like. There are often...sacrifices involved. Painful sacrifices, much like the bleeding, the eye, and so forth. Oh, you might want to step lively back from the portal. Quickly now, lads, or you'll join the dead."

Gabriel and Thetan stepped well to the side of the gateway and in good time for then came an explosion that rocked the valley and knocked them, and every man within two hundred yards, from their feet. The hard black material that capped the closed gateway exploded, shattering into a million shards, though the opening that was the gateway itself endured.

Darkness streamed from the portal like a black tide that rolled in on the air. As fast as it did, it pulled out even faster, but the gateway now lay open again, though no wind or pressure came with it this time. Only a moment passed before they heard a thunderous roar of some otherworldly monstrosity.

"We've got to close it," said Gabriel, "before Azathoth, or something worse, comes through. Otherwise, it will have all been for nothing. Why did it open again? Did we not use enough blood? How do we stop it?"

"Destroy the Sphere's shards," said Thetan. "Some bits of it must yet have power."

"Will that work?" said Gabriel to Lasifer.

The Gnome shrugged. "How would I know? I'm just an old Gnome," he said with a grin.

Thetan took up his battle hammer and searched the ground for fragments of the

Sphere; Gabriel did the same. There were many shards, truth be told, many commingled with the black material that had capped the gateway. Every shard they found, they smashed to bits as fast as they could.

But the gateway refused to close.

The roaring from beyond the portal grew louder by the moment.

"Hurry, hurry," said Lasifer, his tone maniacal. "Something hungry this way comes," he said, a wide grin on his face as he danced one foot to the other.

"Keep searching," shouted Thetan sharply. "Smash every shard."

As they scoured the ground, the portal suddenly grew in size, opening wider, its diameter broadening tenfold in mere moments. A deafening roar burst from the portal, a rush of air with it. Smoke and brimstone assaulted the men's noses.

"Get down," shouted Thetan as he dived to the ground, flattening against the earth. Gabriel did the same. The ground violently shook and from out of the portal flew a huge creature, its underside hurtling by mere inches above the men's backs. Black and serpentine, its size beyond comprehension, its stench, reptilian mixed with sulfur and other noxious fumes that made the men gag. As it passed through the portal, the creature unfolded bat-like wings — wings that went on forever, reaching for the horizon, blotting out the sun. Thetan glanced up, ready to spring to his feet once the thing had passed, but there seemed no end to its long neck, broad body, and giant, barbed tail. In addition to the wings, four legs it had, claws longer than swords, teeth aplenty in a mouth that could swallow the largest Olyphant. A dragon it was, right out of olden legend, but far larger and more fearsome than any storybook creature. The name the Northmen gave it was Nidhug.

Upon hearing Nidhug's roar, the battle across the great valley of Vigrid immediately stopped. All eyes turned toward the dragon, which had scales of blackish red, the deep color of dried blood. Like ticks, upon its vast wings clung the ravenous undead. It rose into the air and as it passed over the battlefield it lowered its serpentine neck, opened jaws filled of fangs, and ejected a great stream of fiery liquid that set ablaze a hundred men and sent them screaming into the afterlife. Beyond that single deadly blast, Nidhug paid the Midgaardians little heed, and flew west until it passed out of sight.

The gateway narrowed to its former size after the dragon passed through, but the portal did not close.

And Nidhug did not journey to Midgaard by its lonesome.

On the dragon's heels came the wretched denizens of the pit, the very hordes of hell. They thundered through the gateway: foot and hoof, wing and belly, claw and boot, roaring in anger, or was it joy -- the world of men for the taking, blood and souls, all they could eat. Lasifer looked on and cackled with maniacal glee.

In those days, people had no names for the

creatures that spewed from that infernal portal, for in large measure such monsters had not existed on Midgaard before that day. First amongst them were great numbers of giants of all varieties: Storm Giants, Formorians, Cyclops, Ogre, Frost and Fire Giants, the sons of Nifleheim, Frostheim, Muspelheim, and beyond. Some were ten feet tall. Others fifteen, twenty, even thirty feet in height. About the Giants' feet loped hell hounds, devil dogs, and great wolves, some few larger than horses. But so too came countless spirits and unnatural beasts of all types, and the worst in many ways, the ravenous undead, walking corpses whose only purpose was to tear apart and devour the living.

And there were more. Dragons of many types came through, though none akin in size to Nidhug; Liches, Lycanthropes, and Blood Lords; Hags and Harpies; Wights and Wraiths; Demons and Devils; Bugbears and Bogeyman; Ghouls and Ghosts; Goblin by the thousands; and every other type of monster you've ever heard of and that truly existed. They were all there. That's how they came to Midgaard. Before that day, if they existed at all, it was in naught but nightmares, fireside tales, or fevered visions. Now, they were real. They were here. And most had but one purpose: to eat our bodies. Some others also wanted to dine on our souls.

JUTENHEIM
ANGLOTOR TOWER
THE TEMPLE OF POWER
YEAR 1267, 4TH AGE

A bovine monstrosity leaped through the gateway from Nifleheim; its two huge hooves slammed to the floor with such force the stone cracked. Two great horns sprouted from the creature's bull-like head; its body, broad and thick with a barrel chest, its bulging arms twice the size of the largest man's. Eight feet tall it was, a spiked war hammer in its grip. Yellow fire burned in its eye sockets and a long black tongue flicked from betwixt its maw.

The bull stepped forward and a Sithian charged it, undeterred by the fear he must have felt. A single swipe from the bull's hammer flung the man through the air to crash against the far wall. A kick sent another knight tumbling through the air. The bull advanced, snorting and growling.

Ezerhauten blocked its path.

The bull's eyes focused on the tall knight with the dragon crest. It knew him at once and grinned.

"Dekkar the traitor," it said in a human voice, though its words were of an archaic dialect. "For an Age, I've yearned to front you again. Your evil deeds at long last come due."

"Mammon?" said Ezerhauten, recognizing the voice, somewhat changed though it was.

"None other."

"What has become of you? You are a monster. A thing."

"What?" said Mammon. He tilted his brutish head to the side, pausing a moment, eyes squinting. "The Traitor yet beguiles you; this place reeks of sorcery. Your eyes betray you; open them wider and see the truth."

"My eyes are ever clear, old friend," said Ezerhauten, "and I pity you. Turnabout now, and I'll let you live, in honor of the good man that you once were. One chance only."

Mammon shook his head and charged, hammer swinging.

Ezerhauten ducked below the weapon, sidestepped, spun, and slashed low as Mammon barreled forward. His sword bit Mammon's ankle deep enough to hobble him, though the bull paid the wound no heed. Ezerhauten ducked another hammer strike but his second slash missed Mammon's other leg, the bull's speed deceptive.

Ezerhauten bounded in close and slammed his elbow to the underside of Mammon's jaw, sending him stumbling back. Ezerhauten tried to close again, but Mammon's kick caught him in the chest, sent him flying twenty feet across the room to crash against the stone wall.

Ezerhauten came down on his haunches and then stood straight up, breathing deeply, an evil smile on his face. "That the best you can do?" he shouted.

Mammon charged Ezerhauten at superhuman speed, head lowered, growling all the while, muscles rippling, horns forward like a bull.

At the last moment, Ezerhauten leapt to the side with preternatural swiftness.

Mammon crashed into the wall.

The titanic impact pulverized the stone, which only stopped Mammon when he'd plunged three feet through its depths.

Ezerhauten spun back and thrust his sword into Mammon's spine, once and then again, precise strikes both. Ezerhauten knew just where to aim, though he couldn't be certain that the bull's physiology was the same as a man's. The blade sank deep, Mammon's armor, and his hide, little defense to that ranal blade expertly used.

Mammon's body shook violently as it staggered back from the hole. He flopped to his knees on rubber legs, his arms limp. He turned his head toward Ezerhauten, a look of disbelief on his inhuman visage. "This cannot be," he mumbled, black foam oozing from his mouth.

Ezerhauten's next slash cut halfway through Mammon's neck and sent black blood spurting. Mammon groaned, collapsed face down to the ground, and did not move again.

VIGRID VALLEY
FIMBULWINTER - YEAR 3
LAST DAY OF THE AGE OF MYTH AND LEGEND

Gabriel took up his horn and blew a warning blast to alert the men about the further incursion at the gateway. Everyone had seen Nidhug, but those far afield did not yet know of the creatures that followed.

Not far away, Wotan, a golden helm atop his head, his spear Gungnir to hand, pulled himself into his saddle, astride Sleipnir, a white horse of regal bearing and mammoth size. The great lord was unsteady from his wounds, but determined to survive the day or else meet death head-on in battle. He planned to set off at once after the dragon. He turned at Gabriel's horn and his eyes widened at what thundered toward him.

The denizens of the *Nether Realms* streamed into Midgaard by the hundreds, by the thousands. As they did, Thetan frantically rummaged about the ground, hammer in hand, and smashed every Sphere fragment that he could find. Beside him, Gabriel did the same. What a strange sight that was, the great knights on their knees, pounding the ground with hammers as the hordes of hell streamed by mere yards away.

"By all that's holy," shouted Gabriel, "there is no end to them. Every moment births a dozen more. If we can't close this portal, all the world will be overrun."

Luckily for the two fallen Arkons, the invaders did not linger on the gateway's doorstep. They plowed forward in a mad rush and paid the two men no heed. Most of the monsters raced away at random, some by their lonesomes, others with countless of their fellows. Any man that dared bar their path they set upon, but most of the monsters had no interest in a lingering fight, though some few rejoiced in it and pounced upon any man, living or dead, that they encountered.

Some of the creatures feasted on the wounded and the dead across the battlefield, but most fled the area with their best speed. Whether that was due to confusion and fear about being suddenly dropped in Midgaard in the midst of a battle, or was part of some devious plan previously laid, no man could say.

Throughout the valley, the former combatants — loyalist, rebel, and Northmen — lined up, shoulder to shoulder, to meet the creatures' charge. Human fought human no longer. Now they joined together as one people against invaders who brought nothing but rage and hunger and offered naught but death and wanton destruction.

Arrayed for war though they were, the men had battled all day long and were weary and wounded, their formations scattered. And though they were experts in battle, their experience came battling other men. They didn't know how to fight monsters, creatures, things.

Not to say that monsters didn't exist in Midgaard before the gateway opened. They did, in far-flung corners of the world, but only in sparing numbers. Only the most learned scholars and widely traveled adventurers had ever seen such things. So the troops, loyalist and rebel alike, as experienced as they were, were quite unprepared for the battle they found themselves embroiled in. A battle not for freedom and independence, but for the fate of humankind.

VIGRID VALLEY
FIMBULWINTER - YEAR 3
LAST DAY OF THE AGE OF MYTH AND LEGEND

THETAN THE LIGHTBRINGER

"**Y**ou did this," shouted Thetan as he fronted the shriveled Gnome, every shard he'd found, pulverized, yet the gateway stood wide. Men screamed in the distance as monsters not meant to walk their world tore them apart and feasted on their blood and souls. "You knew this would happen when I shattered the Sphere; your plan from the beginning. Why?"

"Why?" said Lasifer whose confused expression turned to a grin, his eyes wide and wild. "Each to his nature, don't they say? I do so like to hear folks scream."

That answer shocked Thetan and he hesitated a moment. He'd long known the Gnome was shifty, and being a wizard he wasn't altogether rational, but Thetan didn't think him mad. And certainly not evil. Had his mind suddenly snapped? Or had evil possessed him? It made little sense since Thetan had always been a good judge of character. There was no time to waste. Thetan's hand shot forward to grab the Gnome by the throat. He'd reveal how to close the portal or Thetan would crush the life from him before he could manage more mischief. He didn't want to do that, but the Gnome was dangerous, and that left Thetan few options.

The trouble was, Thetan's hand passed through the Gnome as if he were not there. Shocked though he was, Thetan swatted at him twice more, all to no effect. He stepped closer and bashed the Gnome with his shield. It too passed through him, the Gnome grinning all the while. The old wizard was right there, plain as anything, yet not there, as insubstantial as the wind. Thetan could not touch him.

"Damn your sorcery," shouted Thetan. "If enough come through, you'll die too, Gnome; your magic won't hold out forever. How do I close it? Tell me before it's too late."

"Oh, how dramatic," said Lasifer. "Appealing to my fears, my desire for self-preservation. How quaint, Lightbringer. I have no fear of these things, however fearsome they be. I am no mortal man to be gnawed upon by dark things puked from Helheim."

"You are no mere Gnomish wizard or bumbling court jester, not now, if ever you were," said Thetan, "if even you are the Lasifer I've known these many years. Who or what are you? Some fiend or doppleganger? Name yourself. Show yourself. Or do you fear *me* so?"

"Who and what I am is no business of yours, except that you are correct -- I am far more than I seem, and discerning that, however late, makes you a bit less daft than I feared. I suppose that's good in its way, for entertainment's sake if nothing else. You do entertain me, Thetan. You always have, in your own dull way. That's what this is all about, of course. Entertainment. *My* entertainment. As far as I'm concerned, that's why you all exist. Or at least, why I allow you to continue to exist, though I admit, after today, there will be a lot fewer of you, a shrinking down of the species so to speak. The question is, will it drop all the way to extinct or shall you remain extant? Big words, I know, big words, far more than a warrior's brain can handle. Oh, yes, I know. I suppose it'll have to close eventually. If not, they'll kill you all quite quickly, the fun over lickety-split -- at least as far as your kind goes. Those beasts, left to their own devices, are more boring even than your lot. They'll not keep me in cackles for a single age. That won't do at all. No, not at all."

"How do we close the portal?" said Thetan.

"What a one-track mind," spat Lasifer. "All business, bluster, and bravado. A bit of variety might do you some good, you know. Perhaps, a woman in your life would help? Oh...but who would have you, such an oaf. You're entertaining in your own way, I'll admit. But you'll not like my answer, son of man, but tell you I will, for the fun of it, if nothing else." He peered about conspiratorially, as if to make certain no one else could hear. "The eye and the blood are not yet done," he said and cackled some more.

"Speak not in riddles, creature. I've no time for them. Plain words, nothing but."

"Of course, plain words, of course, in honor of dullards and dunces everywhere." Lasifer slowed his next sentence, enunciating each word. "The sacrifice is not yet complete. The priest and the

356

king must pass through the gateway, down into the *Nether Realms* -- a trip like no other, a journey to be remembered -- well, for a few minutes at least, before he dies, torn to pieces, soul eaten and such. In payment for the trip, the Worldgate will be sated and close completely until called upon to open once more by another ritual sometime in the future, or mayhap the past – it really depends on how you look at things, your...temporal perspective, if you will. Oh, I know, that's all gibberish to you, Monkey Boy, but you asked the question, so don't complain about the answer. Always the complainer; quite annoying."

Thetan turned toward where Wotan fought in a desperate battle against a giant wolf, a beast five times the size of the largest dire wolf Thetan had ever seen."

"Fenrir, it's called," said Lasifer. "A magnificent beast. The northman's match, I'd wager, more so in his decrepit state. Best make haste to his side, hero, for the Worldgate may well not accept a corpse as a sacrifice, and instead remain open for who knows how long. That won't go well for your entire world, methinks."

"How do I know you speak the truth about the sacrifice?" said Thetan as he marched to Wotan's aid.

Lasifer cackled and then spoke a sentence in a voice that almost exactly mimicked Azathoth's, "You must have faith in me, beloved -- this one...last...time. Ha, ha! Make haste, hero. Make haste before his life lay waste. No doubt, you'll

357

soon be dead. The horror, the dread, ha, ha!"

Lasifer stepped back and took it all in, spinning around this way and that as a desperate battle spread across the valley. "And now, the fun begins," muttered Lasifer, the Old One.

JUTENHEIM
ANGLOTOR TOWER
THE TEMPLE OF POWER
YEAR 1267, 4TH AGE

PUTNAM

Sergeant Putnam long ago lost count of how many battles he'd fought during his career. Some of them had been easy — that is to say, he'd had little trouble evading serious injury or death; some were hard, meaning he'd gotten banged up or darned lucky; others, he'd barely lived through, and once or twice, for a while, he'd thought he hadn't. But in all his years there were few battles as dangerous or as frightening as that of the inner sanctum beneath Anglotor keep. It was a wild melee with monsters out of Nifleheim, or some such place, not that it mattered. Fighting creatures from who knows where always dropped you directly into the "hard battle" category, if you were lucky. If not, well, you'd end up dead right quick. Plenty of good men did. Putnam lost more than a few friends that way. That's the way things were fighting with the Sithian Mercenary Company.

Of course, they weren't traditional mercenaries at all.

They were Lord Angle Theta's men.

Always had been; always would be, trickery of late to fool the League, notwithstanding.

The job being what it was, most of Theta's men didn't live to go gray, but they oft went out in a blaze of glory. Some of them longed for that; usually got them a lengthy write-up in the company annals. That got you remembered, talked about and toasted, long after your time. A slice of immortality and respect worth more to a warrior than a buxom queen's weight in gold.

But not to Putnam. He figured that glory was for the young and for the stupid. He fancied the idea of being remembered, but he preferred hanging about this side of Valhalla for as long as practical, so he played things smart. Principled, but smart. That's how he lingered long enough to get the grays at his temples and sprinkled here and there amidst the short cut brown. That, and being one of the scrappiest fighters this side of Ezerhauten.

He needed every bit of scrappyness that day. The Anglotor Nifleheimers were vaguely man shaped, meaning they had a head, a torso, and most of them walked upright and had arms and legs, but not always two of each. There were myriad varieties, some resembling one animal or another, others being lizardish or insectoid, some of them looking like nightmares, but all were hell-bent on killing every human in the sanctum, and given the chance, every human everywhere, the bastards. Probably wanted to eat them too. There were far easier ways to fill one's belly, so why monsters always wanted to eat folks was one of life's mysteries Putnam figured he'd never square away, so he'd stopped trying.

Many times since entering Theta's service, Putnam had fought "creatures" — things most men would name monsters and run screaming from while peeing themselves. He'd also fought most every variety of wild beast, some giants, various and sundry wizards and their ilk, man-eating fish, flying things like giant bats, birds, and worse, and on occasion, he'd fought things that hailed from the *Nether Realms,* Helheim, or some such weird place. Usually, such monsters caused trouble by their lonesomes, sometimes, in small groups, but rarely had he encountered anything resembling an army of them. That day in Anglotor, not only were they an army, but an endless one -- and they were coming straight at him, nothing on their minds except murder and munching man-flesh.

In addition to being afflicted with graying hair, Putnam was also afflicted with courage — two things that rarely strolled side by side. He preferred a stand-up fight and rarely turned tail from one. Those qualities fit in fine with Theta, Ezer, and Frem, which is what got him jumped up to First Sergeant some years back. Putnam didn't think even they knew the extent of his martial skills, for he only put them on full display for those he was about to kill. And in Theta's service, he'd killed more than his share. More than he wanted to remember. Thankfully, they were all bad and had it coming, or so he told himself.

On a good day, Putnam could go toe to toe

with most anybody. He figured he could even hold his own against Frem or Ezer if he had to…maybe. Not that it would ever come to that, for he loved them like brothers, and they were the good guys, Ezer's surly disposition notwithstanding. Actually, calling them the good guys wasn't enough. Frem, Ezer, and Theta were the best men he'd ever met. Not goody goodies, mind you, but men of honor, of justice, of their word. Men would follow them into Helheim if needs be.

And they did.

When the Nifleheimers came at him, Putnam went to work, same as usual, hacking and slashing, swinging and stabbing. In no time, he'd left four bruisers dead, dying, or twitching, pools of blood spreading every which way, mucking up the place. But he knew he'd landed in the deep stuff when he saw Sidriel leap through the gateway. Other Sithians wouldn't have recognized him, or any of Azathoth's Arkons, but Putnam studied the old lore what Theta made available. Best to know one's enemies, he figured. *Find any edge you can and exploit it*, Theta would say. And that was smart thinking.

Putnam knew Sidriel by the crest on his armor — a seven sided star, orange at the tips, black and blood red stripes at the center, and a big oversized helmet atop his head, weird feathers flopping from it. He'd seen sketches of him in one of the oldest annals. Of course, Sidriel looked different back then -- a man, not a monster, but that sigil was so distinct and colorful it stuck in Putnam's head and he knew it at once. That fellow was not just a random beastie with hunger pangs. He was one of Azathoth's Arkons -- one of them that followed him down into the Nifleheim in ages past. Putnam knew he was in for a fight.

VIGRID VALLEY
FIMBULWINTER - YEAR 3
LAST DAY OF THE AGE OF MYTH AND LEGEND

WOTAN

Wotan, supreme chieftain and most storied hero in the history of the northern realms, battled a slavering beast akin to a wolf, but unlike any that had prowled Midgaard before. As large as the biggest ox it was, and twice as strong, yet swift and agile as the fleetest mountain wolf. Its coat was long and black as pitch, lean muscles rippling beneath. Yellow fangs protruded from a mouth cluttered with four inch teeth, claws twice again as long, and as sharp as honed steel. Eyes of red, tongue of black, stench worse than a week-dead beast wafted from it, body and breath. Its disposition, even fouler.

In the coldest mountain passes and deepest northern gorges, Wotan had fought terrible beasts before: dire wolves twice again the size of their common cousins; bears fifteen feet tall that felled trees with a single swipe; boars the size of mules with tusks like spears; sabercats, vicious, quick, and deadly with twelve inch fangs and no fears; and darker things still -- things with names unknown to civilized folk, creatures that instilled dread and haunted dreams, some few with origins beyond the pale, beyond Midgaard, or from blood lines lost to antiquity, long dead and best forgotten. Wotan had faced them all and lived to tell. No man, save perhaps Thetan or Mithron, had ventured farther and seen more of the dark down through the long years.

But even Wotan didn't hunt the most fearsome beasts alone. He and his took them in numbers, with arrows, spears, and dogs, as need be. This time, Wotan fought alone -- his kinsmen scattered, each to their own desperate battles, outnumbered and outsized as they were. And he did so, wounded, weaker than he'd ever been, one eye gone, the other rapidly blinking and half-closed from pain, blood, and tears. The cold threatened to freeze his blood but promised him relief if he but lay down and sleep, give in to the darkness and never awake. As frigid as was that Fimbulwinter, heavy snow swirling about the battlefield, growing deeper by the moment, it was not the weather that brought on Wotan's shivering, but the blood loss. He'd bound his wrist tight and true, but still it oozed red with his lifeblood. Sluggish and weak, he wanted to drown in Asgardian mead to dull the pain and warm his belly, and sleep until it passed. But that must wait until the knife work was done. Enemies were everywhere. And one of the worst, the wolf that stood before him.

Tyr the Just fought a giant hound called Garmr nearby and from the sound of it had similar troubles; Wotan heard the blows, grunts, screams, and yelps, though he witnessed not the action.

Heimdall, and Donar's sons, Magni and Modi, fought the sons of Muspelheim, giants called Jotuns, who were twice and more their height. Wotan heard his kin shout their war cries and felt the ground shake each time a Jotun fell. And fall they did. His warriors cut them down despite their size and skill, yet on they came, no end in sight to their numbers.

Frey fought the most fearsome of the Jotun clan: their king, who was called Surt -- a giant amongst giants, of flaming red hair, swarthy complexion, and mammoth sword that shone with the sun's brightness, flames alive along its length.

Wotan had lost track of Donar and Loki even before the battle had begun. His other kinsmen and karls were scattered. There was no one to stand with him. He'd even lost Sleipnir, his beloved mount of long years. The wolf raked black claws into his side at the first. Sleipnir reared, kicked the beast back, and was game for more, but Wotan jumped off and ordered him away, the wolf far too large and fearsome a foe. He hoped the horse cleared the field and made it to safety where his wounds could be properly tended.

So, he'd stand alone, show the beast his mettle, and send it howling back to Helheim where it belonged.

Fenrir Wolf lunged once again; Wotan sidestepped and bashed its head with Gungnir, his fabled spear of Dwarvish craft, the wood of the World Tree, Yggdrasil, at its core. He spun and jabbed the beast's flank with all his strength...but the wolf leapt aside unharmed, too quick to touch. That blow should have struck home despite Fenrir's preternatural speed but Wotan's injuries badly slowed him and defied the battle rush.

Fenrir barked and gnashed its teeth, and came on again. Wotan stabbed and stabbed again and again with Gungnir's tip, which bit over and again into the wolf's flesh, drawing blood from a dozen wounds about its head, neck, and shoulders. But not a one was deep, its hide too tough for even Gungnir to penetrate. And the beast gave as good as it got. It lashed out with its paws, swiping as would a bear, rending Wotan's leg armor, breastplate, and shoulder steel.

Wotan danced back and to the side, feinting and hopping, light on his feet despite his injuries -- all to avoid those snapping jaws. Jaws that could crush a tree trunk, that could grind boulders to dust. He wanted no part of them. A common wolf, even a Direwolf, would've died a dozen times in that melee, and not done Wotan a bit of damage -- not with that armor on -- the best carbon steel forged by Asgard's master smiths. But that hell-wolf was made of sterner stuff than any Midgaardian beast. Stronger than an autumn bear, faster than a sabercat it was, and so much larger, so much more resilient. And its eyes: intelligent, aware, and malevolent in a way that belied its beastly nature.

Wotan bashed its head, swinging Gungnir as a staff as it came in, searching for an opening to sink the spear's tip into its eye or its underbelly, but the beast crashed through his strike, slammed into his breastplate, and sent him flying across the field. He felt as if he'd been hit by a horse at full gallop, must've been thrown twenty feet, mayhap more.

Stunned, the wind knocked out of him, a terrible pain in his torso, mayhap one or more ribs broken, he ignored the pain and sat up, Gungnir still in hand, his head foggy, his eyes unfocused. He had to get the spear out in front, betwixt him and the beast until his head cleared. Mayhap, if luck were with him, it would choose another opponent, giving him a moment's respite. Before he pulled himself to his feet, he saw the merest flurry of movement, and then the beast's jaws clamped around his torso, front to back, and bit down with power beyond imagining.

The wolf lifted Wotan into the air like a rag doll. He hung horizontal as it bit him and shook its head in a frenzy.

Wotan heard his armor rent beneath those fangs and crush within those jaws.

And then his bones did the same.

VIGRID VALLEY
FIMBULWINTER - YEAR 3
LAST DAY OF THE AGE OF MYTH AND LEGEND

Wotan tried to stab the wolf with Gungnir, but the spear was gone. He punched the wolf in the head about its snout and eyes, but didn't know if any strength remained in his hand.

Wotan would not yield. Would not let the darkness take him. He kept throwing punches, as best he could, no leverage, no strength, but he kept on – or at least he thought he did. He couldn't breathe. In the darkness crept from all sides.

And then a huge Arkon, one of Thetan's rebels, came to his aid. It was Hogar the Invincible, he who in a later age was called Sir Frem Sorlons.

Hogar planted his boot within Fenrir's open jaw, just beside Wotan's torso, and planted his other leg solidly so that the beast could no longer twist its jaw. Try as it might, the beast was pinned.

Hogar pressed both gauntleted hands against the beast's upper jaw. He pushed down with his foot and he pulled up with both hands against Fenrir's jaws with all the strength that any man did ever possess. He grunted and strained from the effort, his mighty thews flexing. And somehow, the beast's jaws opened farther and farther still, though Wotan remained impaled on its lower fangs. The beast tried to shake Hogar off, but he had its head pinned against a boulder and he pushed open those jaws, farther and farther.

Fenrir strained and began to panic.

"Pull him clear," shouted Hogar. "Someone, pull Wotan clear."

At that moment, Thetan arrived at the scene. He scooped up Gungnir and brandished it with both hands. He lunged forward and plunged the spear deep into Fenrir's open maw, up through the roof of its mouth and into the wolf's brain. Fenrir's legs collapsed; eyes rolled back in its head, and the great beast fell dead.

JUTENHEIM
ANGLOTOR TOWER
THE TEMPLE OF POWER
YEAR 1267, 4TH AGE

PUTNAM

"On me, men," shouted Putnam. "We've got an Arkon coming."

That got Sidriel's attention. He locked his red glowing eyes on Putnam and pulled back his lips, displaying snakelike fangs. He held a short sword in each hand and leaped toward Putnam, his speed, shocking.

Moag Lugron hit the bastard with an arrow mid leap. Unlike in silly stories, arrows don't knock you out of the air as they would a little bird. It didn't change Sidriel's momentum one bit. The arrowhead was of common iron or bronze, maybe steel tipped, but no ranal to be found, so it was useless against him. That it stuck in him at all was a testament to the quality of Moag's bow and his aim.

Putnam dodged, spun, and barely evaded Sidriel's initial slash, and then stepped in and worked longsword and dagger. And then they were at it. Their blades clanked and bashed against each other: bang, bang, bang, like a mad drummer, over and over, faster and faster, wild and crazed. Putnam fully expected his sword to break under that pounding, but he was at his finest, and parried every blow. Trouble was, he didn't get in a single lick. All his energy focused on defense, on keeping himself alive. That was the best he could manage against that bastard, outmatched as he was in speed, strength, and probably skill. A few moments more and Sidriel would get him, that outcome inevitable unless he could disengage.

Royce barreled into Sidriel, which probably saved Putnam's butt. Now, Royce was a big man, and wore heavy armor, and he was moving darned fast, but by the gods, he bounced off and went flopping to the ground. There was no accounting for that unless Sidriel weighed at least three or four times what a normal man should. Putnam knew the Eternals were unnaturally heavy for their size, so he figured that Azathoth's Arkons must be all the more so; only explanation. What they were made of, he'd no idea. Too bad Royce hadn't anticipated that. Now they knew.

"On me," shouted Putnam again. He needed more help before his luck ran out.

Trouble was, Royce was still down.

But then Carroll was there, Moag backing him. And Ward waded in. That was more than Putnam could've hoped for since that crew were some of the Company's best.

"Now," shouted Putnam. They charged. Any normal fellow would've got skewered six ways from Sun Day right then and there, but not old Sidriel. He twisted, spun, ducked, and slashed with deftness that you wouldn't believe. It went on for a goodly while before Moag hamstrung him with a cut from that wicked dagger of his, the black ranal one he'd picked up in Tragoss Kell years ago.

That slowed the bastard. But he was still fast.

Carroll came in, stabbed him in the shoulder. Putnam went for the sternum but got blocked.

Sidriel's overhand swing slammed clear through Ward's shield and hard against his breastplate, but somehow it held. That tied up the Arkon's sword and he had to drop it.

Sidriel kicked Moag in the head, sending him reeling.

Carroll returned the favor, planting a powerful kick high on Sidriel's back, which bent him forward. Putnam slammed his elbow to Sidriel's jaw, a signature move that he'd used to drop men as big as Frem.

It only pissed Sidriel off.

Fast as lightning, he grabbed Putnam by the belt and tossed him like a potato sack. He crashed into somebody who broke his fall, but Putnam scrambled up in a flash. He'd have time to lick his wounds later, assuming he didn't get dead. And if he did, nothing mattered anyway.

Sidriel traded blows with Royce and Carroll, fending them off to good affect, despite them being swordmasters both. Ward tried to get in on the fun and Moag lurched about looking for an opening, blood dribbling from an ear.

When their swords were blazing faster than Putnam could watch, Moag dived in and tripped Sidriel.

373

The Arkon fell flat on his rump.

Ward slashed him solid, but the blow deflected off his armor. Sidriel nicked Ward in the leg, and gifted Carroll a cut to the arm as he made his feet.

Putnam charged back in, his enthusiasm and optimism fading fast. Like as not, Sidriel was going to kill the lot of them. But Putnam spied a good opening and took it, for tough as he was, Sidriel didn't have eyes in the back of his head. Putnam's two-handed swing caught the back of his neck. By all rights, that should've taken off Sidriel's head, but it didn't. It sunk in only about two inches, a nasty wound all the same, green blood spurting everywhere. The stuff stunk so badly, Putnam nearly retched. His sword was stuck fast in Sidriel's neck, so he let it go and pulled a short blade.

Neck wound or no, Sidriel had plenty of fight left in him. When he tried to pull the sword from his neck, Moag stabbed his underarm. Carroll kicked the back of Sidriel's knee with all his strength, while Royce tackled him from the flank.

The Arkon went down hard.

The Sithians were on him. They hacked, slashed, and stabbed; must have skewered him thirty, maybe forty times before he stopped fighting back.

As soon as Sidriel went limp, Ward grabbed him by the collar and with some help from Royce, lifted him to a seated position.

"Cut off his head," shouted Ward, "or the bastard will get up on us."

And Royce did just that.

Took him about six cuts, but the bastard's head rolled.

82

VIGRID VALLEY
FIMBULWINTER - YEAR 3
LAST DAY OF THE AGE OF MYTH AND LEGEND

Hogar's face scrunched up in disgust from the wolf's putrid stench, and he shouted, "Pull him clear," as he held open Fenrir's massive jaws, though the beast was surely dead.

Thetan lifted Wotan about the shoulders and carefully pulled him free of the beast's teeth.

"Is he alive?" said Hogar.

"Still breathing," spat Wotan. The great chieftain's hands shook; he pressed them to his midsection. They came back bloody. He was sliced open across his entire abdomen and back. Jagged, deep wounds. His armor shredded.

"Seems I had a bit more blood left after all," said Wotan.

Thetan grabbed a fallen cape and wrapped it tightly around the Northman's torso to staunch the bleeding.

Wotan groaned, agony on his face. "Broken ribs. You must see the day through without me," he said between gritted teeth. "I may yet survive this, but for today I'm done."

Hogar loomed above the warriors, ready to defend them against any creatures that dared venture near while they were vulnerable. But luckily, the battle with Fenrir and the devil dogs had cleared the immediate area of other combatants.

Nearby, but unable to help, Hogar saw the devil hound Garmr tear off the arm of Tyr, one of the greatest of the northern chieftains.

Tyr was determined to take the hound with him to the afterlife. With whatever remained of his strength, he buried his sword in the hound's neck, blood spouting. But the hound was stubborn too. It pounced on Tyr even as its blood soaked the ground. It clamped monstrous jaws on his throat. And tore. And tore.

Kneeling beside Wotan, Thetan leaned down and spoke in his ear. "My friend, I'm told the only way to close that portal is for the priest and the king to sacrifice themselves by jumping through it, into the *Nether Realms*."

"Go grak yourself," said Wotan. "I've done my duty for the day. You go jump through, you bastard."

"There's no other way," said Thetan. "It must be the priest whose eye was sacrificed, the king whose blood was shed. You and no other can do this thing."

"I heard you the first time. Did you hear me?"

Thetan did not reply. He gave Wotan some moments to think.

"Of course that's the only way," said Wotan sarcastically as he winced in pain and held his belly. "It has to be me: take my eye, my blood, and now my life, my everything. Only me! What did I do to deserve this honor? These aren't even my lands. He was not *my* god. Loki warned me that you would be my doom. The doom of us all, he said. I did not listen, I did not believe. I chalked it up to his usual jealousies and mischief, exaggerations and paranoia, but he knew. *He knew.*"

"I know that it's not fair," said Thetan.

"To Helheim with fair," said Wotan, "this curse and these rituals are no random chance. There's a purpose to it, dark and deep. We're being played, in a game not of our making; its rules unknown to us. That Gnome of yours is at the heart of it, but it seems I've no time to untie it. It falls to you to unravel the mystery. And I charge you to do just that, to see it through to wherever it leads. And to exact the proper vengeance. Vengeance, Thetan. Will you do that for me?"

"I will," said Thetan.

"I'll have your sworn vow," said Wotan.

"You just heard it," said Thetan.

Wotan nodded. "And I will hold you to it from whatever afterlife will have me. Know well, that I would gladly step through that gateway if doing so would save all Midgaard — *if* I could but stand and hold my sword or my spear to gird me against the darkness and the devils within. After all, what does my life mean compared to that of all the world? And likely as not, I'm done for anyway," he said looking down at his wounds. "But if I pass through like this, I cannot even defend myself. I'll be torn to pieces by the hordes of Helheim, a calf to the slaughter. I care not for such a death. I don't deserve it. I will die fighting, on my feet, a warrior's death, with honor."

"I will place a short blade in each of your

hands, my friend," said Thetan. "You will have a warrior's death as is your due. I think we have no choice in this. I cannot close the portal otherwise. I've tried everything I can think of. The wizard says this is the only way, though I share your distrust of him. He is more than he seems and has more knowledge than he should. I don't even know if he's the Lasifer that I've known all these years or some impostor. Or maybe I've never known him at all."

"Get me to the breach for all good's sake, and let's be done with it. Get me on my feet and give me those blades, but I'll not sacrifice Gungnir to such a fate. I would not have the hordes of Helheim possess such a treasure, nor my daggers. Gather me common ones on the way. Henceforth, *you* will bear mine. Treat them well; I warrant even *you* have not wielded their like. A parting gift, old friend, my mentor of long ago."

"I will wield them with honor," said Thetan.

Thetan carefully lifted the Northman, which caused Wotan great pain and he cried out despite himself. Thetan carried him toward the portal by a circuitous path, avoiding the Jotuns, hell hounds, fiends and devils, and undead monsters of nightmare that continued to pour from the gateway.

Luckily for them, and for all the warriors on the field that day, most of the creatures paid them little heed, determined instead to scatter to the winds rather than stand and fight. The Jotuns and their minions, however, seemed quite content to engage in a stand-up battle.

Hogar guarded Thetan and Wotan along the

way, felling no fewer than four Jotuns, and several other creatures that Thetan could not name, who dared accost them. By the time they arrived at the portal's edge, Wotan's eyes were closed, his breathing shallow.

"Are you still with me?" said Thetan, though looking at the blue tinge to his friend's skin he did not expect an answer.

"Get me up, and hand me the blades," said Wotan, his voice weak, his eyes still closed.

But Wotan could not stand. He could not hold the blades. His skin had gone cold. He'd lost too much blood. How he was alive at all, Thetan could not imagine.

"If he dies before you toss him through," said Lasifer, who appeared from nowhere, "the Worldgate won't accept the sacrifice, and it will remain open for however long it likes. Shove him through, Thetan, the sooner the better. He's only a stinking barbarian, after all."

"I cannot. I will not leave him to be torn to shreds without even a chance to defend himself."

"Either that or the gate stays open and they tear him to shreds anyway -- along with the rest of you. He'll die either way."

Thetan hesitated a moment, trying to sort things out, trying to make the right decision, or to avoid the wrong one. But every choice seemed wrong.

"Make your peace with it and throw him through," said Lasifer. "There's really no other option. You've practiced being stupid quite enough already."

And then the gateway suddenly grew wider, much wider, and a giant serpent roared through.

"Oh shit," said Thetan.

"Ha, ha," cackled Lasifer, "I warned you. Say hello to the Midgaard Serpent, Lightbringer."

JUTENHEIM
ANGLOTOR TOWER
THE TEMPLE OF POWER
YEAR 1267, 4TH AGE

FREM SORLONS

As the flood of Nifleheimers through the gateway grew faster and thicker, Frem feared he and his would soon be overwhelmed. The Sithians were scattered, no line or formation, each man for himself, most fighting two, three, or four invaders.

They had to get the gateway closed.

And quickly.

Frem figured that destroying the Orb was the best way to do that. He'd lost track of Theta and Ezer, and there was no time to look around and size things up, so he was on his own for the time being and, best as he could tell, *he* was closest to the gateway. It was up to him.

A short distance to reach the Orb, but a hard slog past the hungry Nifleheimers that barred his path. He held his shield close to his torso, sword high. In those close quarters the long blade was a liability, better work for a short-hafted axe or hammer, but none were handy.

Frem slashed the next creature that came at him, shoulder to hip. It howled and dropped to its knees as its guts spilled to the floor. With the backswing, Frem cut the throat of another -- a long-necked, duck-billed fiend with floppy ears and a rat's tail.

Two steps forward and two more came at him: one multi-limbed and spider-like: two black eyes as big as saucers, a pincered maw, furry all over, ugly as sin; the other, humanoid with spiked armor and curvy sword. The spider stabbed with its legs, one after another and over again, a wild frenzy that clanged and clanged against Frem's shield, threatening to pierce it, and jarring his arm and shoulder to the point of numbness, but he deftly moved the shield up and down and side to side to catch each furious blow, all the while parrying Spike's sword with his. Frem's Battle Sight was all that saved him; no common man could have kept up with the speed of those strikes.

Frem spun, sliced the top two inches off Spike's head, and shield-bashed the spider twice, shattering some of its legs, then stabbed it betwixt the eyes. It squealed and went still.

Frem plowed forward, maneuvered around other combatants, and stepped over bodies that lay twitching. The footing, treacherous — blood everywhere, red, green, and more, all blending into a horrific soup. Other fighters jostled him. He backstabbed the fiend that fought one soldier, crushed an ape creature's skull with his sword's pommel, shield-bashed two or three other Nifleheimers, their aspects a blur.

Just before Frem reached the altar, another of Azathoth's Arkons leaped through, and Frem heard the horns of Vaeden sound from beyond the gateway. He'd not heard those horns for years beyond count. Once, a source of pride and confidence. Now they made his blood run cold, a shiver down his spine.

The fabled trumpets announced the lord's approach, the approach of Azathoth. He was coming, following close on the heels of his vanguard. Frem knew that if he didn't get the portal closed within minutes they would lose not just the battle, but the world, for if Azathoth crossed over, all Midgaard would be lost.

But first, he had to get past Gop -- once a tall, proud Arkon, now a hunched, twisted mockery of his former self. Frem recognized his crooked nose and triangular sigil even though his skin was now red, and his face looked chiseled from stone, two black horns sprouting from his forehead, his ears pointed, eyes blood red and glowing. Frem remembered Gop as a brutal fighter, strong and tough, but that played to Frem's strengths. Best to deal with Gop quickly.

"Get thee back to Helheim, demon," shouted Frem.

"What?" spat Gop, his gravelly voice barely understandable where once it was smooth and clear. "You call me, demon, traitor? Yes, I remember your face if not your name. You're one of the Harbinger's sniveling lap dogs. Your death, long overdue."

Frem's sword crashed into Gop's and they pressed each other, strength against strength. Gop's preternatural power surprised Frem. In another setting, Frem would've tested his strength against Gop's, but in that wild battle, with all that was at stake, he had no time. And so, with their swords still locked, Frem stepped in and punched Gop with his shield. The blow was so powerful that it knocked Gop back against the altar with such force that the great stone slab shifted, though the Orb did not fall. Frem shield-bashed him again and Gop's sword clattered to the ground. Frem dropped his as well, used his shield to block Gop's view, pulled his dagger, and plunged it into Gop's armpit. He pulled it back, slick with green blood that stank of death and decay.

Gop howled. "You bastard. A poison blade, you no-good coward. I'll take your soul, I'll devour—"

Frem shield-bashed Gop's face: once, twice, and a third time. Gop tried to block the blows, but one arm hung limp, the other too slow. He crumbled to his knees and his eyes rolled back in his head, green blood everywhere.

Frem wasn't done with him. He slammed his shield down onto the top of Gop's head, again and again, with a strength that few men had ever possessed. The din was so loud, Frem couldn't hear the strikes, but he felt Gop's bones crush.

After he'd mashed Gop's skull to pulp, Frem turned from him and prepared to slam his shield's edge into the Orb, hoping to shatter it, but something grabbed his ankle in a grip like a vise. In a flash, it yanked him from his feet and dragged him from the altar.

A slavering ape-like creature, broader than

the largest man, had Frem by the ankle and hooted and hollered as it hauled him away from the Orb. Frem knew at once that that was no random chance — the creatures had orders to keep Midgaardians away from the gateway. That meant they were more than mere beasts under the Arkons' command; they had intelligence. But it also meant, Azathoth feared the gateway could be closed, so there had to be a way to shut it down, whether that be by smashing the Orb or otherwise.

Frem would find that way.

Before Frem could strike the ape, a toad-like creature with multiple rows of pointy yellow teeth clamped its jaws on his other leg. He felt the teeth pierce his flesh and his leg burned as if seared by a fiery brand. His armor had failed him. He wondered, if that bite carried poison.

Ignoring the pain, Frem sat up, lunged forward, and sent his dagger through the toad's eye, who bit down all the harder for it, even as the ape dragged Frem farther from the Orb.

As Frem struggled to free himself, he discovered that shattered skull or no, Gop wasn't done yet. The Arkon's thick spiked arm clamped down around Frem's neck from behind and squeezed with inhuman strength.

Frem smashed his head back against Gop's forehead, but the Arkon's grip did not slacken. Gop held him fast, as did the toad, but the ape continued to pull his leg with incredible strength. They stretched him like a torture victim on a rack. In a moment, either his neck would break or his leg would tear off. Either way, he was done for.

The horns of Vaeden sounded again, louder, closer this time. The world was running out of time. And Frem was running out of air.

84

VIGRID VALLEY
FIMBULWINTER - YEAR 3
LAST DAY OF THE AGE OF MYTH AND LEGEND

The Midgaard Serpent let loose a deafening high-pitched squeal as it burst through the gateway from the *Nether Realms,* the portal itself forced to expand to permit the creature's entry. The beast was enormous, larger by far even than the dragon, Nidhug. Midgaard had never before seen its like. It was round and limbless like a worm, brown like dirt, its hide like a dragon's, headless, eyeless, faceless and featureless save for a gaping maw that could swallow an Olyphant whole and barely notice, filled with row upon row of innumerable teeth. It was a creature built for nothing but eating, consuming, destroying.

It roared as it passed Thetan at great speed, a putrid wind slamming against him as it did, its earthy stench overwhelming. Thetan watched it for some moments, his jaw slack, disbelieving what he saw, the creature seemingly endless. A hundred feet of it passed in a moment, then a hundred more, and then five hundred, and on and on, no end to it.

Thetan still held Wotan in his arms, the Northman unconscious. Thetan could not tell if he still breathed, if his heart still beat. He had to throw him through; it was the only chance to save the world. Midgaard could not survive such monsters. Thetan had to do whatever it took to stop them. There was no one else. No other way.

A woman's voice, soft and sweet, whispered in his ear, though no woman was near, no one at all save for Lasifer, Gabriel, and Hogar. The old Gnome capered about maniacally, cackling with glee at the sight of the serpent. Gabriel and Hogar stood, mouths agape, paralyzed by the sight of the thing.

"No good comes from an evil deed, my love," whispered the unseen woman in Thetan's ear. Thetan didn't know the origin of that voice, whether real or born of his imagination, but it didn't matter. He knew what he had to do.

He had to save the world.

And if that meant he had to throw his friend to his death, then so be it. Did not Wotan himself say that he'd gladly give his life to save all Midgaard?

There was no other choice.

His eyes met Hogar's.

"I don't know what we should do," said Hogar, "but it feels wrong. We cannot bring about his death."

"I don't know either," said Gabriel, "but death will soon take him anyway. We must do it, I think."

Thetan nodded. "The guilt will be mine alone," he said. He turned and took three long strides to the back of the gateway, even as the serpent still barreled through the front. "I'm sorry, my friend," said Thetan. "Please forgive me." Thetan shouted in anguish as he tossed Wotan through

389

the portal.

At that exact moment, Lasifer stamped his foot and crushed the last shard of the *Sphere of the Heavens*, and the gateway instantly closed. The Fallen Arkons saw not the Gnome's actions, had no notion of them.

VIGRID VALLEY
FIMBULWINTER - YEAR 3
LAST DAY OF THE AGE OF MYTH AND LEGEND

DONAR WOTANSON

Donar smiled even as the ravenous tongues of flame that flitted along the Jotun's nine foot long glowing sword licked the top of his helm. Had he not ducked, that blow would've taken his head. A heartbeat later, he spun, dodged, and sidestepped to avoid another Jotun's sword aimed at his back. He laughed as a slash and three quick thrusts missed him. The next swing came in low; he jumped, and the blade sliced the air beneath him though he felt the heat of its flames through his boots and leggings. An overhand strike crashed down and he backpedaled, quick enough to avoid the blade, but the flames set his breastplate smoking.

Donar figured, they must have doused their weapons in slow-burning oil before they vaulted through the portal. Weren't giant swords wielded by giant men potent enough? They needed flames too? How were the Jotuns so well prepared without notice? Were they lined up at Muspelheim's door since time immemorial, their lives wasted waiting for that foul gateway to fly open? Or were the Midgaardians betrayed? Was someone from our world in league with the

Jotuns and their allies, and did that traitor forewarn them of the gateway's opening? Who commanded the power to speak betwixt worlds, and what was their motive? Donar had no answers and no time to think it through; he'd leave that to his father or Loki. Such machinations were beyond him, but sport to them. He hoped that Loki wasn't behind it, or any part of it. Loki had so often caused all manor of mischief and misdeed, from the small to the sinister, but to betray all Midgaard was beyond Donar's comprehension.

What fools they'd been to assume this unnatural portal to the *Nether Realms* that Thetan had long schemed to open would permit passage only one way. They hadn't planned for an invasion. They hadn't imagined it. Now they were paying the price for that shortsightedness. If enough invaders came though, all Midgaard would pay the price. Donar would not let that happen.

Like their brethren, the Jotuns that Donar dueled had the faces and forms of men: hawk faced, long nosed, shaggy hair and beard, and they stunk. Apparently, monthly baths were unknown in Muspelheim. The Jotuns were much taller, leaner, and more agile than the Hill Giants of the far north that Donar had battled many a time, and they seemed smarter, certainly better trained and skilled with modern weapons.

The Jotuns were twice his height, probably five times his weight, and yet quicker than common men.

Hundreds of their kind had already spewed

from the portal, more every moment, no end in sight. How could the Midgaardians ever stop them all, for each giant was a match for several of their best trained soldiers?

The moment he killed the two Jotuns he faced, Donar planned to march to the gateway and hold it fast. He'd stand at the brink, bar the giants' path, and slay them before they fouled Midgaard's sacred soil with their presence. His men would deal with the Jotuns that had already made it through. He'd guard the breach alone if need be, until victory was his or Old Death took him. No more glorious way could a warrior pass from this life. Donar did not seek death, but he'd never run from it, not while victory was yet possible, no matter how terrible his foes.

But Donar too was no common warrior. He was as uncommon as they come. A great chieftain of the northern lands, second in power and skill only to his father, Wotan. And he wielded the mystical hammer called Mjollnir, crafted by the dwarf Brokkr and imbued with wondrous powers in times long past. Short of haft it was, meant to be wielded one handed, but its metal head was huge and blocky, even larger than the great mauls of Muspelheim. Only Donar could wield it in battle. Some said, only Donar could even lift it. On its sides were inscribed runes of power that bristled with esoteric sorcery known only by dwarven masters.

Donar slammed Mjollnir into one Jotun's massive leg, his blow too quick for the giant to dodge or block. Bone snapped with a terrible crack, loud even above the battle's din. As the

Jotun toppled he attempted to grab Donar, drag him down with him, but the Northman avoided his reach, swung his hammer again. This time, he smashed it into the Jotun's face, and crushed it to pulp.

Donar jumped aside without a moment to spare before the second Jotun's sword came down and narrowly missed cleaving him in two.

Donar's hammer found that one's arm and shattered it. The Jotun roared and staggered back. Donar pressed forward, bashed him in the abdomen with his shield, and planted Mjollnir in the middle of the Jotun's chest with a powerful overhand strike. The hammer staved in the giant's sternum, and Donar had to wrench the weapon free. He spun about just as a sword swung at him, caught his shield and tore through it, nearly skewered him. The Jotun's sword ripped the shield from his grasp. Donar threw Mjollnir from close range and caught the giant in the throat. Its neck collapsed and the Jotun fell back like a tree, dead before he hit the ground. Donar held out his hand and he smiled a broad smile as Mjollnir sailed through the air back into his grip.

Donar heard a loud skirling sound and turned toward the Nether Portal just as the Midgaard Serpent burst through.

"By all that's holy," said Donar. "Comes now a demon lord of the pit."

The great serpent slithered towards him at breakneck speed and crushed everyone and everything in its path -- man, monster, and giant alike -- intent on battling and destroying the

Wotanson. Its gaping maw was so large it could swallow him whole and not even notice.

86

JUTENHEIM
ANGLOTOR TOWER
THE TEMPLE OF POWER
YEAR 1267, 4TH AGE

FREM SORLONS

Frem struggled against the choking pressure, and desperately strained to dislodge Gop's arm, but it was a vise that denied him breath. He could not escape *it* or the toad creature clamped down on his right leg or the ape who tried to tear off his left. He was going to die, and if he did, the gateway would remain open long enough for Azathoth to stride through, and the world would end. The world!

All because *he* was weak.

Weak.

Weak.

The thought of it made Frem's blood boil. He refused to yield, and focused all he had on loosing Gop's grip and taking a breath. It should have been easy. Frem's strength was so far beyond that of common men and even of uncommon Arkons, that he should have broken that grip in but a moment. But Nifleheim had done more to Gop than grotesque his appearance. Its insidious sorceries had gifted him superhuman strength, strength beyond even Frem's, and who knows what more. How it did any of that Frem dared not contemplate. Strain as he might, Frem couldn't get loose. His only chance was to outlast Gop. He kept up the pressure, straining without respite, hampered terribly by lack of air. The struggle went on for what felt like minutes, but was surely only moments.

Even as Frem's vision began to narrow and blur, Gop's strength at last faltered, and Frem pried arm from throat just enough to suck in a sliver of air, then a bit more, and more still, and with that his strength returned and his energies surged.

And then, with a burst of adrenaline, he broke free, and slammed his elbow into Gop's jaw, which sent him reeling. It was plain to Frem, that but for Gop's injuries, he'd have never overcome that embrace. He'd have died there.

Frem sat up, leaned forward, and slammed his fist into the ape creature's forehead. The punch had no effect. Perhaps the blow was feeble, or else, mayhap the creature was immune to pummeling, just as it was immune to common steel.

Frem spied a ranal dagger, fallen close by his side. He grabbed it, and plunged the blade through the ape's forehead: flesh, bone, and brain.

The creature instantly went limp.

Frem kicked the toad in the head with his newly freed leg, over and again, until its jaws slackened, though each blow left his leg in agony.

Ignoring the pain, Frem scrambled to his feet, one leg numb, the other afire. He turned and Gop was there again, the bastard. Frem ducked a punch, then tried to kick Gop in the groin, but his legs betrayed him, collapsed beneath him. He landed on his rump, spun, and swept out Gop's legs. The move probably hurt Frem more than Gop, but it worked. Gop's back hit the stone floor hard and gray matter oozed from his shattered skull.

Frem made his feet on shaky legs, and plowed forward, the battle still raging all around. Nothing would keep him from the Orb. Come what may, he'd get that gateway closed.

As Frem charged toward the gateway, another ape creature leaped through it -- and came straight at him, bounding on bare feet and knuckles. Frem bashed it aside, but another took its place, then a third, a fourth, a fifth. Frem smashed, cut, and barreled his way through, his efforts focused not on killing them, but on getting past them. Once the gateway was closed, there'd be plenty of time for killing.

Frem leaped as he approached the altar and slammed his shield into the Orb with incredible force creating a loud metallic clang -- a booming reverberation akin to a mallet striking a bell. That blow launched the Orb across the sanctum. It hit the ground hard, but did not break.

And the gateway did not close.

"Shit," spat Frem. He wondered whether he hadn't hit it hard enough or if the thing was unbreakable.

Frem made for the Orb; he'd whack it again,

as many times as needed until he smashed the darned thing to bits. There could be no other outcome. But Gop was there *again*, growling, and barring his path. The bastard just wouldn't stay down. Frem dodged a punch that would've felled a tree, then shield-bashed Gop's face again and sent him sprawling. He wanted to finish him, but he dared not spend the time.

Frem made it around the altar as another toad creature jumped through the gateway on the other side — they were coming out both ends of it now. He smashed the toad with his shield so hard that his arm went partly numb. The thing was dead before it hit the ground. Frem turned, searching for the Orb. It rolled about on the floor, men and creatures fighting on all sides, inadvertently kicking it, sending it careening around, in and out of Frem's sight.

Frem went after it, death lurking on all sides.

He pushed aside one creature that blocked his path, smashed his dagger's pommel on another's head, pushed aside two Sithians who got in his way, and then caught sight of the Orb.

A large bipedal creature with the head of a wolf loomed over it, blood dripping from its canine jaws. It was as tall as Frem, and just as broad, huge of muscle, but hairy like a wolf. It had torn the throat from a soldier — Frem prayed it wasn't one of his Pointmen, but couldn't tell from the angle. Something slammed into Frem's arm and his dagger went flying out of reach. Frem bounded forward unarmed and punched the wolf's jaw with all his strength. That rocked the creature's head, spun it ninety degrees; that blow would've dropped the largest horse or broken most any man's neck. But the wolf's face snapped back toward Frem, and it let loose a bellowing laugh as it kicked Frem in the abdomen.

Frem reeled backwards, surprised by that blow, which knocked the breath out of him; his strength momentarily sapped. Another creature, all bristling hair and yellow fangs, lunged at him. He pivoted his torso and shield-bashed it with whatever strength he could muster, his shield arm barely responsive. Luckily, it was enough. The creature staggered back and was lost amidst the wider melee. That gave Frem a fleeting moment to breathe and gather his strength.

Frem reached for his hammer before he remembered it was long lost. All his spare blades were gone too, and his armor, tattered. If this kept up, soon he'd be fighting naked.

The wolf came on again. As fast as it was, Frem was faster, and slashed its face with his shield's edge. That shocked the wolf and stopped it in its tracks. Frem pounded it with his left fist and then slammed it with the shield again and again. The creature punched back with huge fists that hit like iron mallets. Frem's shield buckled and broke under those blows, his right arm numb and barely responsive. They traded blow for blow, pounding each other over and again. Frem could barely see, tears clouding his eyes, but he kept punching and kept getting hit, for he had little room to maneuver.

And then Frem's hand hit the stone wall. For some moments he didn't know if he'd shattered his hand, but the wolf stopped hitting him. He blinked the tears and blood away until he could see straight. The wolf was on the ground, convulsing. Green blood gushed from its skull where his fists had cracked it.

And there on the floor just next to the wolf was the Orb.

And Frem heard the horns of Vaeden sound a third time. His glance revealed the flood of creatures that poured through the gateway, monsters one and all, but no royal banners waved, no horns held to monstrous lips. But so loud were the horns, no doubt they stood on the Nifleheim side's threshold, steps away from breaching Midgaard, Azathoth on their heels.

Frem leaned against the wall to steady himself, lifted his armored boot, and smashed it down with all his strength onto the cursed Orb.

It shattered!

Shattered into a thousand shards.

Frem heard a humming sound, metallic and dissonant, that grew louder and louder -- and then came a crash, as if a huge door slammed closed.

And the gateway to Nifleheim vanished; the wailing from beyond the portal went with it.

Now, there were only the sounds of the battle in the sanctum. Still, a desperate struggle, scores of otherworldly fiends battled weary soldiers, outnumbered but brimming with courage and determination as they fought amidst the heaped dead.

And then from the chamber's main doors streamed a troop of soldiers.

The Eotrus!

With barely a breath of pause at the sight of those horrors, they waded into the Nifleheimers: sword and shield, hammer and axe, honor and glory.

Frem was exhausted. He could barely lift his arms. But he waded back into the fray, killed three or four more Nifleheimers before all the creatures were cleared from his corner of the room. Most of the rest had charged the Eotrus, but they were giving them what for. Frem wasn't needed. He leaned back against the wall and found himself sinking to his rump. He was done for the day and closed his eyes.

VIGRID VALLEY
FIMBULWINTER - YEAR 3
LAST DAY OF THE AGE OF MYTH AND LEGEND

DONAR WOTANSON

Any sane warrior would have run from the Midgaard Serpent. Or at least, gotten out of the way. Instead, Donar laughed. He lifted Mjollnir to his face and spoke to it. "Hammer, your time has come. Slay now this devil of the depths and all glory will be ours."

Donar lifted Mjollnir high and with a running start and all his preternatural power behind it, let the hammer fly along with his battle cry.

When Mjollnir struck the Serpent just above its maw, a sound like a thunderclap rang out and shook the ground for hundreds of yards in all directions, shock waves toppling men and Jotuns far and wide. For all its incredible power, the hammer did the creature no obvious harm, barely slowed its advance for even a moment.

The smile left Donar's face.

He stood rooted, shocked. Mjollnir had never before failed him. Then he held out his hand and recalled the hammer, which flew back at great speed and slowed only when it settled into his grip. He vaulted aside as the Serpent barreled forward, but to his surprise, the great wyrm paid him no heed, as if it didn't even know he was there.

How could that be?

He was the Wotanson.

Surely, the creature desired his death more than any other.

Donar swung Mjollnir with all his strength and slammed it against the Serpent's side as it passed. Another thunderclap sounded, this time to greater effect. The Serpent's vast body rolled over, roaring, and its maw turned back toward Donar.

"Ha! Come forward, devil, and face Donar if you dare!"

It slithered toward him trampling Jotuns and men by the dozens. Donar felt like a bee that had just stung a bear. Without a hundred more bees, he'd do the bear no harm. If anything, he'd make it angry.

But it didn't matter.

This battle was his destiny.

His glory.

He felt that, deep in his bones.

He would see the beast dead, somehow.

He smashed Mjollnir against the Serpent's hide again; this time, his thunderclap brought no reaction.

The great maw raced toward him.

He could dodge aside again and hope the thing couldn't track him, or else maintain his stance and likely be crushed or swallowed at the creature's whim.

There was only one choice the Wotanson could make. He took up a fallen Jotun's still flaming sword and raised it to his shoulder, ready to meet the wyrm, the smile back on his face, his eyes wild, destiny beckoning, the world's fate at stake.

When the Serpent reached him, its maw reared up, high overhead, and turned downward facing him. No doubt, the thing planned to smash its maw down and envelop him, swallowing him in a single bite.

Donar didn't wait for that.

He didn't dodge or flee.

He charged howling his battle cry. He leapt into the air, impossibly high, nine foot long sword swinging. Timing the strike perfectly, he sliced open the Serpent's throat with Muspelheim steel and fire. A six foot long cut did he inflict, through its thick hide and deep into its flesh.

As luck would have it, or fate decreed, and against all odds, he struck a vital spot, perhaps *the* vital spot in the wyrm's anatomy. A thousand other wounds that he or an army of men could have inflicted would not have duplicated that critical strike. From the wound gushed a foul and putrid acid that perhaps was its lifeblood, or else, a venom sack, or who knows. Donar saw it coming as he dropped to the ground after the strike. He didn't know it was any more than blood, but he didn't want to be doused by it, making the rest of the battle all the more difficult. But more than that, he sensed a danger; how, he knew not. So the moment he landed, he dived and rolled as fast as he could to gain distance from the wyrm.

The creature turned toward him, but whether by happenstance or intent, no one could say. The acid blood showered Donar, face and eyes, chest, arms and armor.

For a moment he felt nothing.

Then, all he felt was pain.

He staggered back, blinded, unable even to scream as the foul liquid devoured his flesh.

The serpent wailed in anger and agony from its own wound, and flopped about like a fish out of water, rolling over and over, crushing a score of men and Jotuns.

And then, after but a few short moments, the Midgaard Serpent collapsed, dead.

Donar staggered back, clawing at his face as the poisonous acid afflicted him. Nine steps did he manage before he fell back on his rump and then onto his back and breathed his last.

Donar, son of Wotan, was dead.

JUTENHEIM
ANGLOTOR TOWER
THE TEMPLE OF POWER
YEAR 1267, 4TH AGE

With Korrgonn's blade lodged in Theta's gut, foul creatures converged on him in a frenzy, swarming from all directions, the longed for chance to slay the Harbinger at last at hand.

They dived at Theta, hoping to pull him down by force of numbers, and tear him to pieces.

But Theta was not done yet.

He groaned as he kicked, punched, and pummeled them, and slashed with Dargus Dal, hastily pulled from its scabbard, as his life blood showered the floor. Then he drew forth his falchion blade with his left hand, Dargus Dal now in his right, his face growing pale, his enormous strength draining away.

Korrgonn struggled to his feet, and appeared little better off than Theta, for he bled from a score of wounds to arms, chest, and neck, which the Harbinger had gifted him.

Wincing, his teeth clenched, Theta pulled the Nifleheim dagger from his belly and cast it aside, his gauntlet smoking from the mere touch of it. Without hesitation, he slashed his blades to the left and the right, and over again, and again, and again. Each cut sliced off a Nifleheimer's head or limb. The floor filled with the torn dead; their alien blood bubbled and frothed as it pooled, its stench even more nauseating than that of the creatures themselves. Theta advanced on Korrgonn. "Return now to the void where you belong," said Theta.

Korrgonn thrust out both hands, palms facing Theta, and mouthed quick words in a language unknown. A beam of red fire shot from the amulet of Dagon strung about his neck, and sped toward Theta.

Theta in turn spoke a single word. Instantly, his Ankh pulsed with blue light that sprang forward and intercepted Korrgonn's attack. The mystical beams collided; sparks flew and crackled as they fought, one against the other, continual beams of fiery death either of which would have incinerated any mortal caught within their grasps.

A few heartbeats later, both beams sputtered and died, each the bane of the other. Theta advanced anew, but as he did, he saw the ugly neck wound he'd gifted Korrgonn close of its own accord and instantly scab over. The other wounds about his body healed much the same.

Korrgonn smiled. "You are nothing compared to me, immortal though you be," said Korrgonn. "You are but a human, not a god, not a higher being. Stand against me and survive you cannot."

Korrgonn scooped up a fallen bastard sword and charged at Theta. When their blades met, Theta's falchion shattered the sword into a thousand fragments. Shards of steel flew into

Korrgonn's chest, neck, and face. Theta's next slash came but an instant later. Korrgonn staggered backward, his hands to his neck. Blood spurted from betwixt his fingers.

"Evil cannot win," said Korrgonn, his words gravelly, eyes wide with shock. "Good will always triumph in the end."

"At last you speak the truth," said Theta as he swung his falchion once more and separated Korrgonn's head from his shoulders. As the falchion cut through the godling's neck, sparks erupted and lightning cascaded about the chamber.

Korrgonn's corpse collapsed to the floor. It and his head glowed golden, then orange, then bright yellow, and finally blue, and burst into flames, top to toe.

"The fires of Helheim reclaim their own," said Theta.

Seconds later, the godling's corpse was naught but moldering ash.

VIGRID VALLEY
FIMBULWINTER - YEAR 3
LAST DAY OF THE AGE OF MYTH AND LEGEND

Thetan stood beside Donar's corpse, having arrived far too late to aid him. A bright light caught his eye and he turned toward it. Across the bloody field, beyond broken and twisted bodies of men, Jotuns, and darker things, he spied a duel of titans. Frey, a great chieftain of the Northmen and vassal to Wotan, did battle with the tallest and most fearsome of the giant-kin, Surt — king of the Muspelheim Jotuns. Where Frey was fair of features, skin, hair, and beard, the Jotun's skin was black as pitch, his hair, flaming red, his brow heavy, jaw thick.

Surt's sword shone brighter than the sun, and flames covered it from hilt to tip. Unlike those of the other Jotuns' swords, these flames were not birthed of blazing oil. Above the hilt, Surt's sword was *made* of fire. A product of magic it had to be, hellfire harnessed into a weapon without peer. Its flames could neither be doused nor sated. With every swing, droplets of hungry hellfire flew from it. When they landed, they did not twinkle out, but rather, took root despite the gathered snow about the valley's floor.

And the hellfire spread.

Spread like a virus, flowing here and there like a living thing with no regard for anything save its insatiable hunger to destroy, to consume. It covered the field in Surt's wake, melting and boiling off the snow and burning the frozen ground beneath, flame and smoke filling the air, fumes noxious and thick, spreading, ever spreading. Given time, Surt's hellfire might well consume the world.

Bodies by the dozens were aflame on that trail, some few still alive, screaming, rolling about in the snow trying in vain to extinguish the flames, and calling out for aid that would never come, their only salvation, the cold embrace of Old Death himself. And make no mistake, Death prowled the battlefield that day, joy in his stony heart for all the disparate souls that he did reap, his bounty beyond his wildest expectations.

King Surt battled his way across the field the moment he spotted Frey laying low his kinsmen, a half-dozen Jotuns dead about him, stabbed and cut to the bone. Three more fell to the Northman's skill before Surt fronted him.

But against Surt, the hero faltered. Fatigue afflicted Frey, pressed as he was on all sides by a cadre of skilled and strong, giantish foes, and he, left to his lonesome. His movements were slowing, his breath labored. Already bloodied, head and hand, arm and back, and now he faced their champion, a behemoth five times his height with boundless strength, a magical weapon, and not an ounce of mercy. And to his regret, he faced that monster without his fabled blade, a mystical sword of Dwarven make, lately gifted to his servant, Skirnir. The Asgardian sword he carried that day was common by no account, its steel, the finest in Midgaard; its edge, infallible, and more than capable of slaying a squad of Jotuns. Yet, it lacked the sorcerous dweomer needed to stand against the like of Surt's hellsword.

One of Frey's arms was bloody; more blood ran down his cheek. A bold swing of Surt's sword would've taken off his head, save that Frey ducked with uncanny speed.

Thetan leaned over and picked up Donar's fabled hammer. He held Mjollnir in his hand, a weapon too heavy by weight or magic or both for any but Donar to wield. But in Thetan's hand, it was half the weight of a common war hammer. How that was so, he knew not. But it felt good in his hand. It felt like it belonged there. As if the weapon were meant to be his. Without further delay, he bounded across the field, mystical hammer and spear to hand. With Gungnir, he hamstrung one giant, stabbed another in the neck, a third through the eye, hardly slowing his pace.

While still a goodly distance away, he saw Frey fall to one knee, then lift his sword and parry a mighty swing of Surt's weapon. But that blow shattered Frey's blade into a hundred pieces.

Without a long weapon, Frey had little chance. But Thetan raced toward them at his best speed, ducking blows from this Jotun and that. He had to get to Frey in time, for Frey was important, not personally to Thetan, but to the Northmen. He was a hero, a living legend among them, all the more vital with Wotan and Donar's passing. Thetan was determined to save him if he could, and he risked himself in the doing.

One of Frey's arms was bloody. More blood streamed down his cheek. Another swing of the hellfire blade sliced into Frey's arm. The Northman staggered back even as Surt lunged forward and sank his fiery blade into Frey's chest, the blade so large it nearly cleaved him in two. Still afire, the hellsword's tip exited the Northman's back. Surt smiled an evil smile as he twisted the blade in the mortal wound.

Thetan leaped through the air and slammed Gungnir's tip into the back of the Jotun's head. The razored tip blasted out the front of Surt's face. A moment later, the King of Muspelheim crashed to the snow. He lay dead on the field, his skull staved in, and fair Frey dead and crushed beneath him.

With the Jotun king's death, his sword's flame died and its hilt smoked and melted into the earth until no trace remained.

JUTENHEIM
ANGLOTOR TOWER
THE TEMPLE OF POWER
YEAR 1267, 4TH AGE

THETA

Blood gushed from the deep stab wound in Theta's side and he stumbled back against the chamber's wall. He'd been cut many times before, knew how to weather pain and continue to fight with the injury. He healed so much faster than other men, most wounds meant nothing to him. This one was bad, but nothing worse than he'd suffered a hundred times before.

Except for the poison.

The wound felt afire. He'd been poisoned before, but this was different. Poison it was, but not of this world. It was a dark brew born of the *Nether Realms,* something no Midgaardian had any defense against.

He risked removing the Ankh from about his neck, and placed it directly on the wound, but it had no effect. The Ankh either possessed no magic that could neutralize that poison or refused to gift it to him that day. Sometimes, the Ankh was fickle.

Then he remembered his flask. His hands shaking, he pulled it from its place on his belt. It was as weighty as ever, its thick steel free of corrosion or decay despite its great age. After all the many times he'd used it down through the long years, it still felt nearly full. A wonder beyond words.

Before he opened it, another Nifleheimer was on him, and then another. Both were insectoids of some sort, skittering and clacking as they came at him, legs ending in razored bone, stabbing and slashing.

Theta kicked one, then the other, and went to work with Wotan Dal, ignoring his injuries, but careful to hold tightly to the flask.

In but a few moments, he'd killed them both, then slipped on the blood that pooled at his feet. Went down on his rump against the wall. It was his own blood that betrayed him. Dead gods, how much had he lost? How much could he have left?

He opened the flask as quickly as he dared and pressed it to his lips, his tongue to the stopper to limit his taste, for a single drop was all that was needed. Any more would be wasted. Someone had told him that long ago, but who it was, he couldn't recall.

The elixer felt warm going down, a pleasant sweet taste to it, thick as syrup. Warmth spread from his throat and belly, across his torso, to his head, and finally, his limbs. He felt it working on every wound that plagued his body. Felt it concentrate at every hurt and speed up the healing. But the bulk of the elixer's power sped to the wound on his side. It knew where it was needed most.

The burning soon subsided and Theta felt the wound stitch itself closed from the inside out. It itched more than it hurt now, but the burning was gone.

A miracle. A wonder of magic, though how that boon had come to him, he had long since forgotten. He wondered whether that wound would've killed him. The poison. The blood loss. Would this have been his last day? His final battle. A fitting end it would have been, to die at the hands of a deity -- if that was what Korrgonn truly was. But the drought had saved him, just as it had saved him many times afore. Theta would live to fight another day.

VIGRID VALLEY
FIMBULWINTER - YEAR 3
LAST DAY OF THE AGE OF MYTH AND LEGEND

A heartbeat after Thetan pulled Gungnir from Surt's head, he spun around, and slammed Mjollnir into the head of a Jotun that had fallen wounded to one knee. Its head cracked like a raw egg, blood, brains, and bones flying. Plenty of it splattered Thetan, but no one would notice, drenched as he was in blood and gore, head to boot.

Thetan leaped up onto that Jotun's shoulder before its corpse fell over, sprang high into the air, and slammed Mjollnir into another Jotun's head, that giant near twenty feet tall, gray haired and battle scarred. As Thetan dropped to the ground he spun in midair and stabbed. Four lightning quick spear thrusts felled two giants that had leapt at him from behind. Like so many of their fellows, they tried in vain to crash into Thetan and pull him down. Better that, they must have figured, than face the Lightbringer weapon to weapon. They'd seen what he could do, the piles of their fellows heaped around him. But like their kinsmen, they were too slow. The Jotuns fell hard to the ground, clutching mortal wounds, and rolled about in their death throes, cursing and pleading, trying to crawl away, but Old Death was on them.

Old Twenty Footer, no doubt, one of their chieftains, was not done yet, though a third of his skull was staved in and his jaw was dislocated and far askew. He must have known he was finished, but he was a brave man. By his size and scars, a man that may have never tasted defeat. He wanted to go down fighting and to take Thetan with him to the afterlife. His enormous hands clamped down on Thetan's shoulders and tried to squeeze his neck, wring the life out of him. The giant snarled and drew close to Thetan's face, desperation in his eyes, blood dribbling from his mouth. He muttered some threat or curse in Jotun that Thetan didn't bother to comprehend.

Thetan shrugged off the giant's grip, though power enough yet remained in those fingers to crush a boulder. Thetan swung Mjollnir up into the underside of the giant's jaw. The chieftain's head snapped back with a terrible crack. He fell backward like a tree and crashed to the snow with a thud.

Thetan spun about and slammed Mjollnir into a devil dog's head, mid leap. Broken teeth flying, the thing collapsed lifeless without even a yelp. Two more leapt in its wake, large and powerful enough to bite off a man's head, their jaws snapping and spittle flying. Thetan stabbed one through the neck and pinned it to the ground but not before its jaws clamped down on his leg and tore away what little remained of his mangled armor. The other dog he knocked aside with his hammer. Before the hound recovered, he slammed the hammer down and splintered its spine. A final strike to its head mashed its skull to pulp.

Thetan turned this way and that, sucking putrid air, but ready to meet the next assault. He saw nothing but the heaps of torn dead that surrounded him, a mountain range of ruined flesh and red rivers. For the first time in what seemed like hours, no opponents rushed him. He checked again to be certain, then quickly stabbed each fallen enemy within reach to make certain they were dead. He dropped to one knee to keep out of sight while he caught his breath and regained his strength. He had little left. The battle had gone long. He'd never been so tired, his arms so weary they shook, though the Northmen's weapons took hardly any strength to wield owing to strange magics imbued by their Dwarven makers.

He had trouble steadying his breath; he wasn't used to that. He tried taking in air slower and deeper while avoiding breathing through his nose, the stench sickening. He couldn't afford the chance he'd be caught retching when the next enemy leaped over the dead and came at him. It was harder to calm himself when mouth breathing; his body fought him. He was beyond all limits, beyond all training — only his willpower, his refusal to quit or to be defeated had kept him going. His heart pounded; lungs hurt. He spit blood and mucus and cleared snot from his nose, which made the battlefield stench all the worse, but he had to breath.

His canteen was gone, lost early in the battle. He drained the two mouthfuls of water that remained in his backup flask. That made no dent in his thirst but cleared more blood and grit from his mouth.

Sweat poured from everywhere and mixed with the blood that covered him. It was hard to see, blood dripping into his eyes and nothing to wipe it away with. At least the blood wasn't his, most of it, anyways. He was battered, cut and bruised in at least a dozen places, but everything worked and nothing hurt much worse than anywhere else, so he figured, he likely had no mortal wound.

Wary of any approach, he checked himself and found no grievous hurt, but he couldn't be certain for sword cuts were insidious things, and he didn't know if the Jotuns used poison. It didn't seem so by the look of their blades, but some poisons were sly and slow. He covered a cut on his forearm with a scrap of cloth less bloody than the rest, and applied pressure, though it bled little. Maybe it wasn't too bad, or else, mayhap he had little blood left to shed. Proper tending and any stitching would have to wait.

And then he remembered the sap. Why he called it that, he knew not, for it was a healing drought. He couldn't even remember where or when he'd bought it, but it was in a flask, tucked securely in a pouch at his waist. He remembered being told to imbibe but a drop, any more would be wasted. He drank that drop and felt immediately refreshed and invigorated. His thirst, so powerful, he chanced a second drop, but it had no further effect. He stoppered the flask and carefully returned it to its place, then further assessed his situation.

His helm was long gone; knocked from his head by a blow he didn't see coming. Nearly tore off his ear with it. A dozen shields had served him that day, then broken under countless assaults. Half as many swords met the same fate. Even Thetan's fabled armor had met its match. His breastplate remained, bent and gouged, and punctured near the right shoulder. He still had one grieve, but not much else. The rest, torn away.

But the Norsemen's weapons did not falter. Wotan's spear, Donar's hammer, they were wonders. They clung to his hands where other weapons, common or kingly, would have long since fallen away, so slick with blood. And they refused to break, no matter the assault. No greater weapons had perhaps ever been crafted.

He hadn't noticed the nausea before, but as his heartbeat slowed and breathing eased, it crept up on him. His head pounded; stomach queasy; he wanted to puke, to rid his body of the battlefield stench that clung to him. He wanted to lay down, sleep for a hundred years on a soft bed. He was so tired he'd even sleep right there amidst the dead. He wanted to. He could have...but he wouldn't. There was more knife work that needed doing before the day was done and he expected that some of it only he could do.

He wanted water and wine. He needed water. A gallon of it. And food. Energy. He defied the nausea and pulled a piece of jerky from his pouch, stuffed it between teeth and cheek; the best he could do for the moment. It tasted of blood and grit. He'd scrounge a canteen from the dead.

Still no Jotuns came at him. He could rest a while longer. That wasn't too much to ask for, was it?

The glimmers he'd gotten as he fought were of devastation across the valley. Pockets of men fought in all directions, fewer and fewer as the battle wore on, but last he'd had a good look, he wasn't alone. Wasn't the last. How long ago that had been, he did not know.

And then he realized, he no longer heard the clash of weapons and the wild battle cries. Not even in the distance. But the ringing echo of steel smashing steel remained in his head and wouldn't die, as if a ghostly army still fought on all sides. He knew that was but an illusion, a product of the overloud and overlong clash.

The battlefield had its noises though. They always did. Never quiet, not unless and until the wounded are cleared from the field and the dead burned or buried deep. There is always the moaning. The crying. Pleading. Begging and bargaining. It came from all sides. Not many voices. Far fewer than there should be with so many fallen, but enough to create a din. The voices of men, he heard, though very few, and horses too. Most were Jotun's and some few of their devil dogs and great wolves, yelping and whimpering.

He had to get out of that hole and join up with whatever survivors remained, but he knew that many of the wounded enemies, down or not,

422

were still dangerous; he had to be wary. *On a battlefield, a reckless man is a dead man,* he muttered — one of the many lessons he'd taught his men.

And he had no idea how many Jotuns and their pets still stalked the Valley of Vigrid. There could be a thousand within a half mile. If any had marked his position and gone for reinforcements, they could be closing in on him even now.

Or were they all dead?

Were his men all dead?

Was everyone dead?

Was he the last?

He couldn't think of that. That couldn't be possible. He couldn't bear that guilt. He pushed the thoughts aside. He'd look around soon enough, and then he'd know. He'd help whoever he could, whoever was still alive. And then he'd get clear of that killing field. He'd get clear and never look back.

A few more breaths and he stood. But he could see no farther than a dozen yards in any direction, less in most. He climbed over the heap of bodies and gazed on the valley of death. Thetan's throat constricted, the hairs stood on the back of his neck, and he shuddered at the sight.

Countless dead lay in all directions for as far as he could see, moaning wounded soon to join them. Smoke rising everywhere, a bit a flame, broken weapons, fallen lances and helms, and blood. Blood and guts aplenty. A sea of death and destruction.

All his brethren were gone, Fallen and Loyalists, both.

But then a breeze dissipated the smoke and he saw farther and his heart leapt for here and there in the far distance stood groups of men. Soldiers. And no giants.

He was not the last.

He had not gotten them all killed.

A grunt behind him grabbed his attention and spun him around. To his surprise, but a hundred yards away stood the closed gateway. He'd thought the battle had carried him much farther afield, ten times at least that distance.

His back against the gateway, stood Hogar. Hogar! The big man held aloft a huge hound, twice again as large as him, and brought it down across his knee. The sound of its spine snapping was loud even at that distance. Hogar was covered in blood and gore, and was barely recognizable. In fact, only by his physique did Thetan know him.

"Hogar," shouted Thetan, but the word barely got out, his mouth so dry, voice raspy.

A rangy man emerged from behind the gateway, backpedaling, sword and shield working, a Jotun stalking him, its mammoth axe carving the air. The man ducked and spun and his sword danced, and the giant's axe fell to the ground, his arm with it, and the Jotun howled. The man stepped forward, stabbed and sliced, and the giant's head came free from its neck. The head bounced and rolled a goodly ways while its body remained upright until the warrior bashed it with his shield, which promptly fractured and fell from his arm.

Thetan moved toward them, stabbing fallen Jotuns as he went. The two men held their positions but waved at him. When he drew closer, he saw that the second man was Gabriel Hornblower and Thetan's heart rejoiced. When they came together, the three embraced. It may be that a tear or two of joy was shed, but no one would know owing to the blood and sweat that masked their faces.

92

JUTENHEIM
ANGLOTOR TOWER
THE TEMPLE OF POWER
YEAR 1267, 4TH AGE

JUDE EOTRUS

Jude gasped in horror when he witnessed the Harbinger murder the son of Azathoth. He couldn't believe his eyes.

It couldn't be true.

Evil could not prevail. The son of a god could not be killed.

To Jude's eyes, Korrgonn fell in slow motion, head and body, blood spraying, his golden form collapsing, wings limp. The terrible thump Jude heard when the godling's corpse struck the floor haunted him forevermore, though how he heard it at all in that din was inexplicable.

His eyes played him false, owing to weakness, blood loss, it had to be. He didn't know what he was looking at. He was confused. Or else...it was a clever ruse that Korrgonn employed to convince the Harbinger he'd won so he'd lower his defenses, all the easier to defeat him.

It had to be so.

But Thetan now appeared to Jude's eyes to be a man — a tall knight in glinting armor and accouterments — not a monster. Gone were the

426

batlike wings, the spiked tail, the horns, and inhuman pallor. What did that mean? Jude's head spun.

VIGRID VALLEY
FIMBULWINTER - YEAR 3
LAST DAY OF THE AGE OF MYTH AND LEGEND

"**C**omes now Bose and Raphael," said Hogar, excitedly as he, Thetan, and Gabriel shared what water they'd scrounged, and tended the worst of their hurts. "And Blazren walks with them, Silver circling. Nine lives, those two."

"We as well," said Gabriel. "For all our wounds, not a one is mortal."

"Another group marches toward us from the north," said Hogar. "The tall one at the van, thank the Norns, is Azrael. He leads a squad of a dozen strong." A smile filled Hogar's face as he announced their names: "Uriel...Tolkiel...and Dekkar."

"Any sign of Mithron or Steriel?" said Thetan.

"Yes!" said Hogar, "She's with them."

"Eleven of our thirteen," said Gabriel. "How unlikely."

"All but Mithron and that no-good traitor, Arioch," said Hogar.

"The gateway claimed Arioch," said Gabriel. "Just as it did the false god. We've seen the last of them both."

"We must find Mithron," said Thetan. "Alive or dead, I'll not abandon him to this field. And there must be more survivors."

"We'll find him," said Hogar, "And alive, I'll

wager."

"No one will take that bet," said Gabriel. "Only a fool would bet against Mithron, no matter the odds."

The battle's survivors flocked to Thetan's position over the next hour, from across the valley. They grew to two hundred strong in fighting shape: Fallen, Loyalists, and Northmen. A hundred more were too injured to fight. Few Loyalist Arkons survived: Dardan, Mythilox, Kullmid, and Protiel amongst them. Of the Northmen, several chieftains remained, including Hoener the Silent; Modi the Brave and Magni the strong, the tall and powerful sons of Donar; Vidar and Vali, sons of Wotan; Forseti the Just, Hermodr the Messenger, and Uller the Hunter. Together, under a begrudging truce, the group set off toward Vaeden to rest, take shelter, and tend their wounds; slow going with so many injured.

Crows descended by the thousands on the battlefield, cawing and pecking at the dead in a wild frenzy. Wolves howled in the distance.

"More devil dogs?" said Uriel.

"Common wolves, I think," said Tolkiel.

"We shiver in the heart of Fimbulwinter," said Gabriel. "From where come these birds?"

"My grandmum warns that carrion crows are the servants of Old Man Death," said Hogar. "He whispers to them the where and when of battles and his birds speed there to collect their due. It's not flesh they're after, my brothers, it's souls. I don't believe all that, grandmum being a teller of tall ones, but I figure, best not die with a crow

429

near my eye. No good can come of it."

"Best not die at all," said Thetan.

Just then, a large black bird landed on a pennant that was stuck into the ground along their path. Hogar growled and waved it off, but it held its position and stared at him, defiant. A moment later, another bird set down beside it.

"Begone, rancid soul suckers," said Hogar as he readied his shield to bash them both.

"Hold," said Thetan. "Those are no carrion crows. They're Wotan's ravens, Huginn and Muninn. Mark the collars, the sigils."

"What of it, he's gone," said Hogar. "They're scavengers now."

"They're smarter than any horse, or dog, by far," said Thetan, "or so claimed Wotan. They were his messengers and scouts, much as Silver is ours."

"Will they work for us, I wonder?" said Gabriel. "You carry their master's mystical spear."

Thetan stepped close to the birds and spoke in a quiet voice. "Do you understand my words?"

Both birds nodded.

"Can you check for us if the path to Vaeden is clear? And the city secure?"

Another nod from both.

"Good, go," said Thetan with a waive of his arm, and the birds took flight, headed west, the direction of Vaeden.

"Ridiculous," said Bose. "Birds can't understand human speech. This is no time for parlor tricks, Lightbringer."

"Maybe they understood," said Hogar,

"because he spoke to them in bird speech."

Bose rolled his eyes. "They're animals, they don't have speech. Anyway, I understood every word he said to them."

"Perhaps, that's because you speak bird too, even if you don't know it," said Hogar with a smile. "You've always been a bit flighty and you do have quite an impressive beak."

Bose closed his eyes and shook his head.

"Best give up now, Bose," said Uriel. "You're outwitted."

"You mean, dimwitted, I trust," said Raphael.

"Indeed," said Uriel.

"Tark off, the lot of you," spat Bose.

Azrael cleared his throat to draw the men's attention. "Some animals of ancient age, long around people, understand our words," he said. "We've all known dogs with such skills."

"Dogs aren't birds," said Bose. "Enough of this. Let's get moving, the sun sinks, my energy and patience with it."

"Didn't he keep pet goats too?" said Gabriel to Thetan as they set off again.

"Aye, a boar. The Northmen keep close to nature. Serves them well."

A mile west of the gateway they came upon an area piled high with the dead. A group of Arkons had made their last stand, fighting back to back. A hundred Jotun lay broken and lifeless around the small circle. A hundred! Twenty of their hounds lay dead beside them. A dragon's corpse overshadowed them all, a hundred feet long, tail excluded.

"See if there are any survivors," said Thetan

to Hermodr, the swiftest and most agile of the Northmen.

"He must be there," said Gabriel. "Who else unaccounted for could kill so many? Could he still be alive?"

Thetan shrugged.

"Someone killed the dragon," said Hogar. "One less for us to hunt down." That got the group's attention and all eyes went to Hogar and Thetan, but Thetan did not react, he merely stared after Hermodr at the circle of the dead.

"It's a wyvern, not a dragon," said Azrael.

"A what?" said Hogar.

"Wyvern resemble dragons," said Azrael, "but they have no front legs, only wings and back legs. Dragons have four legs, plus the wings."

"I don't care how many legs it has," said Hogar, "so long as it bleeds. And it looks like a dragon to me."

"One lives," shouted Hermodr from atop a giant's corpse.

As one, the Fallen sprinted toward the battle site.

When they crested the heap of giantish dead, they saw him.

Mithron.

JUTENHEIM
ANGLOTOR TOWER
THE TEMPLE OF POWER
YEAR 1267, 4TH AGE

"**Y**ou're telling me that the League's mercenaries, the Sithians, were your men from the beginning?" said DeBoors to Theta, Ezerhauten, and Frem as they stood amidst the inner sanctum's carnage shortly after the battle's end.

"Trained them myself," said Ezerhauten, "except for the newer recruits."

"Unconventional," said DeBoors as he stroked his upturned mustache, "but there's a wisdom to it. You knew the League's every move, your agents all over their camp. Why not just set upon them in the night, put them to the sword? You could've been done with this business long ago; must have had a hundred chances."

"They knew the Worldgate's location," said Theta. "We didn't, but we needed to. The only way to be certain was to follow them here."

"You want this place for its connection to the Grand Weave?" said DeBoors. "Even I can feel its power, and I barely dabble."

"We're here to take it off the board," said Ezerhauten.

DeBoors raised an eyebrow. "That's bold. Still

playing the long game, I see. Cloak and dagger, move and counter move, but against who this time? There's a good deal more to tell, methinks, and perhaps more of my help you'll need."

"We've shared enough secrets for today," said Theta. "And they're for your ears only. I figured, I owed you that much."

"Fair enough," said DeBoors, "for today, but tell me this, how did Ezer communicate with you, keep you apprised of what went on?"

"He didn't," said Theta. "I trusted him and Frem to handle things however they needed to be handled. To improvise. Who better than they?"

"But with all those archwizards and Korrgonn himself," said DeBoors, "how did you keep your identities secret? Didn't the wizards sense the deception? And Nifleheim lords can read men's minds say the rumors, or is that just fiction?"

"Korrgonn could read your mind as readily as you can a book," said Ezerhauten. "But we had sorceries placed over us that blocked our memories even from ourselves. They could read our minds all day long and we wouldn't expose ourselves, for none of us, save me, knew we were Theta's men."

"How did *you* deceive them?" said DeBoors.

"My talisman," said Ezerhauten as he pulled out his Ankh from beneath his breastplate. "You tried to buy it from me once."

DeBoors nodded. "Keeps out mind readers too, does it?"

"If you know its secrets," said Theta.

"I should've offered more," said DeBoors.

"Not for sale, then or now," said Ezerhauten.

"None of them are," said Frem.

"One of us had to remain with the full knowledge of who they were to make certain that the whole venture stayed on course," said Ezerhauten. "It made the most sense for it to be me."

"So say you," said Frem. "I found no fun in my mind being muddled. It did more than cloud my memories, it dimmed my wits. Only lately have I been myself again, though even now I'm a bit foggy, but I still say my Ankh could've shielded me as well as yours did you. I know, you'll argue we'd have been twice as likely to be caught if we both kept our memories, but I still disagree, not that it matters now."

"How did you keep the men in line and your plans on track?" said DeBoors.

"We trusted to their natures," said Ezerhauten. "And our boys stayed true to them, one and all. And, we hired a bunch of men shortly before the mission, men who knew nothing of our true background and purpose. Planted seeds of a false history, we did. A narrative that told of our singular reputation in Lomion and parts foreign. The Leaguers didn't investigate us thoroughly. Because of their magical proficiency they thought they could not be outwitted or outmaneuvered, the fools. We played them from the start."

"And when your soldiers saw Theta and the rest of us in the woods as we approached," said DeBoors, "the veil of sorcery lifted? That was the trigger?"

"Aye, on first sight," said Ezerhauten.

"Bold," said DeBoors. "And ingenious, but your plan could've gone awry a hundred ways."

"Risks that we had to take," said Theta, "and we paid a weighty price in lives and blood on both sides. But it was our best chance to destroy the League and serve my ends. And it worked, despite the twists and turns along the way. Here at the end, it was my men that filled the room and overwhelmed the last of the wizards. We didn't know how we were going to get here, but we knew if they made it this far, this is how we wanted it to end. This was our strongest play."

"And overall it worked," said Ezerhauten. "Another epic tale for the annals."

"Overall," said Frem as he looked down at Uriel's corpse.

95

VIGRID VALLEY
FIMBULWINTER - YEAR 3
LAST DAY OF THE AGE OF MYTH AND LEGEND

Mithron sat atop a Jotun's shield, another propped behind his back. A sword in his hand; his leg wrapped with a tourniquet.

"You're late," said Mithron, his deep voice as commanding as ever. Six Arkons lay dead in the circle, and five score giants and their pets. Plus the dragon.

Thetan and the others picked their way to his side. Medical pouch in hand, Azrael knelt and examined Mithron's leg.

"Do you know how long I've carried this blade?" said Mithron as he displayed his sword, only half its blade remaining. "I thought it unbreakable. Darned dragon snapped it."

"It's a wyvern," said Hogar.

Thetan drew close to Mithron and whispered, "You've been productive."

"None of ours died easily," said Mithron. "Brave men. Rezrael is among them; killed one of their chieftains before they cut him down; took a dozen to do it. He was a long time dying, and I could do nothing. You didn't tell us that the Nether door opened both ways."

"I didn't know," said Thetan speaking louder so that the others could hear.

"It was more than one door," said Dekkar.

"And not just because it opened front and back. Didn't you notice?" he said looking to each of his brothers. "Any of you?"

"What do you mean, more than one door?" said Tolkiel. "I saw one opening only."

"Fire Giants of Muspelheim," said Hogar, "and Frost Giants of Nifleheim. Is that what you mean? I thought it odd those old enemies were lying in wait for us together, if the old tales be true."

"Maybe they're not," said Gabriel. "Mayhap both giant clans hail from the same place."

"A land at once of fire and of ice?" said Raphael. "That's the stuff of song and story only."

Gabriel shrugged.

"The giant clans gave each other wide berth," said Dekkar. "They were not friends or allies. The other creatures, those hordes of dead things, demons, ghosts, goblins, ghouls, and gremlins, and whatever else they were. They hail from Helheim, not the giants' lands. And the giants fought them. I saw several kill each other."

"I saw the same," said Blazren, "though I could make little sense of it. It seemed as if they were as shocked to see each other as we were to see them."

"Exactly," said Dekkar.

"I hadn't time to think it through before," said Azrael, "but you're right. The Sphere didn't open a single door to Nifleheim, but many doors, to many worlds, each with creatures lying in wait for the veil betwixt the worlds to be lifted. Each group prepositioned there. All of them, enemies

438

to us, and some to each other. That explains it all except who organized it."

"The old Gnome betrayed us," said Thetan. "I always thought him little more than a dabbler in the arcane; a few tricks up his sleeve to please the court. But he's much more than that. What he is, I do not know."

"He knew what would happen," Thetan continued. "He planned this invasion, then fled rather than face my wrath."

"Who is the man that did this?" said Mithron.

"Lasifer," said Thetan. "Lasifer."

"I know not that name," said Mithron. "Who is he?"

Thetan wrinkled his brow and looked confused. "Azathoth's court wizard. The Gnome. Were you hit on the head?"

"Check him," said Thetan to Azrael.

"How long ago did he serve in the court?" said Azrael.

"What?" said Thetan. "Is that a jest? He looked around, but found no support from the others. They all looked confused.

"Do none of you remember the old Gnome?" said Thetan.

"I recall no Gnome in the court, wizard or otherwise," said Gabriel. "Could he have been there before our time?"

Thetan was slow to respond, looking at the confused expressions on his friends' faces. "Sorcery is at work here," he said. "No doubt, it's the Gnome's doing. Lasifer was there from the beginning, before any of you, but he served until the end. He left with us. You all knew him. Knew him well. It was he that told me about the Sphere of the Heavens, how we could use it to banish Azathoth. He planned the whole thing. We thought him our ally. But he betrayed us. A foul plot from its birth."

"You told us that you'd discovered the Sphere in Azathoth's vaults," said Gabriel, "and after long study, you'd discerned its power to open a portal. It was *your* plan."

"We followed *you*," said Mithron.

"I remember it as Gabriel says," said Raphael.

"As do I," said Bose.

Uriel, Dekkar, Tolkiel, and Steriel all said the same.

Azrael nodded his agreement. "Sorcery is at work, as Thetan says. We cannot sort it out here. We need time and shelter and clear heads to think it through. Let's put aside this debate until we rest safely in Vaeden's halls."

"Aye," said Hogar. "That is wise."

"I don't know what goes on here," said Mithron as he looked at Thetan, "but we need your head on straight. All Midgaard is at far greater risk now than before. Those creatures — thousands of them, mayhap tens of thousands. Dead things. Demons out of Helheim. Dragons. Jotuns. We unleashed them onto the world. This is a thousand times worse than if we'd done nothing and let Azathoth continue his rule. How many of the invaders even stopped to engage us? One in ten? One in twenty?"

"Fewer than that," said Dekkar.

"And yet they destroyed our armies," said Mithron, "though we were decked for battle and at the ready. And now they're roaming the countryside, probably killing everyone they encounter, and here we stand, impotent, and all you speak of are phantom Gnomes. I don't understand this. I don't know what to say to this."

"You've said too much already," said Hogar.

"Wait until we're in Vaeden," said Azrael. "We're too vulnerable here."

"We're losing the light," said Dekkar.

"What darned difference does that make?" said Mithron. "The Jotun have fled the field, the cowards. They'll not trouble us tonight, and we can travel in the dark; we know these paths like the backs of our hands."

"It's not the Jotun I'm concerned about," said Thetan. "It's the other creatures that spewed from the portal."

"They ran from us," said Hogar. "Even in their numbers. Why should we fear them?"

"They ran from the sun," said Azrael. "That's what they fear, not us. When the darkness comes, so will they. The demons."

"Oh shit," said Hogar.

96

JUTENHEIM
ANGLOTOR TOWER
THE UNDERHALLS
YEAR 1267, 4TH AGE

JUDE EOTRUS

"**Y**ou still with me, Judy Boy?" said Teek as they trudged along the dark passageway that led to the base of the great stair in Anglotor's underhalls, Teek supporting most of Jude's weight. Brother Donnelin shuffled just behind, moaning quietly in pain and helped along by Par Keld. Donnelin's head was wrapped with several layers of thick cloth, blood staining through where his eye had lately been.

"I'm cold," said Jude, his words slurred as if he were drunk. "I can barely keep my eyes open. What's wrong with me?"

"It's the blood loss," said Teek. "The wine and the bite of rations I gave you will help. We'll get you something better when we're out this hell hole; then you can rest. But for now, you've got to be strong, keep one leg moving after the other. It's a long way to them stairs and an even longer trek up; I'd rather not carry you the whole trip. But be happy, Judy Boy, because it's over. You made it through. You're a free man again and you're going home to your cushy castle and frilly clothes."

"You were on my side all along, weren't you?" said Jude.

"Lord Theta had me sign on with the League a ways back so that I could watch them up close and personal. When you got nabbed, I figured I best keep you alive. And I did."

Jude halted and turned his face toward Teek, his eyes wide with alarm. "You work for the Harbinger? You're one of his?"

Teek sighed. "You saw when the godson got dropped. Minute he did, Theta didn't look like no demon anymore, did he? Just a man, a knight. That's the real Theta. Old Korrgonn sold you his snake oil, sugar on top. And you lapped it up like a starving dog, damn fool boy. We could've got out a might sooner, and you'd have kept more juice in your veins, and the priest his eye."

"He had me convinced," said Jude. "He said all the right things. Everything made sense. I thought he was..."

"Best to judge a person by their actions, Judy Boy, not be their fancy rhetoric or their reputations."

Jude was startled when he realized that Par Keld was supporting Donnelin.

"Yep, that's right," said Keld, a smile on his face, but a dash of vinegar in his voice. "I'm Theta's man too, Mister Eotrus. Always have been, and always will be. I'm loyal, loyal to the core. If I wasn't, do you think I'd have taken this assignment? Nobody else wanted it. But I took it because I knew I'd get it done where others would've failed, so here I am in this stinking hole in the ground, hauling along this Cyclops and babysitting you. No doubt, Teek will get all the credit, and I'll get none. But that's okay. I'm used to it, getting no respect. I do what I need to do, same as Theta. That's why we get on so good; that's why we're so close, like brothers. He depends upon me and that's why I'm here."

"You're here because nobody else will work with you," said Teek.

"Everyone loves me," said Keld. "It's you that got exiled. I didn't do anything. Don't blame me."

"What about Brackta?" said Jude.

"What about her?" said Keld. "A Leaguer through and through. Good riddance."

"Keld, your tongue wags more than a wee dog's tail," said Teek, "and you've even less sense. I'm sorry to say, Judy, but Brackta was one of them, a true believer. Brainwashed by their old religion and Ginalli's silver tongue. But she was a decent lass, and she loved you."

Jude's jaw hung low. "Did she tell you that?"

"Her eyes told me, Judy Boy. They're more reliable than words — you'd do well to remember that. She's gone, so it's best you forget her, sooner than not."

"What a mess," said Keld as they came upon the chamber at the base of the great stair. There were Stowron bodies everywhere, many missing limbs or heads, others crushed to pulp, the floor awash with blood. Great scorch marks marred the walls and floor where desperate sorceries had sought to hold the Harbinger back. Stones great and small had fallen from the ceiling and littered the killing ground. Stev Keevis and Par Rhund had not yielded their position without a fight.

But the men's attention was drawn to one thing more than anything else. And when they looked at it, they shuddered. At the base of the stair was a Stowron staff stuck upright into the stone floor, and atop that staff hung the severed head of Mort Zag, the last Red Demon of Fozramgar, an expression of terror forever frozen on his face.

When at last they reached the top, having encountered several more of Theta's men going up and down the stair about their business, they made their way through the tower's entry hall, now half cleared of bodies, and out into the light of day.

Not far outside they spied another uncommon sight. Two Golems lay flat, one on its belly, one on its back, mere yards from each other, ropes and chains aplenty wrapped around their necks, arms, legs, and torsos. The largest man Jude had ever seen was dressed in sailor's garb and sat on the chest of one of the Golems, a mammoth hammer as a large as Theta's, with a much longer half, in his hand. Beside him lounged a rotund swashbuckler with long white hair, a garish hat, and an evil grin.

Each Golem's binding was pulled tight and staked deep into the ground and tied off to great boulders, some few still being hauled into place by a squad of soldiers. And not just any soldiers. Eotrus men!

"Jude!"

Jude turned toward the voice as Claradon hobbled toward him at best speed, battered, bruised, and bandaged, Ob at his side.

"You're here?" said Jude, confused. "You came for me?"

Claradon embraced him. "Of course, brother."

"Donnelin?" said Ob. "I...I thought you were dead. Donnelin!" The Gnome and the priest hugged each other.

"By Odin, I'm not the last after all," said Ob.

"You look like shit," said the priest.

And the Gnome laughed. They all did.

VIGRID VALLEY
FIMBULWINTER - YEAR 3
LAST DAY OF THE AGE OF MYTH AND LEGEND

"**I** stopped the bleeding and I've got the wound closed," said Azrael. "Now I need to bind it to keep it that way."

"Finish up, and help me to my feet," said Mithron. "I'll need a serviceable weapon."

"No problem there," said Raphael. "Plenty of spares lying about. I'll even scrounge you a new leg if you want, though it might be a few sizes small."

"If you walk on that leg, bound and stitched though it be, you'll tear it open for certain," said Azrael, "and bleed all the way to Vaeden, or until you run dry, whichever comes first."

"Anyone up for carrying a grumpy mountain, badly used?" said Raphael.

No one spoke up.

"Fine," said Mithron. "Then I'll bleed. My Targon is dead thanks to the damned dragon—"

"Wyvern," said Hogar.

"So unless someone finds me a big horse, walking is the only way."

"I'll help you, brother," said Bose, "though my back will long regret it."

"And I," said Hogar even as Steriel worked frantically with dagger and cord, transforming a spear into a crutch.

"We move out in five, whether you're done or not," said Thetan. "I'll not face those things in the open again. Not today."

Mithron's eyes went to Thetan's weapons: hammer and spear.

"The northern chiefs fared worse than we, it seems," said Mithron.

"They fell as heroes," said Thetan. "Their deeds will be long remembered."

"Will their kin let you keep them?" said Mithron.

"Donar's sons said no man but their father had strength enough to wield Mjollnir in battle. But I did, and they saw it. They said the hammer chose me as its new master, and so, it be rightly mine. They renounced their claim. Much the same was said of Wotan's spear, though if Loki still lives, he will not agree."

"He'll claim them?" said Mithron.

"I'll not hand them over. Not these weapons. Not to that trickster."

"And if he tries to take them?" said Mithron.

"Then we hope the others back me," said Thetan. "Or else, our alliance may well be short lived."

"You value two weapons that much?" said Azrael.

"I must," said Thetan, "for they have powers beyond compare. Without them, we may well not defeat the worst of the beasts."

"So you *do* plan to hunt them down," said Mithron.

"Every last one," said Thetan. "Even if it takes me a thousand years."

"Longer than that, I fear," said Hogar, "judging by their numbers."

"They may well decide to hunt us down," said Mithron.

"Then it'll be over all the quicker," said Thetan.

"No matter the time it takes," said Hogar, "my sword is yours, my brother. We'll see it through together, to the end. I'll follow you into Helheim itself, if need be."

"Let's hope it doesn't come to that, my friend," said Thetan as he clasped Hogar's shoulder.

"Helheim has followed us home," said Raphael. "The dawn will never be as bright again."

A half hour later, as the group trudged along, Huginn returned without Muninn. The bird hopped from one leg to the other, croaking and chattering.

"What's he saying?" said Hogar to Thetan.

"Ask Bose," said Thetan. "I don't speak raven."

"He's warning us, you fools," said Bose. "Something's not right in Vaeden. Maybe it's under attack."

"Or mayhap, the bird merely needs to pee," said Raphael. "You hop much the same when you can't get your armor off."

"Grak off," said Bose.

"Make ready," said Thetan, "we should have a clear view of Vaeden over the next rise."

"Someone should go aloft and check it out," said Bose.

"Silver's up," said Thetan. "I'll not give away

449

our position scouting with Targon. That's why I sent the ravens."

"Form a line and draw your weapons," shouted Dekkar. "Combat ready. Wounded to the center."

"Blazren," said Thetan, "what do you see?"

Through Silver's eyes, he peered, the mechanical bird high aloft. "Smoke, black and thick. There are fires. We're losing the light, I can see little more."

When they reached the hilltop, the Vale of Vaeden came into view, an opportune breeze clearing some of the smoke. Plumes of gray and black rose from every district. Flames assaulted various buildings, though whatever conflagration had befallen Vaeden had run its course. Nothing alive moved within their sight, though bodies aplenty heaped behind the sundered city gates; others, fallen from the walls.

They saw nothing human alive. But they did see a dragon.

"Oh shit," said Hogar.

"Oh shit," said them all.

And it was not just any dragon, it was a Nidhug, the large blood-red dragon that rocketed from the gateway when it opened. Five or ten times the length of the one Mithron had slain. It was entwined about Vaeden's central tower as it dined on the bodies heaped atop a lower spire's roof. Demons of the pit clung to its hide as they too devoured the flesh of the recently living.

The soldiers stood in silent shock for some time taking in the horror.

"There's more besides the dragon and its

fleas," said Dekkar. "Somebody busted down the gates. The dragon didn't need to do that, and couldn't have fit if he tried. He would've went overtop."

"There would have been at least five hundred guardsmen left on duty," said Bose.

"Well, if we move back in, we'll get to hire some new guardsmen," said Raphael. "The old ones are a bit charred and gnawed upon."

"What in Helheim do we do?" said Bose.

"We brought this on ourselves," said Azrael. "Maybe we were duped by Thetan's Gnome, or ensorcelled by him, or maybe this was all our own stupidity. It doesn't matter now, because the doom of Midgaard is upon us. It's right there," he said pointing at the dragon. "Right there! We brought that here, and all the others. We didn't want to, but we did. We're responsible. All the blood and souls of Vaeden will not sate that thing or its brethren, not for a day. It's not going to leave. They're not going to go back. They'll kill everyone they find, for killing's sake, or for food. They will destroy everything we've built. Everything everywhere. No one will be safe."

"We will stop them," said Thetan.

"How?" said Bose.

"There's no fighting something like that," said Raphael. "It's beyond us, beyond anyone."

"Mithron killed a dragon by his lonesome," said Thetan. "Donar did the same with the giant serpent. And *we* together will find a way to kill this one. And all the rest. Every last one. We will purge Midgaard of the Nifleheim scum."

451

"A fitting penance for unleashing this horror upon the world," said Azrael.

"It was a mistake," said Steriel.

"We have to fix it," said Thetan. "There is no one else. We must do this no matter the difficulty."

"We must hunt down your Gnome," said Gabriel.

"Who cares about Thetan's ghost-Gnome?" said Bose, "The damage is done. The *Nether Realmers* are here. What more mischief can an old Gnome do, if even he exists, and I'm not convinced of it?"

"He exists because the Lightbringer says he exists," said Hogar.

"We've no idea what more damage the Gnome can do," said Azrael. "We need to take him off the board."

"He needs to pay," said Dekkar. "A few hours under one of Iblis's paring knives would be a start."

"We kill him on sight," said Thetan. "We can't take any chances, for he is far more than he seems. I fear that we may find the dragon an easier foe to slay."

"Nonsense," said Bose, "an old Gnome trickster, a blade or a bow will end him quick enough."

"When we launched our rebellion," said Thetan, "one of you said that I was the harbinger of our doom. I say to you all, that was wrong. It was never me. Lasifer the Gnome, or whatever he is, is the Harbinger of Doom, and I will not rest until I cut out his black heart and stick his head on a pike for the crows to nibble on."

"I think the dragon has spotted us," said Raphael.

"What?" said Bose as they looked toward Vaeden.

"Oh shit," said them all.

Thus ended the Second Age of Midgaard, known to all as *The Age of Myth and Legend*. And thus began the Third Age, the span now called *The Age of Heroes*. But in those days of yore, it was known far and wide as *The Age of Monsters*.

JUTENHEIM
ANGLOTOR TOWER
THE TEMPLE OF POWER
YEAR 1267, 4TH AGE

DOLAN SILK

Dolan Silk's entire body hurt. One eye, swollen shut and throbbing. He bled from three or four places but not badly enough to kill him, and his right leg wasn't working properly — something strained or torn. But it was his duty to return to Lord Angle's side, so he picked his way across the inner sanctum's gruesome floor. There wasn't anywhere to walk clear of bodies. He had two choices: tread on the dead Nifleheimers, or step between them into the pools of Nifleheimer blood — putrid ichor of various colors that stunk up the place. He'd never seen so much blood; he figured you could fill a small river with it, and wondered whether it would eat through his boots and burn his flesh — he'd seen *that* before, but no one else was howling about it, so he figured it was safe enough. But he prayed he didn't slip, and stepped carefully to make certain of it. He didn't want that ooze touching his bare skin, especially not his face. Getting dirty didn't much bother Dolan, usually, but that slop was demon blood, and guts, and who knows what else — he wanted no part of that. And, it had been a long day. A long journey. He was tired.

He knew the moment he passed the sanctum's threshold that he'd entered a chamber that predated humankind. It was something built by an olden race, the ones who created shapes and patterns, angles and curves, that tricked the eye and confounded the mind. Every time he ventured into such a place, and he'd been in more than a few with Theta, he felt queasy. It came on sudden and always threatened to make him puke, though he rarely did. His eyes would grow blurry and he'd have to concentrate to focus his vision and his attention; his ears would feel plugged up, sounds dulled, and his thoughts muddled like after a few drinks. Happened every time. That time was no different.

He'd missed the final battle, the showdown with the leaders of the League and the Nifleheim Lord that they followed. Disappointing was that. But he figured he'd done his part along the way. After he got battered at the base of the big stair, Lord Angle ordered him to hang back and went on alone. The truth was, for some minutes, he couldn't even stand up, and Lord Angle knew it, and was just being respectful, so that he didn't feel guilty for not continuing on.

As he traversed the room, the only spots where Dolan could see the stony floor were ones where *men* had died. Someone ordered the survivors to gather up the fallen soldiers and carry them from the room for a proper burial topside, under the sun, where men were meant to be, not down in those depths.

Who was going to carry them up the stairs, Dolan wondered. He didn't figure any of them had the strength for that, not after the trials they'd been through. It was a long way up. Very long. Maybe after a good night's rest some of them would find the strength for it. But that would mean coming back down. He didn't figure anyone would have the gumption for that. He knew that after he made it up those stairs he wouldn't even want to look back.

Several soldiers stalked the room with spears, and jabbed the demon carcasses, making certain that none of them were playing possum, that every one of them was good and dead. Smart move, probably Lord Angle's idea. Dolan knew that that might not be enough. They probably needed to cut off their heads. Or else, burn them. Or both. The boss knew all about that sort of thing. He'd make the call.

Theta, Frem, Ezerhauten, and DeBoors were gathered around a body off to one side of the chamber. Dolan couldn't tell who it was, but he figured it must be Uriel since those four all knew him well from back in olden days.

When Dolan was halfway to them, Ezer, Frem, and DeBoors turned to depart. Ezer paused as they met each other, nodded but no smile, and put a hand on Dolan's shoulder. "Good to see you, boy. Glad you're in one piece," he said, and then moved on.

Frem nodded as he approached and the two embraced, a warm hug, but no words passed between them.

DeBoors didn't bother acknowledging him at all and Dolan didn't much care.

Theta was on one knee beside Uriel's body looking down at him. Dolan gasped despite himself, despite all the horrors he'd seen that day and in days past, for Uriel was tied down to a wooden cross, chunks torn out of his arms, legs, and torso, and a gaping hole in the center of his chest. Dead gods, he never had a chance.

Dolan squatted across from Theta. "He should've gone down fighting, not trussed up," said Dolan quietly. "Who did it?"

Theta shook his head.

Dolan figured that meant he didn't know or didn't care to say.

"It was already done by the time I arrived," added Theta. "I was late."

Because Theta offered that, Dolan's spirits lifted a bit despite the grim situation. Good to know that the boss thought well enough of him to say more than he had to. A sign of respect that Lord Angle didn't gift everyone. That made Dolan swell with pride, though he made certain not to let it show on his face.

"Jude Eotrus is alive," said Dolan. "I passed him on the stairs. Teek was helping him up. Who would have figured?"

"He got lucky," said Theta. "Luck plays a greater part in life and death, success and failure, than people give it credit for. Random chance decides our fate, my friend. Random chance. Or the hand of the gods."

"Which gods?" said Dolan.

"Who knows," said Theta. "But to think, if we'd arrived five minutes earlier, before they cut Uriel open, he might've lived through this the same as the Eotrus boy. Five minutes mayhap would've been enough. Should've been enough to keep that gateway from ever opening. More of our men died because I wasn't faster, because I wasn't here. Because I was late."

"We were as fast as could be," said Dolan. "No one else would've been faster, or near as fast, if there were anyone else, and there isn't."

"We could've pushed harder," said Theta. "We could've carried on longer the last few nights. We could've quickened our pace a bit, one less rest, a quicker meal, an earlier start. Any of that would've made the difference. Would've saved lives. Would've saved Uriel."

"Mayhap it would have," said Dolan. "Or maybe not. Maybe something else would've happened had we been a bit quicker. Maybe something else would've gotten in our way or slowed us down. There's no second-guessing these things. You know that better than me. We got here in time for what was most important. To get the gateway closed before Azathoth came through with his armies. And we did that."

"Barely," said Theta. "I heard the trumpets. I heard the wheels of his chariot. One or two more minutes and he'd have been through, back in Midgaard, here with us. Do you understand how close we just came to ruin? He'd have killed us all to a man. And his armies would've marched through by the thousands and conquered all of Midgaard. He would've enslaved our entire race just as he sought to do in times past. It would've been the end of everything, of all we hold dear. Firstly, our freedoms, then our lives, perhaps even our very souls."

"We stopped that and that was our true mission," said Dolan. "Call it the hand of fate and be done with it, Lord Angle. We cannot control everything. We can only do our best."

"So *you* are the fountain of wisdom now, my friend? Giving *me* the advice?" said Theta, a small smile on his face.

"You've done the same for me more times than anyone could count," said Dolan. "And for everyone else. We all need a reality check, a bit of a pep talk here and there, every now and then."

Putnam appeared beside them. "My Lord," said Putnam, "all the Nifleheimers are confirmed dead, and all our dead are cleared out. We left the Leaguers where they fell, the bastards. And I have men waiting to carry him out," he said gesturing toward Uriel, "when you're done, but if you don't mind, I'll have them wait outside, and I'll be heading topside. My head is spinning in this place, my stomach flopping."

"No need," said Theta. "I will carry him up myself. I owe him that."

"As you wish, my lord," said Putnam. He turned and made his way from the room, leaving Theta and Dolan alone amidst all that death.

They remained in silence for several minutes. Dolan did his best to breathe through his mouth, striving to stave off the nausea. After a time, he had to pinch his nose closed, and even then his stomach churned.

"He was with me from the beginning," said Theta of Uriel. "One of the original thirteen rebels."

"I've enjoyed those stories," said Dolan, "…a thousand times."

"And you'll hear them a thousand times more before I'm tired of telling them," said Theta.

They lingered in silence for a while before Dolan spoke again. "Is it over? Are we done with this business, these gateways? Can we finally rest? Can we go home?"

"There are more Worldgates scattered about the corners of Midgaard," said Theta, "but unless someone's seeking to use them, and knows the methods, they'll remain closed forever. But still, even closed, they are centers of power from which great sorcery can be drawn."

"Best we destroy this place," said Theta.

"Fire?" said Dolan.

"Aye, for this room, but we'll bring down that stair, close the passage well and good, forever. I'd bring down the whole cavern if I could, but we don't have the tools or the manpower left unless we camp out here for weeks, maybe longer, and I'm not interested in doing that. I think the men would mutiny."

"Not our men," said Dolan.

"Aye, but the Lomerians probably would. Slaayde's men certainly will. I'm surprised they've stayed with us this long. We need his ship to get back."

"What about DeBoors' ship?" said Dolan.

"Aye, that gives us options. But best we get

going now, a long trek up the stairs."

"Sitting here, like this, Uriel the Bold dead before us," said Dolan, "I feel like we should say some words about him. A prayer. Isn't that proper?"

"And who would we pray to?" said Theta shaking his head.

"Who indeed?" said a deep voice from behind Theta and Dolan.

99

JUTENHEIM
ANGLOTOR TOWER
THE TEMPLE OF POWER
YEAR 1267, 4TH AGE

Theta and Dolan whipped their heads around to where someone stood but where no one should have been, since they'd sensed no movement.

And yet there he stood.

Tall and regal, flowing robes of white; a shock of long white hair, mustache, and huge bushy beard; his skin, pale, lined, and yet flawless; his features, chiseled and strong; his age, old but indeterminate. His eyes were ancient and piercing, bright...glowing...green, and haunting. He held his hands out to his sides, palms forward, his face forlorn.

He was Azathoth, the one true god.
"Oh, shit," said Dolan.
"Oh, shit," said Theta.

END

Thanks for reading *Blood of Kings*. While you're waiting for the next volume in the series, please consider trying the Audiobook versions, or one of the related short works (available from most retailers in ebook and paperback), all set in the Harbinger of Doom universe and featuring some of your favorite characters.

THE HERO AND THE FIEND
(A novelette set in the Harbinger of Doom universe)

THE GATEWAY
(A novella length version of Gateway to Nifleheim)

THE DEMON KING OF BERGHER
(A short story set in the Harbinger of Doom universe)

THE KEBLEAR HORROR
(A short story set in the Harbinger of Doom universe)

ABOUT GLENN G. THATER

For more than twenty-five years, Glenn G. Thater has written works of fiction and historical fiction that focus on the genres of epic fantasy and sword and sorcery. His published works of fiction include the first twelve volumes of the Harbinger of Doom saga: *Gateway to Nifleheim*; *The Fallen Angle*; *Knight Eternal*; *Dwellers of the Deep*; *Blood, Fire, and Thorn*; *Gods of the Sword*; *The Shambling Dead*; *Master of the Dead*; *Shadow of Doom*; *Wizard's Toll*; *Drums of Doom*; *Blood of Kings*; the novella, *The Gateway*; and the novelette, *The Hero and the Fiend*.

Mr. Thater holds a Bachelor of Science degree in Physics with concentrations in Astronomy and Religious Studies, and a Master of Science degree in Civil Engineering, specializing in Structural Engineering. He has undertaken advanced graduate study in Classical Physics, Quantum Mechanics, Statistical Mechanics, and Astrophysics, and is a practicing licensed professional engineer specializing in the multidisciplinary alteration and remediation of buildings, and the forensic investigation of building failures and other disasters.

Mr. Thater has investigated failures and collapses of numerous structures around the United States and internationally. Since 1998, he has been a member of the American Society of Civil Engineers' Forensic Engineering Division

(FED), is a Past Chairman of that Division's Executive Committee and FED's Committee on Practices to Reduce Failures. Mr. Thater is a LEED (Leadership in Energy and Environmental Design) Accredited Professional and has testified as an expert witness in the field of structural engineering before the Supreme Court of the State of New York.

Mr. Thater has written and edited numerous scientific papers, magazine articles, engineering textbook chapters, and countless engineering reports. He has lectured across the United States and internationally on such topics as the World Trade Center collapses, bridge collapses, and on the construction and analysis of the dome of the United States Capitol in Washington D.C.

To be notified about new book releases and any special offers or discounts regarding Glenn's books, please join his **mailing list** here: http://eepurl.com/vwubH

BOOKS BY GLENN G. THATER

THE HARBINGER OF DOOM SAGA

GATEWAY TO NIFLEHEIM
THE FALLEN ANGLE
KNIGHT ETERNAL
DWELLERS OF THE DEEP
BLOOD, FIRE, AND THORN
GODS OF THE SWORD
THE SHAMBLING DEAD

MASTER OF THE DEAD
SHADOW OF DOOM
WIZARD'S TOLL
DRUMS OF DOOM
BLOOD OF KINGS
VOLUME 13+ (forthcoming)

HARBINGER OF DOOM
(Combines Gateway to Nifleheim and The Fallen
Angle into a single volume)

THE HERO AND THE FIEND
(A novelette set in the Harbinger of Doom
universe)

THE GATEWAY
(A novella length version of Gateway to
Nifleheim)

THE DEMON KING OF BERGHER
(A short story set in the Harbinger of Doom
universe)

THE KEBLEAR HORROR
(A short story set in the Harbinger of Doom
universe)

To be notified about my new book releases and
any special offers or discounts regarding my
books, please join my mailing list here:
http://eepurl.com/vwubH

Made in the USA
Middletown, DE
15 November 2019